CW01433455

TO CAGE A WILD BIRD

www.penguin.co.uk

TO CAGE A WILD BIRD

BROOKE FAST

TRANSWORLD PUBLISHERS

UK | USA | Canada | Ireland | Australia
India | New Zealand | South Africa

Transworld is part of the Penguin Random House group of companies
whose addresses can be found at global.penguinrandomhouse.com.

Penguin Random House UK, One Embassy Gardens,
8 Viaduct Gardens, London SW11 7BW

penguin.co.uk

Penguin
Random House
UK

First published in Great Britain in 2025 by Wayward TxF
an imprint of Transworld Publishers
001

Copyright © Brooke Fast 2025

The moral right of the author has been asserted
This book is a work of fiction and, except in the case of historical fact,
any resemblance to actual persons, living or dead, is purely coincidental.

Every effort has been made to obtain the necessary permissions with
reference to copyright material, both illustrative and quoted. We apologize
for any omissions in this respect and will be pleased to make the
appropriate acknowledgements in any future edition.

Penguin Random House values and supports copyright. Copyright fuels creativity,
encourages diverse voices, promotes freedom of expression and supports a vibrant culture.
Thank you for purchasing an authorized edition of this book and for respecting intellectual
property laws by not reproducing, scanning or distributing any part of it by any means
without permission. You are supporting authors and enabling Penguin Random House to
continue to publish books for everyone. No part of this book may be used or reproduced
in any manner for the purpose of training artificial intelligence technologies or systems.
In accordance with Article 4(3) of the DSM Directive 2019/790, Penguin Random House
expressly reserves this work from the text and data mining exception.

Typeset in 12.5/16pt Granjon LT Std by Six Red Marbles UK, Thetford, Norfolk
Printed and bound by CPI (UK) Ltd, Croydon CR0 4YY

The authorized representative in the EEA is Penguin Random House Ireland,
Morrison Chambers, 32 Nassau Street, Dublin D02 YH68.

A CIP catalogue record for this book is available from the British Library

ISBNs:
9781911751007 hb
9781911751014 tpb

Penguin Random House is committed to a sustainable
future for our business, our readers and our planet. This book is
made from Forest Stewardship Council® certified paper.

MIX
Paper | Supporting
responsible forestry
FSC
www.fsc.org   FSC® C018179

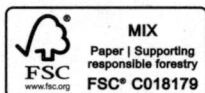

To my hunny. Life with you is a dream come true.

I

ONE HUNDRED TWENTY-SEVEN.

That was the number of lives I'd traded for a full belly over the years.

Today would make one hundred twenty-eight.

I'd been holed up in the shadowed alcove of the alley since midday, the reek of piss and rotting trash making my eyes water.

My muscles were stiff, begging to be stretched, but I resisted, keeping my gaze fastened to the entrance of the safe house.

The ramshackle townhouse was tucked between two crumbling apartment buildings, its front door worn enough that it might have crumpled from its hinges with a well-aimed kick.

What was taking so long?

Typically, before the sun dipped below the tops of the skyscrapers and continued its descent toward the horizon, I'd have a fugitive cuffed, dragging their feet as I pulled them toward the city jail. From there, the fugitive would be transported to End-lock, the prison that lay over a hundred miles from the city border.

At Endlock, they would await their fate – death at the hands of Dividium citizens.

But even though Aggie's informant had said the fugitive would move from the safe house before dark, there had been no sign of him, and at this time of evening the Lower Sector buzzed with activity. Vendors shouted and pushed rickety carts through the streets as they attempted to make their final sales to the day-shift laborers rushing to spend a bit of their meager wages, while dark-hooded figures skulked through the crowds, hoping to overhear information they could trade to the authorities for extra credits.

Wary pedestrians shot fleeting glances my way as they slipped by my hiding place, likely mistaking me for a patrolling guard.

I was worse.

A bounty hunter – a traitor.

The safe-house door creaked open an inch. I pressed myself farther into the alcove, breath caught in my throat, for fear that the slightest sound would send me home empty-handed.

A heartbeat later, the door yawned wide, and a finely clothed figure ventured out, braving the alley in hopes of blending into the wave of Lower Sector commuters.

I abandoned my hiding spot, and a grim smile spread across my face as I stepped toward the retreating form.

This would all be over soon. I could already imagine the credits on my wristband creeping from a few dozen into the thousands. Enough for several months' rent and a pantry full of rations to get my brother, Jed, and me through the winter. Maybe even enough for a new pair of boots to replace the ones falling apart on my feet, and a winter coat for Jed.

'Torin Bond,' I called.

The figure halted mid-stride, craning his neck. His hood slid back to expose a mop of brown hair streaked with gray. His weary eyes were underscored with deep purple and lined with faint wrinkles.

'Stop,' I commanded as he took another step, my hand reaching for the set of handcuffs secured at the belt of my black cargo pants. 'I don't want to hurt you.'

A half-lie. There would be some small satisfaction in getting into a fistfight with a citizen from the Upper Sector – one of the wealthy who took and took, even as they watched us starve.

'Then don't.'

With that, Torin vanished into the bustling crowd of commuters, a shadow swallowed by a river of moving bodies.

Shit.

I'd lose my advantage if he made it to the border checkpoint that controlled the flow of movement between the Lower and Middle Sectors. Thousands of commuters were lined up on either side of the checkpoint, waiting for the patrol guards to scan their wristbands to verify their identities and confirm they had the correct permissions to cross the sector border. If Torin got there, I would either lose him in the masses, or one of the guards would recognize him and wind up with *my* credits.

The boundary dividing the two sectors was unmistakable – the structures in the Lower Sector stood as crumbling remnants of the world before, unchanged since the Council partitioned the city into three sectors after the second Civil War.

A few blocks from where I was positioned, on the other side of the checkpoint, the Middle Sector was full of newly constructed buildings and well-dressed citizens. Their pressed suits and flowing dresses were only the beginning of the divide between us and them.

I caught sight of Torin among the stream of commuters. He elbowed through the masses, but the throng of bodies slowed his progress.

I raced along the outskirts of the crowd, pushing myself to move faster.

The cuffs at my waist clanged against my thigh with each stride, nearly drowned out by the soles of my boots slapping against the packed dirt.

Glancing over his shoulder, Torin exhaled in apparent relief when he didn't see me behind him.

Just like I planned.

I chose that moment to step directly into his path.

His jaw went slack, and I might have laughed at the look on his face had he not pulled back his fist and swung it at my nose.

I ducked, charging into his legs, sending him crashing forward onto the gritty street. Some of the commuters jumped back, gasping, while others merely glared and stepped around us.

Torin cried out, scooping up a handful of dirt and gravel and hurling it at me.

I yelped, shielding my eyes, but felt the sting of the debris nicking my cheeks.

The move gave Torin enough time to scramble to his hands and knees, but I launched myself onto his back before he could stand, sending both of us tumbling to the ground in a heap.

Torin rolled until he was on top of me, subjecting me to heaving gasps of putrid breath. I rammed my head into his face before he could work out his next move, his yell muffled as his teeth cut into my forehead.

'Fucking bitch!' he screamed, spitting out a tooth and a mouthful of blood, a glob landing on my cheek.

'Original,' I muttered, grimacing as the blood trickled across my skin. 'If only credits could buy wit.'

I entertained the thought of pocketing Torin's tooth. It was customary for hunters who visited Endlock to collect the teeth from their kills and wear them on chains around their necks, or shaved into strings of pearls. I'd seen teeth worn as cufflinks or as the centerpiece of extravagant, diamond-encrusted rings. They were morbid trophies – status symbols. Those who weren't skilled in hunting went so far as to buy teeth from vendors in back-alley markets to fit in with their peers – I'd seen my neighbors pull their own teeth to sell to the wealthy during especially harsh winters when they couldn't make rent or afford rations for their children.

Torin's hands clamped around my throat, cutting off my air supply and any coherent thought. I flailed about, seeking a weapon, but my fingers found only dirt. On instinct, I kneed him between the legs before delivering a pointed jab to his throat. I shoved him off me, forcing him onto his stomach, and pressed my knee into his back, gasping in lungfuls of air as I caught my breath.

I unfastened the handcuffs from my belt and secured them tightly around Torin's wrists.

He spluttered but still managed to twist his neck until his eyes found my face. I didn't meet his gaze.

Never make eye contact.

That was the first rule of bounty hunting.

'I have children,' he whimpered.

I swallowed.

So did my parents when the Council sent them to Endlock.

Dividium was ruled by a Council that had formed in the aftermath of the war – three leaders elected by a board of officials from each sector.

Each Councilor was assigned to a sector to enforce regulations: Councilor Elder to the Lower Sector, Councilor Baskan to the Middle Sector, and Councilor Peña to the Upper Sector.

They all resided in the Upper Sector in homes that were vast enough to house dozens of people.

'Please. I don't want to die.' Torin's words were a mere whisper.

He overestimated my character if he thought begging for mercy would help him.

'Neither do I,' I murmured. Empathy wouldn't keep Jed alive.

The mass of pedestrians continued to weave around us, unfazed, a testament to the number of people arrested and sent to Endlock every day.

Many of the most frequent visitors to Endlock paid to hunt the lower-level criminals – that was typically all they could afford. But the wealthy loved nothing more than the chance to stick it to one of their own. And a prisoner like Torin? The hunters from the Upper Sector would be itching to take a shot at him.

My heart had nearly stopped when I'd checked the criminal database that morning using the ancient tablet I'd scraped up enough credits to purchase second-hand a few years prior. An advertisement had popped up, urging me to visit the Lower Sector's Endlock Experience office to discuss booking a budget-friendly hunting package featuring a meal plan and two nights' accommodation at a campground within view of Endlock's grounds.

Book now for a free photo package and weapons upgrade!

I'd snorted as the text scrolled across the screen, and swiped the ad away to reveal an updated list of bounties. Next to a grainy picture of Torin, the reward for his capture was set at ten thousand credits.

It was the highest reward I'd seen for a criminal, and the prison would make at least twice that from selling his life to a hunter.

I'd never had the funds or the desire to partake in a hunt, though I'd sent enough people to the prison to hold myself responsible for signing their death sentences.

I figured hunting was an addiction, like gambling or spirits. It gave people a sense of power, a perception of control in a society that constrained us with unending rules. Rules for the times of day we were allowed outside our homes. Rules that dictated where we could step foot within Dividium – we weren't permitted above the Lower Sector without documented authorization.

I exhaled, hauling Torin to his feet and shoving him toward the city jail.

*

'What have you got for me today, Raven?' Captain Flint asked, his voice gruff and unfeeling as the concrete walls that surrounded us.

The jail was the newest structure in the Lower Sector but also the least inviting. The front room was nothing but gray walls and barred windows, bare save for the desk occupying the middle of the space and the blood-red flag covering the wall behind it. In the center of the flag were three black interlocking circles – one on top, two below. Three circles. Three sectors. Three Councilors. The flag of Dividium.

The heavy entrance doors cut off the chatter of the streets, immersing us in a tense silence broken by the tinny voice emanating from the small screen of the tablet Captain Flint held.

'We have a breaking update on the attack on the western quadrant of the crop fields that occurred nearly two weeks ago. After a tireless investigation by city guards, the Council has reported findings that Eris Cybin, known terrorist and leader of the rebel organization called the Collective, is the culprit behind a fire that destroyed a large portion of the city's coming harvest and resulted in the death of several field workers, as well as the death of Silas V. Elder, the husband of Councilor Caltriona Elder.'

I squinted at the tablet.

That couldn't be right.

Eris was the leader of the Upper Sector's cell of the Collective. Though Eris had led dangerous rallies and attacks against the Council in the past, none had focused on the city's harvest. Damaging the crops would hardly impact the Council – it was the Lower Sector that would suffer. The Collective's responsibility for the death of Councilor Elder's husband would mean more patrols and arrests in the Lower Sector, warranted or not.

'Guards are still investigating what Elder was doing beyond Dividium's border wall in the first place, with the leading theory being a

meticulously planned kidnapping and execution by the Collective. Eris Cybin remains at large.'

The news stream faded into a commercial for a Middle Sector jewelry shop that specialized in shaving teeth from Endlock into charm bracelets.

Flint's bulbous form hunched over the device, his eyes never lifting from the screen, even as I shoved Torin before me.

Torin had dragged his feet on the short walk to the jail, only relenting when I'd pulled out my dagger and threatened to remove his favorite appendage. After that, I could hardly keep up.

'Torin Bond,' I announced, handing him over to the guards beside Flint's ornate desk.

Flint's device fell, his attention fully captured by the man now in his custody.

'Council above, you went after a fugitive from the Upper Sector?' His blue eyes held mine, but I couldn't tell whether he admired my bravery or found humor in my stupidity.

'Flint, we're talking about ten thousand credits here.'

He scanned a piece of parchment, searching for Torin's name. 'What did he do?'

'His wife had an affair last year. When Torin caught her, he reported her lover to the guards – told them he'd stolen a valuable watch. The man was sent to Endlock for it. Killed. And then, a few weeks ago, Torin's wife found the watch hidden in his study and reported him.'

Flint let out a whistle. 'Juicy.'

'The bitch set me up,' Torin snarled, and the guards yanked at his arms until he quieted.

I curled my lip, addressing Flint but speaking loud enough for Torin to hear. 'Even if he hadn't done that, isn't watching children starve while having more food than he could ever eat crime enough?'

Perhaps that wasn't fair. Maybe I was a touch bitter that Torin had been born into a family that knew nothing about the lengths most of us had to go to for survival.

But food wasn't the only thing that separated the Lower Sector from the Upper. In the Lower Sector, getting arrested was nearly as easy as breathing. But in the Upper Sector, most citizens got a slap on the wrist for anything other than the most heinous of crimes.

And what Torin had done was as good as murder.

Flint grunted, not keen to say anything untoward about the Upper Sector when one of the Council's spies might be listening.

The guards disappeared behind a door with Torin. They would lock him in a holding cell until the next transport to Endlock was ready.

Flint shook his head at me before swiping at his tablet, typing in a passcode to access the reward system. 'Slow day. You're the first to come in.'

He hit a final button, and my wristband vibrated. I tilted the face toward me and watched as the credits on the small screen steadily increased, relief flooding my body.

I'd been down to my last fifty credits, left from the bounty I'd turned in a month before. A woman named Perri.

There were plenty of illegal operations running rampant in the Lower Sector, but Perri's had been the most lucrative. Mostly because it preyed on desperation. She'd sold counterfeit medication. Antibiotics that failed to treat infection, knock-off heart medications – you name it, she sold it. Aggie had heard rumors that Perri's arrest had done little to end the business, and I was still working on tracking down the other people involved.

I narrowed my eyes as the screen on my wrist stopped at a number just north of eight thousand. I turned back to Flint. 'Eight? It's supposed to be ten.'

He shrugged, grimacing. 'You brought me damaged goods.

He's missing a tooth, and he has a black eye. You know the broken ones bring in less for Endlock.'

He spoke as if the prisoners' injuries, their *lives*, were an inconvenience to his bank account – but voicing that thought would only make him a witness to my hypocrisy.

Their deaths funded my existence as well.

'Jed's eighteen now,' I blurted instead, hoping maybe he'd take pity on me and throw in a few extra credits. My brother, Jed, was why I'd gotten into bounty hunting in the first place – he relied on me, and I would do anything to keep him fed.

'Already?' Flint whistled, logging out of the reward system and sealing away my chances of more credits. 'I remember the day you first walked in here.'

Jed was eleven then, and I was sixteen.

The jail had seemed terrifying to my innocent eyes. Sterile cement walls and hulking guards who shouted through the locked door when inmates got too rowdy on the other side. Captain Flint had printed me a list of wanted fugitives without batting an eye. I dropped out of school the next day and began scouting for my first target.

But for all Flint's shortcomings, I was indebted to the man. Without his help, Jed and I would have starved on the streets, unable to scrape together enough to pay the rent on our run-down apartment.

'He grew up fast,' I said weakly. And he had. I'd been responsible for Jed since our parents' deaths seven years ago.

Now, Jed would be considered a fully-fledged member of society, sentenced as an adult for any indiscretions instead of receiving a strike.

Minors were afforded three chances to stay within the bounds of the law. Three strikes, and then they were sent to Endlock to be selected as hunting targets, no matter their age.

With each crime committed by a child, the city guards slashed a long, deep line into their shoulder with a standard-issue switchblade – the scars were how they kept track of how many chances each child had left.

I reflexively rubbed at the two strike marks carved into the back of my left shoulder, the scars thick and permanently raised.

'Better get going.' Flint made a shooing motion in the direction of the door, already bored and ready to get back to watching the news stream. He put his stockinged feet up onto his desk. 'May the Council watch over you.'

I waved to Flint, pushing past the guards who stood watch at the entrance to the city jail as I muttered the required response. 'May they guide us to eternal peace.'

2

'GIVE ME A pint, Vern.'

'Not until you go see Aggie,' the barkeep growled, wiping the worn wooden counter with an oily rag. 'She's in the back with the others.'

'And I can talk to her just as well with a mug of ale in my hand, even *better* with a mug of ale in my hand, as a matter of fact,' I said, waving my wristband in his direction, showing off the screen full of credits. Calling it ale was a stretch – a compliment, really, for the homebrew that Vern illegally concocted.

The plump, wiry-haired man had owned the musty basement tavern – aptly known as Vern's Tavern – for as long as anyone could remember. He was perpetually grouchy and a man of few words, but as long as his patrons paid their tabs and shut their mouths when the patrols came around, he couldn't have cared less about the insidious activities they got up to under the comfort of his leaky roof.

Vern scanned my wristband and shoved a mug into my hand, the ale sloshing over the sides and soaking my skin.

'Now get back there,' he demanded, turning his prickly gaze toward the next paying customer.

I raised the mug in a mock salute but stopped short, narrowing my eyes when I saw Jed descending the steps into the tavern.

At eighteen, he was all sharp angles and lanky limbs, the spitting image of our father with his light blonde hair, wide blue eyes, and the constellation of freckles that danced across his ivory cheeks.

Though I had five years on him, I was often mistaken for his younger sibling.

I'd inherited our mother's features – gray eyes and long, dark brown hair that fell in waves down the middle of my back. The only trait Jed and I had in common was our complexion.

'What are you doing here?' I snapped, grabbing him by the elbow and yanking him into an unoccupied corner of the tavern. 'You should be at work. It's almost curfew.'

'I'm on my way there.' Jed rolled his eyes, pulling his arm from my grasp. 'I needed to make a quick stop.'

'At *Vern's*?' I pressed, raising a brow. 'For what?' I glanced around but no one seemed to be paying us much attention.

Jed tried to push past me, but I held an arm out, refusing to let him by.

'You know what I'm here for, Raven,' he said in a whisper, nodding in the direction of the private meeting room. 'I'm eighteen now. I can start initiation.'

'Absolutely not,' I seethed, fighting to keep my voice down. 'You're not getting involved with them. It's not safe.' Panic clawed at my chest when I pictured him getting caught and sent to Endlock. I'd gotten us this far by having as little to do with the Collective as possible, but, of course, he would want to follow in our parents' footsteps by joining the rebel group.

'I don't need you to keep me safe.' Jed's voice shook, his hands fisting at his sides. 'I need you to stop using me as an excuse to arrest people to pay the rent.'

'Jed, I—'

'For every person you turn in, you're aligning yourself with the Council. Taking their side. You're no better than the hunters who get off on putting a bullet through a prisoner's head.'

My mouth snapped shut, his words cutting into me like a thousand shards of glass. I knew he disapproved of my job, but it was something we almost never talked about. Just like our parents.

'There is no other side,' I whispered, my voice brittle. 'There is the Council's side or death.'

'You sound just like them,' Jed spat. 'You're not even willing to *try* anything else.'

'If I hadn't taken a strike for you, maybe I'd have the option of trying something else,' I hissed. As soon as the words left my mouth, I wished I could take them back.

It was true I'd taken a strike for Jed, and that having two strikes made me unhirable at the factories, but that wasn't his fault. It was mine. I'd take it again in a heartbeat. Take all of his pain if I could.

Jed stared at me for a moment, lips pressed into a thin line, and then turned on his heel and marched toward the exit.

'Where are you going?' I asked, shoving a strand of hair from my heated cheek.

'Work. I can't look at you right now.'

Jed stomped up the stairs and out of the tavern without a backward glance, and I tipped back my mug of ale, drowning everything out with the sour liquid.

'Getting drunk so you can live with yourself, Thorne?'

I groaned, looking up to see Aggie's son, Graylin, leaning against the bar. His brown hair, streaked with gold, was curled up at the edges from the damp humidity of the room, and he twirled a dagger between his fingers.

Self-righteous prick.

There had been a time when my mother and Aggie would

whisper behind their hands and shoot each other conspiratorial looks when they saw the way Gray teased me and how I blushed in turn.

Then, there was the stolen kiss, a week after my sixteenth birthday. The sticky heat of summer had given way to a deliciously cool breeze as we sat watching the sunset from the rooftop of my apartment building. Gray had transformed the barren, concrete space with a blanket and the nubs of some of Aggie's homemade candles, their gentle glow softening his features as the sky faded from blue to orangey-pink, then velvet black and glittering with stars.

Gray had leaned in, emerald eyes intent on mine as he cupped my chin. I'd let out a shaky breath, and he'd closed the distance between us, our lips brushing as we jumped over the line of friendship into something new.

The next day, my parents were arrested.

A few days after that, they were dead, and I became a bounty hunter to take care of Jed.

A choice that Gray had never forgiven me for.

If we all look out for each other, we might have a fighting chance of survival. That's how they win, Raven, when we only look out for ourselves.

His words had started out earnest, an entreaty. But when he saw that something had shifted in me, that I would do anything to ensure Jed's survival, and his survival alone, Gray had turned cold and distant. It was like he didn't know me anymore, and I didn't know him. Like all those years faded into nothing in the face of empty cupboards and overdue rent.

I shook my head to clear the memory. 'Maybe drunk is the only way I can withstand your company.'

Gray barked out a laugh, wielding a bright smile that didn't reach his green eyes. 'Where'd Jed go?'

I looked away from whatever emotion was swimming in his gaze, some combination of sadness and disgust, to examine the myriad small scars that dotted the tanned skin of his cheeks and hands. Some were faded, like the long gash on his left temple from when he'd fallen through the floor of our makeshift fort in an abandoned factory when he was twelve. Others were fresh enough that he'd likely gotten them from his involvement in a Collective mission. He was as tall as Jed, though no one would describe Gray as lanky – he filled out his worn shirt well enough that I didn't have to imagine the hard planes of muscle that lay beneath.

'Stay away from him, Gray.'

I slammed my mug on the bar and waved my wristband at Vern, snatching the pint of ale he was passing to another patron. When he cursed at me, I winked, strolling across the tavern until I reached the door that led to the back room, Gray on my heels.

'Hetty was killed in the last hunt.' Opal's words reached me as soon as I slipped through the door, my eyes adjusting until I could see the woman was speaking to Aggie's wife, Loria. 'We need to send in a replacement if we have any hope of getting Kit out. Someone with combat experience, preferably, if we're going to get her across the Wastes alive. Besides the harsh conditions, we've had reports of scavengers stealing from travelers, sometimes even kidnapping them.'

My brows knitted together. Attempting to travel across the Wastes was as much of a death sentence as a stint at Endlock.

Loria's eyes shifted to me as she held up a hand to cut off Opal's words.

'Drinking away your problems?' Aggie asked in the silence that followed. What was it with this family and their focus on my ale intake?

Aggie sat at the head of a long table, smoking a clay pipe. Loria sat to her right, her arms crossed over her chest, and her eyes narrowed as she watched me. Most of the other dozen chairs surrounding the table were filled with people of varying ages, save the

chair to Aggie's left and one at the opposite end of the table that
Gray promptly slipped into.

A collection of candles brightened the space, casting each face
in an orange-hued glow. Aside from the factories that were kept
running at all hours, our sector had to resort to candles and oil
lanterns after curfew when the electricity cut out for the night.
The Lower Sector had the highest rate of criminal activity, which
the Council used as an excuse to enforce the nightly curfew. They
said the curfew was to protect us, but it was mostly to ensure the
Middle and Upper Sectors had access to as much electricity as they
wanted from the limited power grid.

The Lower Sector had the highest population – nearly a hundred thousand people, as many as the Middle and Upper Sectors
combined – but we were crammed into the smallest section of the
city, packed into tiny apartment buildings like colonies of ants.

'Nothing like a room-temperature mug of ale to chase away the
guilt of sending another man to his death.' I raised my mug and
took a large swallow. Besides, Jed was working until dawn. When
I stumbled back to our apartment, he wouldn't be home to see my
disheveled state.

Or condemn me further.

When Jed turned eighteen, he'd been forced to pick up a grueling night shift at a water treatment facility. The position paid less
than scraps, but it was all that was available, and he didn't have a
choice until something opened up elsewhere.

'He deserved it, dear,' came Aggie's soft reply as she tucked a
graying strand of hair back from where it had fallen from her
braid. Her face, tanned and heavily lined, held a sad smile. She
already knew I'd turned in Torin – she had people everywhere.
'Come sit with us.'

I did as she asked, nodding to the other members of the Collective as I took my seat and pulled a folded sheet of parchment from
my pocket. I slid it across the table to Aggie.

'Here,' I whispered so the others couldn't hear. 'Tacha Vanil. Single mother. She was left homeless when her apartment building collapsed last year. She's wanted for stealing a few ration bars from the market. I found her digging through the rubbish bins in the alley behind the facility where Jed works.'

It was an agreement Aggie and I had. In exchange for her providing me with intel on the whereabouts of fugitives who'd committed serious crimes, I helped her track down those who didn't deserve to be arrested, let alone killed at Endlock. The Collective took them in, and helped hide them. I didn't know how they did it, and I'd never asked.

Aggie nodded her thanks, tucking the paper into her shawl as she said softly, 'We'll take care of it.'

'So, to what do we owe the pleasure of your company this evening?' Gray asked from the other end of the table. 'Leaving the dark side behind to officially join us?'

'In your dreams.' I leaned back in my chair, kicked my booted feet up on the table, and watched as pieces of caked mud flaked off onto the scarred wooden surface. 'I'm only here because Aggs said she had a job for me. One that pays handsomely.'

Aside from my deal with Aggie, I usually stayed far away from the Collective. After all, it was our parents' involvement with the rebel group that had gotten them sent to Endlock.

And my big mouth.

But Aggie was my mother's dearest friend, a fixture in my life. Between the payout she offered and the reward I'd gotten for turning over Torin, I might have enough credits to stock our pantry *and* bribe the overseer at the water treatment facility to move Jed to the day shift.

'Of course,' Gray spat, as if he'd heard my thoughts. 'Credits are the only thing you care about. Your parents would be—'

'*Graylin*,' Aggie scolded her son as if he were still a child and not a man of twenty-five years.

My face grew hot at the mention of my parents, but I didn't rise to his bait. 'That's simply not true.' I tipped my mug back, taking a large swallow before slamming it on the table. 'I care a great deal about myself, too, Gray.'

He moved to stand, but stopped short when Aggie held up a hand.

'Enough,' Aggie said, taking a long pull from her pipe. 'There's enough violence in this world to last a dozen lifetimes. I won't have any of it here.' Tendrils of smoke slipped from her lips as she spoke, wrapping me in the floral-sweet smell of the smoldering ironroot leaves she puffed on to keep her joint pain at bay.

Graylin nodded and closed his mouth, but that didn't stop him from leveling a glare in my direction.

'Speaking of violence' – I scanned the table, noting that one face was absent – 'wasn't Eris supposed to be here tonight?'

The other cell leaders joined the Lower Sector meetings on occasion to keep up to date on news they didn't trust messengers with.

'You really think he'd be here after the news stream today?' Gray's words were heavy with condescension.

'So it's true, then?' I'd held out hope that it was someone else. That Eris wouldn't have gone as far as destroying food.

'It's true that part of the harvest was burned,' Aggie said, lips downturned at the corners. 'But we haven't been able to get in touch with Eris to confirm his alleged involvement. Some Collective members believe the Council ordered the fire.'

My jaw dropped. 'The Council? Why?'

'To frame the Collective,' Gray said.

'The public's opinion of us has changed in recent months,' Loria chimed in. 'For the better. The recruits in the program Gray's heading have managed to hand out thousands of extra rations, and made it known that they were coming from the Collective. Zael and Opal's crew have been renovating one of the abandoned factories to put roofs over more families' heads. Citizens are associating us with safety and protection.'

I shook my head. 'It's one thing for the Council to want to gain back public favor, but another for them to destroy food. We're starving as it is. And Silas Elder died in that fire. Why would they allow that to happen?'

'We don't *know* that the Council is behind it,' Opal insisted. 'It's just a theory.'

'They'd rather all of us starve than think we could survive without them lording it over us,' Gray spat. 'And nothing could make people hate us more than letting them believe we destroyed their food.'

But that didn't answer my question about Silas Elder.

'We'll discuss this later,' Loria cut in, casting a meaningful look in my direction before I could question them further.

Aggie already said too much in front of me for Loria's taste, especially as I'd always refused to officially join the cause.

'What's the job, Aggs?' I asked, changing the subject and cutting through the tension in the air.

Aggie coughed, hacking until Loria leaned forward and slapped her on the back. Eventually, Aggie took a gulp from the mug in front of her, and clasped Loria's hand in hers before speaking.

'I need you to intercept Councilor Elder's communications, specifically the letters she's been sending to a contact at Endlock.'

For a moment, the only sound in the room came from Graylin stabbing his dagger into the table, over and over.

I laughed.

'Are you mad?' I pushed back from the table and got to my feet. The only thing I wanted more than credits was for the Council to know nothing of my existence. 'I'd be sent straight to Endlock.'

'Not if you don't get caught,' Aggie replied. 'Councilor Elder hasn't confided in any of our agents who have made it into her inner circle. She keeps her cards close to her chest, but she sends frequent communications to someone at Endlock. And all written communications are sent on the daily transport with the new inmates – you'd just need to find a way to get her letter off the transport.'

'Why is she sending written communications in the first place?' I frowned, the question forcing its way past my lips against my better judgment. 'Why not send an encrypted message from her tablet?'

Gray smirked. 'One of our recruits in Elder's inner circle was able to hack into the Council's secure messaging platform. They didn't see much before they were locked out, but Elder has been sending written communications to Endlock ever since while her team shores up security.'

I shook my head. That was . . . I hadn't realized the Collective had such major connections. Even still, there was no way I was going through with something so risky.

'It's important, Raven,' Aggie said softly, as if reading my thoughts. 'My source from the North Settlement said Councilor Elder has been in contact with their leaders, insisting they let her and her entourage visit.'

'Why?' I asked, my sense of reason shoved aside by my curiosity.

'She *says* it's to study their crop growth and see if there's anything our scientists can learn from them to improve our own yield.'

The land around Dividium was dying.

When I was young, my family hadn't worried very much about food. As far as I remembered, it hadn't exactly been plentiful, but I'd rarely gone to bed hungry. But ten years ago, something had changed. The soil had revolted – some dormant side effect that arose from the earth's radiation poisoning during the war. Now, our crops were resistant to growth despite our most experienced scientists and farmers battling against the infected soil.

As food grew scarcer, prices soared, and we were driven closer to starvation.

'You don't think that's what she actually wants from the North Settlement?' I asked, mulling over Aggie's words.

Aggie shook her head, but it was Loria who spoke. 'If she cared so much about making sure we didn't starve, she'd regulate the waste and overconsumption running rampant in the Upper Sector and pay our people fair wages. There's more than enough to go around if it's allocated correctly.'

I didn't know about that, but there was no use arguing with Loria.

'What else could she want with them?' I asked.

'That's what we're trying to find out,' Aggie mused.

I shook my head. 'Aggs, you know I'd do anything for you, but this . . . this is a death sentence.'

'If anyone can do it, I know you can,' Aggie said around a yawn. The ironroot helped her pain, but it was also a sedative. She wouldn't last at the meeting much longer.

I was silent for a moment, thinking. 'Bar Jed from joining the Collective, and I'll consider it.'

The hushed conversation among the other members came to a standstill.

Gray barked out a humorless laugh and opened his mouth to speak, but a glare from Loria stopped him.

'Raven,' Aggie said, shaking her head. 'He's an adult. You can't protect him forever. He has to make his own choices.'

'It's the only offer you can make me. That and the credits.'

'Raven . . .' Aggie started, but her eyelids were drooping.

'We need some time,' Loria said, cutting in and nodding in my direction. 'Go on. We'll talk tomorrow.'

I was seated at the bar, halfway through my third mug of ale, when the hair on the back of my neck rose. I swiveled on my stool, scanning the room until I found the source of the feeling – a man seated in a dark booth in the corner, staring at me with no attempt at discretion.

He was young, maybe a year or two older than my twenty-three years, outfitted all in black. His golden-brown skin was smooth and unblemished, and he had pulled his long, ebony hair back into the knot that many men in Dividium favored. A few rebel tendrils had escaped the tie that held his hair, and soft waves framed his high cheekbones and defined jaw. Though his shirt concealed his arms and broad shoulders, the fabric was tight enough to suggest that he held a physically demanding position. I guessed he might be a carpenter, or even a farmer, one of the few professions that granted citizens access to the world outside of Dividium's walls – under the watchful eyes of city guards, of course.

I glanced away, willing to consider that I might be overestimating the intensity of his gaze. But each time I turned in his direction, his eyes were still fastened to my form.

I hopped off my stool, hand going to the handle of the dagger strapped to my thigh, and sauntered across the tavern. More patrons had filtered in since my time in the back with Aggie, and I had to elbow my way through them, cringing away from the feeling of their sweat-soaked skin against mine.

The man's eyes remained impassive, like my approach didn't surprise him in the least, though his lips twisted into a slight smirk.

It only made me more wary.

I took a final step and slid into the booth, close enough to the man that our shoulders touched, and then held up my dagger so that he could see the razor-sharp point.

I opened my mouth, but a shout cut through the room before I could speak.

'Kill the lights. Patrol sixty seconds out.'

Within moments, the lanterns were snuffed out, plunging the room into darkness. The groups of rowdy patrons fell into a hush while the bleary-eyed guitar player in the corner stopped her song mid-strum.

Wedged into the worn booth, startled by the sudden loss of sight, I pressed my dagger firmly against the man at my side.

He let out a low, rumbling chuckle that raised goosebumps on my arms, but he didn't speak. His warm breath filled the air around me, heady with the perfume of mint leaves and mead.

Outside, the boots of patrolling guards crunched on gravel, their flashlights making passes over the windows above our heads and leaving dancing shadows on the basement walls in their wake.

But then, as quickly as they'd come, the guards moved on.

The tavern staff relit the lamps, the musician croaked out her melancholic tune anew, and the room returned to its usual state of noisy chaos.

'What do you want?' I asked the man.

His eyes flicked over my face slowly, lazily, resting on my lips for a beat too long before he met my gaze with eyes like molten honey, fringed by lush lashes. 'This,' he said with a grin. 'Though preferably without your dagger digging into my side.'

'This?' I repeated, drawing out the word and arching a brow.

'Mm-hmm,' he hummed. 'A beautiful, dangerous woman pressed up against me in this booth.'

He was *flirting with me*? My face heated. An evening of bounty hunting followed by Aggie asking me to interfere with the Council's communications had put me on edge, and I'd immediately clocked this man as a threat. But maybe he wasn't. Maybe he was exactly the distraction I was looking for.

I abandoned responsibility, letting my eyes roam his body, taking in the finely stitched fabric of his clothing. It appeared brand new, without a stain in sight. There were no patches covering worn elbows or knees, and when I glanced beneath the table, I beheld a pair of scuff-free boots. Not a farmer, then.

'You're not from here,' I mused, my eyes narrowing. 'Middle Sector? What are you doing here?'

'I was supposed to be meeting someone, but he hasn't shown up,' the man said, glancing around the room.

'I know most people that frequent Vern's. Who are you look-ing for?'

He stared at me intently for a moment, rolling his lips together as if weighing the merits of confiding in me. 'Eris Cybin.'

I forced myself not to react. 'Friend of yours?'

'I need to repay him.'

I raised a brow. 'You're indebted to Eris? You're a bigger fool than I thought.'

'You know him?'

'I know *of* him.'

'Is he here?' the man asked, hardly breathing.

I shook my head, echoing Gray's words from earlier. 'You really think he'd show up after the news stream today?'

The man's face fell, but his lips twisted into a smirk. 'That's too bad. But I'd say your company is a generous consolation prize.'

'A *consolation prize*?' I rolled my eyes. 'You really know how to make a woman feel special. Please don't tell me that line actually works for you.'

'You'll have to let me know. It's my first attempt.'

His leg knocked against mine beneath the table, and my breath hitched.

'Well, I guess that depends.' I gestured between us. 'What do you think the outcome of this is?'

'I was hoping to use my charm to convince you to follow me back to my place,' he said with a wink.

My pulse quickened.

'Awfully presumptuous of you,' I drawled, sheathing my dagger and letting my shoulders loosen. 'Just because I'm not going to stab you in the ribs doesn't mean you're going to get me naked in your apartment.'

'Naked?' His eyes darkened. 'Here you are, attempting to corrupt me when all I wanted was for you to walk me home. It's not safe out there alone.'

I snorted and finished my ale, the alcohol going straight to my head and pushing thoughts of Torin and Eris and empty pantries from my mind. 'Why do I get the feeling there's nothing left of you to corrupt?' I breathed, leaning in until there were mere inches between our lips.

The way I saw it, I could go back to my sad, empty apartment and ruminate over the blood on my hands, or I could let a handsome stranger help me forget all about it.

Not a terribly difficult choice.

'It's funny,' he said, eyes not leaving my mouth. 'I have the same feeling about you.'

'I'm Raven,' I told him, wanting him to know *something* about me before I kissed him.

He hesitated but finally said, 'Vale.'

I moved forward, a breath from eliminating the last distance between us and shutting out the final remnants of my horrible day, but there was an uproar of raucous laughter beside us, and then I was drenched – warm, sour liquid ran down my face.

I shot to my feet, running my hand over my face to wipe the ale from my stinging eyes.

'Sorry,' a man slurred, stepping close. 'I was only trying to get your attention.'

I took a deep breath in through my nose and let it out through my mouth in a slow *whoosh*. Just another drunken man. Not a threat.

But then his hand locked onto my wrist.

'Let go,' Vale growled as he got up from the booth.

I rolled my eyes at him, my hand going for my dagger.

'I saw you getting all cozy with him,' the man said. 'But if you're looking for company, I'd wager I have more to offer than he does.'

'Tempting,' I got out through my teeth, ripping my wrist from his grip and turning back to Vale. 'But I'm not interested.'

'Bitch,' he mumbled under his breath.

After that, it was hardly my fault he wound up lying on the floor unconscious with a black eye and a broken nose.

I shook my hand out in an attempt to lessen the pain in my knuckles.

'Like I said' – Vale's words tickled the shell of my ear as he leaned in – 'I'd feel much safer if you walked me home.'

I couldn't help the laugh that slipped from my lips.

'Aren't you going to clean that up?' Vern called when he saw me eyeing the exit.

'Talkative tonight, aren't we, Vern?' I crooned, making my way over to the broom closet. I braved the cobwebs and roaches to snag a mop and bucket that had certainly never seen the light of day.

I tossed them onto the unconscious man's chest. 'He'll come around soon enough. Make him clean up his own mess.'

Vern grunted, but I'd already motioned to Vale and skipped up the steps and out the door into the slumbering city.

3

'*THE LOWER SECTOR curfew is now in effect. Citizens are not permitted to leave their homes under any circumstance until morning. If found in the streets, you will be arrested on sight.*'

Councilor Elder's monotone voice droned from the speakers on repeat, cutting through the silent streets.

'How much farther is it?' I asked.

We'd been walking in the dark for several minutes, sticking close to the buildings and scanning the shadows for patrolling guards.

My heart thundered in my chest, and only now, as I was following a stranger down a dark alley, did I realize my stupidity.

The ale and the way Vale's lips had looked in the lantern light had gone to my head, but now, with the cold breeze slipping its fingers beneath my worn jacket and the threat of patrols, I knew I should be safely tucked in bed back at my apartment.

'It's just a bit farther,' Vale said, reaching out and grabbing my hand. His warm fingers curled around mine, igniting something inside me.

Maybe it would be all right, then.

Maybe, this once, I could take the night off from thinking about Jed and rent and my next payout. I could do something for myself.

A clatter came from the street at the end of the alley, and I froze.

'I heard something over there,' a light voice, too close for comfort, called from the street.

'Just leave it, Glin,' a rumbling baritone answered. 'Our shift's almost up. If we find someone, there'll be paperwork, and we won't be home for hours.'

I felt a tug on my hand, and Vale pulled me backward, holding a finger to his lips.

With my next step, I kicked an empty bottle, which shattered against the bricks of the nearest building. I turned to Vale, wide-eyed.

Silence.

And then the sound of quick footsteps.

I took a deep breath, exhaling slowly as I scanned my surroundings for an escape route.

The alley was lined with apartment buildings, but there were no emergency exit staircases or ladders to climb. No lower-level windows to slip through, and nothing large enough to hide behind.

I felt for the dagger strapped to my thigh.

'A blade will be no use against their guns,' Vale whispered.

I paused.

If I couldn't fight, it was over.

The only way out of the alley lay in front of us, or far back the way we'd come.

My throat tightened, and I froze, unable to draw breath.

I was going to die at Endlock, just like my parents.

And Jed would be left to fend for himself.

I clamped my shaking hand harder around the handle of my dagger, pulling it from its sheath. I wouldn't let them take me alive.

Then there was a hand on my arm.

'Do you trust me?' Vale was close enough that I could feel his breath on my cheek.

'Not at all,' I breathed.

He walked toward me, and I backed away until my shoulders met brick, and there was nowhere left to go.

'I promise I can get you out of this,' Vale whispered. 'Let me kiss you.'

I nearly laughed at the absurdity of the suggestion, but paused as everything seemed to clarify around me.

My hands trembled, the guards' footsteps pounding closer as I drew what I knew were my last breaths.

There was nowhere to run or hide.

No chance of making it out of this alive.

But I could decide to live my final moments in pleasure instead of fear.

I slipped my dagger back into its sheath.

'Okay.'

If Vale was surprised, he didn't show it. His large hands slid up the sides of my neck until his fingers framed my face, his thumbs beneath my jaw. And then he pressed his lips to mine.

He groaned as my mouth parted beneath his, and his tongue traced over my lips before delving into my mouth.

I pulled him closer, my pulse ratcheting up as I ran my hands up the back of his neck and into his hair until I reached the tie holding the smooth locks back from his face. I yanked the tie free and tangled my fingers in his hair, relishing the softness.

Someone was speaking in the background, but I couldn't make out their words.

Adrenaline filled my veins, fear merging with lust as I lost myself in Vale, kissing him harder, breathing him in. One of my hands slipped beneath the hem of his shirt and over the smooth plane of the muscles of his abdomen. Molten heat pooled in my core as I let out a soft moan, and he bit my bottom lip in response.

'Careful, Little Bird,' he growled. 'You'll make me forget we're not alone out here.'

I'd already forgotten.

'Face the wall and put your hands up.' A flashlight pierced the darkness, momentarily blinding me.

'Don't move,' Vale whispered, running his thumb over my still-parted lips. Then he turned to face the guards, his body blocking me almost entirely from view.

'I said—' the guard began.

'I heard you,' Vale interrupted, voice low. He was doing something with his hands that I couldn't see, rolling up his sleeve to show them something on his wrist, a watch or his wristband or—

'Vale, I think you should listen to them,' I urged, using his body to shield my movements from the guards as I pulled my dagger free once more. 'They'll hurt you.'

But both of the guards had gone quiet, and the flashlight fell from my face.

'We're sorry. Please, carry on.'

I froze, knowing I must have heard them wrong.

But the two guards turned and practically ran back to where they'd come from, leaving me in stunned silence, staring at Vale's back.

Nausea churned in my stomach as I realized what I'd done. Who I'd kissed. Because there was only one thing that would keep someone in the Lower Sector from being arrested after curfew.

I didn't speak until a minute later when the guards' footsteps vanished, and Vale finally turned to face me.

'You're a guard.' The words shook as I pushed them past my lips, even though I was sure I was right. Vale hadn't shown a hint of fear while the guards were rushing toward us.

He was one of the Council's minions and I'd *kissed* him. My hands shook around my dagger, itching to stab him. Only the thought of Jed had me sheathing the weapon instead.

'Something like that.' He grimaced at whatever he saw in my eyes.

I reared back and punched him square in the face. I heard a *crunch* and a grunt, but I ran before I could see how he'd react.

When I returned to my apartment, the building was dark – the electricity was still out from curfew. I stumbled up the stairs with the beginnings of a headache thrumming along the back of my skull, and dug in my pocket for my keys.

I jiggled the broken doorknob, angling it the only way that it would accept my key, but instead of catching on the lock, the door creaked open without resistance, and I had to grip the doorframe to keep from face-planting on the cracked tiles of the kitchen floor.

Jed had forgotten to bolt the door.

I looked around, noting that nothing seemed to be disturbed. That, at least, was a stroke of luck in my shitshow of a night.

I stumbled into bed without bothering to change and woke up on my lumpy mattress a scrap of hours later to a pounding headache.

Or what I thought was a pounding headache, until I heard Aggie slamming on my front door and yelling at me to get out of bed.

The bed creaked as I got to my feet.

'I'm coming!' I yelled. 'Will you stop with the banging?'

By the time I reached the kitchen, Aggie had let herself in using her key and had my kettle heating on the stove. She sat in one of the mismatched chairs that ringed the shaky dining table, her face illuminated by the low light of dawn filtering in through the window above the sink, bringing out the dark circles that framed her eyes.

'For strike's sake, Aggs. What are you doing here?'

'Sit down,' she responded, ignoring my question.

'What's wrong?'

'Sit down,' she repeated, and my heart dropped. I'd thought she must have come over to convince me to help the Collective, but that didn't explain why her hands shook at her sides.

'Okay.' I held my hands up in surrender and sat on one of the rickety chairs. 'But keep your voice down. Jed will have just gotten to sleep after his shift. You don't want to wake him.'

'Jed was arrested last night, Raven.'

I let out a shaky laugh. 'That's not funny, Aggs.'

'It wasn't meant to be.'

'Jed's sleeping,' I said, but as I spoke, I noted the empty hook by the door where his jacket should've been.

Aggie shook her head at me, and her lips turned down at the corners. And maybe I still wouldn't have believed her if it hadn't been for her eyes and the tears that welled in them.

Panic clawed at me as I stood and sprinted for Jed's room, heart pounding in my throat.

I flung the door open, flinching as it slammed against the wall, and scanned the space.

His bed was still made, the sheets smooth and untouched.

My gut twisted, my insides turning to ice. Jed was clever. Cautious. He always stayed out of trouble and he never came home late. If he wasn't here . . .

I returned to my chair in time for Aggie to set a mug of steaming tea on the table before me.

'I saw him at Vern's right before his shift,' I whispered, my hands forming into fists and resting on the tops of my thighs. 'What happened?'

'Drink,' she insisted, pushing the mug toward me.

I lifted the cup, breathing in the scent of mint tea and letting the warmth from the mug seep into my hands and chase away some of the chill that had settled in my bones.

'Tell me.'

'It was just after curfew. He'd only been on shift for an hour when Torin Bond's son found him,' Aggie began, leaning toward me as if she could feel I was barely hanging onto my wits.

'Torin Bond's son,' I repeated numbly, taking a sip of the scalding tea and letting it burn down my throat.

Aggie nodded. 'Torin's son is a friend of Councilor Baskan's son, Roald. Leif told me the two of them walked into the water treatment facility with a patrol guard, and no one stopped them.'

Leif was another member of the Collective. He was the same age as Jed, and they had most of their shifts at the facility together.

'What did they do?' I set the mug back on the table before my trembling hands could drop it.

'They attacked him. Had him arrested as soon as he fought back.'

'But he was defending himself! That's not a crime,' I cried, slapping the table.

'If the Councilor's son says it's a crime, it's a crime,' Aggie said, gripping her mug of tea so hard her knuckles turned white.

'But why hurt him? Why not me?'

'Leif said they taunted Jed. Told him they came here to your apartment, but when you weren't home, they figured sending him to Endlock in your place would be the next best thing.'

The unlocked door.

They'd come to find me, and instead of being here to take their wrath, I'd been drinking at Vern's with the intention of warming a stranger's bed.

I hadn't protected Jed.

I stood, reaching for my jacket. 'We can talk to Captain Flint,' I told Aggie. 'I'll do a few jobs for free. Let him keep the credits in exchange for freeing Jed.'

'It's too late, Raven.' Aggie touched my shoulder. 'They put Jed on the evening transport. He'll have already reached Endlock by now.'

Her words hung heavy in the air, running through my head on an endless loop. Jed was at Endlock.

I sucked in a deep breath. My hands trembled, and the room spun around me as I struggled to draw in enough air. 'We have to do something.'

Aggie watched me spiral out of control and, realizing she'd have to be the calm one of us, quickly ushered me back to my seat and sat across from me.

'I have to get him out,' I whispered.

'And you will,' she answered without hesitation, and some of the tension left my body.

'How?' I asked. My voice was small, almost childlike.

'I spoke with the Collective before I came here. They've agreed to help you get Jed to safety, in exchange for your assistance. You do us a few favors, and we'll get you into Endlock.'

'How am I supposed to help Jed if I'm locked up alongside him?' I asked, disbelief sharpening my words.

'My dear, the only way to break out of Endlock is from the inside.'

'Break him out?' A humorless laugh burst from my lips. 'No one's ever escaped.'

'Yet. We have someone on the inside who's been working on it for quite some time. Between the two of you, with the Collective on your side, you'll be able to do it.'

'So that's it, then?' She made it seem so easy, but I knew that no one who entered Endlock as an inmate had ever left. 'I do you a few favors, and your contact helps me break out of Endlock? And then what? Where would we go?'

'No,' Aggie said. 'The favors include you helping Jed *and* our contact escape. Then the three of you make the journey to the North Settlement, and you make sure our contact gets across the Wastes unharmed.'

'Are you *insane*?' I hissed. 'It will be impossible to get Jed out as it is, and I'm supposed to walk in there and escape with him *and* a total stranger and make it all the way to the North Settlement?'

Aggie closed her eyes and took a deep breath before speaking. 'I don't think you understand this situation, Raven. I had to call in all the favors I'm owed within the Collective for them to agree to allow you to go with our contact to the North Settlement. The only reason they agreed is because I convinced them the combat skills you've acquired as a bounty hunter will be invaluable in protecting our contact while you travel across the Wastes. They don't care about you and Jed. *I* do. I told them you'd never join us if we didn't help Jed, too.'

She was right, of course.

And I'd never be able to get out of Endlock on my own.

A plan with a high likelihood of death was still better than the certain death Jed would face if I didn't try.

I sighed, rubbing my eyes. 'What's so special about this contact that the Collective is willing to risk it all to get them out?'

'Need-to-know basis, Raven.' Aggie took a swallow of tea from her mug. 'You're not one of us.'

Fair enough. 'How do you know your contact will still be alive by the time I get there? They could be killed in a hunt any day.'

'She could.' Aggie nodded. 'But she'll be alive. She's been chosen a few times, but for the most part she's good at keeping her head down during hunt selections. And we have people on the inside that intervene from time to time.'

I reached a hand up to stroke the locket I wore around my neck, a mindless, comforting gesture that I'd repeated thousands of times since my mother had given me the necklace.

'I don't understand,' I finally said, when I'd managed to calm myself a bit. 'Why are you asking me to do this if you have people on the inside?'

'Kit isn't their main focus. They only help her when they can do so without compromising their missions.'

Missions.

Apparently, Aggie had kept more from me than I'd realized over the years. For her to have assets inside Endlock . . . it was unfathomable to me.

'Can you tell me who they are? In case I need help?'

She shook her head. 'No. If someone caught you with that information . . .'

'I wouldn't give them up,' I insisted.

'You've never been tortured,' Aggie whispered, and my mouth dropped open. 'And I believe you'd give anyone up if it meant sparing Jed's life.'

I looked away, not wanting her to see the truth of her words on my face. 'Okay. I understand. Need-to-know basis.'

Aggie nodded, and I blew out a long breath, still boiling over with questions.

'And the North Settlement's leaders will let us in when we arrive? Just like that?'

Dividium was one of five cities that had formed fifty years ago, after the second Civil War tore apart what had once been the United States. Two of the other cities were on the East Coast, like Dividium, though they were hundreds of miles away, inaccessible across the Wastes. The other two cities were on the West Coast. All of the cities were self-governed, operating separately from each other, with their own leaders and laws. From what I knew about the other cities, which admittedly wasn't much, none of them had a prison system like Endlock.

Aside from the cities, I'd only heard whisperings – hushed con-versations in forbidden basement taverns – of settlements where people lived with more freedom. Places that hadn't been hit as hard by nuclear warfare, where the land had been able to bounce back more quickly and could sustain small populations of people who preferred to live in a more rustic setting, away from the modern infrastructure that the settlements didn't have the materials to erect.

The North Settlement was the closest settlement to Dividium, and while I knew it existed, until I could lay eyes on it myself, my brain insisted it was a complete fantasy.

'The North Settlement's leaders don't allow just anyone inside,' Aggie said. 'But if you're with our contact, they'll let you in. We've worked out a deal.'

'A deal?'

'Need to know,' Aggie repeated pointedly.

I couldn't help but roll my eyes, but I nodded all the same.

There wasn't any choice.

'Melody and Keaton would be proud,' Aggie whispered, and my breath caught.

My parents.

I hardly ever heard their names anymore. My father had led the Lower Sector cell of the Collective before his and my mother's arrests, and that era of the Collective had been more focused on keeping people out of Endlock than waging any attacks on the Council.

They were peacemakers, and they would've hated that I was a bounty hunter.

But I imagined Aggie was right – they would've been proud of me for daring to save Jed.

I took a deep breath.

'Okay. I'll do it. When do I go to Endlock?'

Aggie swallowed the last of her tea, and pushed herself to her feet.

'Today.'

4

WE STEPPED OUT of my apartment and into the congested square, passing citizens spending their hard-earned credits on food and supplies, all of which would barely stretch to sustain them through the week. Their eyes carefully evaluated the most affordable produce and grains as merchants packaged up bruised vegetables and loaves of steaming seed bread.

I passed a salesman who attempted to reel in customers by shouting about heavy discounts on last season's Endlock merchandise, and waving around pamphlets that outlined financing options for those who couldn't afford to pay up front for a visit to Endlock.

'This isn't all I have, miss!' the man shouted, practically in my ear, as he latched onto my arm. 'If you have information on someone who's committed a crime, you can report them here. I'm a representative from the Endlock Experience office, so I'm authorized to give you credit toward a hunt at Endlock in exchange for any information that leads to an arrest.'

My lip curled, and I shook off his touch. The Endlock credit program was just the latest scheme to ensure citizens didn't trust each other.

I glanced to my right, giving my back to the salesman, and caught sight of Graylin. He walked among a group of children, handing out ration bars from a satchel.

When we were children, Gray and I used to accompany my mother and Aggie on similar missions. On one of those days, we'd run out of rations and Gray had given his own breakfast to a young boy who'd missed out.

The Collective had grown its numbers significantly since we were young, with a few thousand recruits spread throughout the city. That meant more resources, and that the satchel Gray carried today was comically large.

If I hadn't been so nervous, I might have smiled, but I looked away before he caught me staring.

Run-down buildings encircled the square, their once proud windows cracked or entirely missing their glass, bandaged with tarps and scraps of fabric that flapped in the breeze.

Many of the merchants kept a wary eye on me as I wound my way through their stalls. They knew who I was and that I sent people to Endlock to pay my bills. They couldn't afford to turn down my credits, but didn't offer smiles or polite conversation.

Smoke and spices filled the air, and my mouth watered. One merchant cooked giant grubs over an open fire, and I watched as fat dripped from the skewers and sizzled when it hit the flames.

She caught me looking. 'Five credits.'

'No, thank you.' I shook my head and kept walking. Grubs and insects were standard fare in the Lower Sector, more affordable than fresh meat, and not half bad if cooked by the right vendor.

Aggie walked ahead of me, dressed the part of a wealthier Middle Sector citizen, with a forged wristband that stated her reason for being in the Lower Sector as visiting a relative, in case a guard stopped to check her story. She was far enough away that no one suspected her of accompanying me.

I stepped around a building, and the jail came into view. In front of it, a transport idled. Exhaust clouded the space around the rig, and the scent of fuel was heavy in the air. Fugitives shuffled out the side door of the jail and up the stairs to the transport – a task made difficult by the chains binding their ankles. The guards barked at them, urging them to move faster.

I paused, counting the seconds as they ticked away until—

Aggie stopped in view of the guards, carrying a basket laden with goods from the market – small bags of flour and oats, and a few vegetables wrapped in brown paper.

I continued walking and, when I passed her, I deliberately elbowed her hard enough that she dropped her basket, and all of its contents fell to the street.

She grabbed my hand once and squeezed. I pretended not to see the tears slipping from her blue eyes as I turned my back on her, running, half-heartedly, in the other direction.

'Guards! Guards, come quickly! She's stolen from me!'

The guards were close enough that they were there in an instant, grabbing my wrists and hauling them behind my back as they dragged me toward Aggie. They took one look at her in her new pants and neat button-up, and me in my stained, threadbare clothes, and I could tell they'd immediately made up their minds about who to believe.

One of them reached into the pocket of my jacket and pulled out my mother's silver locket, and I bit my lip.

'Is this what she stole?' another one of the guards asked, his grip cutting off the blood flow in my arm.

'It is,' Aggie said, her voice unrecognizable in its disdain. 'The girl nearly made off with a family heirloom.'

The locket was the last thing my mother had gifted me. Her mother had given it to her, and she'd ripped it from her throat when the guards were banging on our apartment door to drag her off to Endlock. I knew Aggie would protect it while I was away.

'Captain!' the guard called toward the entrance to the city jail, handing the locket to Aggie and pulling me away from her. 'We've got another one. Want her on this transport?'

Flint glanced over, bored, but when his eyes landed on me they widened almost comically. 'Raven Thorne? What's happened?'

'She was caught stealing from another citizen. There's still time to process her and get her on today's transport to the prison,' the guard reported. If he noticed the change in Captain Flint's expression, he ignored it.

'Damn it all,' Flint huffed. 'You'll cost me a good chunk of my commission, girl.'

His . . . commission?

I waited for him to say he'd misspoken. To demand evidence that I'd committed a crime. To at least have the decency to look *sad*.

But he only stared, seeming to look through me like he didn't know me at all. Like he hadn't saved me from starvation when my parents died. Like he hadn't seen me weekly for years, and asked after me and Jed.

I thought it had been because he'd seen a struggling child and cared enough to step in, but I swallowed against the sudden realization that he'd only ever seen me as a paycheck.

I blinked away the ridiculous tears prickling at the back of my eyes, and cleared my throat.

'Sorry to inconvenience you, Captain,' I retorted, my voice dripping with forced sarcasm. 'Would you like to escort me onto the transport now, or would you prefer to keep on with this stunning display of compassion?'

'I've never been one for pretty, hollow words,' he said, glancing at his tablet and swiftly scanning the information on the screen. 'There's still room for her on this transport. Get her prepped.'

And then he turned on his heel and walked back into the jail.

Another guard approached with two sets of manacles.

She fastened the shackles over my limbs. After that, walking became nearly impossible. My steps were slow and faltering, an agonizing shuffle, as the guard pushed me up the transport steps. The cuffs chafed at my ankles within moments.

Inside, an aisle ran the length of the transport, flanked by rows of bench seats stretching toward the rear. I lurched toward the first vacant spot.

'Isn't that the bounty hunter?' a voice called from the back of the vehicle, their words cutting through the sound of the rumbling engine.

The question froze me in my tracks, and a shiver traced its way down my spine.

Terrible fates awaited people like me in Endlock, not just at the hands of the hunters. The prisoners would view me as their enemy, no better than the guards who kept them under lock and key.

Maybe worse, since I was supposed to be one of them but had chosen the life of a traitor.

'It *is* the bounty hunter,' a woman chimed in. 'I saw her talking to Flint.'

I forced my lips into a smirk. I couldn't let them see my fear. If I did, I wouldn't stand a chance.

Soon, the transport was a cacophony of jeers and taunts as the rest of the soon-to-be prisoners told me exactly what would befall me once we arrived at Endlock.

I was about to ease onto a seat when a leg shifted into the aisle, blocking my path. I didn't have time to dodge the limb, and lost my footing. Since the shackles effectively immobilized my hands and feet, there was nothing to break my fall. I landed face-first, my forehead hitting the floor with a resounding thud.

A groan slipped past my lips, and a dizzying array of stars swam in my vision as I rolled onto my side, drawing my knees up to my chest to get back to my feet. I could feel the beginnings of a splitting headache.

'Oops,' a gravelly voice called to me. I looked up to find a fugitive leaning precariously over the aisle, a triumphant sneer on his bearded face. 'Better watch where you're going. You wouldn't want to break any bones before your first hunt.'

I met his eyes, rage coating my throat. 'I've broken plenty of bones, but none of them were my own.'

Then I painstakingly hoisted myself upright and slid into the nearest available seat. My nose throbbed, but a quick touch assured me it remained unbroken.

'They're all going to hate you,' the man called. 'The other inmates, I mean. They'll kill you before the hunters get a chance.'

'They can try,' I said, with more confidence than I felt.

5

THE GUARDS WAVED the transport through the city's barrier wall, and then the vehicle crawled over the potholed road that threaded between the fields of scraggly crops that sustained Dividium.

The fields dwindled until the only thing that could be seen for miles on all sides was cracked, bone-dry dirt. Not a living creature or shrub in sight.

The Wastes.

After some time, the rumbling of the transport's engine lulled me into a fitful sleep.

In my dreams, Jed was a child again, and we were on the hunting grounds at Endlock. Only I was chained down, forced to watch as Jed died a hundred deaths at the hands of hunters, their faces twisted into monstrous grins as they shot him in the back. They laughed maniacally, parading around with his corpse like it was some kind of grotesque trophy, even as I screamed and screamed.

I woke, panting, when the transport went over a nasty bump in the road and I nearly flew into the aisle. Bleary-eyed, I jerked my body upright, my manacles grating against the raw flesh of my wrists as I turned toward the windows lining the side of the vehicle. My breath hitched in my chest.

Instead of the crowded buildings and towering structures customary in Dividium, a sprawling expanse of forest stretched out on either side of the road. Trees, lush and brilliantly green, crowded the terrain. Rays of fading sunlight trickled through the branches, painting everything with a hint of gold.

A few scattered trees, wisp-thin and sickly, stood in the Lower Sector.

In the Middle and Upper Sectors, with everything spread out generously, I knew residents had access to carefully manicured parks filled with hardy trees and shrubs that managed to survive the contaminants in our soil – places they could go to escape the endless maze of concrete.

Still, the flourishing greenery before me was a far cry from those uninspired spaces in the city. I hadn't realized such untamed nature had continued to exist after the war.

We drove past a turnout with a sign that said *Turn here to visit the new campground accommodations, Camp Endlock*.

A few minutes later, the trees gave way to a gleaming five-story hotel and resort. Guests dined at outdoor tables in the courtyard, and others lounged by a pool at the side of the building, sipping cocktails while their children splashed in the water and laughed. Lower Sector citizens dressed in polished uniforms walked between the guests, handing out drinks, folding towels, and taking food orders.

Some guests stood and pointed as they watched our transport rumble by, excitement widening their eyes.

The vehicle continued up the road, past a childcare center, shops, and several restaurants.

The buildings consumed me so thoroughly that I failed to notice the slowing of the transport until we came to a standstill, the brakes screeching loud enough to make my ears ring. I tore my gaze from the window to take in the view through the windshield, which revealed a daunting set of iron gates flanked by watchtowers.

The driver gestured to a uniformed figure perched in one of the watchtowers. A buzzer sounded, and the gates began their slow swing inward. Once we passed through, they closed with a metallic clang behind us – and then my attention was drawn to the structure ahead.

The first sight of Endlock stole my breath.

The building was a fortress. It rose scarcely higher than a two-story building in Dividium, yet it stretched across the property and out of my sight. It was made up of bare concrete walls studded with narrow, barred windows.

I imagined an endless layout of grid-like rooms with low ceilings that would push down in a claustrophobic embrace. My breaths came in short spurts as my gaze swept over the property.

Outside, a fence sliced through the landscape, a metal serpent emerging from the forest and coiling protectively around a vast field and the perimeter of Endlock.

Every hundred yards or so, watchtowers punctuated the fence, each manned by guards, their rifles held at the ready.

Beyond the chain-link fence, there was no sign of activity. Instinctively, I knew the field was part of the hunting grounds – a two-mile-long forested cage where visitors to Endlock were released upon their chosen targets.

The growl of the vehicle's engine died out, and my eyes tracked a uniformed figure that slipped from the prison's front entrance. He approached us with brisk, stiff strides, mounting the transport's steps to stand at the end of the aisle. His assessing gaze swept over us.

He wore a uniform consisting of a starched black shirt that reached his throat, a matching pair of black cargo pants, and tightly laced leather boots. *Warden* was stitched onto the breast

pocket on the left side of the shirt in bold white letters, and the
flag of Dividium decorated his right shoulder. He was balding,
with a salt-and-pepper beard framing his round face, and skin
pale enough that it bordered on translucent. He wore three short
strings of teeth around his neck – he hadn't opted to shave them
down, so they maintained their natural shape.

At least a hundred teeth.

I fisted my hands on my thighs, swallowing against the bile
rising in my throat.

'Welcome to your new home,' the man said, a serpentine grin
curving his thin lips. 'I'm Warden Larch.'

A chill slipped beneath my skin, turning my blood to solid ice
in my veins.

'I'll be leading you through the building until we reach the processing area,' Warden Larch continued. 'Remain behind me at all
times. We will encounter guests. If you try to harm them, we will
kill you without hesitation. And if we kill you, we'll lose out on the
fee a hunter would have paid for the opportunity to take your life.'

His concern for our well-being was touching.

'Is that understood?' Warden Larch asked curtly, demanding
our acknowledgment.

I nodded my head along with everyone else, my pulse kicking
into gear.

'Let's get you checked in, then,' Larch said, exiting the transport.

We filed out behind him, a group of guards surrounding us.

Endlock didn't have a separate entrance for prisoners.

As soon as we stepped into the front lobby, I understood why.

A group of hunters stood next to a check-in counter, crowded
around a life-sized cardboard cutout of Pharil Coates, the CEO of
Endlock Enterprises.

Coates was a celebrity in Dividium. He was wealthy, and powerful from the success of Endlock, and had a mansion in the Upper

Sector that was larger than any home owned by the Council. He was handsome enough that he couldn't go anywhere without a group of fans following him and proclaiming their love. There'd even been a famous reporter a few months back, Blythe Levine, who had been arrested and sent to Endlock for stalking Coates.

When the hunters saw us, they stopped what they were doing, pointing at us and whispering excitedly as Warden Larch motioned for us to stand against a wall painted with a mural of trees.

'Warden, sir!' A woman in a pink skirt suit and a gold-plated name tag that read *Rina* stepped out from behind the check-in desk and walked toward us, heels clacking against the white marble-tiled floor as she spoke to the group of hunters. 'You bunch are in luck. Not everyone gets to meet Warden Larch.'

Larch stepped up as if playing a rehearsed part.

'Welcome to Endlock,' he said to the guests, his smile threatening to split his cheeks. 'As you can see, this new transport of prisoners has just arrived. They haven't been processed yet, so you can't officially select them as targets, *but* . . .' Here, he paused for effect.

Officially? My mouth went dry. Was there something worse than being selected as a target? Some sort of off-the-books execution package the hunters could purchase?

The other sounds faded away as I scanned the lobby for a weapon. There was a paperweight on Rina's desk, but the nearest guard would shoot me down or knock me unconscious with the wooden baton hanging from their belt before I could make it that far. But . . . I looked down at the shackles binding my wrists together, and the corners of my lips twitched.

The guards had unwittingly armed me with everything I needed to strangle them, or the hunters, should I need to defend myself. Of course, I wouldn't be able to take them all down, but I wouldn't die without taking a few of them with me. Not if they weren't going to give me the chance to see Jed again.

I widened my wrists, the chain between them going taut, readying for an attack.

The hunters leaned closer, hanging on Larch's every word as he continued. 'If you've purchased the photo package, you can step right up for a photo opportunity with these prisoners.'

The photo package?

My brow furrowed. Surely, we weren't exciting enough for the hunters to be willing to spend their credits on—

The hunters rushed us, jostling me hard enough that I stumbled into the prisoner standing next to me. He glared as I righted myself.

A photographer came forward, directing the hunters. 'One group at a time, now. Quickly, quickly. Don't worry – they're restrained. They can't hurt you.'

I fought the urge to bare my teeth.

Keep your head down. Get to Jed without getting yourself killed.

'Photography and cameras of any kind are prohibited during hunts and on the hunting grounds, so this is one of the only opportunities to have your picture taken with inmates,' Larch announced. 'If you want to add on the photo package so you don't miss out, Rina can help you out at her desk.'

I rolled my eyes as a gaggle of hunters rushed to Rina's desk, waving their wristbands in her face.

'Warden, sir.' A middle-aged woman in a T-shirt with the slogan *Endlock: The Thrill of a Lifetime* sidled up next to Larch, resting a hand on his bicep and batting her lashes. 'I was wondering if I could get a photo. Just the two of us.'

Larch gave her a smarmy smile, smoothing back the few strands of hair on his head before posing with her, his hand resting dangerously low on her back.

When the photo op was over, the guards walked us down a long hallway past a gift shop flaunting Endlock-branded apparel and trinkets, intricately drawn maps of Endlock and the hunting grounds, and countless other souvenirs. After the gift shop, we passed a set of locker rooms that I guessed were meant for the hunters.

We stopped at the next door and were thrust into a dark room, and forced to stand as each prisoner was led, one by one, behind a black door.

Inmates stepped behind the door, and none reemerged.

I gripped the fabric of my cargo pants tightly between my fingers to hide the shaking in my hands.

'Landis Caraga,' a guard called out.

The man from the transport, the one who'd tripped me, took an unsteady step forward but stopped short when a distant, muffled scream came from behind the door.

'No,' Landis whispered, shaking his head. 'Fuck this. I'm not going back there.' And he made a break for the exit.

Four steps.

That's how far he made it before a guard lifted her gun and buried a bullet in the back of his head.

My mouth flapped open on a silent scream, and I brought my chained hands to my ears in a futile attempt to stop the ringing there.

Around me, inmates dissolved into a mixture of shouts and sobs and silence, but none of us moved toward Landis.

None of us tried to escape. We just watched as a growing pool of red seeped from Landis's lifeless body.

'Raven Thorne.'

My head snapped up at the summons, my gaze colliding with the hulking guard who'd called my name. My feet were rooted to the spot.

My hesitation pressed the guard's patience, and before I could take a step, I felt the prod of his rifle against my spine, the metal barrel cool through my threadbare shirt.

I shuffled forward as fast as my manacles allowed and stepped through the door.

Blinding fluorescent lights assaulted my eyes.

Then, rough hands were on me, unshackling my restraints and letting them clatter gracelessly to the floor.

'Take your clothes off.'

My gaze shifted toward the source of the voice, and my newly freed hands went to my neck, reaching for a locket that was no longer there.

'Take. Your. Clothes. Off,' the guard repeated, her tone thick with irritation. She fidgeted with the collar of her uniform as she spoke, her hair pulled back so tightly I half expected the strands to pluck themselves from her head. Behind her, in the upper corner of the room where the wall met the ceiling, a camera was pointed directly at me, its red light blinking to show it was recording.

I didn't ask why. Not now that I realized the only protection I'd thought I had – Endlock caring enough about making money off me to keep me alive until my first hunt – was non-existent.

The guard didn't avert her gaze until my trembling hands touched the hem of my shirt.

I tried to keep my eyes clenched shut, but I saw Landis every time I closed them, his blood spreading across the concrete floor.

Breathe, Raven.

In*, two, three, four.*

Out*, two, three, four.*

I lifted my shirt over my head and dropped my pants, then my undergarments, using my hands to hide myself as best I could.

I'd never felt so exposed. So vulnerable. I could feel the guard's hateful gaze and struggled not to let my mind focus on the camera watching my every move. This was a violation, cold and sterile.

I shivered as the guard examined my body. When she was finished, she grabbed my wrist, removing my wristband – effectively removing my identity and every credit I had to my name. She replaced it with a new, black wristband, one that didn't have a screen. Once clamped on, secured tightly enough that it pinched the skin on my wrist, the device was void of any hinge point or visible clasp. The number 224 was printed in white across the smooth, seamless exterior and a small green dot of light glowed next to it.

I didn't bother to ask what it was for.

The guard tossed my clothes into a metal bin in the corner and handed me a new set of undergarments and a backless medical gown.

Reading the confusion in my eyes, she let out a huff and said, 'The doctor needs to conduct a physical examination. It contributes to your ranking.'

'What – the faster I can run, the more I'm worth to the hunters?' The words slipped out before I could stop them, and I froze, my heart in my throat as I waited for her to pull her gun on me.

But she barely glanced at me as she said, 'Something like that.'

The guard ushered me into an adjoining room, where a woman lounged on a rolling chair, her pen scribbling across a clipboard.

Her silver hair swirled about her tawny cheeks, curls bouncing with every move she made. Adjusting her spectacles, she glanced at me with a bright smile that raised my brows. It felt like a trap.

'I'm Dr Amelia Row.' She extended her hand toward me.

I flinched at her sudden movement.

Dr Row's smile wavered, and she retracted her hand without touching me. 'I'm going to examine you for injuries and ask you a few health-related questions. Okay?'

I nodded, biting my lip as I waited for her to revert to the cruelty or disdain I'd encountered from the other prison staff.

'Excellent.' She gestured toward an examination table draped with a sheet of medical paper. 'Take a seat for me, Raven.'

I quirked a brow at the unexpected use of my name, and she

lifted her clipboard in explanation. The paper sheet crinkled beneath my bare thighs as I jumped up on the table.

'Do you have any pre-existing health conditions?'

I scanned the walls until my eyes landed on a camera identical to the one I'd seen in the previous room.

I frowned. 'None that I'm aware of.'

'When was the last time you had a medical examination?'

'I've never had one.'

She looked unfazed as she jotted down my reply with her pen.

I'd focused on medical studies in my final years of school and learned enough to provide basic aid for my family, so we'd managed to avoid paying for professional care.

Over the next fifteen minutes, Dr Row performed my examination with far more professionalism and kindness than the guard in charge of my strip-search.

At the very least, there seemed to be one friendly face in this hellhole.

'You're a remarkably healthy young woman, Raven. You could survive a long time in here.'

I suppose she meant to comfort me with the words, but they did nothing to soothe the sharp edges of my worry. My health would offer me little defense against rifles and blades.

'Lucky me,' I said under my breath.

Dr Row rapped on the door, and it opened almost immediately. The guard on the other side grasped my arm, yanking me away from the brief respite the examination room offered.

The guard led me to a third room, where another guard stood at a counter, his back to me, fiddling with some sort of device.

My escort left me inside the room, and the door slammed.

Papers crinkled as the guard set down the device and picked up a clipboard.

'Arrested for theft,' he read off my record, sounding bored. 'Parents were rebels.'

He stiffened as he read the second part, and so did I. He finally turned to face me.

Both of us froze when we made eye contact.

'Raven?' The guard's mouth fell open, and I noted the fresh cut across the bridge of his nose and the bruising under his eye where I'd punched him the night before.

Vale.

6

'WHAT ARE YOU doing here?'

We spoke the words simultaneously, and I stepped back toward the door.

Vale glanced up at the corner of the room before answering, and when I followed his gaze, I caught sight of yet another camera.

He cleared his throat, looking away from me. 'I work here.'

The nausea I'd experienced the night before returned with new intensity. The only thing worse than kissing a patrol guard was kissing one of Endlock's guards.

Which begged the question of what a guard from Endlock had been doing in the Lower Sector the night before, at Vern's of all places. He'd said he was indebted to Eris, but why would someone who worked at Endlock be mixed up with a Collective leader?

'Raven Thorne,' he read from his clipboard, interrupting my thoughts. His lip curled. 'You're a criminal. A *rebel*.'

I shrugged, not wanting to mention his *own* connection to the rebels and give up the information to anyone who might be watching us through the camera. Not when I might be able to use it to my advantage.

Vale took a deep breath and pinched his lips together. After a long silence, he cleared his throat, shifting his attention back to the contraption on the counter.

'Sit,' he ordered, his voice a deep growl.

My eyes darted to the lone seat in the room – a gray metal chair, bolted to the floor, the armrests and legs equipped with restraints clearly meant for securing limbs.

Next to the chair, a silver bucket sat on the floor, filled to the brim with water.

I rolled my shoulders back, my head warring between following his orders and staying as far from the restraints as possible. Landis had been killed for defying the guards and trying to escape, but Vale . . . I didn't think he'd kill me. Not when he hadn't bothered to pull his gun on me when I'd punched him the night before. Not when the memory of our lips touching was still fresh.

'Looks inviting.' I cleared my throat. 'But I'd prefer to stand.'

His posture grew impossibly rigid, and he grumbled something unintelligible under his breath but didn't answer me. He didn't even turn around to meet my gaze. Instead, one hand fell to his outer thigh, and he patted his holstered gun in warning.

I jolted, internally cursing myself for being so stupid. He was a guard. Of course he'd shoot me without blinking.

But.

He hadn't shot me. He'd only threatened to. And while that wasn't *great* for me, it was certainly a step up from some of the other guards I'd encountered.

'You know what? It's been a long day,' I said, sitting without further argument. Crossing my legs at the ankles and resting my hands in my lap, I maintained as much distance from the restraints as possible. The cool metal of the chair pressed into my skin, raising goosebumps along my arms.

I felt utterly exposed in the skimpy medical gown that barely grazed my thighs.

'What do you know about Endlock?' Vale asked.

I looked up to find him leaning against the counter, facing me again, his jaw clenched and his arms crossed over his chest.

His gun rested safely in its holster on his thigh.

'I know that citizens pay to hunt inmates here. For entertainment,' I bit out. 'And that you let them.'

His eyes shuttered. 'Citizens pay to hunt *criminals* here,' he corrected me. 'For the betterment of Dividium.' A muscle ticked in his jaw as he spoke.

'So you say.'

'Do you know what life is like for inmates here?'

'Wretched, I'd expect.'

He nodded. 'For some of them. But there are rankings – Lower, Middle, and Upper, just like in Dividium. All inmates, with a few exceptions, start at the Lower level. Cramped quarters. Shit food. Low price on your heads.'

With a few exceptions. I rolled my eyes. He meant people from the Upper Sector, like Torin, who'd probably have wealthy hunters lining up, willing to pay any price to hunt him.

'You're really selling it,' I managed through gritted teeth. He clearly enjoyed rubbing reality in my face. I wondered if he was embarrassed now that he realized he'd been associating with a true criminal. A rebel.

'If you do well in the hunts, you can move up. Moving up means more food. More freedom – a higher cost to hunt you.'

'Why are you telling me this?' I asked. 'Do you think you'll still have a chance of crawling into my bed if I make it to the Upper level? Is that the freedom you're referencing? Because I'd die before I touched you again.'

I clapped a hand over my mouth as soon as the words escaped. *Fuck.* I hadn't meant to get that heated. I'd pushed too far.

But Vale didn't so much as flinch at the venom in my voice. 'Don't flatter yourself, inmate. I'm required to go over the logistics with each new arrival.'

Oh.

My cheeks flamed.

'Vale!' a muffled voice called through the door.

'What?' Vale turned from me.

The door opened a crack.

'Larch wants to know what the holdup is.' The new guard's eyes flitted over to me. He opened the door wider, and a wolfish whistle slipped past his lips. 'Must be because you're having some extra fun with this one, eh?'

The guard had a gray tint to his skin, like many of the drunks who frequented Vern's. He was shorter than me, maybe up to my nose if I was standing at my full height, and his stomach strained against the buttons of his uniform shirt. He had a toothpick dangling from his cracked lips, and a single tooth hung from a chain around his neck.

'Don't be ridiculous, Mort. I would never touch an inmate,' Vale snapped.

'Might as well have a good time with her before the other prisoners rip her apart.' Mort shrugged, and a chill snaked down my spine at his words.

'Why would they rip her apart?' Vale asked, arching a brow in my direction.

'Because she's a *bounty hunter*,' Mort said, chewing his toothpick. 'She's put more than a few of them in here. I'd want a piece of her if she did that to me.'

Vale's eyes snapped to mine with something like confusion in his gaze. I met him with a hard stare, unflinching, daring him to judge me.

'Is that true?' he asked, his voice deadly soft. He scanned the clipboard, and I knew the moment he read the evidence. His eyes narrowed. 'Must have been a cover to keep the guards from real-izing you were a rebel all these years.'

'Why don't you come a little closer,' I purred, batting my lashes. 'Find out for yourself.'

And then something hit my face, so hard that my head snapped to the side and my teeth cut into my cheek.

I blinked, stars swimming in my vision as I looked up to see that it was Mort who'd delivered the blow. Not Vale.

'Watch your mouth when you're talking to your superior,' Mort spat, the veins in his neck bulging.

I shut my eyes and blew out a long breath through my nose to keep from snapping back at him.

Vale took a half-step forward and then stopped, his hands form-ing fists at his sides and his gaze hard and impassive. Ice cold. 'Give her a uniform, Mort.'

An unnerving glint flashed in Mort's yellowing eyes. 'But you haven't given her an identifier yet.'

'An identifier?' My brows drew together. 'What do I get, a name tag?'

'I can do it.' Mort took a step toward the counter, the fluorescent lights making the back of his bald head appear shiny. 'Hyde and I have a bet going to see which one of us can leave it on the skin the longest without burning through to the bone. He's not off to the best start – the last inmate he marked passed out and had to be sent to the infirmary.'

Mort grinned at the memory, and I swallowed, trying to figure out what horror they were about to inflict on me that had the potential to burn through to my *bones*. I was starting to wonder how anyone survived Endlock's check-in process to even make it to a hunt.

'No,' Vale snapped, his eyes turning wild for a moment. He cleared his throat at the startled look on Mort's face. 'No. I'll do it.'

He sauntered over to me, bending down, his eyes inches from mine. They'd looked so warm and inviting when I'd met him, but now I realized they were a honeyed trap. He didn't meet my gaze as he positioned my trembling arms, one at a time, on the armrests, strapping them tightly with my palms face up. His skin was a shock of warmth against mine, nearly feverish against my chilled skin.

He was close enough that I could've spat in his face, but I didn't fight him. If I died, Jed would be left to face the hunters alone.

Vale moved to my ankles, repeating the same motions until I had no hope of escaping from the bolted-down chair.

'It doesn't matter what your name was before you got here,' Vale declared, voice frigid. Almost mechanical. 'Your new name is 224. It will remain your name until you die. And then a new inmate will come through, and your name will pass on to them.'

'How sentimental,' I responded. 'And do you plan to tattoo my new name onto my skin? If that's the case, at least let me have some input on the stylistic elements.'

If I kept talking, maybe I could ignore the fear coursing through my veins.

'No. I won't be tattooing you,' Vale murmured. But the noticeable pause before his response had my hair standing on end.

He returned to the counter and retrieved the device he'd been tinkering with earlier.

It was long and thin, tapering toward the top, while its base, embellished with the number 224, was flat. The instrument resembled an oversized stamp, save for a switch on its side.

'What is that?' I asked, my voice wavering, as I jerked my wrist to test the chair's bindings. I couldn't budge an inch.

With a flick of his thumb, Vale flipped the switch, and the digits on the device morphed from an inky black to a blistering, radiant orange.

'It's a branding iron,' Mort announced, a grotesque grin stretching across his face.

Vale turned to face me. Without a hint of hesitation, he brought the searing device down onto my forearm.

And then my skin was on fire.

7

I SCREAMED.

I might have been embarrassed by such a vulnerable display if it hadn't felt like my flesh was melting from my bones.

I inhaled, trying to count my breaths, but my nose filled with the stench of charred skin instead of clean air. I swallowed against the bile that climbed my throat.

When I managed to tear my gaze from the sight of my searing arm to confront Vale, I found him averting his eyes as if my weakness repulsed him enough that he couldn't bear to watch.

In my delirious haze, I almost spat in his face.

But then he lifted the branding iron away from my raw flesh, removed the restraints from my arms, and submerged my blistering forearm in a bucket of water so cool that an involuntary moan of relief escaped my lips.

Steam wafted from where my skin met the water.

'To keep it from burning too deeply,' Vale muttered, too low for Mort to hear.

'Fuck you.' My voice came out humiliatingly weak. So soft I could barely hear it.

It was reckless to provoke a guard, especially after the treatment Mort had shown me, but I hadn't prepared for the pain that came with Endlock's intake process, and my composure slipped.

Vale's eyes flicked up to my face and then away, but he didn't raise a hand to strike me for my disrespectful words. *Interesting.*

A sudden, nauseating realization swept over me.

Jed.

They had branded my little brother. I pictured him strapped to the chair, cowering and defenseless.

Every instinct screamed for me to leap up and sprint from the room to locate him, but my arms were the only limbs freed from the chair's restraints, and Vale, now hovering a few steps away, still had a gun fastened to his thigh. Even if I managed to get past him, Mort blocked the door. And there'd be more guards beyond that.

It won't do Jed any good if I'm dead.

So I remained seated, my scorched arm soaking in the bucket of ice water for what felt like an eternity, then allowed Vale to gingerly bandage the number freshly burned into my skin.

224.

My new identity.

Vale unstrapped my legs, and Mort tossed a dull gray standard-issue jumpsuit in my direction. I used the scrap of material that passed for a medical gown to shield my body from Mort's roaming eyes as I hastily pulled on the clothes. The number 224 stood out in bold font on the back of the jumpsuit, and the vivid red of Dividium's flag adorned the front, just below my right shoulder.

A pair of utilitarian boots landed at my feet, and I laced them in silence.

I stared at my injured arm. I wasn't sure why they bothered branding us if the jumpsuit covered the mark from view.

'Warden Larch wants to make sure you remember who you belong to,' Mort said, as if reading my mind.

I jerked my head up to find him watching me, and clenched my teeth against the words I wanted to hurl in his direction.

'Take her to the mess hall, Mort,' Vale commanded.

It was time to face the other inmates. Time to find Jed. That thought alone was enough to cut through some of the rage and fear clouding my mind.

Mort's hand clamped around my elbow, roughly pulling me upright and dragging me out of the room and down the corridor.

'Listen careful now,' Mort grumbled. He shot a lingering glance my way, stirring an uneasy feeling in my gut. 'No talking back. No starting fights. No physical contact with other inmates. You're only allowed out of your cell for work, meals, showers, and hunts.'

'Yes, *sir*.' I forced the words through my teeth. 'What happens if I . . . *someone* breaks a rule?'

Mort smirked. 'Remember that friendly slap on the cheek I gave you earlier?'

My hands clenched at my sides, but I made myself nod instead of using my fists to wipe the smile off his face.

'That was a warning blow.' Mort gave a fond pat to the wooden baton hanging from his belt. 'If you break the rules, I get to beat you with this. Or worse.'

How fun. 'Any other rules I should know about?'

Mort smiled wider, showing all his teeth as his eyes scanned my body with excruciating slowness. He licked his lips. 'Always obey the guards.'

I swallowed, looking away before he could read the fear and revulsion on my face. I turned my focus to memorizing my surroundings.

There'd been some kind of office directly across from the examination room we'd left, and Mort had had to swipe his keycard against a locked door flanked by a pair of guards standing with their hands placed ready on their batons. The lock had clicked, and the door opened into a new part of the prison.

In the next corridor, we passed a stairwell, and two doors on opposite sides of the corridor labeled A and B. The doors were adorned with narrow, vertical windows, and, as we walked by them, I was able to catch a glimpse through the glass. Behind the doors were long hallways, lined with cells – cellblocks. I didn't have much time to look, but I estimated there were at least fifty cells in each block.

Aside from the guards, the halls outside the cellblocks were lined with dozens of cameras watching our every move. Even if an inmate made it out of their cellblock, they wouldn't get far before running into trouble.

We turned left and passed more doors, with larger windows. I craned my neck, taking in as much detail as I could through the glass. Some of the doors led to maintenance rooms or offices with prison staff sitting behind desks. Through one window, I saw inmates in varying colors of uniform – gray, brown, and green – loading sheets and garments into washing machines, while others folded freshly cleaned laundry.

Based on what Vale had told me, I imagined the uniform colors corresponded with Endlock's ranking system. The inmates in gray must have belonged to the Lower level, like me.

We reached the end of the corridor, and Mort scanned his badge on a reader, unlocking a final door and leading us into what looked to be a cafeteria.

The room was reminiscent of a massive cave encased in cold cement, the low ceiling pressing close, threatening to crush what was left of my composure. Artificial lights bathed the space in an almost blue glow, casting shadows. The raucous chatter of countless inmates echoed off the walls, and plastic utensils clattered against bowls and trays.

The noise faded into the background as I scanned the room for Jed's blonde head and lanky form.

Long, rectangular tables with benches on either side crowded the space, and were occupied with inmates in gray, brown, or green uniforms.

Near the front of the room, a large screen hung at the top of the wall. There were three columns on the screen, with a symbol next to each number. The numbers in the third column all had a yellow circle next to them, while the numbers in the first two columns had either a red X or a green checkmark.

What the hell was this?

Below the screen, more inmates floated in and out of the kitchen with steaming trays of food. They served the food to a line of waiting prisoners.

Guards kept watch from the edge of the room, hands resting on the batons hanging from their belts, and I noted a camera in each of the four corners of the space.

But there was no sign of Jed.

It doesn't mean anything. It's a big prison. He could be anywhere.

The words played on a loop through my mind, like if I focused on them enough, I could keep from panicking.

My gaze shifted to the guards surveilling the room.

I couldn't fathom how Aggie expected me to aid in a prison break beneath so many watchful eyes. It didn't seem like anything went on in Endlock without being recorded.

Mort touched my shoulder, leaning close to whisper in my ear. 'Let me know if there's anything I can do for you. I'm sure we can work out some kind of exchange.' He winked.

I shook myself out of his grasp, my heart pounding against my ribs as I gripped the fabric of my uniform to keep myself from slapping him.

'412!' Mort barked, and a strikingly tall prisoner with rich copper-brown skin and a halo of curls approached us. I noted his green uniform and that he looked to be in his early thirties. He didn't spare me a second glance, his brown eyes resting warily on Mort.

'Fresh meat.' Mort shoved me toward the inmate, and I righted myself before I slammed into him. 'Cell 224 – take her when dinner is over.'

The inmate nodded, turning on his heel and disappearing back into the throng without bothering to see if I followed.

I hesitated for half a second before racing after him, much preferring the company of a fellow prisoner.

'I'm Raven,' I called, practically jogging to catch up to him.

'August,' he said without turning.

I committed the name to memory, even as I scanned the room again in case I'd missed Jed the first time around.

But I hadn't.

'August?' I began, then hesitated.

It was clear Jed wasn't in the mess hall, but the contact Aggie had told me to be on the lookout for might be.

Sure, it was rash to bring up the Collective in front of others, but if I couldn't find Jed right away, my next best option was to locate Kit. Every second I waited brought Jed closer to death, and, as it was, the sound of the other inmates talking should keep the cameras from picking up anything I said.

I lowered my voice. 'Do you know an inmate called Kit Casey?'

August stopped so quickly that I slammed into his back.

He spun on his heels, putting his hands on my shoulders to steady me. 'What?'

'No touching!' a guard hollered across the room. August dropped his hands back to his sides but didn't step away. His brown eyes were steady on mine.

'I'm looking for someone named Kit Casey.' My voice was a whisper now, and August tilted his head closer to hear me.

'No, I—' He looked around, but none of the inmates nearby seemed to be paying any attention to us. 'I heard what you said. What do you want with Kit?' The last part came out rough, almost threatening, and his eyes narrowed on me, taking in every detail.

So he did know her.

And he was obviously protective of her.

I weighed my words carefully. 'We have a mutual friend. And a shared interest in staying alive.'

August's eyes widened, and he stared at me for a long moment. 'I know her, yes.'

I had to fight to keep my mouth from dropping open.

A million thoughts raced through my mind – I could talk to her now. Today. I'd barely been at Endlock for more than a few hours, and I was about to meet Kit and see how close she was to finding an escape route. 'Where is she?'

August pointed to the screen at the front of the room. 'She's not here. She was selected for a hunt today, so she'll have dinner late with the other survivors.'

Understanding dawned on me. 'The screen tracks the inmates being hunted?'

The numbers on the screen were three digits each, like the one that was branded on my arm.

August nodded. 'There are three hunts a day, and up to ten targets are selected for each hunt. The first two hunts were already completed, that's why—'

'The Xs mean an inmate died, and the checkmarks mean they survived?' I concluded, nausea churning my stomach as I counted the number of Xs on the screen. Seven. And the third hunt of the day hadn't even been tallied yet.

'And the yellow circles mean the results of the third hunt haven't been posted yet,' August explained.

My stomach sank. My ticket out of Endlock was currently being hunted by bloodthirsty citizens with *guns*.

'But what if Kit doesn't—'

August cut me off. 'She'll be fine.' He sounded confident about her odds of survival. More than confident – he sounded *sure*.

I narrowed my eyes.

'This isn't the place to talk, anyway,' August said before I could speak. 'Get yourself a tray and some grub from the front. They'll put the food away if you don't hurry, and you can't afford to lose weight here. I'll introduce you to Kit tomorrow.'

I hesitated for only a moment before nodding my thanks to August, hiding my nerves behind a wobbly smile as I rushed to the front of the cafeteria, dodging the glances of curious inmates. Some of the prisoners bore signs of abuse from the guards – split lips and black eyes or, more subtly, in the way they shrank into themselves when they sensed me walking by them. Others met my gaze head-on, asserting their dominance. Everyone was sizing up the new prisoners. I recognized a few people from the transport and even caught a glimpse of Torin. He was wearing a brown uniform, which meant he was one of the exceptions Vale had mentioned – a new inmate who started out with a higher rank because he was from the Upper Sector.

I snagged a tray from the depleted stack and placed a bowl on top.

The platters of food were nearly empty, but on the first table I noticed the remnants of roasted vegetables and . . . was that meat? I leaned toward it, but an inmate with a hairnet and apron stepped into my path.

'Greens only,' the inmate said. 'Gray food is over there.'

She pointed to the last table in the row, and I walked over, remembering what Vale had said about the food for different ranks.

When I reached the table, another inmate ladled a scoop of brown, watery slop into my bowl, and I managed to snag a bruised apple from an otherwise vacant platter.

I'd had much worse.

The workers distributing the food wore brown uniforms, like Torin, which I assumed signified the Middle level. I wondered if all inmates were assigned jobs during their sentences. A stint in the kitchen might not be so bad, especially if it meant access to extra rations, but it must have been a sought-after job if no Grays occupied the space.

Back at the table, August half-heartedly introduced me to some of the inmates sitting on the benches nearby, a blur of grays, browns, and greens, none of whom were Jed or Kit.

'Wait. It's you.'

A voice, two seats down from me.

I turned to find a woman with a green uniform and gritted teeth staring me dead in the face, and I gritted my own teeth.

Of fucking course.

It was Perri.

She was tall and muscular, eyes as gray as the steel skyscrapers in Dividium.

I didn't normally take joy in bounty hunting, but the day I'd turned Perri in had been different – I'd thought it meant no more fake birth control on the streets of the Lower Sector. No more vials of dyed water that she swore would stave off nutrient deficiencies in children.

Unfortunately, it had taken her arrest for me to realize she was only the face of the operation that had infected the city.

'I'm sorry?' I responded, stirring my food and feigning confusion while my mind raced to find a way to defuse the situation.

'You're the reason I'm in here,' Perri seethed, getting to her feet and stalking closer to me. 'She's a bounty hunter, August. She's not one of us.'

I looked around the room, hoping no one had heard, but several inmates were looking on, glaring at me, the anger in their eyes rivaling Perri's. *Great.* I gripped my plastic spoon. If I snapped it in half, it should be sharp enough to break skin, or at least gouge an eye.

But no one moved to attack.

August cast an icy glance in my direction. To my shock, he stared at me for a beat before he pronounced, 'She is now.'

My brows knitted together. He had no reason to draw attention to himself, *especially* not to come to my defense.

I relaxed my grip on the spoon.

'You deserve to be here more than most,' I told Perri, my confidence bolstered by August's words. 'You probably have more blood on your hands than I do.'

Her neck reddened, and the flush crept into her cheeks.

'Not yours. Not *yet*,' she spat back at me, her threat clear.

A bell tolled, snapping the tension, and all the inmates stood.

I gulped down a few hasty mouthfuls of what I now realized was porridge and tucked the apple into the pocket of my jumpsuit before hurriedly clearing my tray and exiting the mess hall on August's heels, keeping a wary eye out in case Perri intended to launch an attack.

I *needed* to find Jed.

'Did you notice any other new arrivals last night?' I asked August, unable to hold the question back any longer. 'I'm looking for my brother – he's tall and lean with blonde hair.'

'That's your brother?' August nodded. 'I know who he is. Kit told me what he did.'

I drew in a breath, skeptical. 'She met him?'

August nodded again. 'She's been at Endlock for months. She tends to befriend the newbies, especially those rumored to have punched Councilor Baskan's son in the face. That'll make him some friends.'

I breathed a sigh of relief, even as I tucked away the new detail about Kit. She'd been at Endlock for a *while*. The Collective had made it clear that they needed my combat skills to get her across the Wastes, which had led me to believe that Kit wasn't able to defend herself. But she clearly had a strategy for survival out on the grounds – one that made August certain he didn't have to worry about her out there.

I shook my head, returning to the conversation at hand. The one in which I'd learned Jed had punched a Councilor's son. I fought a grin. 'That's him. Jed.'

'I can't say you won't have enemies, especially with your background, but that boy? He'll do fine here. Word gets around fast, and people will look out for him as much as they can outside the hunts.'

'We'll see,' I said. But the idea of anyone but me looking out for Jed was ridiculous – they'd be too busy taking care of themselves.

We turned, entering a new corridor. The right side of the passage was lined with cellblocks, six of them in total. We stopped at the very end of the corridor, outside the final cellblock. The letter H was painted, blood-red, on the gray wall next to the card reader.

A guard stepped up, scanning his card and waving his arm to usher the inmates ahead of us into the hall. He stopped when he reached me. 'I don't recognize you. You lost?'

I stiffened, waiting for the guard to draw his baton. But August stepped in front of me, catching the guard's attention.

'It's 224's first day. I'm on orders to show her to her cell.'

Recognition flashed in the guard's eyes at the sight of August, and he grunted, waving us through. I sucked in a relieved breath.

'You don't often hear of people standing up to the Council, especially when those of us from the Lower Sector know how easy it is to get arrested. I've never heard of anyone being that brave,' August continued once we were out of earshot of the guard, admiration seeping through his words.

I felt a surge of pride welling inside me, even as I wished that Jed had chosen safety over bravery. Instead, I found myself glancing around a cellblock, surrounded by the stomping footsteps of dozens of prisoners, searching for a glimpse of his face.

The cells we passed at the beginning of the cellblock were void of any outside decor, and the prisoners within them were all dressed in the same basic gray uniforms.

Above all the cells that I could see, lit up on digital displays, were the inmates' rankings – numbers one through three. The rankings were associated with the price placed on each prisoner's head – the cost of hunting them.

'The rankings for Lower level inmates only go up to three,' August explained when he saw me looking. 'The Middle level is four through seven. The Upper is eight through ten.'

We made it about a third of the way down the hall, and August motioned for me to enter an empty cell. The display above the cell showed a ranking of three.

'Your examination with Dr Row must have gone well if you're already at a three,' he said.

I shrugged, looking into the cell.

A slim cot hugged the wall, draped with a frayed blanket and a thin wisp of a pillow blotted with questionable stains. Opposite, a steel toilet provided an introduction to Endlock's version of privacy. The cell extended a few feet beyond the end of the cot but was narrow enough that I wouldn't have been able to lie across the width of the space. A camera was the only adornment on the otherwise empty walls.

Lovely.

I turned to August, motioning toward his green uniform. 'You've made it to the Upper level. How long have you been here?'

'Two years,' he replied, emotionless. 'But it doesn't take that long to get your rank up. You'll move up to the Middle level if you do well in your first hunt or two. Most people don't survive that long, so the Lower level is basically a rotating door of new inmates. I'd imagine you'll do well and move up, given your history.'

My mouth dropped open. 'You've been here for *two years*?'

'I hold the record.' A sheepish smile curved his lips. 'I'll see you at breakfast. Cellblocks share the same meal shifts.'

Then he left me alone in my cell and walked off.

Two years was impressive, but I knew it painted a massive target on August's back. The wealthy took pride in their hunting skills, and a prisoner who managed to elude their bullets for a year would've been tempting to any of them.

I stuck my head into the corridor, watching August's back as he walked deeper into the cellblock.

'What's your ranking?' I called to him. It was obviously high if he'd made it to the Upper level. But it couldn't have been—

'A ten,' he said without looking back. He entered a cell at the very end and, based on what Vale had told me about Upper level inmates, I had to imagine it was a lot larger, and far more comfortable, than mine.

The guards made their rounds to secure us in our cells, and I was jolted out of my thoughts when a low whistle sounded. A tall, rail-thin guard with a bushy mustache and beard, and what seemed like a permanent slouch, sidled up to my cell. A tooth that had been shaved to a sharp point dangled from one of his ears, and his sleeves were pushed up so I could see what looked like tally marks tattooed across the olive skin of his forearms.

'What have we here?' the guard drawled, gaze flitting up and down my body. 'I haven't seen you around before.'

'No fraternizing with the prisoners, Hyde,' a familiar voice warned, and then Vale was standing next to the guard, his eyes narrowed.

Hyde. The guard who'd taken pleasure in melting through an inmate's skin with a branding iron. Perfect.

Hyde licked his lips, not taking his eyes off me. I fought to suppress the shudder crawling up my spine.

'Careful,' a slimy voice intruded, and Mort stepped into view, still chewing his toothpick. 'That's the bounty hunter. I'd be wary of your *appendages* if I were you.'

Like I'd touch any of you.

The words begged to break free, but I pressed my lips tightly together, glaring at the guards instead. I wasn't used to holding my tongue, but I'd have to learn fast if I wanted to stay alive.

Mort grinned, leaning so close that I could see the food stuck between his teeth from his last meal. He pinched his forefinger and thumb together and then drew them across his lips to mime zipping them. 'Fast learner. You're much prettier with your mouth shut.'

My lip curled, and my nails bit into my palms, the sting keeping me grounded even as I imagined all the ways I could incapacitate the guard. A jab to the throat would do the trick, but it wouldn't be nearly as satisfying as driving my knee into his balls, over and over.

The image brought a smile to my face, and Mort's eyes narrowed. He reached for the handle of my cell door. 'What's so fun—'

'Enough,' Vale commanded, voice dangerously low. 'Mort, I need you to secure A and B Block. Hyde, you take C and D, and I'll be checking your work. No slacking.'

'What crawled up your ass?' Hyde asked, raising a graying brow.

Vale pinched the bridge of his nose. He let out a long breath, as if fighting to keep from throwing a punch at the pair of idiots. 'We want to be ready in case Larch decides to spring an inspection on us. Does he strike you as a man who tolerates anything less than perfection?'

Mort and Hyde hobbled off toward the barrier door without additional argument.

'So sweet of you to step in,' I crooned, nodding after Mort's retreating form. 'But I'm more than capable of taking care of myself.' What made him think I wanted his help, anyway? His choice of profession didn't exactly align with keeping people alive.

'Don't take it personally, 224.' Vale leaned close. 'I'm not in the business of helping rebels out of the kindness of my heart. My job is to make sure everyone is following the rules – inmates and guards alike. Though with you being a bounty hunter, it's going to be hard to enforce the rules around you. Particularly the one that says inmates aren't supposed to engage in fights.'

The fresh burn on my arm pulsed at his proximity.

I ignored the threat in his tone, forcing my lips into a smirk. 'Such a fine example of a law-abiding citizen. Makes me wonder what you owe Eris – something big enough for you to be skulking around the Lower Sector after curfew, hmm?'

Vale's face twitched, but otherwise he gave nothing away. 'Careful. Don't you have enough enemies, Little Bird?'

Then he was swallowed by the shadows of the corridor.

8

I LAY AWAKE for hours on the tiny cot, its worn mattress scratchy beneath me, metal springs poking into my back as I stared at the blinking red light in the corner of my cell.

Amid a chorus of snores from the nearby cells, I formed a mental map of all the parts of Endlock I'd seen – the intake rooms, a maze of locked corridors, the mess hall, and my cellblock. The concrete walls of the prison had to be at least twelve inches thick.

I needed to find Kit and figure out how far she'd gotten into planning, but based on Endlock's security, the most likely escape route lay on the hunting grounds, where there were no cameras and far fewer guards.

There'd been talk of televising the hunts when Endlock first opened, but Pharil Coates had quickly shot the idea down. He said it was for customer privacy, and that allowing the public to view hunts would cheapen the experience. He didn't want anyone to have access to any facet of Endlock unless they had the credits to pay for it.

Luckily, his greed worked in my favor.

I needed to be chosen as a target for a hunt so that I'd have time to explore the hunting grounds unsupervised and learn what I was working with. *And* I needed to keep Jed safe in the meantime, which could prove difficult, considering I didn't even know which cellblock he was in.

Eventually, exhaustion pulled me into a fitful sleep.

Morning came far too quickly, and I rose to the toll of a bell, rubbing at eyes that felt encrusted with sand.

The cell doors slid open with a hiss, and I followed the herd of prisoners toward the mess hall.

Inside, steaming food trays rested on tables for the Middle and Upper level inmates, while the food table for the Grays was stacked with paper-wrapped ration bars.

I'd eaten something similar during the biting winter months when the prices of grain and preserved produce soared beyond what I could justify on my measly income. The ration bars were gritty and bland and had the consistency of cardboard, but they had sustained Jed and me through some tough times.

I scanned the mess hall. There was still no sign of Jed, but I noted Perri glaring at me from the other side of the room. I gave her a wave and a bright smile, and she scowled, squeezing her plastic spoon so hard it snapped in half.

Choking back a laugh, I snatched a ration bar from the pile and veered toward an unoccupied table. Another inmate walked by, driving their shoulder into mine, hard.

'Sorry,' they said, but they smirked, and there was a round of low sniggers from the other inmates nearby.

I bit my lip, weighing the consequences of dropping my ration bar and throwing a punch at them.

'Attention, inmates!' a voice commanded from the front of the room, stopping me in my tracks. 'The new arrivals will be split into different groups for orientation. When I call out your number, step forward.'

Vale. My lip curled.

I hadn't expected any formal initiation into prison life, but the bounty hunter in me knew getting any kind of tour was a good opportunity to familiarize myself with Endlock's layout — anything that would help me find a path out of the prison.

Vale announced a string of numbers as I stuffed the ration bar into my mouth, remembering what August had said about eating enough food to stay strong.

A group of inmates I vaguely recognized from the transport left the mess hall with the first group, following a guard who snapped at them to keep up.

'In group two. Inmates 210, 219, 224 . . .' I tuned out the rest of the numbers but made my way toward the front of the room with my group.

'This group will be with me,' Vale said.

I blanched, my stomach tightening. Of all the guards, of course, it had to be *him*.

He wore the same uniform as Larch — black cargo pants, black boots, and a collared, long-sleeved black shirt with the flag of Dividium on his shoulder. His shirt didn't have his name stitched onto it, and as far as I could tell, he wasn't wearing any teeth around his neck.

He looked up, catching my eyes, and glared.

Happy to see me, then.

Vale pushed open the heavy metal door that led out of the mess hall. 'Don't fall behind.'

The words may have been meant for the entire group, but his piercing gaze lingered on me as he spoke.

Vale led our group through what my mind had begun referring to as the main corridor, its walls stained with age and neglect and decorated with Endlock's signature cameras. The scent of antiseptic, mingling with sweat and fear, hung in the air in a palpable vapor.

As we walked, I noticed the other inmates distanced themselves from me, not wanting to be associated with a bounty hunter. Some snuck stares at me out of the corners of their eyes, but most ignored me entirely, which was just as well – hopefully it meant fewer people scrutinizing me as I tried to find a way out of the prison.

We came to the end of the hall and turned right, stopping short at a barrier door. Vale scanned his badge, nodding to the guards posted on either side of the doorway as we were waved through.

I immediately recognized the exam room entrance on my right, and shivered, the burn on my wrist pulsing. We walked past the room and up to a set of towering steel doors.

Vale scanned his badge again, and I stared when he ushered us through the opening and into an expansive hall. We were met with the slightly sulfurous scent of gunpowder. The heart of the room boasted a firing range, complete with human-shaped targets. I scanned the myriad bullet holes that riddled the targets. Numerous weapons lined the walls: guns and blades and other instruments I couldn't name. A circle of training rings, cushy mats lined with rope, sat a few paces from where we stood, and a large screen took up the wall on the far side of the room with scattered folding chairs resting before it.

'This is where we bring our guests before their hunts officially start,' Vale explained as our group moved into a loose semicircle before him. 'It's designed to prepare them for what to expect and to assist with weapons training for those who have never wielded a knife or firearm.'

The space seemed perfect for training soldiers and preparing armies, but instead I pictured wealthy citizens laughing their way through target practice, anticipatory grins stretching their faces as they placed bets on which of them would take down the most formidable prey.

'After they finish with the shooting range, the hunters who have purchased weapons upgrades are allowed to select their weapon of choice from the wall, while those who haven't are given a standard-issue rifle.' Vale motioned to the weapons. 'The hunters who have purchased additional combat training are also offered a class that teaches basic techniques.'

'Combat training,' I repeated. Vale's eyes snapped to mine, a warning burning in them. But if I could gain any knowledge that would give me an advantage on the hunting grounds, I had to ask. 'I'm surprised they would pay for that, considering they already have guns. Has an inmate ever managed to get the upper hand over a hunter?'

I phrased the question as innocently as I could, but I felt the collective intake of breath from the other inmates.

Vale took a step toward me. 'Physical confrontations between hunters and targets are rare, but they do happen if an inmate manages to disarm a hunter. But inmates are only allowed to engage in a fight with a hunter if it's self-defense – one on one with no other inmates around.'

Vale drew closer, his chest just inches from mine as he spoke. 'Trust me when I say, you don't want that to happen. If it does, and you beat them, your ranking will rise to a ten, and then every hunter with something to prove will want to take a shot at you. *All eyes will be on you.*'

The last part came out as a whisper, and Vale's golden eyes bored into mine. I swallowed, and his gaze flitted down, tracking the movement of my throat.

He coughed, turning away and leading us toward the screen on the wall. The overhead lights dimmed, and the other groups of inmates filed into the room through the door by which we'd entered.

Larch followed close behind.

'Everybody find a seat!' Larch shouted across the space, voice ricocheting off the walls. 'The video you're about to see is the same one that our guests are shown before every hunt.'

Hyde sprang into action, fumbling with a remote until the screen flickered to life and a new voice filled the room. One I recognized from news reports and city-wide video streams.

'A century ago, the human race teetered on the edge of extinction,' Councilor Peña narrated alongside striking imagery – barren riverbeds once overflowing with life and forests rendered skeletal by endless wildfires.

'As natural disasters wiped out food sources, the government implemented strict measures for rationing to keep citizens alive and fed, and implemented martial law to maintain order. But protesters accused the government of hoarding resources for itself. The government tried to appease them, but they only demanded more, even though what they demanded did not exist. When the government did not, *could not*, meet their demands, terrorists launched an attack. And then another. And then the attacks grew in size and ferocity, and the government was driven to retaliate with nuclear warfare. Most of the country perished in the destruction that followed.' The screen showed deserted towns and cities reduced to rubble.

'As the remaining population of the United States emerged from the aftermath of the war, our Founders gathered with like-minded survivors of all backgrounds to create Dividium. The sanctuary city we now call home.'

All citizens knew this history. It was taught in our schools and ingrained in us from a young age.

'Dividium was split into sectors. The Lower Sector, for those skilled in trades – the backbone of our city. Lower Sector citizens provide us with necessities for everyday life. The Middle Sector is for our protectors and innovators: doctors and patrol guards, artists and entertainers, engineers and educators. And our Upper Sector, of course, hosts the guardians of Dividium: your Council and city officials, our army's leaders, and our scientists. Together, we're dedicated to maintaining a city committed to peace and regrowth.'

The camera panned to modern-day Dividium with its sleek skyscrapers and protective wall, and then to the expanse of the hunting grounds and Endlock.

'Each citizen has the opportunity to apply for residence in a different sector than the one they are born to, provided they complete the necessary education and credentials for the position they're seeking outside of their home sector.'

A pretty lie. Lower Sector citizens couldn't afford the required education. The degrees from our schools didn't meet the qualifications needed to attain a position in another sector.

'Our Founders introduced strict laws, with consequences to match, to protect our people, knowing that leniency with law-breakers is what allowed violence to escalate enough to force the government's hand in the second Civil War. If one fails to uphold these laws, we cannot count on them to look out for the betterment and future of our society, and we cannot waste our limited resources on them. Criminals will be imprisoned, regardless of the nature of their crimes. Loyal citizens must aid in the extermination of these criminals to prove their unwavering allegiance to Dividium. We continue our traditions for collective peace. Those who cannot uphold our traditions forfeit their lives and their place in Dividium.'

Councilor Peña droned on, listing the Founders and recounting their contributions until the screen went black.

'There you have it,' Warden Larch said, clapping his hands together loudly enough in the ensuing silence that I jumped. The legs of the metal chair I occupied screeched against the ground with my movement. 'The hunters, our guests, should be seen as guardians tasked with protecting our city. Even as criminals, you can still play a part in supporting the peace of our society. You'll be an example to your loved ones and the very hunters who chase you – a reminder of the consequences of defiance, and what must be done to ensure continued peace.'

I swallowed the dark laugh that bubbled up in response to his words.

'I'll let you get on with your orientation,' Larch said. 'You won't be seeing the hunting grounds today – in fact, you won't be seeing them until your first hunt.'

It made sense that they wouldn't want us to get our bearings. Without a preview of the grounds, we'd be left purposely disoriented and vulnerable when they released us for the first time.

'My group, let's go.' Vale's voice sliced through my thoughts.

I trailed dutifully after him and the rest of our group.

We left the training area, passing back by the examination room and through the barrier door. Vale turned left, leading us into a stairwell. We descended a lengthy staircase until we reemerged in Endlock's underbelly. The temperature dropped noticeably, and I wrapped my arms around myself to ward off the chill.

Corridors tunneled off to the left and right of the stairs, but Vale led us straight ahead.

Sporadic, dusty wall sconces illuminated the underground passage and cast wavering shadows along the walls and the doors nestled within them. Though there were cameras, they were fewer and farther apart than in the other parts of the prison I'd seen.

'Down here, you'll find the infirmary,' Vale said, gesturing to a door with a nameplate that read *Dr Amelia Row*.

A small smile lit my face when I recalled Dr Row's warmth, though it seemed wrong for such a kind person to be secluded in the darkest part of the prison.

The hair on the back of my neck rose, and I looked up to see Vale staring at me, his eyes narrowed.

I broadened my smile, and his lip curled, but he averted his gaze.

My brows drew together. Even as I danced between the lines of obedience and defiance, he didn't lash out at me, or react the same way other guards did. What I didn't understand was *why*.

'The workshop is farther down the corridor,' Vale continued, speaking to the group as if we hadn't just had a silent standoff. 'As I'm sure you've noticed, each inmate has a set of duties within Endlock. Those assigned to the workshop handle repairs and maintenance.'

'When will we get our work assignment?' I asked.

An assignment in the workshop would be ideal. There was a definite advantage in having easy access to so many tools.

'Inmates aren't assigned their positions until they survive their first few days at Endlock. We wouldn't want to waste the training.'

At dinner, after confirming Jed wasn't in the mess hall, I loaded up with a bowl of watery broth – the only thing I could get my hands on, as the inmate on duty at the Grays' table had yanked away the tray of beans when I'd reached for a scoop. My reputation continued to precede me.

My steps guided me toward the first relatively friendly face I recognized, which happened to be August's. With our mutual interests, I didn't think he'd attempt to murder me over dinner, unlike Torin or Perri or any of the other inmates who were staring daggers at me across the room.

August was conversing with a woman who looked to be a couple of years older than me, maybe twenty-five or twenty-six. She had sleek black hair cropped at her chin and twinkling hazel eyes.

'What's the *point* of wearing accessories if no one can see them?' she grumbled, pulling at the zipper of her green jumpsuit until the pendant she wore around her neck was on full display. It was a golden butterfly, and I'd have wagered it cost more than a month of my earnings in the Lower Sector.

'*You* know it's there,' said a woman across the table with a smooth, russet-brown complexion and hair braided close to her scalp in even rows. She also wore the deep-green uniform of the Upper level inmates.

'Yes, but I can only give myself so many compliments, Kit,' the first woman continued. 'What if I want a whole gaggle of admirers?'

Kit. It was her – the person important enough to the Collective that they were attempting to make history by breaking her out of Endlock.

I averted my eyes, trying not to seem too interested. It wasn't the right place to explain who I was. Not while everyone was watching.

'Well, I don't know about a *gaggle*,' Kit laughed. 'But you have at least one admirer.' She winked, and the first woman's face went from olive-toned to scarlet in a matter of seconds.

'Hi,' I said to August as I slid my tray onto the table next to him. He had been chuckling at the women's antics, but fell silent at my greeting.

August stared at me for a long moment but finally scooted over to make a bit of extra room. 'Raven, this is Yara.' He pointed at the woman with the butterfly necklace sitting on my other side.

I nodded at her.

She stared at me in silence, then turned her focus back to her food.

She knew I was a bounty hunter, then.

Across the table, Kit stabbed at her solid biscuit until the tines of her plastic fork snapped clean off. She sighed and dropped the ruined utensil.

'That's not food,' Yara addressed her, reaching across the table to grip Kit's hand, stroking her thumb over her skin. 'I'm starting to believe you're lying about being an engineer. You should know that thing is strong enough to be used as building material.'

An engineer. I wondered if that was related to her importance to the Collective.

Kit's wide green eyes glittered with amusement, and she squeezed Yara's hand in return. 'Very funny,' she said, her voice so soft that I had to lean in to make out her words.

August set down his napkin and cleared his throat before Yara could continue. 'Now you've met Yara, and that's Kit.' He gestured to the girl across the table. Kit gave me a hesitant smile, and I returned it, almost too eagerly.

'And this is Momo.' August motioned to the scrawny, wide-eyed boy with brown skin and hair shaved close to his scalp. The boy was sitting on Kit's other side, wearing a green uniform. He looked at me from beneath his lashes, and I guessed he must have been about twelve years old.

Which meant he'd taken three strikes to earn his spot at Endlock.

'Food,' Momo told me when he saw me staring. 'I stole food. I was the oldest of my four siblings, and we were starving. That's why I'm here.'

I clenched my jaw, looking away, and blowing out a long breath to loosen the tension in my chest. After growing up in Dividium and hearing hundreds of stories like Momo's, I shouldn't have been able to feel any rage at all.

'I heard your brother punched Roald Baskan in the face.' Momo changed the subject, his voice filled with awe.

August glanced at the boy with a broad smile that crinkled the skin around his eyes, and I watched as he slipped the biscuit from his tray and placed it onto Momo's.

I softened at the exchange. Where Momo was all skin and bones on a narrow frame, August towered over the rest of us, his broad shoulders suggesting that he'd be bulging with muscle if he had access to adequate rations. Giving up any bit of food would cost him.

'He did,' I replied.

'For strike's sake. *Please* tell me he broke Roald's nose.' Yara leaned forward, deigning to speak to me. 'I wish I could have seen the look on that smug son of a b—'

'*Yara*. Language,' August interjected before the curse could leave her mouth, his eyes flitting to Momo.

'*Language*,' Yara repeated, mocking. 'Okay, Dad. Don't make me poison you too.'

My eyes widened, but I withheld my questions. *For now.*

August narrowed his eyes.

Kit cleared her throat, breaking the tension. 'I think what Gus's trying to say is that Momo's already seen way more than he needs to at his age. Let's try to preserve some of his innocence.'

Ah. The peacemaker of the group. I sifted through what I knew about her – late twenties from my best guess, an important asset to the Collective, potentially because of her knowledge as an engineer. She'd managed to survive Endlock for months, and, if I was right about the lingering stares and subtle touches they were exchanging, she was in a relationship with Yara.

'It's okay,' Momo said around a mouthful of soggy biscuit, interrupting my thoughts. 'I've heard the word *bitch* before.'

August covered his face with one humongous hand and let out a sigh. Kit and Yara made eye contact and dissolved into a cackling fit.

I snorted, then reared back, surprised at myself, and cleared my throat. 'Do any of you know where my brother is? I've looked for him at dinner, but he's not here, and I—'

I broke off, eyes snapping to the screen at the front of the room, and the targets listed there with their Xs and checkmarks and circles. I didn't even know the number Jed had been assigned. *Branded with.* What if he was—

'He's not out there. He has the first dinner shift,' August said, and when I turned to him, his eyes were soft. Sympathetic.

I shook my head. 'How do you know?'

'Because I saw him going into Block A his first night here, and that cellblock has the first dinner shift,' he explained. 'And his number is 203. It's not up there.'

'Thank you,' I whispered, blowing out a long breath, and letting the tension drain from my body as I committed the number to memory. The knowledge made me feel more in control, but Jed being in a different cellblock, and having a separate meal shift, would make communicating with him nearly impossible.

'For siblings, you two couldn't be more different,' Yara piped up, looking down at her jumpsuit and picking off a speck of lint. She pretended not to see Kit's pointed stare.

'I know.' I toyed with the fork on my tray. It was true. Jed was generous and brave, and I was closed off and selfish. I had to be.

'Well, you're both here now,' Kit said, softly. 'Do you know how the hunt selection works?'

I hated the pity in her eyes, but I wouldn't turn away any knowledge she was willing to share. I shook my head.

'There are eight cellblocks, and Endlock runs three hunts per day with a maximum of ten targets per hunt. For each hunt, they rotate through the cellblocks. So if the morning hunt starts at Block A, the next selection is at Block B, and so on. It means we get at least two days off between each hunt. More if you can lie low.'

'Fat chance,' Yara murmured, earning another glare from Kit.

'It's strange,' August added, eyes moving to the live screen. 'For the entire time I've been here, I only remember there being one or two days where the hunts weren't filled up. But for the last month, there's been at least one hunt a day with less than ten targets selected.'

I glanced at the screen again, counting the targets.

He was right.

Only nine inmates were listed under the first column, and eight under the second.

Kit hummed. 'I bet Coates is about to blow a gasket over it. I heard he invested a ton of credits into advertising a few weeks ago.'

I didn't doubt that Endlock's CEO had spent more on ads

recently – my tablet had been bombarded with pop-ups before I was arrested.

Yara nodded. 'Especially if the rumors are true that Coates is preparing to launch a campaign against the Council. Endlock would have to be doing well for him to stand a chance. I'm sure he'll, very predictably, run on the platform that because he's the wealthiest man in the city, he's a great candidate, but it will be hard for him to claim he's a competent businessman if Endlock is hemorrhaging credits.'

I blanched. 'Coates is planning on running against the Council? *How?*' Dividium only held elections when a Councilor passed, and the Council would never let Coates gain that title. He already held too much power for their liking.

'With enough credits, he can make anything happen,' August chimed in. 'But for now, we should be safe from seeing Coates on the Council. Endlock's definitely losing income – he has enough to deal with here.'

But the slight drop-off in revenue for Endlock didn't make me feel any safer. There were still three hunts a day, even if they weren't filling up.

'When is our cellblock up next in the hunt rotation?' I asked, though I didn't really want to know the answer.

'Tomorrow morning,' August answered.

I nodded. I'd have to be ready.

I ate the rest of my meal in silence, content to listen to August's friends chat away, and attempt to glean more information about Kit.

A sense of relief washed over me when the bell rang for us to return to our cells. I needed a break from the hatred-filled eyes of other inmates that I'd felt boring into my back during our meal.

But as I was settling in, waiting for Vale or some other guard to secure the barred door of my cell for the evening, another bell rang out.

'Showers!' a guard bellowed, his voice carrying easily through the cellblock.

I merged with the mass of inmates, the crowd pushing me forward. At least there was some protection in staying with a group – I had no interest in remaining alone in my cell while Mort and Hyde skulked the halls.

A droning buzzer signaled the opening of the thick steel door dividing our cellblock from the rest of Endlock, and I followed the group through until we arrived in a new corridor, lined with doorways.

The Upper level inmates streamed in through the farthest door, the Middle level inmates made for the center entrance, and I was pushed through the closest door with the other Grays, into a communal bathing room.

Iron sinks, stained and rusted, lined the space. Showers stood at the center of the room, sterile stalls that held no luxuries – no soap or towels, or even curtains for privacy. But with the grime and weariness of the last day and the dried sweat coating my skin, standing under a stream of hot water sounded heavenly.

There was one camera in the corner of the room, but, curiously, it was pointing directly at the floor – positioned so it couldn't possibly track any of our movements.

Clothes fell to the floor around me. I hesitated.

'Five minutes!' a guard shouted from the bathroom entrance, impatient. I hurriedly peeled off my jumpsuit under the watchful gaze of the flickering fluorescent lights, fingers shaking slightly.

I left the garment draped precariously on the edge of a chipped sink to keep it out of the water pooling on the tiled floor.

Using my arms to cover myself, I slid into an unoccupied stall with my back to the room.

The other inmates had mastered an efficient routine of showering within the allotted time, and several of them were exiting their stalls by the time I stepped under the scalding stream.

A groan threatened to escape my throat at the feeling of the cascade of hot water on my tired skin, and, for a moment, I forgot where I was.

'*Get to the Blood Tree. Get to the Blood Tree. Get to the Blood Tree.*'

The words floated to me from the stall next to mine, where an inmate was repeating the same bewildering phrase over and over, her voice quivering as if her body were wracked with shivers.

'Get to the Blood Tree. Get to the Blood Tree. Get to the Blood Tree!'

Her voice picked up speed and volume, and I resisted the urge to ask whether she was all right.

It was best not to draw attention to myself.

'Shut it, loon!'

Perri's voice cut through the misty air.

The inmate gasped, and the stream of water in her stall abruptly stopped. She skittered from the shower, shuddering as she hopped into her uniform, soaking the fabric through. She ran from the room, hunched in on herself and still whispering about the Blood Tree.

'She's gone batshit,' Perri laughed, speaking to another inmate. 'I heard she was sent here with her lover, and she watched him die during their first hunt. She hasn't said anything but "*Get to the Blood Tree*" since. I can't wait until one of the hunters finally puts a bullet through that lunatic's head.'

My fists shook at her vile words.

It wasn't until Perri left the room that I realized she shouldn't have been there at all.

Greens had their own showers.

But I didn't have time to ponder her whereabouts – I could see the other inmates were filing out of the room, and I finished up quickly, not wanting to fall behind. Shutting off the water, I wrung the moisture from my tangled hair. With the absence of the steamy water, an icy chill permeated the air, raising goosebumps along my arms.

The bathroom had grown quiet, and I noted even the guard was absent from the door.

I was alone.

I reached for my jumpsuit, trying not to let the silence unnerve me.

And then a few things happened at once.

The lights clicked off, plunging the room into darkness, and a sharp blow to my gut sent me crumpling to the wet floor, gasping for breath.

9

HANDS AND FISTS, more than I could count, rained down on me – punching my face, arms, and torso, pulling at my hair, and scratching my skin.

I lashed out, my bare foot connecting with a knee. A deep voice cursed, but the blows kept coming. My fists swiped at the air, connecting with soft stomachs and sharp bones alike, and grunts and cries filled the air around me as I fought back.

I was a more-than-decent fighter. I had to be to succeed as a bounty hunter. But my skills were laughably inadequate against an onslaught from multiple assailants in utter darkness.

I might die here.

The thought came after several minutes when my limbs were tiring, but my attackers showed no signs of stopping.

And what a ridiculous death it would be, having risked everything to save Jed, only to be murdered in a bathroom by a handful of vengeful prisoners.

It was what I deserved.

Blood trickled across my face, and my ribs ached with every

breath I took. I rolled, curling into myself and giving up on fighting back in favor of protecting my head and vital organs.

But as abruptly as the assault had started, it ceased. Footsteps retreated until I was sure only one person remained in the bathroom aside from me. The stench of sour breath enveloped me as they leaned close.

'This is Perri,' the high, lilting voice said. 'Go ahead and tell the Warden what happened to you here. He won't do shit to me. No one can protect you, bounty hunter.'

I lay on the floor for what felt like hours, every breath coaxing a sharp ache from my bones. I'd survived one battle, but if I couldn't fight back against a group of inmates with a vendetta against me, how would I ever get away from a hunter armed with a rifle?

Eventually, I drew in a shaky breath, ignoring the stabbing pain in my abdomen, and managed to haul myself onto wobbling hands and knees.

Groping my way to the sink, I found that my discarded jumpsuit had fallen to the watery floor. The fabric was drenched, but I pulled it over my raw skin, the chill seeping into my fresh cuts and scratches. With my luck, I'd wake up with a raging infection.

Hands trembling, I felt for the faucet, wrestling with the stubborn handle until cool water trickled out. I splashed water over my face to remove the blood, while taking a mental inventory of my injuries.

I felt like shit, but I was standing and able to move my arms and hands. No broken bones, but definitely a few bruised ribs – not to mention the cuts and what would surely be dozens of bruises on my skin come morning.

I tried to take a deep breath but the pain in my ribs flared up, and my head spun. I grabbed the sink, lowering myself to the floor and leaning my back against the wall.

'What's going on here?' A voice in the hall, slightly muffled. 'I just took roll in Block H, and we have an inmate missing.'

My head lolled to the side, and my eyes blinked shut. They were too heavy to hold open.

'I . . . We didn't realize how late it had gotten,' another voice answered.

'It's nearly time for lights out,' the first voice seethed. 'Wait here. I'm not done with you.'

The room flooded with light, bright and blinding, and I squeezed my eyes shut to block it out.

'Fuck.'

Rushing steps, and then a hand brushed my cheek.

I flinched, wondering if this would be the person to kill me.

I forced my eyes open.

'You're alive,' Vale whispered, blowing out a long breath.

'Very astute,' I croaked out. 'No wonder they hired you.'

I could have sworn his lips quirked up then, but I blinked, and any amusement was gone. His eyes hardened.

'What happened?'

'Some light sparring. Seven on one, from my best guess. Don't worry. I got in a few hits of my own.'

'Of course you did.' His mouth flattened into a tight line. 'Do you know who it was?'

I paused, considering. 'No.'

Vale's eyes narrowed, and he opened his mouth, but I cut him off before he could argue.

'What's it matter? I'm a bounty hunter. I knew this would happen.'

He raised a brow. 'You said it was seven on one. That's not a fair fight.'

I barked out a laugh and then hissed, my hand flying to my ribs and pressing down over the stabbing pain there.

Vale's jaw clenched as he watched my face. He reached a hand into his pocket and pulled out a clean napkin, pressing it against the line of blood that seeped from my temple.

'You work at Endlock,' I reminded him. 'And you're worried about a *fair fight*? What do you call a hunter with a rifle up against an inmate with no weapon?'

He chewed his lip as he seemed to weigh something in his mind. But when he spoke, he looked away, not meeting my eyes. 'Inmates come to Endlock knowing what happens out on the hunting grounds. That's the risk of breaking the law. Of being a *rebel*.'

The words came out flat.

I rolled my eyes. 'You still think I'm a rebel? I'm far too self-ish for that, *guard*. Call me a criminal, and I won't argue. But I'd never do anything to put my brother at risk.'

I froze as soon as the words left my mouth.

Shit. I hadn't meant to mention Jed – to alert Vale to my weakness.

But he just stared at me for a long moment, assessing.

A throat was cleared by the bathroom entrance and Vale jumped to his feet, yanking his hand from my face like I'd burned him.

Kit and Yara stood in the doorway.

'What is it?' Vale asked.

'The Warden asked us to get you,' Yara told him, meeting his eyes. 'There's been a fight in Cellblock D. It's bad.'

Vale paused, glancing back at me for one moment, two. 'Right. You two help 224 to the infirmary.'

And then he was gone.

'What happened to you?' Kit asked, her quiet voice at odds with the alarm lighting her eyes. She rushed to my side, holding her arm out to pull me to my feet. I was in too much pain to refuse the help.

'Just a little initiation,' I got out through clenched teeth.

'They must really like you,' Yara said, her disdain for me still plain in her voice, though it was hard to miss the pity in her eyes. 'I didn't get any special treatment when I got here.'

Yara walked over to the corner of the room and pointed to the camera there. 'You should have known something was up.' She glanced at me over her shoulder. 'The guards changed this camera's position. They only do that if an inmate's managed to bribe them.'

I *had* found it strange that the camera was pointing at the ground, but I was still getting my bearings at the prison, my mind going in too many different directions to focus on the details for long.

I was going to get myself killed if I didn't get it together.

'What could an inmate possibly have to offer in trade that a guard doesn't already have?' I asked. Because if I could take anything of value from this exchange, it was to learn what passed for currency between inmates and guards.

Yara laughed. 'Are you really that naive, bounty hunter?'

'If they're lucky, they trade in information,' Kit told me. 'We hear a lot as prisoners. Sometimes, the guards are bored enough that they focus on us, but most of the time they forget we're even there – forget to filter themselves around us. We learn a lot about them. Some of it can be used to blackmail them, other bits we trade to other guards.'

'But the unlucky ones,' Yara added when Kit trailed off, 'trade their bodies for favors. After you're here for a while, if you manage to stay alive, you'll come to understand that more.'

I shivered at the memory of Mort telling me we could work out an arrangement if I ever needed anything.

'I can't believe Perri hates me enough that it was worth it to her to trade in on a favor just to hurt me.' Certainly, she could've gotten something more valuable.

Kit sighed. 'Don't underestimate the power of revenge as a motivator. It makes people dangerous. Irrational.'

I shook my head in disbelief, and a wave of dizziness over-
took me. I stepped forward to keep myself from falling, and Kit
grabbed my arm to keep me upright.

Kit glared at Yara until she stalked over and grabbed my free
elbow. She grimaced as the soaked fabric of my jumpsuit pressed
against the cream-colored sweater she wore over her uniform. She
was one of the fortunate inmates, then – someone with a wealthy
family on the outside to keep her comfortable during her time at
Endlock.

'Don't mind her.' Kit gave me a small smile. 'She's wearing a
new sweater, and she just finished painting her nails.'

I glanced over at Yara and couldn't help but admire her perfectly filed, lavender-polished nails.

'Well, excuse me for maintaining a modicum of individual-
ity,' Yara huffed. 'I might have to follow their rules, but at least I
haven't let them rip away my personality or fashion sense.'

I respected that. At first glance, maybe I'd misjudged Yara based
on her appearance. But she remained unbroken by Warden Larch
or the Council, unlike many other inmates who stooped beneath
the weight of their fear. Every garment she chose, each accessory
she wore, was a quiet act of defiance.

Kit leaned forward to meet Yara's eyes. 'It was a compliment,
darling. I would never mock you.'

'You don't have to help me,' I added, addressing Yara. 'I know
you don't want to.'

'Yeah, well. I don't want to be locked up in this prison, either,
but here I am.'

'Yara acts tough, but once you get past her prickly shell, she's the
sweetest person you'll ever meet,' Kit told me in a loud whisper
that sent Yara's eyes rolling into the back of her head.

'Why are you being nice to me?' I asked, averting my eyes to
hide my suspicion.

'Because Kit's making me.' Yara shrugged.

'Because we have a *mutual friend*,' Kit chimed in before exchanging a lingering look with Yara. 'And I like to get to know a person before I form an opinion about them. Now come on.'

I had to fight to keep the shock off my face. August must have told her what I'd said.

They clamped their arms around mine, gripping me carefully, though my injuries still screamed beneath their gentle touches. I tried not to let the pain show on my face.

As we exited the bathroom, we passed through the pair of guards flanking the entrance.

The pair of guards that must have stood there, listening, as I was attacked.

Yara saluted them. 'Keep up the good work, boys.'

One of the guards reached for his baton, raising it to slam into Yara, but she lifted a hand, palm out, stopping him. 'Next delivery is tomorrow, Bax. If I remain uninjured, that is.'

Bax grumbled but lowered his baton. 'Don't push it. There better be extra for me this time.'

'You can count on it,' Yara answered as we turned down the hall.

Evidently, she had something of value to trade for immunity from a beating.

'I thought you weren't getting another package until next week?' Kit whispered, brow arched.

'I'm not.' Yara smirked. 'But I saw the look on Vale's face. Those guards won't have a job here come tomorrow.'

I chewed my lip. Vale was a guard, and a young one at that – why would he have power over the other guards? But my thoughts were interrupted when I noticed we weren't walking in the direction of my cellblock. 'Where are we going?'

'Infirmary,' Kit said. 'Like Vale ordered. You're bleeding all over the place.'

'No.' I stopped walking. 'No. Then the others will think I'm weak, and more of them will come after me.'

'It was Perri, wasn't it?' another voice asked. Turning, I found August had sidled up to us, Momo tailing him.

I blinked at his words. 'Yeah. It was.'

'She does have a pretty good reason to hate you,' Yara said, her gaze accusatory.

'And I have a pretty good reason to hate her,' I snapped. 'She lied and stole from Lower Sector citizens. Sold them fake treatments. People *died* because of her. They still do. None of it stopped when she was arrested.'

I stopped, breathing hard. Even though Perri was terrible, and deserved to be jailed . . . no one deserved to be hunted for sport. And I'd sent her to that fate when I'd turned her in. I couldn't blame her for hating me as much as I hated her.

Yara's mouth dropped open. '*That's* why the guards do her so many favors. I thought it was just because she was Larch's favorite, but I bet she's still managing to run things from in here – she probably has the guards on her payroll.'

My stomach churned. If she was right, that made Perri nearly invincible.

'We should tell Larch,' Kit interjected, before Yara could answer. 'Inmates aren't supposed to hurt each other. Even if he doesn't care about us, he'll care about losing out on credits if they kill you before you're selected for a hunt.'

'Don't worry about me,' I insisted. 'I'm already a bounty hunter. I'm not interested in anyone thinking I'm a rat, too.'

Kit looked like she wanted to argue, but she said nothing.

'Larch won't do anything, anyway.' August sighed. 'Perri is his pet. She does whatever she wants. You've seen how rarely she's selected for a hunt. Her favors for him let her get away with being a bully. Though this was aggressive, even for her.'

'So, we won't tell Larch,' Kit conceded. 'But we can still bring you to the infirmary. Dr Row doesn't ask any questions.'

'It looks worse than it is,' I lied. 'Besides, we all know I had it coming. If Perri hadn't done it, someone else would have eventually.'

They couldn't argue with that. They'd all seen the way almost every inmate in the place hated me.

'But your injuries—' August started.

'No.' I took a few steps back toward the bathroom. 'I'll clean myself up. Things will only get worse if the others think that Perri hurt me badly enough to warrant a visit to the infirmary.'

'I'll help,' Kit said, setting off for the bathroom ahead of me. I opened my mouth to tell her I didn't need help, but she added, without turning around, 'Don't argue with me. I've made up my mind.'

Yara muttered something under her breath, grabbing Momo's hand and walking in the opposite direction. 'Come on, Gus. We don't need everyone to know we're associating with the bounty hunter.'

August winced but didn't say another word as he followed her.

10

'GOOD MORNING, INMATES. Glad to see you're all looking well,' Warden Larch said as he strolled into our cellblock the next morning. He was escorting a woman decked out in tactical gear.

She wore cargo pants and heavy-duty boots, and a pair of custom pink pistols were holstered on her hips. Her wrists were stacked with bracelets of beaded teeth, and matching necklaces adorned her neck. Rings, embedded with teeth or diamonds or a combination of both, twinkled from each of her fingers.

Her glacial blue eyes landed on me, and her lips spread into a small smile at what she saw. Besides a black eye, a split lip, and a cut above one eyebrow, the rest of my injuries were hidden beneath my uniform – a blessing, as that's where the real damage was.

'Today's hunt brings in a fine group of hunters, most returning guests.' Larch paused, seeming to savor the nervous shifting of our feet and the dread that seeped into the air. Then he frowned. 'Only nine of you will have the honor of participating.'

His words sent a shiver down my spine. Nine of us might die today.

'Now. I don't take part in every selection, but I have a very special guest with me today.' Larch motioned to the woman at his side. 'Verona Shields holds the record for the most kills at Endlock, so I'd say she's worthy of an escort.'

Verona preened at his words, tossing a flame-red braid over her shoulder.

'The rest of our esteemed guests will be entering the cellblock momentarily. You will keep all of your limbs inside of your cell. Any attempt to harm our guests will have severe consequences.' His eyes narrowed, his words a promise.

What kind of punishment could Endlock offer that was worse than *death*?

A low buzz droned as the secure door at the end of the corridor unlocked.

Vale strolled in, a group of guests on his heels, their animated conversations at odds with our silence. Armed guards formed a protective ring around them as if *we* were the threat.

'Welcome, honored guests,' Larch boomed, a smile stretching his ruddy cheeks, though I noted it didn't reach his eyes. He spread his arms wide, gesturing to the inmates as if showcasing prized cattle. 'We're so pleased to have you with us today.'

One of the hunters cut in, 'How does this work?'

My eyes darted to the speaker, and my stomach dropped when I saw it was a young boy, no older than Momo.

He stood next to a man, whom I assumed to be his father – all sharp angles and silver-blonde hair.

'Ah, a newcomer. Your first hunt is something you'll always remember!' Larch's false enthusiasm grated on me. 'Each of you gets the pleasure of selecting one target – either from this section of the cellblock or one of our more *challenging* inmates farther down. Once out on the grounds, all targets are fair game, but we often find that hunters try to go after their own selected target.'

The boy pushed past Larch, and his eyes sparkled as they flicked to each cell, scanning his options. He bounced on the balls of his feet, and his fingers twitched at his sides as if he were envisioning the feel of a rifle in his hands.

The man in the cell next to me was the first to be selected, chosen by a hunter about my age who was swathed in a black jacket and pants and had a wickedly curved knife at their side.

But nothing could prepare me for the moment when the young boy who'd spoken to Larch came to rest in front of the cell of a girl about Jed's age. The boy tilted his chin, inspecting her.

I leaned against my bars, sticking my head through as far as the metal allowed. The cool rods pressed at my temples as I fought to see what was happening.

'I think she might be the one,' the boy said softly to his dad, pointing his bony finger toward the girl's chest. If I had been in the corridor with him, I would have ripped the finger clean off his hand.

The girl, to her credit, stood her ground. But I saw the way she chewed at her lip and hunched ever so slightly, as if she could disappear.

I cracked my neck and rolled my shoulders back.

'So, you're one of those hunters who goes after easy targets?' I drawled. I needed to be selected for a hunt to get my ranking up and gain the privilege of a looser leash to explore the prison – there was no use in waiting.

The space fell into a weighted silence.

The boy and his father snapped their faces in my direction.

'He's never been on a hunt before,' the boy's father spluttered, striding toward me, crimson-faced. 'And who do you think you are, speaking to *my* son like that?'

'If you want me to stop speaking, you're going to have to put a bullet in me,' I retorted, stepping back from the bars. I didn't want to break any of Larch's rules this close to a hunt. 'It's fitting that you would allow your son to choose a weak target for his first hunt, since I'm sure you've never taken down anyone higher ranked yourself.'

My rank sat at a three, the highest possible for a Lower level inmate. If I could make the hunters angry enough, I knew they would choose me.

I felt the weight of Vale's glare from down the hall but ignored him. If he didn't like how I spoke to Endlock's *esteemed guests*, he was welcome to try to stop me.

'I'll have you know I'm one of the top-ranked hunters in the Middle Sector,' the man hissed, taking my bait. He reached a hand down to his belt, clenching a silver chain adorned with a dozen polished teeth.

I lifted my hand and inspected my fingernails. 'I bet,' I said, my smile sugary sweet. 'I'm sure none of those teeth were purchased on the black market.'

'Her,' the man said to Larch, drops of spit flying from his mouth. He jabbed a finger in my direction. 'We want her.'

Larch clasped his hands together with a smug smile. 'Excellent choice.' He turned to address the rest of the guests. 'If you'll all follow me to the prep room, our guards will have your targets ready for you momentarily.'

They streamed out of the cellblock, chattering excitedly.

'You didn't have to do that.'

I looked up to see the girl staring at me, her hands clamped around the bars of her cell so tightly that her knuckles were white.

'I know.'

'I'm going to die anyway,' she insisted, voice sharp. 'Now, it will just be another day.'

'Best get to enjoying breathing while you can, then,' I grumbled. It came out harsh, my nerves getting the better of me as the guards came around, unlocking our cells and shepherding me toward the barrier door along with the other chosen targets.

'I'll be fine,' I whispered. To myself. To Jed – wherever he was.

My hands trembled, and I balled them into fists to hide the shaking.

'Not really what I would call keeping a low profile, bounty hunter,' Vale murmured, breaking me from the cloud of fear as I brushed past him.

His jaw clenched, and some unnamed emotion flitted through his eyes, faster than I could decipher it.

I batted my eyelashes at him. 'I can hardly help that I'm noticeable.'

The guards corralled us into a cramped room, and I turned, taking in all nine targets. I'd seen the Lower level inmates that had been selected, as well as Torin in the Middle level, who'd had the misfortune of attracting Verona's attention, but I'd been too far from the Upper level of the cellblock to see which inmates had been chosen from there. Now, I noted August and Momo were among them.

Someone had selected a *child*.

I looked away, taking in the details around me to keep from screaming.

The room we stood in was nearly empty except for a handful of guards standing against one side of the space, and a pair of cameras on the walls.

At the far end of the room was a metal door. My thundering heart told me it led to the hunting grounds.

Vale ordered us to line up against the wall, and Hyde approached to pat each of us down in search of unsanctioned items – anything we could use to defend ourselves.

I gritted my teeth, struggling to ignore the feeling of Hyde's meaty hands on me, but with Vale nearby, the repulsive guard didn't linger.

'Endlock's weapons are programmed so that they'll only fire at someone wearing a wristband with a green light,' August whispered, leaning against the wall beside me and holding up his own wristband, printed with the number 412. 'It's a safety precaution. There were incidents in the past when hunters wound up on the wrong side of their guns.'

I nodded toward Vale and the wristband he wore above his identity wristband, noting that there was no number printed on it. 'Then why is he wearing one?'

'Everyone on the grounds wears a wristband for tracking purposes,' August explained. 'The guards and guests wear them in case of emergency, but their bands glow red – Endlock's guns won't fire when pointed at them.'

Ingenious. And terrible news for me. I'd have to figure out how to get mine off if I had any hope of escaping without being tracked and dragged back to Endlock.

'Targets. Listen up.' Vale's voice commanded the attention in the room, and we all stood straighter, craning to hear his words.

Vale looked at me pointedly. 'Most of you know this, but for the benefit of our first-timers, let's go over what you should expect.'

I attempted a glare, but the trembling was back, and I was sure I came off more defeated than defiant.

His gaze lingered on me longer than was necessary, roaming over my face as his fists clenched at his sides.

He seemed to shake himself before continuing his speech. 'We'll release you onto the hunting grounds. You'll have a two-minute head start, and I suggest you use that time wisely if you want to survive. Some of you are fast runners, some are good climbers, and some are skilled at melting into your surroundings. The targets that will stand out to the hunters are those who don't possess these skills. If that sounds like you, you better have a backup plan.'

It was possible, then, that none of us would die today. If we were quick and clever, maybe the hunters wouldn't find any of us. But the odds of that seemed low.

'Along with the fence surrounding the hunting grounds, a magnetic force field is synced with your wristbands. It adjusts every thirty minutes, keeping you trapped within a segment of the hunting grounds. For the first thirty minutes, you'll be confined to the outer edge of the grounds – between the perimeter fence and the force field's boundary. Then, the boundary will move in, forcing you closer to the center but not yet allowing you to reach safety. You'll stay in that second segment for thirty minutes before the boundary moves in a final time, and that's when you can attempt to reach the Blood Tree.'

The Blood Tree. The term the inmate from the showers had repeated over and over. I felt sick.

'What's the Blood Tree?' one of the inmates asked, shaking so hard they could barely get the words out.

'The Blood Tree is the landmark you must reach to survive the hunt,' Vale explained. 'You're attempting to get there alive, and the hunters will be trying to kill you before you reach it.'

I narrowed my eyes. So the force field was to stop us from sprinting directly for the Blood Tree as soon as we were released onto the grounds. Two minutes was a big head start, and with the weapons the hunters carried, they would be slower than us. Without the force field in place, I bet most targets could make it to the Blood Tree alive.

But that'd be no fun for the hunters.

I gritted my teeth.

August elbowed me, breaking me from my thoughts as he tilted his head to whisper in my ear. 'The Blood Tree has sensors. As soon as you touch it, your wristband will turn red, and the hunters will no longer be able to shoot at you.'

Vale cleared his throat, looking pointedly in our direction until August closed his mouth and faced the front of the room again.

'The order in which you reach the Blood Tree impacts your rank. The faster you get there, the more your rank will increase.'

There was no way I'd be the first one there, not when I needed as much time as the force field would allow to explore the hunting grounds and try to find a weakness in the security for our escape.

One part of Vale's explanation didn't make sense to me, though. 'The magnetic field,' I blurted. 'How will we know that it's closing in? Or that we're at the boundary?'

Vale frowned, his eyes flitting over my face. 'You'll feel it. Move as quickly as you can, and you won't have cause to worry about it.'

I looked around the room, sizing up the other inmates, and my eyes caught on Torin. He was trembling, and great rivulets of sweat trickled from his hair onto his forehead.

I swallowed, turning away.

Vale scanned his keycard and unlatched the steel door that lay before us, confirming what I'd suspected – it was our entrance to the hunting grounds. The door opened to reveal a few feet of open space and a metal wall blocking out what lay beyond, though the dreary gray of the sky remained visible.

'There is one rule once the hunt starts,' Vale said. 'Do not physically engage with any hunter who isn't attacking you. No starting fights or intervening on another inmate's behalf. No ganging up with other inmates to take down the hunters.

'Once you step through this door, walk to the end of the passageway until you reach your designated stall,' he continued. 'You'll be closed into your stall during the countdown. When the countdown ends and the buzzer goes off, you'll be released onto the grounds, free to follow any strategy you wish.'

An inmate ahead of me collapsed, falling to the floor, their arms and legs jerking about wildly.

'He's having a seizure!' August called out, dropping down next to the inmate.

'Great,' Hyde growled, rolling his eyes as he walked over. He pushed up his sleeves, displaying his bony arms and tally tattoos as he reached for the inmate. 'Now we'll have to start late.'

'We're not starting late,' Vale snapped, striding up to him. 'Bring him to the infirmary.'

Vale turned, scanning the room until his eyes fell on another guard. 'Anya!' he called to her. 'We need a replacement. Ignore the rotation and get me someone from Block A – it'll be faster.'

Anya raced off but the other inmates pressed at my back, pushing me along through the door into the open-air, metal-lined passageway before I could see more.

I hesitated before a stall, and Hyde shoved me forward. I stumbled until I caught myself against a cold steel wall. A door slammed shut behind me, sealing me into the tight metal box. My chest constricted, my breathing turning shallow and rapid.

'No,' I whispered. The walls were too close. Too tight.

I gazed upward, feeling the oppressive, cloud-covered sky pushing down on me, suffocating me. The humid air caught in my throat, and sweat trickled down my back, tickling my skin. Would the hunters be waiting on the other side of the door, fingers twitching, rifles held, ready to shoot us down as soon as we came through?

My heart pounded like a frantic bird beating its wings against the cage of my ribs. I scanned the stall for an escape route, but the gleaming walls towered above me, their surfaces polished smooth and free of grips or footholds.

Vale's voice broke through my panicked slew of thoughts. 'Targets. In a few moments, you'll hear the start of a timer. You'll have ten seconds to prepare yourselves, and then a buzzer will sound, and we'll release you from your stalls. At that point, I suggest you run. Two minutes following your release, you'll hear an alarm that signals the hunters have been allowed onto the grounds. Good luck.'

The countdown began, each tick of the timer syncing with my beating heart, pulsing through my veins, burrowing into my very bones.

And then the buzzer pierced the air, and the metal before me slid away to reveal the hunting grounds.

11

AS SOON AS I saw the grounds, my breath steadied, each inhalation deeper than the last as I shoved my panicked thoughts to the back of my mind.

A sprawling field lay before me, stretching until it met the edge of a thick curtain of trees and the ancient conifer forest beyond. The other inmates had left their stalls and were racing for the facade of a sanctuary that the shadowy branches offered.

I broke free of my stall, sprinting out into the open field. Rain soaked into the fabric of my jumpsuit, chilling me to the bone. I only made it a few steps before I felt hands on my back, shoving against me, and I fell face-first into the wet grass. I lay there for a moment, heaving as I tried to get the air to return to my aching body.

'Your turn to die, bounty hunter,' the inmate who'd shoved me shouted, her braid slapping against her brown uniform as she sprinted toward the forest.

I jumped hastily to my feet, spinning wildly as I searched for August. He'd survived Endlock for years, making him my best bet for getting through this hunt. I scanned the field to my left, and my eyes landed on—

Jed.

My heart jumped into my throat, and I realized that a part of me had thought I might never see him again.

But it was him. He was alive.

Ahead of me, his damp blonde hair streamed behind him as he ran toward the forest. The cuffs of his uniform were high on his wrists, too short for his long limbs. My throat tightened, and I nearly cried out before panic surged within me again.

He must have been the selection from Block A. Chosen to replace the other inmate.

If he made it to the forest before I caught him, I might not be able to find him before the hunters did. I might lose him again – this time, forever.

'Jed!' I yelled, my voice cracking as I raced after him. His legs were so long, and each step he took extended the gap between us. *'JED!'* The raw scream tore from me with a force that grated against my throat.

Jed turned, his eyes meeting mine and widening. He tripped over his feet, falling to the ground.

I sprinted to his side, my breathing ragged. Hauling him back to his feet, I scanned him for any sign of injury, taking in his wide blue eyes and freckled cheeks, but aside from the dark circles beneath his eyes and the bandage on his forearm that covered what must have been his brand, he seemed unharmed.

'What have you done?' Jed whispered, looking at me wildly as if I might be a figment of his imagination.

I wanted to hug him, to assure him that I would take care of him and it would all be okay now that we were together – but we had to go. I grabbed Jed's hand, giving it a quick squeeze before I released it and stepped back.

'Follow me,' I commanded.

I spun, finally locating August's retreating form, and setting off after him.

Jed's steady footsteps beat against the slick grass beside me.

After years spent chasing fugitives and sneaking around, I usually had speed and stealth on my side. But today my scrapes, bruises, and sore muscles slowed my stride.

My breathing grew ragged, my lungs burning with exertion as each step welcomed a fresh wave of throbbing pain.

Though I knew the trees offered no real safety, I still felt a thread of relief pass through me when we crossed the forest's threshold. At the very least, the tree branches above helped ward off the rain.

August widened the distance between us, carrying us deeper into the trees as he easily hopped over fallen logs and roots. I picked up the pace, pushing past the ache in my ribs.

A glint of metal at the edge of the forest caught my eye.

The perimeter fence.

We'd unwittingly followed August almost to the border of the hunting grounds, and were now running parallel to the fence.

A piercing alarm rang out, high and keening, signaling that our two minutes were up. The hunters were out on the field.

Only twenty-eight minutes remained until the force field pushed us deeper into the grounds.

But the fence called to me, and I didn't know if I could truly trust Kit to help me escape with Jed. She had her own motivations, and nothing was keeping her from leaving without us.

I stopped, and Jed skidded to a halt next to me.

Could there be a weakness in the fence? If the force field pushed inmates toward the center of the hunting grounds, that meant no one spent much time looking around the physical perimeter fence. Why would the guards need to be meticulous about upkeep if an invisible barrier would herd us closer and closer to the Blood Tree?

'Raven? What are you doing?' Jed asked, eyes darting around nervously.

I looked in the direction August had run, but he was out of sight now. The only movement came from some small, unseen animal, rustling the branches at the base of a shrub laden with red berries.

I pointed to an ancient tree with thick branches and plentiful pine needles. 'Climb up there.'

'Are you going to follow me?'

'No.' I shook my head. 'Not yet. I need to look at the fence and see if there are any weaknesses.'

'I'll go with you,' Jed said, stepping toward me.

I threw an arm out, blocking his path. 'You can't. I'll be quieter on my own. You're not used to sneaking around and staying out of sight.'

He opened his mouth, presumably to argue, but I placed my hands on his shoulders. We were wasting time, and I nearly snapped at him before I saw the look in his eyes. He was *terrified*, and barely keeping it together, though no one but me would've noticed his tell — because it was the same as mine. He breathed in for a count of four, and then out for a count of four. It was something our mother had taught us to do when we were children, to calm us down when we were scared or anxious or overwhelmed.

Both of us had needed to use the breathing technique more times than I cared to remember.

'I know you don't understand what I'm doing here,' I whispered, softening as I stared intently into Jed's eyes. 'But if you listen to me now, I promise we'll be okay, and we can talk after the hunt.'

Jed shut his eyes for a moment, and when he opened them, his breathing had evened out, and his eyes were calmer. He nodded. I let out a breath, relief coursing through me. It didn't matter that the last time we'd spoken, we'd argued. That we were being *hunted*. Jed trusted that if he listened to me, I'd keep him alive, just like I always had.

He hauled himself up into the cover of lush pine needles, and I cut through the woods until the trees turned to saplings that eventually dwindled to weeds and grass. I approached the towering chain-link fence that enclosed the hunting grounds. Rust stained its surface, and it was bent in certain areas as if an animal or an inmate had smashed against it, but for the most part it was unscathed.

I briefly wondered if the fence was electrified before I spotted a squirrel climbing across the metal without pause.

High as the fence was, one could theoretically climb to the top. But its crown was a halo of barbed wire, capable of cutting through clothing and flesh alike. If Jed and I managed to get to the other side without falling to our deaths, we'd leave a trail of blood that'd be easy for the guards to follow, even if we didn't have tracking devices clamped around our wrists.

My pace slowed, pain giving way to fatigue. Breathing became a struggle. I allowed myself shallow inhalations through my nose, knowing the deep, panting breaths I craved would be a dead giveaway of my position to any nearby hunter.

Outside the shelter of the trees, I had no protection from the rain. My teeth chattered, and my soaked jumpsuit clung to my skin, leaching the warmth from my body.

Indecision kept me rooted to the spot as my gaze swayed between the forest's canopy and the fence.

The fence sat ten feet from the cover of the trees, open and exposed. If someone saw me, I'd have nowhere to hide.

And I didn't know how much longer I had before the force field would push in on me.

But I'd made a vow to myself that I'd get Jed out of Endlock or die trying, and I didn't know when I would have another opportunity to examine the fence. The longer it took me to figure out an escape route, with or without Kit's help, the higher the likelihood that one of the hunters would kill me before I could save Jed.

I took off running parallel with the fence, losing track of time as the rusted links blurred together and my legs grew heavier.

After a few minutes, doubt began to creep in. I was being foolish. Of course I couldn't expect there to be some break in the fence, conveniently waiting for me to stumble upon it. Not with Endlock's reputation. Not when no one had ever escaped.

I slowed to a walk, and was on the verge of giving in, when something caught my eye — an area where the forest had grown particularly wild, merging with the fence in some areas. A bush grew against the metal and some sort of climbing vines snaked up and through the chain links.

I stopped, staring at the fence.

Every rustling branch and chattering squirrel had me flinching, nearly jumping out of my skin, and I kept all of my senses on my surroundings.

Time was running out.

But an idea began to take root, and I grabbed the fence, wrapping my fingers around the metal.

I could dig under the fence, a gap big enough for Jed, Kit, and me to slip through. Given the force field and how far this section of fence was from Endlock, it might take a few hunts to dig a hole that was big enough, but the foliage should keep my progress hidden until it was done.

My lips turned up, ever so slightly.

I'm going to get Jed out of here.

But the not-so-distant sound of a snapping branch shattered my fantasy.

I needed to run.

More snapping twigs, this time accompanied by steady footsteps and laughter. Dread turned my stomach into a swirling mess.

I let go of the fence and it sprang back, the sound of metal against metal filling the air like a hawk releasing a shrill cry to alert others to easy prey.

I froze, suddenly feeling like I was back in that Lower Sector alley with Vale, after shattering a bottle and alerting the patrol guards to our presence.

'What was that?' a deep voice asked, and the footsteps in the woods stopped.

'I don't know,' another voice responded. 'But if it's a target, I want the kill.'

I held my breath. My heart hammered against my ribs, so loud I was sure it would give me away.

The thudding boots grew closer.

'There's a target over there!' the first voice called, and all strategy went out the window as I took off into the woods at a full sprint.

'Quick! She's getting away!'

I picked up the pace, clearing the line of trees and hopping over roots and fallen logs, zigzagging through the forest in case they had their rifles trained on me.

Heavy boots pounded the ground behind me, accompanied by laughter. I didn't dare turn to see how close they were as I raced up a hill.

Don't stop.

I cleared the hill, and the ground began to slope downward. I lengthened my strides, looking for a place to hide before the hunters crested the hill behind me and had a good vantage point from which to shoot at me.

This couldn't be how it ended. Not before Jed was safe.

My wristband began to vibrate, startling me. I narrowed my eyes, but kept running, only for the vibrations to intensify.

I nearly stopped in my tracks when I realized what it must mean – I was almost up to the boundary of the force field.

With nowhere to go.

I inhaled a deep, shuddering breath and pivoted to the right—

A hand clamped over my mouth and a strong arm banded

around my waist from behind, yanking me against an unyielding chest.

My scream was muffled behind the hand, and the scent of mint and soap filled my nose as my captor pressed their back against the bark of a tall pine, still holding me tight.

I didn't think as I opened my mouth and bit down on their finger.

'*Fuck*,' a voice hissed in my ear, though their hand stayed pressed to my lips. 'It's *me*, Little Bird. Is that the thanks I get for helping you?'

I froze, going limp in his grip.

Vale.

The hunters' footsteps pounded closer, coming dangerously near to the tree we stood behind, and then pausing.

My heart stopped and I tensed, feeling all the places where my body was pressed against Vale's. I didn't dare breathe, and his hand stayed firm against my lips.

Another step toward us and then—

In one smooth motion, Vale released my waist and drew his arm back. I tracked the movement and realized he'd been holding something. A *rock*.

He threw the rock, hard, in the opposite direction from us, and it landed a few dozen yards away, thudding among the pine needles.

And then Vale's arm was back around my waist, pulling me tightly against him, and into the shadow of the tree.

'Over there!' one of the hunters cried out, running toward the rock.

Their footsteps faded into the distance, and I shut my eyes, taking a long inhalation through my nose.

'I'm going to remove my hand from your mouth before I bleed to death,' Vale whispered. His lips brushed my hair as he spoke and his breath tickled the shell of my ear, raising goosebumps along my skin. 'If you scream, those hunters will turn around and kill you.'

He lifted his injured hand from my mouth, though his arm stayed around my waist, his long fingers splaying over my hip.

'You'll need stitches,' I murmured, not fighting my smirk, even as my thoughts raced, trying to wrap my mind around what had just happened and figure out how to extricate myself safely and get back to Jed. 'Let's call it payback for the brand, shall we?' I said, twisting until we were face to face, a breath apart. There was a loud, tearing sound as I ripped the flimsy cuff from the sleeve of my uniform and handed it to him.

He arched a brow at me.

'For the blood,' I explained, rolling my eyes.

His eyes roamed over my face and then narrowed. He shook his head, pressing the fabric to his wound.

'What?' The question I really wanted to ask was *why*. Why keep the hunters from killing me?

'Most inmates are consumed by fear when they're sent out here. They hunker down and hide, and then beg to be spared once they're found. The hunters get off on it. But you . . . you still have some fight left in you. I can tell you're afraid, but you're using the fear to your advantage, somehow.'

'Ah.' I rolled my lips, letting out a low laugh. 'The world has been trying to kill me for years. I won't cower and scream for those rich fucks just because it entertains them.'

'I suppose anyone foolish enough to cage a wild bird shouldn't expect them to sing for their captor,' he mused. 'But even now with your bravado, you're just biding your time, aren't you? You pretend you have nothing to lose out here, but I can see right through your act. You're planning something. I see how you weigh every word before you set it free. How you hold yourself back from acting on your impulses and letting us see you for what you really are.'

'And what am I?'

'For starters?' Vale leaned in until his lips brushed my ear. 'Deadly.'

I shivered. 'I don't know what you're talking about.'

'Hmm,' he mused, crumpling the scrap of fabric from my torn uniform. He slid his hand between us, his knuckles brushing against my thigh. My breath caught, but he only reached for my pocket, tucking the soiled fabric inside. His molten eyes met mine. 'The hunters are gone. You should go.'

He was right: the force field would be closing in at any moment, and I had to find Jed before it did.

I took a step backward, but paused, finally working up the nerve to ask the burning question out loud. 'Why are you helping me?'

Vale held my eyes for another moment, seeming to weigh something. 'You didn't tell the Warden about Eris and me. Now we're even.'

His veiled eyes scanned the forest, and then his gaze flicked to his wristband. His eyes widened. 'Go. Head toward the center of the grounds. The force field will be moving in soon.'

I didn't have time to question him further.

I darted into the forest.

Without knowing which way the hunters had gone, I risked running right into them if I wasn't careful. While part of me itched to confront one of them – tear their weapon from their hands and see how mighty they felt when facing me with nothing but their fists – I knew it would be foolish. This was about more than my pride. Jed was counting on me.

My pulse thrummed in my ears, making it difficult to differentiate between the forest's natural sounds and any potential threat.

When I was certain I was alone, I moved forward, keeping the fence in my line of sight to retrace my steps back to Jed.

Eventually, the towering tree came into view.

'Jed!' I cringed at the sound of my voice, hoping everyone else had already moved closer to the Blood Tree and wouldn't be around to hear me.

Jed poked his head between the branches, a strand of hair flopping over his forehead, and some of the tension left my body. He was okay. Still alive.

'The force field is moving,' I told him, swallowing the lump in my throat. 'We need to go. Now.'

He worked his way down the tree far more quickly than I'd thought him capable of, then landed on the leaf-covered forest floor beside me.

Without another word, we set off at a jog toward what *seemed* like the center of the grounds. It was hard to know for sure – the trees all looked the same to me, not like the buildings and street corners in Dividium that I was so accustomed to.

Jed's long legs put distance between us until he was several steps ahead. I was about to tell him to slow down, thinking that we were safely within the new border, when my wristband started vibrating again. Only this time, I knew it was because the boundary was behind me, creeping closer, pushing us into the next segment of the grounds. I picked up the pace, but it was too late. I felt a searing pain from beneath my wristband as if someone had stabbed a needle into my skin.

But what felt like one needle morphed into hundreds as the sensation traveled up my arm and into my body. There was a buzzing in my ears, and suddenly I didn't feel as if I were in control of my movements.

I took a staggering step forward, fighting through the metallic taste in my mouth and the spots of light dotting my vision.

I cried out, and Jed stopped, looking back at me.

I tried to tell him to run, to keep going, but I couldn't form the words. My chest grew tight as I stumbled toward Jed, taking step after agonizing step on shaky legs until, as suddenly as the pain had started, it vanished. I fell to my knees.

'The force field,' Jed whispered.

Though the pain was no longer an active presence, my skin was flushed red, and my breath came in short gasps as my heart tried to return to a normal rhythm. 'So that's what Vale meant when he said we'd feel it.'

I'd thought he'd meant the vibration, but it was clear now that he'd been referencing the pain.

'Vale?'

'The guard. The one who told us what to expect out here.'

'What did it feel like?' Jed asked.

I shivered. 'Like electricity coursing through me. I think the force of it could've killed me if I hadn't gotten out fast enough.'

Jed rolled his shoulders back, and then reached a hand out to me. 'Then we have to keep going. Before it closes in again.'

I nodded, clasping his hand and letting him pull me back up, ready to move toward the Blood Tree.

But then, a low whistle came from the trees ahead of us, beyond our sight.

12

THE HUNTERS HAD found us. We hadn't been quiet enough, and now we had nowhere to run.

Jed's eyes met mine, and I held a finger to my lips. My heart was beating out of my throat as I scanned our surroundings, looking for . . . There.

I pointed to a nearby tree with low hanging branches.

Jed nodded and got to work climbing the tree, swinging from branch to branch like he'd been born in the forest.

I cracked my knuckles, reaching out and ascending the tree with steady movements.

I'd done my fair share of climbing as a bounty hunter – scaling the sides of buildings to reach balconies and windows to enter houses after a bounty had barred their door against entry.

Still, my muscles shook from Perri's beating and the shock of the force field. I didn't know how I'd summon the energy to reach the Blood Tree if we survived this hunter.

Peering through a curtain of leaves, I made out two figures

below. I held my breath, straining to hear any sound over the pattering rain.

It was August.

He was striding confidently across the forest floor toward another figure. As the second person turned, their face became clear: Vale.

I felt my forehead wrinkle as I stared, taking in their seeming familiarity with each other. Their heads were bowed close together, and they spoke low, their whispers blending with the sounds of rustling tree branches.

I couldn't make out their words, but I noted August was oddly relaxed, as if having a conversation with a friend, not an enemy.

Outside of ordering us around, Vale shouldn't have bothered speaking to inmates at all.

Yet, he'd helped me when the hunters had been moments from finding me.

Jed's foot slipped from where it rested on a branch, and a cascade of leaves fluttered toward the ground. I froze, my muscles tensing so tightly that they cramped.

The conversation fell silent below our perch.

I leaned forward, ready to drop to the ground and lead them away from Jed—

A scream tore through the silence.

August and Vale reacted without hesitation, breaking off in opposite directions and vanishing from the clearing, leaving no evidence they'd been there in the first place.

My mind raced, working to piece together what I'd witnessed. Maybe August had struck a deal, selling out the other inmates and their locations on the hunting grounds in exchange for his safety?

That would explain how he'd survived Endlock for so long — by throwing others to the wolves before the hunters even had a chance to look in his direction. It would give him time to make it to the Blood Tree.

A different scream split the air, this one much closer to our hiding place and accompanied by sobs. My grip on the branch tightened, knuckles whitening. Above me, Jed stared down into the clearing, his face drained of color.

A gunshot rang out, and a gasp slipped from between my lips.

I'd known what happened out on the hunting grounds. My parents had died at Endlock. But it hadn't seemed *real* until now.

Another shot, followed by footsteps, had my heart slamming against my chest.

I hoped the second shot meant the hunter had missed whichever target they'd aimed at.

Momo dashed into the clearing, and my stomach lurched. Wild-eyed and panting, the boy began a clumsy scramble up a nearby tree.

No, no, no. He's so young.

Momo's green uniform meant he'd survived at least a few hunts. Even still, panic radiated off him in waves, and he didn't climb very far up the tree – the leafy canopy didn't cover him at all, and if the hunter bothered to look up, they'd plainly see him. Momo settled on a branch, breathing heavily and wringing his hands.

Jed pushed away from the trunk, watching Momo intently.

From my hiding spot, I reached an arm out, frantically motioning for Momo to climb higher, but the branches cloaked me too well for him to notice.

Not. Your. Responsibility.

I had to survive to protect Jed and get him out of Endlock. I couldn't risk thinking about anyone else.

The rain continued its drizzly descent, the hunter's footsteps growing closer, his cheery whistle splitting the air.

'Come out, come out, wherever you are,' the hunter called out.

Momo stiffened in his tree.

'I know you're over here. I heard you. And besides, I studied tracking – like the game hunters from before,' the hunter said. 'Did you know they used to train hounds to follow scent trails for their prey? Unfortunately, Endlock doesn't allow dogs, or you'd already be dead.'

Momo was visibly trembling, each tremor threatening to send him falling from his perch and directly into the hunter's clutches.

'Don't be afraid,' the hunter called, his voice low and almost soothing as he paced between the trees. 'I'll make it fast. I was never one of those people who enjoyed prolonging pain. I only want to maintain Dividium's peace. You broke the law, and now you must answer for your crimes. I didn't hit you before, but this time, when I take a shot, I won't miss.'

I watched in horror as Momo's trembling became full-body shakes that jostled the branches he was clamped onto for dear life. Leaves fell from his tree like rain, pooling around the hunter, a puddle at his feet. A sparrow chattered from a nearby tree. A warning call.

The hunter looked up, and I saw the lines of black paint he'd applied to the pale skin beneath his milky eyes.

'There you are.' The hunter tutted at Momo. 'Why don't you come on down from there? I could shoot you right out of that tree, but that could turn messy. We don't want that, do we? Don't you want a quick death?'

To my utter disbelief, Momo began a hesitant descent. He must have been in shock. That, or he was afraid of prolonged pain and perceived death as an escape far better than our current existence.

Jed tapped my hand.

I turned, bewildered, and he jerked his head toward Momo, his eyes wide and imploring.

No. I shook my head furiously.

Jed's eyes narrowed, his mouth flattening into a thin line. He jabbed his thumb toward his own chest, and I heard what he said without words. *If you're not going to help him, I will.*

He stretched his leg out, searching for a foothold below.

My hand shot out, gripping his shoulder, and his head snapped up. He met my gaze, his eyes round and hopeful.

'My, you're young, aren't you? I've never had a kill as young as you. The others will hardly believe this,' the hunter remarked with barely suppressed glee. He released a low, appreciative whistle as he watched Momo's slow descent.

Revulsion churned within me. I shut my eyes for a long moment and then looked at Jed, intently. I held my hand out to him, my palm flat. *Stay here.*

He nodded.

Before I could think better of it, I climbed down from my hiding spot with quick, deft movements. I strained to stay silent, but the hunter's back was to me, and he seemed so absorbed by his own voice and the imminent victory before him that he no longer cared to pay much attention to his surroundings.

Pretend he's another bounty. You've taken down plenty of men. He's no different.

Except he had a gun.

And I had nothing. Not even a single blade.

Momo's eyes darted to me, and I saw the flash of recognition as his foot slipped on a branch.

My breath hitched.

He caught himself, averting his eyes from me and trying not to alert the hunter to my presence.

Smart kid.

He slowed his movements to a crawl, and the hunter grumbled, growing impatient.

I dropped from the lowest branch of my tree and landed softly with bent knees, cat-like, on the plush pine needles that cushioned the muddied forest floor.

A branch creaked above me, but Jed didn't follow.

I scanned the ground for anything that I could use as a weapon. There was a smattering of stones, but all of them were smaller than my fist and wouldn't do me much good against the hunter's gun if he saw me coming.

My eyes snagged on a large branch discarded behind the tree I'd climbed out of, thick and at least the length of my arm.

The leaves attached to the end made a soft, swishing sound, but it blended in well enough with the leaves waving in the wind far overhead.

Spinning on my heel, I walked with the branch step by slow step toward the hunter's back.

I gripped the end of the branch, rearing back and swinging it forward with all my might, aiming for the hunter's head.

But at the last second, he turned – I'd never know if it was because he was alerted by some slight sound or whether he felt a shift in the breeze, but instead of hitting the back of his head, my branch collided with the barrel of his rifle. The collision jarred my injured body, but the force of the impact wrenched the gun from the hunter's grasp and sent it skittering across the forest floor.

I nearly grinned, my gaze narrowing in on him, predatory.

Weaponless, he paused for only a moment before lunging at me, twigs snapping and leaves crunching beneath his stomping boots. His fist caught the bruised flesh of my shoulder, and I gritted my teeth, dropping my branch but refusing to stumble.

I slammed my elbow into his jaw, and he cursed, blood leaking from his mouth where he'd bit his lip.

'You'll regret that,' he spat, circling me.

I spied a small boulder over his shoulder, mostly buried in the ground. If I could just—

The hunter swung another fist in my direction, and I ducked, barely missing a jab to the face.

'Raven!' Jed yelled from the tree. He was climbing down, inching toward the ground, and the hunter whirled around at the sound of his voice.

It might be the only chance I would have.

I swiped my leg out, kicking the hunter's legs from beneath him and shoving him hard in the chest. He went flying backward, his head meeting the boulder with a satisfying thud. He didn't move.

I knelt beside him, feeling for a pulse. I frowned. He would likely survive. Hopefully, he'd at least hit his head hard enough to induce memory loss and make him forget me entirely.

I heard Jed's booted feet hit the ground. Momo rushed into my arms, clinging to me, his small frame trembling. I stood, paralyzed, my hands hovering in the air briefly before I returned his embrace.

'Hey,' I said, disentangling myself and crouching to look him in the eyes. I used my thumbs to wipe the tears from beneath them. 'Hey, it's okay now. You're okay. But we have to get to the Blood Tree before another hunter finds us. We'll keep you safe. Can you be brave for me, just for a little longer?'

Momo gave a shaky nod, sniffling and wiping more moisture from his cheeks.

'Good.' I rose, snagging the hunter's discarded rifle from the ground. I knew now that the weapon wouldn't do me any good since it wouldn't discharge at anyone wearing one of the red wristbands. Still, it might be valuable later – I'd find a place to stash it in the meantime.

'Raven . . .' Jed said. 'W—'

'Not right now,' I interrupted, ignoring the emotion flitting through his eyes. We would talk about it after we survived.

Guiding Momo's hand into mine, we took off into the trees, stopping every few paces to listen for the sound of approaching feet.

At one point, a distant gunshot echoed through the forest, sending the three of us diving for cover behind a nearby bush, but we quickly got back to our feet.

I stowed the stolen rifle in a hollow tree, my mind wandering to the gunshot. Had another inmate been killed?

But the warmth of Momo's palm nestled in mine kept me grounded during our trek to the Blood Tree.

Eventually, the monstrosity came into view in the distance, in the middle of a large clearing. I'd wondered if I'd even recognize the tree, but now it was obvious how it had gotten its name. From the roots to at least ten feet off the ground, the trunk was stained in varying shades of red. Red that I knew came from the blood of inmates who had been mere feet, *inches*, from touching the tree and surviving.

Some of the stains were nearly rust-colored after fading with time. Other stains looked fresher, though I didn't care to linger on that thought.

At the base of the tree, August knelt with his back against the trunk. I saw a red light emanating from his wristband. He was the first to make it to safety.

I pulled Jed and Momo behind the trunk of a large tree before we could get too close to the Blood Tree.

'I don't hear anyone around. That doesn't mean there aren't any hunters lurking in the shadows waiting to get lucky,' I whispered. 'But we don't have a choice. The force field will kill us eventually – I think making a run for it right now might be our best bet.'

'Okay,' Jed said, laying a steadying hand on Momo's back.

Momo swallowed and nodded.

Getting to the tree meant stepping out into the clearing with nothing to hide behind. I stood, looking both ways, and then—

Pounding footsteps. Coming from the woods directly across the clearing from us.

I froze, one hand clamped around Jed's bicep, the other resting on Momo's shoulder. I peered around the trunk of our tree just as a man broke into the clearing. He was breathing heavily and limping even as he struggled to run.

The rain had slowed to a mist, relenting enough that I could see clearly.

Torin Bond.

Verona entered the clearing not far behind, stalking him. She seemed to be stretching out Torin's fear for her enjoyment.

Torin stumbled, the tall weeds at the edge of the clearing ensnaring his foot, and fell to his knees.

He let out a jagged cry as he pushed against the ground. When he tried to stand, his leg twisted beneath him, so he clawed at the mud, crawling away from Verona. Her long strides ate up the distance between them with every inch Torin gained.

'We have to help him,' Jed whispered, urgent. His eyes were wet.

I shook my head, even as nausea curled in my stomach. 'We can't.'

'But she's going to kill him.' He looked horrified, like he didn't know me at all.

I'd managed to save Momo even as the hunter had pointed his gun, ready to fire. I'd risked my life – and Jed's chances of freedom, and I didn't regret it. Momo was alive and breathing next to me. But I wouldn't risk us for Torin.

It made me a bad person, but I already knew that about myself – I had long since made peace with it.

'Please,' Torin begged, tears carving tracks through the grime coating his face. 'Please don't do this. I don't want to die.'

'Then you shouldn't have broken the law,' Verona said, licking her lips and hefting her rifle. 'I'm doing my part to bring justice to Dividium.'

I knew I should look away, but I *couldn't*.

Torin stretched out his arm, reaching for the safety of the Blood Tree.

A shot rang through the woods, followed by silence.

Or what I assumed was silence – perhaps water still dripped from leaves and wind still rustled branches, but I couldn't hear anything.

Torin fell to the ground, lying lifeless in a growing pool of crimson.

I bit down hard on my knuckles to muffle my sudden sobs, my stomach churning as I tried to breathe through the cloud of acrid gunpowder. But the air got stuck in my throat, and my chest clenched. *I couldn't breathe.* It was my fault. I was responsible. I was the one who had sent him to Endlock, and now he was dead.

My ears were ringing, and the sounds of the forest were muffled. With a triumphant whoop, Verona retrieved a radio from its strap on her belt, and muted static filled the air.

'Got him,' she bragged into the tiny speaker. 'Nice set of teeth on him, too – only one missing. You owe me a thousand credits.'

A slew of curses came from the tinny voice on the other end of the radio.

Verona stalked over to Torin's body, wrapping a length of rope roughly around his ankles and dragging him away, back toward Endlock.

Jed made a choking sound but didn't speak.

I spent the next minute dry-heaving.

It was one thing to send fugitives to the city jail, knowing they'd be transported to Endlock. It was another to watch someone murdered in cold blood purely for the amusement of some wealthy wretch who'd grown bored of frolicking about in the Upper Sector. She'd made a bet on a person's life – laughed about it, even.

I thought back to all the bounties I'd taken into custody. Wondered how terrified they'd been when they died.

My breath came in panicked spurts, and my dizziness threatened to send me tumbling into a heap on the ground. I forced my trembling fingers to grip the slick tree trunk.

'You need to calm down.' Jed uttered the words softly. 'Slow your breathing.'

Jed was comforting *me*. I was the one versed in violence, the older sibling who should've been in control of the situation.

Momo took my hand and gave my fingers a gentle squeeze. 'We have to go,' he said. 'Before another hunter gets here.'

I clenched my fists hard enough that my nails bit into my palms, the sting restoring some clarity.

'We have to get to the Blood Tree,' I whispered, remembering myself.

They were counting on me.

I blew out a long breath and peered around the tree trunk – our final cover before we risked the crossing to the Blood Tree.

August still sat at the base of the tree, his mouth pulled into a tight line as he desperately surveyed the woods, as if searching for something.

I knew the moment he saw me from behind the cover of my tree. He stopped, just for a second, and then continued scanning the line of the forest as if nothing had happened. And then, nearly imperceptibly, he nodded.

'Now,' I said, shoving Jed and Momo before me.

We sprinted across the clearing, only looking ahead.

August didn't shy away from watching us now. His eyes were intent on Momo.

'Faster,' August said softly. Then his eyes widened at something over my shoulder, and he stood, his back still pressed to the Blood Tree. 'Faster!' he said. But this time, there was nothing soft about it.

I knew then. Knew that if I looked over my shoulder, I'd see a hunter.

But we were a few yards from the tree now. Seconds.

August reached out an arm as if he could pull us to safety.

I shifted to the left, positioning myself directly behind Jed and Momo, hoping that if the hunter aimed true, I'd take the hit for them.

But then Jed and Momo touched the tree. The lights on their wristbands flickered and went red.

I stretched out my hand, glancing over my shoulder as I did so – and saw the hunter that had selected me, with his son steps behind him. He'd cleared the trees and raised his gun, taking aim. His finger slipped over the trigger, and he pulled—

My fingers brushed against the bark of the tree, and I heard the hunter's rifle click.

His brow furrowed as he stared at the gun, then pulled the trigger again.

Nothing.

He stared at me, his eyes traveling from my face to my arm, to my hand pressed against the Blood Tree.

To the wristband glowing red on my arm.

I mustered all the bravado left in my aching, terrified body and smirked at him.

Behind him, the hunter's son threw his rifle to the ground, stomping his foot. 'It's not fair!' he shouted. 'You said it'd be easy!'

I didn't listen to the rest of his tantrum. I slid my back down the blood-encrusted tree until I reached a sitting position on the ground.

Next to me, August pulled Momo to his side, placing a soft kiss on top of the boy's head. I turned to Jed, and his eyes met mine, tears streaming down both of our cheeks. He reached a shaking hand toward me and I threw my arms around him, clutching him tightly against me as he took in shuddering breaths.

But we were *alive*.

I shut my eyes.

13

ONLY ONE MORE target reached the Blood Tree alive.

Afterward, we made the long hike back to the prison surrounded by guards.

When Endlock finally edged into view, my heart kicked up an erratic beat in my chest. More guards stood against the cement of the prison's exterior wall, waiting for us.

I didn't dare glance at Momo for fear of the guards becoming suspicious.

Jed whispered through barely moving lips. 'Momo, if they ask: you were alone for most of the hunt. The hunter who selected you attacked, and you were able to knock him unconscious in self-defense. No one was with you. Then, you ran into us on your way to the Blood Tree and asked if you could stick with us because you were scared. Okay?'

'Okay,' Momo muttered through clenched teeth, equally intent on not drawing attention. I could see how Endlock had aged him even during his short sentence.

'Inmates, against the wall!' Vale shouted when we approached.

'Put your palms flat against the building and spread your legs apart.'

We complied. I wound up next to the surviving inmate I hadn't spoken with before and looked around, whispering, 'Do you know what's going on?'

She narrowed her eyes at me, tossing her head to move a lock of blonde hair away from them, but finally relented and said, 'I heard the guards talking. They found one of the hunters knocked out cold.'

I nodded, ensuring my face remained neutral.

I imagined Larch was seething, out of his mind about the stain this would leave on his reputation, and the effect it could have on his job. The board had fired several of his predecessors for causing Endlock embarrassment or attracting bad press. And now a hunter had been knocked unconscious on Larch's watch.

The blonde inmate next to me retched, bile and remnants of her breakfast spewing from her mouth. I followed her gaze and nearly doubled over beside her. A guard held Torin's body up, and another guard prised the teeth from Torin's slack mouth with a pair of pliers and dropped them into a velvet pouch. Nearby, Verona waited with her arms crossed and mouth pressed into a thin, impatient line.

'She's a friend of the Council,' August whispered after seeing what I was staring at. 'She specializes in going after targets from the Upper Sector. Usually people she knew in real life that fell from the Council's grace.'

I shivered, imagining Verona sitting at a table hoping one of her friends would be arrested so she could hunt them down.

'How did you evade the hunters today?' Larch asked Momo, startling me with his sudden arrival. 'The hunter who selected you as a target was found unconscious.'

'I . . . I defended myself,' Momo answered, though his lower lip wavered under the weight of Larch's gaze. 'He was about to kill me, so I tripped him, and he hit his head on a rock.'

Larch hummed, his lips stretching into a cold smirk. 'Do you know what happens to inmates who lie to me, young man?'

Momo shook his head, his fragile frame trembling. My fingernails scratched against the rough wall before me as my hands clenched into fists.

'I'm telling the t-truth, Mr Warden, sir.' Momo's voice held a brittle kind of courage. 'I tripped him and then I ran. 224 and 203 found me and let me stay with them until we got to the Blood Tree.'

'I see,' Larch said, gaze pivoting from Momo to me, lips curling into a sinister smile. 'Though I've never heard of a bounty hunter *helping* a criminal.'

I bit my tongue, holding back the retort I wanted to spit at him as I met his stare.

'Get them back inside!' he barked at the guards, stomping away from us and toward the hunting party, likely devising the best way to break the news of the injured hunter to the rest of his paying customers.

I turned to find Vale's eyes locked onto me. I faced him, silently challenging him. But to my astonishment, one corner of his lips quirked up ever so slightly, a fleeting moment that vanished as quickly as it had come before he herded us back into the building.

That evening, as I entered the mess hall and snagged a tray from the stack, something felt off. I'd already learned to brace myself for whispered insults and outstretched legs attempting to trip me as I walked past, but when I looked out over the room, I only found assessing stares.

I claimed a seat at an empty table, casting an uneasy glance around, making sure to avoid looking at the live screen at the front of the room.

I didn't want to be reminded of everyone who hadn't made it to the Blood Tree.

Before I could take a spoonful of my lukewarm stew, August sauntered over.

'Thorne,' he said with a nod, sliding his tray next to mine and digging into his heartier-looking stew.

'Hi.' I cast a sidelong glance in his direction. 'Worried I'm coming for your survival record? I can give you some tips if you'd like.'

He chuckled and rolled his eyes good-naturedly but didn't answer.

Momo approached with Kit and Yara close on his heels.

Kit hadn't brought up our *mutual friend* since helping me after Perri's attack, and I knew I'd have to find a time to talk to her soon, away from the others.

Momo sat next to me and glanced over with a shy smile. 'Hi, Raven.'

'Hi, Momo,' I said cautiously, pushing past the bewilderment coursing through me. 'How are you feeling?'

His reply was cheerful, as if his near-death experience was already a distant memory. 'Oh, I'm fine.' He leaned toward me and lowered his voice to a whisper. 'I keep thinking about the look on that hunter's face when you shoved him. I bet he'll never visit Endlock again.'

Momo dissolved into a fit of laughter.

August cleared his throat, and I looked over at him. He was staring at his tray on the table, his hand gripping a napkin tightly.

'I wanted to say we appreciate what you did for Momo. When he didn't meet me at—' His voice cracked, cutting him off. 'I thought I'd lost him forever.'

My throat tightened, but he continued before I could form words. 'To be honest, we didn't expect you to do something like that.'

Warmth crept into my cheeks under the weight of their stares.
'It was nothing.'

'No.' Kit spoke up from her spot across the table, her gaze
connecting with mine. 'It wasn't. You put yourself in danger to
save him. Most people in here, even the ones that care for Momo,
wouldn't have risked their skin for him. Thank you.'

I offered a nod, my usual wit failing me. I was used to lashing
out against insults and taunts, not accepting gratitude.

Even Yara hadn't leveled a glare in my direction.

'Oh.' August swallowed a bite of his stew and turned to look at
me again. 'Vale had Jed's mealtime and cellblock changed to align
with ours. He should be here soon.'

My mouth fell open. 'Why would he do that?'

August shrugged, not meeting my eyes. 'I pulled a favor.'

A favor?

My eyes narrowed. Vale didn't seem like the type to trade in
favors – I'd seen the way he'd berated Mort and Hyde for breaking
the rules. Certainly changing someone's schedule at an inmate's
request went against those rules.

But—

I had seen August and Vale whispering during the hunt.

They'd looked comfortable with each other. Almost like friends.

It didn't make any sense.

I turned to August. He was laughing at something Momo had
said, looking at the boy like he was his entire world.

Whatever his deal was with Vale, August had used that connection to help me.

The backs of my eyes pricked, and I had to blink several times.

A throat was cleared behind me and I turned to see Jed, standing there with a tray.

I gripped the table to keep from jumping up and throwing my
arms around him – we'd barely survived the hunt, and attracting
a guard with a baton was the last thing we needed.

'Hi,' I said instead, the wetness returning to my eyes. I slid over and patted the empty space on the bench beside me.

In the prep room after the hunt, I'd managed to fill him in on a rushed version of Aggie's plan and how I'd wound up at Endlock. He was frustrated that I'd risked my life for him, but I knew he was relieved, too. That he didn't have to go through this alone.

Jed dropped onto the bench beside me and set his tray down. 'Hi.'

His fingers gripped mine beneath the table and I squeezed back. *We're okay. We're alive.*

We didn't speak the words, but I read them in the warmth of Jed's eyes and the steadiness of my heartbeat.

But the calm I felt was only momentary. A pair of guards kicked off the wall at the edge of the mess hall, marching across the room toward a table a few rows over from ours, batons in hand.

August leaned in close to Momo, putting his hand over the boy's eyes.

'You there!' one of the guards, the one Vale had called Anya, shouted at a tall inmate with a shaved head. '377! We've been informed you took an extra ration.'

The inmate looked around, seemingly confused, before answering, 'Nat gave me the rest of her stew. She didn't want it.'

'That's not what we heard,' Anya answered. And then, before I could blink, she drew back her baton and slammed it into the inmate's head.

My mouth dropped open, and I gripped the edge of the table for support.

The inmate crumpled to the ground, unconscious, and then the other guard, a short, stout man with a black mustache, was on him, raining blows on his back and ribs.

Nausea curled in my stomach, and I fought the urge to rip the baton from the guard's hand and use it against him. It was one thing to know inmates were going to be killed on the hunting grounds, and another to see someone beaten half to death for *sharing food*.

'You're going to kill him!' Kit shouted, echoing my thoughts.

Anya held up a hand, and the other guard stopped his blows, spittle flying from his mouth as he tried to catch his breath. Once he did, each guard grabbed one of the inmate's arms, and they dragged his still body toward the mess hall exit.

Mouth hanging open, I looked around the mess hall, taking in the stricken faces of the other inmates.

Kit made to stand, but August reached across the table and clamped a hand around her wrist. 'What are you doing?'

Kit shook her head. 'They didn't even have proof. He didn't do anything.'

Yara touched Kit's free hand. 'There's nothing you can do to help him.'

'I can't just sit here,' Kit said through her teeth.

'You can,' August insisted. 'Remember what's at stake.'

My head snapped up, looking between them, but as I did, my eyes caught on the green light glowing from Kit's wristband.

'My wristband,' I whispered, horrified. 'What about the tracking device in my wristband?'

August's brow creased, and he turned to me. 'What about it?'

'Even if I get lucky and the hunter doesn't remember me when he wakes up, won't Larch be able to see that I was near him?' I asked. 'He'll know that I was behind the attack.'

August frowned, seeming to think over my question for a few moments. 'Momo told him he was the one to knock the hunter unconscious, and there's no reason for Larch to think otherwise. And besides, they hardly ever check the tracking.'

'Why not?'

August shrugged. 'The prison's overcrowded. They had to move the servers off-site to make room for another cellblock, and they don't have much use for the tracking data outside of when someone goes missing.'

I exhaled, the information loosening some of the tension in my

TO CAGE A WILD BIRD

shoulders. But . . . I tilted my head, staring at him. 'How do you know that?'

He blinked and turned back to Kit. They exchanged a long look, some unspoken question passing between them, and then she nodded. 'We should tell her.'

My eyes narrowed. 'Tell me what?'

'You're sure?' August asked Kit, ignoring my question. It was impossible to miss the apprehension in his voice.

I gripped the edge of the table to keep from grabbing his uniform and shaking him.

Kit cast a meaningful look in Momo's direction before she nodded at August again.

My heart galloped in my chest, beating against my ribcage.

August sighed and scooted closer to me, lowering his voice. 'I know about the Collective. And that you're here to help Kit escape.'

My mouth dropped open, and my hands clenched into fists. 'I don't know what you're talking about.'

Even though August had whispered the words, it felt like he'd shouted them.

Jed narrowed his eyes, leaning in to hear, and I fought the urge to cover his ears. I wanted to keep him as far from our escape plans as I could.

I glanced around at the others. Momo and Yara were still eating their food, utterly unfazed as they watched my face.

'It's okay, Raven,' Kit whispered. 'They know. They're helping, and they're coming with us to the North Settlement.'

The last part came out firm, leaving no room for argument, at least not while we were sitting at a table with the subjects of the argument I wanted to have.

My mission was to get into Endlock and avoid drawing attention to myself while I figured out a way to leave with Jed and Kit, and now Kit wanted to add *three more people* to the deal? It was impossible. More than that, she'd revealed herself to them, revealed *me* to them. Effectively putting Jed in more danger than he already was.

Jed's gaze was still boring a hole in the side of my head, so I faced him.

'Maybe working with a group is a good thing,' he whispered, so only I could hear. 'We can all look out for each other on the journey.'

I pinched the bridge of my nose. Jed's heart was part of the reason I didn't want to bring him in on detailed planning. I was used to making cold, calculated decisions behind his back to keep him alive in Dividium, but he already seemed determined not to let that happen here.

'We'll talk about it later. Not here.' And hopefully he would understand that I only wanted to keep him safe.

'I know about Endlock's servers because of Kit.' August spoke up after a few moments of silence, answering my earlier question. 'That's why the Collective is working so hard to save her. She was an engineer in Dividium and helped develop Endlock's recent tech before she was arrested. The security system, wristbands, the force field . . . you name it.'

My eyes widened. Kit's position as an engineer *was* what made her valuable to the Collective. And if the Collective needed information about Endlock's tech badly enough to risk an escape mission, it could only mean they were planning something huge – maybe even a strike against Endlock.

'And you?' I asked, turning to August. 'My Collective contact told me the North Settlement doesn't like outsiders. Why would they take you in?'

He frowned. 'The North Settlement will have no issue taking me in. I'm a doctor. Their medical care is rudimentary at best.'

Aggie *had* told me a bit about the lack of modern medicine in the North Settlement the morning after Jed was arrested.

I dropped my fork as something else dawned on me. Aggie had said the Collective had other people at Endlock. I'd thought she'd tell me if anyone else was involved in our escape, but maybe not. She'd said I was on a need-to-know basis, and perhaps it was too dangerous for her to reveal anyone else's identity.

'Did the Collective ask you to get yourself arrested on purpose?' I asked. 'Like—'

'Like you?' August smiled, but then his mouth pulled down at the edges. 'No. One of the officials on the Middle Sector board suffered a severe heart attack. They brought him into the medical center I worked at and . . .' He gritted his teeth. 'I tried my best, but I couldn't save him.'

I reared back. 'They arrested you because someone died in a way that was completely out of your control?'

August sighed. 'I think we've established it's not a fair system, Thorne. But what I was getting at is that no one asked me to help Kit. I'm helping her because she's my friend. And because I want to get out of this place alive, with Yara and Momo.'

'You might be a doctor, but how will you get the leaders of the settlement to let Yara and Momo in with you?'

'Simple,' Kit piped up from across the table, standing up as the alarm sounded to signal the end of dinner. 'We're a package deal. They take all of us or none of us.'

I had a feeling it wouldn't be that easy, but that argument would have to wait until more pressing matters were dealt with – namely, figuring out an escape route.

The inmates began gathering their trays, and I stepped up next to Kit, leaning close to her ear as the others walked toward the front of the room.

'I think I may have a way out,' I whispered. 'There's a section of fence that's covered in foliage. I think I can start digging a hole under the fence, and the shrubs should keep it hidden until it's finished.'

I watched her face, expecting her to grin, but instead she gave me a sad smile. 'August and I thought of that, too, a few months ago. When we started digging, we realized they had buried several feet of fence beneath the ground to keep us from digging out.'

I closed my eyes. *Of course they had.* Of course it couldn't be that easy. I didn't know how I'd let myself think I'd found a solution so quickly.

'Okay,' I said eventually. 'We'll think of something else. But what about the wristbands?'

'Yeah. They're a problem. Leave it to me, though – once we have a way out of here, I'll work toward disabling the wristband tracking.'

My mouth dropped open. 'You can do that?'

'Raven,' Kit laughed. 'I was on the team that *created* the wristbands, remember? As long as I have the right tools, I'll make it happen. But there's no use disabling the tracking until we have a definite way out of here. How about you work on the escape route, and I'll focus on the tech?'

So they hadn't had any leads on a way out of here, yet.

That, or she didn't trust me enough to give away the details.

'Deal,' I said. It wasn't as if I had a choice.

I cleared my tray and was heading back to my cellblock when a foot shot out, nearly tripping me. I caught myself, managing to regain my balance.

Unsurprisingly, the owner of the leg was Perri. A man sat beside her, his mousy brown hair slicked back and a smirk curling his lips cruelly to one side – Cyril, Perri's sidekick, whom Kit had pointed out to me that morning at breakfast.

Of course.

'I heard what you did,' Perri spat. It was the first time she'd spoken to me since the bathroom incident.

'I don't know what you're talking about,' I drawled, picking a speck of lint off my jumpsuit as I spoke. I didn't want the truth of today's events getting back to Larch. 'Unless you're referring to my record as a bounty hunter? In which case, you're right. I did bring in more fugitives than anyone else in Dividium.'

'You know that's not what I meant,' Perri said, standing up and getting close enough to me that we were chest to chest, though not touching. She had to lean down to look me in the eyes.

'Go ahead, hit me,' I said, stretching to my full height and not backing down. 'Or are you afraid I'll beat you if I'm not outnumbered?'

But she knew better than to lay hands on me in front of witnesses.

Cyril came to Perri's side, her constant shadow. 'You're still scum, bounty hunter,' he spat. 'Saving one life doesn't make up for the hundreds you've ended.'

I put a hand to my chest. 'Your mathematical prowess is un-matched, Cyril.'

'This doesn't change anything,' Perri said, ignoring my words entirely. 'You did one thing that anyone would have done, and now you want to act like you're better than the rest of us? I don't think so, Thorne. Watch yourself.' With that, she turned on her heel and strutted away.

We'd only been back in our cells for a moment when the guards came around to usher us to the showers.

This time, I didn't hesitate to strip my uniform off and jump beneath the hot stream of water, even though the camera pointed almost directly at me. I scrubbed myself and dressed quickly. I was among the first inmates to finish and head back to Block H.

Only, when I got back, Jed had beaten me and was standing just inside my cell.

'Hi,' I said, sticking my head back into the corridor and noting the guards were far enough away that they shouldn't hear us. 'Are you okay?'

Jed snorted.

I bit my lip. 'Stupid question, I know.'

'If we make it out of here, ask me again,' Jed murmured. 'For now, I'm glad to be alive.'

'You know I'd never let anything happen to you.'

'But you'd risk your own life.'

I didn't need to respond to that. We both knew it was true.

'It's my fault you're in here, Jed. Even if it wasn't, would you really expect me to let you go through this alone?'

He blew out a harsh breath, then leaned against the wall and looked down at his feet. 'No. And I never thanked you.'

'I— What?' My brows knitted together at the conversation's abrupt change in direction.

'I didn't even know how,' Jed continued, wrapping his arms around himself. 'One moment, Mom and Dad were there, and then they were gone, and you took that strike for me without even hesitating.'

'Jed,' I began, stepping toward him. Taking that strike wasn't something he had to thank me for. I had deserved it – it was my fault the guards had found out about the fugitives our parents were hiding. My fault our parents had been arrested and killed. If only I'd known then not to give my trust so easily.

Jed finally looked up, meeting my eyes. 'No, Raven. I need to say this.'

I stopped, reading the emotion alongside the urgency in his eyes, and then nodded, stepping back and sitting on the edge of my cot.

'You've always been willing to do *anything* for me. Whether I wanted you to or not. You being here at Endlock proves that more than anything I could say. And don't get me wrong, I'm grateful for it. For *you*.'

He ran a hand roughly through his hair and blew out a breath. 'But when Mom and Dad were alive, you and I ... we were friends, you know? You used to know how to laugh and joke and have fun. And then we lost them, and it was almost like I lost you too. Or at least the version of you I'd always known.'

The backs of my eyes pricked, and I blinked furiously to keep tears from welling up and spilling onto my cheeks.

'The way you changed. The things you did for me—' He coughed, the words seeming to stick in his throat. 'The guilt of it is eating me alive. And not just because you're here. It's been eating me alive for *years*. Before everything happened, I grew up in awe of you and the dreams you were working toward. You were going to be a doctor. And then I watched you quit school, watched you sacrifice your wants and your needs and your fucking *humanity* when you became a bounty hunter. All of it, just to keep me safe and fed.'

A few tears slipped free against my will, my throat so tight I couldn't speak. Being a bounty hunter was the only thing Jed and I had ever gotten into true fights over. He'd begged me to find another job. *Anything* else. But with my strikes, there were no other jobs available in the Lower Sector that would've kept us afloat.

He rubbed furiously at his eyes. 'You never would've had to do any of it if it weren't for me.'

'No. I made that decision, not you,' I choked out. I couldn't take any more gratitude for the blood on my hands. 'You're my brother. You had no one else left but me.'

Jed stepped toward me. 'I was a child when Mom and Dad were taken. I get why you thought you had to become a parent to me overnight. I wish it hadn't happened, and I'm so fucking sorry about everything you gave up for me. I can't change any of that.'

'I wouldn't want you to.'

'I can't change any of that,' he repeated. 'But I'm not a child any-more. You're not in this alone. You're not responsible for taking care of me. We're here together, Raven. We can take care of *each other* now.'

His eyes flicked up to the camera on my wall. He was being careful with his words, but I understood his meaning well enough.

He wanted in on planning our escape.

It was like I'd watched him grow up before my eyes, from a small, fragile child to the brave man standing in front of me now.

I nodded, using all of my will to hold back a sob. 'That sounds nice.'

It meant opening up. Asking Jed for help. Something I would struggle with.

My first thought coming into Endlock had been to keep Jed as far from the escape planning as I could, not wanting to risk him getting caught sneaking around with me.

But now that he'd opened up to me – now that I knew how he *felt*, I knew Jed was right. He wasn't a child anymore, and I had to stop treating him like one. I needed to stop acting like I was solely responsible for what came next. We were in this together.

A guard hollered at an inmate down the corridor, and we both jumped, brought back to the present.

'You should go,' I whispered as more inmates returned from the showers and rushed through the cellblock.

'I love you,' Jed said before he stepped out of my cell and down the corridor, headed for his new cell.

'I love you,' I whispered back.

14

THAT NIGHT I slept more soundly than I had in years.

It was as if a weight, one I hadn't even realized I bore, had been lifted from my chest, and I could breathe fully again.

Jed and I had never talked about the night our parents were arrested, or how things had changed between us afterward. Now that we had . . . Despite being in Endlock, I couldn't help but feel hopeful.

When I opened my eyes the next morning, I found Yara lounging gracefully at the end of my cot. She wore a delicate set of pajamas, their soft fabric a pale blush. The pants and long-sleeved top matched perfectly and looked like they'd be more helpful in warding off the chill than the standard-issue prison jumpsuits.

Anyone who could afford clothes like that was definitely from the Upper Sector, especially considering Endlock added an exorbitant tax to pass gifts from families in Dividium on to the inmates.

She had a book propped in her lap, hazel eyes engrossed in the words.

'You lost?' I ventured, squinting to be sure she was really there, and pushing myself into a sitting position to be ready to fend off any attack she might throw my way.

The soft rustling of pages ceased as Yara looked up, a flash of surprise in her gaze as if I'd jolted her from another world. Her eyes, ringed with black liner and framed by lush lashes, settled on mine. A cross between a grimace and a smile spread over her heart-shaped face, disarming me – especially considering her icy demeanor towards me and her detached reaction to finding me nearly unconscious on the bathroom floor.

'Don't play games with me, Thorne,' she said. 'I still haven't decided if I like you.'

'At least that's a step up from hating me.'

'A small one.'

'Which begs the question of what you're doing in my cell,' I pressed, crossing my arms over my chest. My eyes flicked to the camera in the corner and then back to where she was sitting.

Her eyes followed mine and she let out a small laugh. 'They don't actually have the cameras running all the time. Coates is far too cheap for that, and it would pull too much energy from the grid. The Warden runs them on rotation around the prison to avoid causing a blackout in Dividium.'

'How do you know?' I asked, not daring to believe that we might have a reprieve from the guards' prying eyes.

'Guards talk. You can tell which ones are on by whether there's a blinking red light. Some of them, like the ones in the basement, are hardly ever on – that sounds like a good thing, but it also means you don't want to find yourself alone down there with a guard. Especially Mort or Hyde.'

I looked back at the camera and noted that the blinking light I'd seen when I was first shown to my cell was missing. She was right.

I cleared my throat, returning to the question at hand. 'What are you doing in my cell, Yara?'

She huffed. 'If you *must* know, I felt the need to thank you for what you did.'

'What I did?'

'For Momo, obviously,' she said, exasperated.

I flushed, pink staining my cheeks. 'August already did that. It's not a big deal.'

Yara scoffed and snapped her book shut. 'Not true. Most people here wouldn't even do that for someone they loved, let alone someone they barely know.'

'Well . . .' I faltered. I didn't know what to say to that. I cleared my throat. 'Maybe I did it because I love hearing people gossip about me. I'll be all anyone cares to talk about for the next week.'

She barked out a laugh. 'You're right about that. But look, I came to bring you some things. I have way more than I need. My mother seems to be overcompensating for her guilt – she's constantly sending me gifts. Really, how many outfits could a girl need in a prison where her days alive are numbered?'

'You don't need to do that. I have this.' I gestured to my dingy jumpsuit. It was covered in dried mud and probably smelled like a Lower Sector sewer.

Yara's nose wrinkled with distaste as she surveyed my outfit. 'Take them. If you're going to help my friends, then at least have the courtesy not to subject us to your terrible smell.'

I took a subtle sniff of my uniform and cringed.

A neatly folded set of pajamas had been laid out on my cot, mirroring Yara's but in a gentle shade of green. Below it was a pair of tactical pants and a matching long-sleeved shirt that were similar, though of far superior quality, to the set I wore back home when I was tracking bounties. Alongside the garments were a plush blanket and an assortment of soaps.

In Dividium, turning in several bounties wouldn't have been enough to afford all of Yara's gifts.

'Is this you playing nice?' I asked.

Yara waved a dismissive hand. 'It's nothing. I've never worn the clothes. They're just gathering dust in my dresser.'

My jaw dropped. 'You have a dresser in this hellhole?'

'Upper level inmate.' Yara shrugged, pointing her thumb at her chest. 'And like I said, my mother is constantly sending me things.'

Yara had mentioned her mother twice, but I knew it was too soon to pry into the guilt she had touched on.

'Okay. I'll take them. But only because I have nothing to wear besides this monstrosity.'

I pulled at my gray jumpsuit. The color was the only unoffending part of the outfit – and I suspected the colors chosen for each level of ranking had to do with allowing prisoners to blend into their surroundings to prolong the hunts. If they'd given us the gaudy orange prison garb of the Old World, the hunters would find us within moments.

Yara rolled her eyes. 'It's not like I was giving you a choice.'

I bit back a laugh, an unexpected warmth spreading in my chest. I realized with a start that I already liked Yara. 'Thank you.'

Her smile grew wider, but she pressed her lips together, wiping it from her face as she remembered herself. 'Yeah, whatever. You can wear these clothes while in your cell or during rec time once your rank is better. The rest of the time, Larch mandates the jumpsuits.'

'At least I don't have to sleep in this rag any longer. You didn't say what you did to convince the guards to let you into my cellblock, though.'

'Cigarettes,' Yara said. 'I get them by the carton, and I keep the guards supplied. In exchange, they give us a bit more freedom. At least when the Warden and Vale aren't looking.'

I'd heard that cigarettes had been commonplace in the Old World, but in Dividium they were a luxury. Our fields could hardly sustain enough food to last the city through the year, which made planting non-necessities like tobacco unrealistic.

'That's why that guard didn't hit you,' I said, nodding. 'The one you talked back to outside the bathrooms when you helped me.'

She grinned.

'Did you work in fashion?' I asked, gesturing to all the clothes. 'Before you were arrested, I mean?' Some of the Council and wealthier citizens paid stylists to choose their outfits.

Yara gasped, slapping a hand over her heart. '*Okay*, bounty hunter, maybe I do like you. But no. Maybe in another life. In Dividium I was an agriculturist – most of my job was studying the soil and trying to figure out a way to make it fertile again. The pay was shit and it wasn't glamorous but . . . it felt worthwhile.'

Damn. Not what I'd expected, and yet it was probably one of the most important jobs in the city. Yara had been in charge of the future of our people.

I arched a brow at something she'd said. 'You said it paid shit – how do you afford all of these things, then?' Blunt, but Endlock had removed any manners I'd possessed.

'My mom's super rich,' Yara said with a shrug.

'What does she do?'

That made her laugh. 'She married the man who became the Chief Financial Officer of Endlock Enterprises.'

I blanched. 'Your *father* is the CFO of Endlock?' That made him one of the richest, and most powerful, men in Dividium. I couldn't believe Yara had wound up at Endlock – anyone in her father's position should've been able to keep their daughter out of jail, no matter the crime.

'Was, bounty hunter,' she whispered, standing and leveling a wicked grin at me. 'Until I killed him.'

My mouth dropped open, but somehow her revelation made me feel less wary of her, not more.

She'd taken down the CFO of Endlock. Her own father.

'Yara, you coming?' Kit called from the entrance of my cell. She gave me a small wave, seemingly unfazed by the look on my face.

Yara nodded, backing toward her. 'Yeah. And don't worry, Raven – he deserved it.' She walked past Kit and into the hall.

An asshole who'd got filthy rich off killing us for sport? I had no doubt that he'd had it coming.

Kit lingered for a moment, a shy smile playing on her lips. 'I think you might be getting past that prickly shell I mentioned.'

I'd decided not to ask August what he'd been doing with Vale out on the hunting grounds.

Even though August had called in one of his favors to get Jed moved to my cellblock, and had admitted to working with Kit, I couldn't bring myself to trust him yet.

But the mystery of Vale . . . so far, even though he hated my guts, he was the only guard who'd shown an ounce of mercy and a capacity for empathy.

And I needed to know *why*.

If Vale was someone who could be called on for favors, I needed to get on his good side.

Make him like me. Trust me, even.

That morning at breakfast, he approached me in the mess hall to take me to my work assignment.

'How long have you been a guard?' I blurted as he swiped his keycard and led me into the main corridor.

Very casual.

Vale looked at me with raised brows, a hint of suspicion in his eyes. 'A year.'

I flicked my eyes up, scanning the cameras lining the wall. After noting none of them had a blinking red light, I continued speaking.

'At Endlock the whole time? Or did you patrol the city streets before?'

At least asking questions was better than wielding sarcasm. *Much friendlier.*

'I've been here the whole time.'

He wasn't giving me much to work with. I swallowed a sigh.

'And did you always know this was what you wanted to do with your life?' I continued, badgering him.

'I always knew this was where I would end up,' he snapped bitterly.

Both of us fell silent as we turned a corner and met a pair of guards standing before a locked door. I mulled over Vale's words as he nodded at the guards and swiped his keycard, ushering me through the door and into another hallway.

The door clicked shut behind us, and Vale stopped short in the middle of the empty corridor. 'What are you doing?'

My pulse thrummed. 'What do you mean?'

'Why are you asking so many questions?' he asked, stepping close enough that I felt the cool stone wall meet my back, the chill bleeding through my uniform. He rested his hands against the wall on either side of my head, caging me in, and I had to crane my neck to look into his molten eyes. 'You don't strike me as some- one who's interested in small talk. On the contrary, I distinctly remember skipping straight past the small talk the night we met.' His eyes glittered wickedly.

I took a deep breath, willing my face not to flush crimson at his words or the memories from that night. But it was next to impos- sible with his eyes on me.

'You saved me out there yesterday,' I breathed, our chests nearly touching. 'That's not something an enemy would do. I'm attempt- ing to call a truce.' I nearly cringed at the foolishness of my words and waited for him to call me out on my lie.

He stared at me, eyes narrowed as if he could see past my fore- head and straight to the thoughts swirling through my mind. 'You're a criminal.'

But he didn't call me a rebel.

'Yes, and I'm paying for that by being here,' I answered, trying to select the words that would win him over. 'Isn't that enough? Or do you need to continue hating me, too?'

He lifted his hand to my face, and the pad of his thumb brushed against my full bottom lip, swiping slowly from the middle to the corner and lingering there. I held my breath, my mouth parting, and he smirked, lifting his thumb into my line of sight to show me the crumb he'd removed, a remnant of my breakfast.

I flushed again.

'Did *you* grow up dreaming of being a bounty hunter?' His voice cut through the charged air as he turned from me to continue walking down the hall.

The sudden loss of proximity left me chilled.

I rolled my eyes, jogging to catch up to his long-legged pace. 'Yes. I always wanted to track down fugitives and turn them in, knowing they'd be killed.'

Our arms brushed, and my skin prickled.

'You always do that,' Vale murmured.

'What?'

'Hide behind sarcasm.'

I turned, expecting to find him smirking, but instead he was studying me intently.

'Are you so afraid of the world finding out that you're not heartless like you pretend to be?' he asked.

I missed a step and nearly fell flat on my face. 'I—' I took a deep breath, steadying myself. 'No one *wants* to be a bounty hunter. But I was the sole provider for Jed, and I needed a job that would make me enough credits to keep him fed and . . .'

Safe.

My words dissolved into a heavy silence between us, the only sound the steady tread of our shoes on the cement.

'You know, I read your file,' Vale finally said. 'The criminals you turned in did some heinous things. All of them. As far as I can tell, you never apprehended anyone for petty thievery.'

'The Council would consider petty thievery equal to any other crime,' I reminded him. And no matter the crimes of the fugitives I'd turned in, I'd enabled the hunters who visited Endlock.

A memory surged of Verona dragging Torin's corpse through the hunting grounds, and my breath caught as I shook the image from my mind.

Vale looked away, not meeting my eyes. 'All crimes open the door to disorder. Disorder leads to chaos, and chaos leads to war.' The words came out rough.

I narrowed my eyes.

Vale opened the door to the stairwell, and we descended into the depths of Endlock. To my disappointment, we passed the infirmary without pausing – some part of me had still harbored a sliver of hope that I might train in medicine again, mending the inmates that escaped the hunts without mortal wounds.

We reached the workshop, and the door creaked open to reveal a room lined with neat rows of workbenches. They were covered with chisels and hammers, and most everything was coated in a fine layer of wood shavings. Tools of all shapes and sizes hung from the back wall – wrenches, hammers, screwdrivers, and—

I froze, staring, my mind flashing back to the fence.

I rolled my lips together to keep from smiling.

Wire cutters.

'You'll be assigned here,' Vale announced, arm sweeping over the room. 'Jed will be in the laundry room.'

I was being assigned to a position that would give me access to the wire cutters. If I could find a way to smuggle them out . . .

I fought to keep from getting my hopes up again. Even if I managed to steal a pair of the cutters from the workshop, I'd have to figure out how to get them onto the hunting grounds.

I made a mental note to talk to Kit and August about it at dinner.

Vale stared at me, waiting for a reaction.

The workshop *did* seem like a cushy job for a Lower ranked

inmate, and, beyond that, I knew Kit and Momo worked in laundry. Had Vale purposely placed Jed there with them?

I met his eyes. 'Thank you.'

'You'll be promoted to the Middle level if you get through another hunt, you know,' he responded, ignoring my thanks.

The pounding of footsteps in the hallway outside the workshop kept me from answering.

Larch appeared in the open doorway, his face flushed. A pair of guards flanked him, and two more followed behind.

Vale tensed, his eyes narrowing. 'Warden?'

Ignoring Vale, Larch's eyes found me. '224. You attacked a hunter yesterday – not in self-defense, but on behalf of another inmate, when your life wasn't in danger. That's against the rules.'

I froze, my heartbeat thundering in my ears. August had eased my fears about being found out by the tracking in my wristband, and between learning he was in on the escape plan and my conversation with Jed, I'd put what I'd done on the hunting grounds out of my mind.

'I thought inmate 447 knocked the hunter unconscious,' Vale said, a flicker of something I couldn't quite discern passing over his face. A muscle ticked in his jaw.

I looked sideways at him. Most of the guards I'd encountered wouldn't make eye contact with the Warden, let alone speak to him out of turn. Vale, on the other hand, addressed Larch like an equal.

'224 must have threatened him to get him to lie,' Larch said, lips forming a straight line.

'How can you be sure?' Vale asked, skeptical. His fingers beat a staccato against his thigh, and my eyes flitted back and forth between the two men.

Larch smirked, stepping aside to reveal the hunter I'd knocked unconscious the day before. 'The hunter just woke up. His weapon was never recovered from the grounds.'

My stomach dropped at the sight of the hunter, and I pictured the hollow tree where I'd stowed his stolen rifle.

The hunter glared at me, his teeth bared and fists clenched at his sides. His lip was swollen, and a strip of gauze was wrapped around his head. 'That's her,' he said through his teeth.

I stepped back involuntarily, gripping the fabric of my uniform to stop my hands from shaking.

'As I suspected,' Larch hissed. 'And now, 224, I'm going to show you how we deal with inmates that defy Endlock's rules.'

I swallowed, remembering my first day at Endlock, and Landis, the inmate who'd been shot down by a guard when he tried to run.

And what I'd done was worse.

I'd attacked a guest. Damaged Larch's reputation, which I guessed was the gravest misstep of all.

A slow, self-congratulatory smile spread across Larch's face, and I fought the urge to slap it away. He got off on the terror that this miserable place inspired in its inhabitants.

I shoved down my fear, refusing to give him the satisfaction of seeing it on my face. There was nowhere to run. If these were my last moments, I wouldn't spend them cowering, no matter how badly I wanted to curl up and hide.

For some inexplicable reason I found my eyes drawn to Vale. I let them roam his face freely, even as he shook his head, eyes wide with fear and an unspoken warning.

Don't provoke him.

But it was too late.

I hid my sweating, trembling hands in the folds of my uniform, and rolled my shoulders back.

'What are you going to do? Kill me?' I drawled, forcing the words out and letting a smirk pull my lips to one side.

Larch faltered, a slight frown marring his face. But he quickly replaced it with a serpentine grin.

He leaned in until his stale breath filled my nose. 'Do you think there aren't worse things than death, inmate?'

15

I WONDERED IF this was what dying was like.

Floating in a dark abyss, devoid of sound and sensation, not conscious of time or space.

Larch had dropped me, unceremoniously, into a dank hole in the basement that served as Endlock's solitary confinement.

At first, I'd found the punishment laughable.

The worst he could offer was to leave me isolated with my thoughts, but I'd spent a lifetime alone with my burdens, sorrows, and pain – unwilling to dump those feelings on Jed. I knew all of my wretched and ugly parts. I didn't have to like myself to live with who I was.

For the first few hours, I saw the punishment as more reprieve than anything.

But then Larch had entered, Hyde at his side carrying something that looked like a toolbox.

I squinted against the harsh light of the corridor, staring unabashedly at the two of them.

'Miss me already?' I asked, not bothering to stand up.

Larch leaned down and backhanded me hard enough to send me sprawling onto my back. I sat up and spat a glob of blood onto the floor. My head spun, my vision going blurry.

'Where's the gun, 224?' he asked, leaning against the wall and crossing his arms over his chest.

Next to him, Hyde set the toolbox on the ground and got to work undoing the latches.

'The gun?' I asked, stalling, waiting for the room to stop spinning.

Hyde flipped open the top of the box, revealing all manner of horrifying tools. Pliers, like the pair that had been used to prise Torin's teeth from his mouth. Rope and tweezers and knives of varying sizes.

My stomach churned.

'Don't play coy with me, girl,' Larch sneered. 'The gun the hunter brought out with him on the hunting grounds was never recovered. Since you were the one who knocked him unconscious, it's only reasonable that you would know the whereabouts of the missing weapon.'

'I never saw a gun.' I swallowed against my dry throat, unable to look away from the toolbox.

Larch chuckled, kicking off the wall. 'I hoped you'd say that. Now I can give Hyde permission to coax the truth out of you.'

Suddenly, I couldn't take in enough air, my breath coming in short spurts as I clawed at the ground, trying to put some distance between myself and Hyde.

'Yes, sir,' Hyde said, a grin widening his face. He plucked a small knife from the toolbox and stepped toward me, using the blade to motion to the tattoos on his forearms. 'You know what these are?'

I slid my hands along the floor, searching for something, *any-thing*, to use against him.

When I didn't answer Hyde, he frowned, but it didn't deter

him. 'In case you're getting any ideas that I might go soft on you, you should know that the lines are to keep track of the number of targets I've killed at Endlock.'

I clapped a hand over my mouth. There were *dozens* of tallies.

'Don't kill her,' Larch interjected. 'Might as well get a few credits out of her first.'

He stepped toward the door but stopped at a sudden commotion on the other side. From the sound of it, two people were arguing. It went on for a few more moments until Larch flung the door open.

'What are you halfwits shouting about?'

'Warden,' one of the guards answered, though I couldn't see who it was, 'I came to tell you that the weapon has been recovered.'

I strained, desperate not to miss a word she was saying.

'That can't be,' Larch spluttered. 'We've been looking since the hunt ended.'

'The latest patrol found it tangled in some underbrush near where the fight took place,' the guard explained.

My eyes narrowed. I hadn't stowed the gun in the underbrush.

Larch stared out at the guard, and then looked back at Hyde and commanded, 'Come with me, Hyde. We've got things to do. You – you stay here and guard the prisoner. She's still owed a stint in solitary.'

This last part was directed at the guard in the hall.

'Yes, sir,' she said to Larch, and then he left with Hyde and slammed the door behind him, leaving me in the dark, with just the barest hint of light trickling in under the door.

A shadow traced its way along the bit of light, and I crawled closer to the door, just as a scrap of paper was pushed beneath it, into the cell.

'Destroy it after you read it,' the guard said, her voice muffled.

Unease swept over me, but it couldn't beat my curiosity. I unfolded the paper and angled it into the dim light.

Familiar, *annoying* handwriting greeted me, in a secret code the two of us had developed when we were children. No one would know it was in code if they weren't looking for it: we swapped out each substantive word for an alternative one, so it made sense without revealing the true meaning. Once I deciphered the letter, it read:

Thorne,

You're lucky we were willing to replace the firearm you stole before the Warden could permanently mar your pretty face. It would've been a shame – it's your only redeeming quality.

You're running out of time. The North Settlement is giving you two months to escape before they rescind their deal.

Stop fucking around.
– G

Graylin.

I stuffed the note into my mouth, swallowing without bothering to read it a second time.

How had he managed to get a letter through to me before I'd been promoted to the Upper level? Obviously the guard on the other side of the door was one of the people Aggie had been referencing when she'd said the Collective had people on the inside. I hadn't expected her power to extend to *guards*.

I wished I had been able to see the guard's face, at the very least. No matter what Aggie said, knowing who you could trust was worth the risk.

The dark was torturous.

The weight of it pressed against me from all sides, a velvet blanket so thick it felt tangible as it slipped along my skin. It was impossible to tell how long I'd been locked away.

I'd known hunger before the prison and had gone days without eating during some of the worst winters. But this hunger was deep and grating, eating away at my very soul for lack of alternative sustenance.

The thick steel door that isolated me from the rest of Endlock never budged. While that meant I wasn't fed, it also came as a relief – it meant Hyde hadn't returned with his box of torture instruments.

Things were not going well if the lack of torture was the one positive I could come up with to keep my mind from lingering on scarier thoughts – like how Jed might die in a hunt before I was released.

My fingers explored every inch of the cell in the dark, scraping against the grit-covered floor. There was no cot to sleep on or blanket for warmth. A flaking faucet stood sentinel in one corner, begrudgingly offering droplets of iron-tainted water if I wrestled with the rusted knob long enough.

It would keep me alive. And I had to stay alive long enough to get out and find Jed.

For hours or days, I sprawled on the frigid stone beneath me.

I should've used the time alone to formulate a foolproof escape plan, adhering to Gray's instructions to *stop fucking around*. Instead, I fell into a state in which I wasn't entirely within Endlock but suspended in living nightmares.

I watched Torin die a thousand deaths, knowing I could have stopped it. I could have saved him. *Why hadn't I saved him?*

I relived all the arrests I'd made over the years with a more thorough understanding of what would befall my bounties at Endlock.

Worst of all, I recalled my parents and the night they'd left. How they'd died horrifying deaths, and how it'd been my fault they were sent to Endlock.

Aggie had asked us to house a man and a woman, fugitives, until she could find a more permanent situation to keep them safe. They'd been with us a few days when our rations began to dwindle. My parents could hardly afford to feed Jed and me, let alone the extra mouths.

At school, my friend Aysa had asked where my food was. I had replied, without thinking, that we had people staying with us, and had to share.

Family friends, I'd lied, when she'd pushed for more information.

I'd thought nothing of telling her. It hadn't been until much later that I'd thought of her sick mother, and her expensive medication. Of the extra credits Aysa would receive if she gave the guards information that led to the arrest of a criminal.

By then, it was too late.

I was in a dead sleep when the pounding came.

Jed snuggled into my side, using my warmth to fend off the gusts of wind that crept through the single-paned window in my room. Raindrops beat against the glass.

At first, when I heard the sound, I thought it was distant thunder rumbling through the clouds.

But when I woke fully and could comprehend the voices hollering on the other side of our front door, I knew the guards had come for us.

I yanked Jed from the bed and half dragged him to where our parents were stumbling from their room, wearing their nightclothes.

I gripped my mother by the shoulders, tugging her until my lips met her ear.

'The fire escape,' I whispered fiercely, referencing the rusted metal staircase outside the kitchen window. 'If you and Father go now, I can take the blame. I'll tell them I hid the fugitives in my room and kept it a secret from you. They'll give me a strike. It will be fine. You can hide with Aggie. Take Jed.'

I found that the prospect of a strike didn't scare me. Not at all. Not compared to the life-altering thought of losing my parents to Endlock.

My mother shook her head, tears glinting in her soft eyes. She pulled me into a hug as she whispered, 'There's no time, my brave girl. I love you.'

It was as if someone had run my heart through with a freshly sharpened blade.

She was accepting her death. Because that's what it was. It was imprisonment with an expiration date.

'Please,' I begged, tears streaming freely down my heated cheeks.

But she tore her mother's locket from her neck and pressed it into my hand as the guards burst through the door, and my scream collided with Jed's until it was the only thing I could hear.

'Raven.'

I sat up with a start, my throat constricting in panic.

I couldn't *see.*

The sudden burst of light blinded me, and my pupils contracted painfully from its intensity.

What if it was Hyde, back with his box of tools?

My breath came in short spurts, my hands going to the floor on instinct, searching for a weapon I knew I wouldn't find.

When I came up with nothing, I resorted to flinging my fists out wildly, attempting to ward off the threat.

Large hands caught my wrists, holding them tight.

'Raven, breathe. It's me. It's okay.'

A cloud of mint and fresh soap enveloped me, blocking out the smell of the moldering cell.

Vale?

Some of the tension left my body, and I stopped fighting.

His warm hands pressed into my skin, large and calloused and sure.

'What are you doing here?' I croaked, my voice a ragged whisper, strained from what must have been days of disuse.

As my eyes adjusted, I realized the illumination was nothing but a sliver of light from the basement corridor seeping through the cracked cell door.

Vale's form gradually solidified before me, and his hold on me loosened, though he didn't pull away entirely. 'I heard you screaming. I . . . I thought one of the guards might have snuck in here, and . . .' He trailed off, his eyes darkening.

He didn't have to finish. The possibility of what a guard could have been doing to me in the darkness of an isolated cell turned my stomach. I'd seen the looks Mort and Hyde gave me and the other women.

Vale released my wrists, reaching into his pocket and freeing a cloth pouch.

'I'm sorry, it's not much,' he said, pulling out the contents. 'I couldn't risk bringing an entire tray. The other guards would've noticed and told the Warden.'

But the biscuit and pair of ration bars Vale held out to me might as well have been a lifetime supply of credits.

I held my breath, eyes flitting to the door, wondering if this was some new form of torture and Hyde or Larch would barge in at any moment and rip the gift away just before it passed my lips.

But Vale handed the food to me, his fingertips brushing against mine and sending tingles shooting up my arm.

My brow furrowed, even as I nodded my thanks.

Vale was here, giving me food. Breaking the rules for me again. It was becoming impossible to ignore the cracks in his story.

At first glance, he came off as a staunchly loyal guard – someone who hated rebels and corrected his peers when they weren't playing by the rules. He'd sought out a position at Endlock, which had led me to assume he was a true believer in what happened at the prison and what the Council stood for.

But if that was the truth, why had he broken the rules for me so many times? He'd been in the Lower Sector after curfew, seeking out a rebel leader. He was close with August. He'd saved me from death during my first hunt and gotten Jed assigned to my cell-block, and now . . . now he was making sure I was as comfortable as possible in solitary.

He hadn't *needed* to do any of that.

'You're going to have to keep your head down from here on out.' Vale's eyes caught and held mine, oblivious to my churning thoughts. 'There are only so many ways I can intervene.'

I shook my head. 'It doesn't make sense.'

'What?'

'*You*, Vale. You don't make sense. You said you saved me during my first hunt because you owed me a debt, but I don't buy it. I don't buy that anyone who decides to work here would concern themselves with returning favors – if you'd let those hunters kill me, you wouldn't have to worry about anyone finding out that you were looking for Eris that night in the Lower Sector. Your secret would've died with me. And more than that, I *know* you think I'm a rebel.'

When he'd first read of my involvement with the Collective, there'd been no mistaking the disgust on his face.

Vale looked away, rubbing his hand over the back of his neck, the muscles in his arm rippling with the movement. I swallowed.

'I don't know what I think anymore. I looked further into your records after what you said that night in the bathroom, after you were attacked. Your parents were rebels, but you were still a kid when they were arrested. Became a bounty hunter right after. There was no proof that you'd joined the rebel cause.'

'Even still,' I murmured, when he finally met my eyes. 'I'm a criminal, and you're a guard.'

And I'd heard him spout the Council's propaganda several times now.

'I didn't expect you to help Momo like you did during that hunt,' Vale said instead of addressing my words. 'I didn't expect a bounty hunter, of all people, to be anything but selfish – to help anyone but themselves. It got me wondering about the chances of you committing a crime less than twelve hours after your brother arrived here. About whether you were actually a selfish person or just someone willing to do anything for the people you love. I can understand that.'

'Vale . . .'

He still hadn't told me what I wanted to know.

'Are you a rebel?' I asked, before I could convince myself to keep the words inside. I was sick of his evasive answers, and the idea of Vale being part of the Collective was the only thing that came close to making sense at this point. Even if he'd made his disdain for the organization clear.

Vale let out a harsh laugh. 'No.'

Fuck. I didn't know why I'd allowed myself to get my hopes up.

'But I'm not loyal to Endlock, either.'

My mouth flopped open. 'Meaning?'

Because there was 'not loyal to Endlock' as in *the pay and hours are shit so I'd take a job elsewhere if the opportunity arose*, and 'not loyal to Endlock' as in *I fundamentally disagree with what they do to people.*

'It's complicated.'

I groaned, covering my eyes with my hands. 'Enigmatic is not a good look on you.'

'Liar.'

I heard the smile in his voice and dropped my hands, glaring at him. 'It's not funny. I'm completely in the dark here.'

'I have no love for Endlock,' he murmured, serious once more. 'But my position here is . . . important. I do the right thing when I can, but I can't draw attention to myself. Or make Larch suspicious.'

'I don't understand. You're not a rebel, but you want to . . . what, help inmates?'

He arched a brow. 'Do I have to be part of the Collective to want to do the right thing?'

I frowned. He was right, but I'd grown up with the Collective and had never thought of there being free agents working against the Council and Endlock.

'Maybe not, but why help *me*?'

'I think you're worth saving, Little Bird.' His golden eyes searched mine.

My face flushed at his words, momentarily distracting me from the fact that he hadn't given me a real answer. By the time I opened my mouth, his eyes had shuttered, and I knew he'd give nothing else away. Not yet, anyway.

'Is Jed okay?' I asked, instead.

'He's fine. He was selected for another hunt, but Gus helped him, and he reached the Blood Tree first. He's been promoted to the Middle level.'

Gus. Vale's casual use of August's nickname startled me, but I was too consumed by relief at Jed's survival to point it out.

A rush of emotions washed over me – panic at the idea of Jed facing a hunt without me, but more potent than that was my pride. He'd not only survived, but he'd been the strongest on the grounds. He'd have more rations and freedom for the rest of our time at Endlock.

Vale's gaze landed on my cheek, where I imagined a mottled bruise where Larch had struck me. His eyes narrowed. 'What happened?' he growled, the venom in his voice making my breath catch.

'It's nothing.' Nothing he could do anything about, anyway.

His warm fingers caught my chin, tilting my face until the light from the corridor spilled across my cheek. 'It doesn't look like nothing.'

'Just the price of talking back to Larch.'

He clenched his jaw, opening his mouth to respond, but faint footsteps sounded in the hall, and we both shot to our feet.

Vale's hand closed around my fingers, the contact a blaze of heat against the chill residing in my bones.

'They can't find me here,' he whispered. 'I'll bring you more food as soon as I can. I promise.' He squeezed my fingers before slipping away.

And then he stepped out of the cell, the door sealing shut behind him and leaving me alone in the never-ending darkness once more.

But I felt Vale's touch long after he was gone.

One week.

That was how long they'd left me to rot in solitary.

Vale had made another food drop, and I'd found the courage to ask him how much time had passed. Seven days seemed both like too much and not enough.

It felt like I'd been in the dark for years, though, rationally, I knew Larch wouldn't take me out of the hunting lineup for too long. In his eyes, I was a walking paycheck. What good would I do him wasting away in the basement?

Vale's news had given me the strength I'd needed to make it through another night – I was getting out today.

A metallic shriek pierced the air as the door was thrust open. Bright, unfiltered light spilled into the cell.

'On your feet.'

Of course, it was Mort, with his ever-present toothpick and leer. Aside from Vale's face, this was the first one I'd seen in a week, and it wasn't a pleasant sight.

I hobbled to my feet, legs shaking.

Mort reached for my arm, impatience deepening the lines on his face. I recoiled, slipping from his grasp.

'I can walk,' I said through my teeth. I'd crawl before I accepted his help. In the dim basement light, I took in my grimy state – the wet, foul scent that clung to me was as putrid as a Lower Sector back alley. Hopefully, my stench alone would keep Mort's crude comments and wandering eyes at bay.

I may have oversold my capabilities because I found myself limping instead of walking. The winding basement corridor seemed to stretch on forever, each of my steps more stilted than the last, until Mort reached an arm out and slammed me against the stone wall.

A strangled gasp escaped me, the breath flying from my lungs. I pushed against him, but I was weak, and his arm was like a vise.

'Get your hands off me,' I snarled.

His lips opened to reveal a rotten smile, his brown teeth glistening in the dim glow from the nearby sconce as his toothpick fell, forgotten, to the ground. 'You don't mean that.'

I spat in his face, watching with satisfaction as his smile dropped and my saliva slipped down his cheek. Then he backhanded me hard enough that my neck snapped to the side. Stars swam before my eyes.

'Behave, and I won't have to do that again,' he whispered. He lifted his fingers, reaching for the zipper of my jumpsuit.

No.

I glanced around desperately, but none of the cameras within sight bore a blinking red light. None of them would witness what Mort was trying to do to me.

I clawed at his arm, tearing into his flesh, feeling his skin open beneath my nails. He growled, rearing back to deliver another blow—

'Mort. Let her go.'

Vale stood in the corridor, his hands clenched into fists at his sides, so tight his knuckles were turning white. The veins in his neck pulsed as his eyes bored into the arm Mort had banded over me.

I held my breath.

'Come to join me?' Mort's eyes flitted to Vale.

As soon as his eyes were off me, my instincts kicked in, and I drove my knee up, into his balls.

'Ahh!' Mort cried out, dropping his hands from me and leaning over to cradle himself.

I couldn't help the cruel smile that twisted my lips.

To his credit, Mort recovered faster than I'd anticipated, and I wasn't ready when he stood, drawing his fist back.

He swung it forward and I flinched.

But the blow never came.

I opened my eyes to see Vale's hand clamped around Mort's wrist.

'Leave,' Vale said, voice rough. A muscle feathered in his jaw.

Mort finally seemed to take stock of Vale's mood and ripped his arm from his grip. I scuttled away from him instead of giving in to the urge to claw his eyes from his disgusting face.

'Come with me,' Vale said to me without taking his eyes off Mort.

'I'll . . . er . . . get back to my duties,' Mort spluttered, eyes flitting between us for a moment before he hustled toward the steps that led to Endlock's main level.

Vale turned, gripping me by the elbow and pulling me after him.

'Where are we going?' I managed to say in a grating whisper, betraying the uneasiness that scraped beneath my skin.

We'd reached the stairs but instead of taking them, we veered right, heading down another dark corridor.

'There's a locker room for the guards down here,' Vale murmured, his soft voice at odds with the tension that filled his body. 'There aren't any shift changes for an hour, so it should be empty. You can shower in private, and I'll keep watch.'

Another kindness, but still no answers about who he truly was. *Why* he was helping me.

'The cameras?' I asked, looking down the hallway. There were many more of them that we'd pass on our way.

'Off,' Vale said without missing a beat. 'None of the basement ones are on rotation at this time of day. Energy conservation.'

I tucked away that bit of information.

I needed to scrub the filth of the last week and the feeling of Mort's touch from my skin, and I knew I'd be too nervous to shower in the communal bathroom where Perri could launch another attack on me while I was weak.

But the thought of showering in a locker room where a guard could walk in without warning had another finger of dread clamping around my heart – Mort couldn't be the only one of them who liked to corner inmates in the dark.

But Vale would be there.

I was jolted by the realization that Vale being with me made me feel *safe*. When had that happened?

I fisted the fabric of my jumpsuit in my hands to stop them from shaking as we made our way down the hall in silence. I pushed Mort from my mind, refusing to linger on what might've happened in the gloom of the corridor if Vale hadn't found us. I told myself that even if Vale hadn't arrived, I would have killed Mort before I let him have me.

'What else is down here?' I asked, noticing the hall veered off in another direction at the end.

'The shared dormitory for the guards, and some private quarters.'

'Who gets private quarters?'

'Larch has his own upstairs. Down here it's mostly senior guards.'

'Does that include you?'

He nodded, then looked away, as if the revelation embarrassed him.

Vale had his own room, and was considered a senior guard when he'd only worked at Endlock for a year. I was missing something. Another piece in an inscrutable puzzle.

We reached a door that swung inward and didn't seem to be protected by any kind of locking mechanism. Vale poked his head into the room, confirmed it was empty, and then placed a hand on my lower back to usher me inside, the warmth of his skin seeping through my uniform.

An L-shaped wall of lockers took up most of the space, some sealed shut and others with doors hanging off their hinges, garments spilling out onto the floor. The benches in front of them stood littered with stockings, a moldering tray of food from the mess hall, and all manner of rubbish.

Vale led me past a dividing wall toward a line of showers that were mercifully fitted with curtains. He motioned me toward the nearest shower, and I stepped inside fully clothed.

I let out a breath when I found the stall much cleaner than the rest of the room had suggested.

'Give me your uniform,' Vale commanded from the other side of the curtain.

I blanched but recovered quickly. At least he couldn't see my reaction – I could feign arrogance much more easily this way. Hide the fear that had overtaken me in the corridor. 'Okay. But don't even think about peeking. Seeing me naked is a privilege, guard. And not one that can be bought with a hot shower and a couple of ration bars.'

He choked, and I bit my lip.

I unzipped my jumpsuit and stuck my hand through the curtain to hand him the saturated uniform, surrendering the filthy garment without bothering to ask what he planned to do with it, and stepped under the stream of water.

A sigh slipped past my lips as the first scalding droplets kissed my skin.

There was *soap*.

I placed my palms flat on the tiled wall and hung my head under the spray of water, letting my hair curtain around me as I took deep breaths and tried to fight the images barreling through my mind.

In, *two, three, four.*

Aggie in my apartment, telling me Jed had been sent to Endlock.

Out, *two, three, four.*

Momo on the hunting grounds with a rifle pointed at his head.

In*, two, three, four.*
Torin crawling, begging, then taking his last breath. A guard pulling the teeth from his unmoving mouth.
Out*, two, three, four.*
The Blood Tree, covered in crimson stains.
In*, two, three, four.*
The endless darkness.
Out*, two, three, four.*
Mort with his hands all over me.
I counted, over and over, until my breaths slowed, and it didn't feel like my heart was going to beat out of my chest any longer.

I stayed under the stream for as long as I could rationalize, scrubbing at my skin until it was red and tingling, working at my hair until the worst of the knots were untangled. I even let a few tears leak from my eyes. Then I pushed the curtain aside, snatching a towel from a nearby hook and wrapping it around my body.

'Vale?' My voice echoed softly in the open space of the locker room. 'Are you still here?'

He appeared from around the corner, stopping in his tracks upon seeing me in the towel. His eyes darkened, and he ran a hand through his hair to push it off his forehead. 'I threw your uniform away. You don't need it now, anyway. Larch upped your ranking to an eight while you were in solitary. You're in the Upper level now.'

My mouth dropped open. 'What? How?'

'Don't think of it as a good thing, Little Bird. I told you that hurting a hunter would make you seem more dangerous – Larch is counting on it. He's advertising what happened, in an attempt to save his ass. And promoting you to a Green means he can make more credits off of you.'

Vale extended a new, forest-green jumpsuit toward me. I reached for it, but a creaking sound interrupted us before our hands could meet – the sound of the locker room door swinging open.

My heart leaped into my throat.

We stood, frozen.

The showers were hidden by the partition wall, out of sight from the rest of the locker room, but there was no telling whether the intruder would come around the corner and spot us.

Before I could work out what to do next, Vale's arms snaked around me, drawing me back into the shower stall I'd vacated. The curtain fell closed, shrouding us in semi-darkness. We stood chest to chest.

Footsteps stomped around the locker room on the other side of the curtain, each step threatening to bring the person closer to discovering us.

I felt the rhythmic rise and fall of Vale's chest against mine, his chin grazing the top of my head. Each breath he took sent a cascade of warmth through my wet hair.

My breath quickened, my heartbeat surging. Only a thin scrap of material stood as a barrier between Vale and my bare skin.

His fingers firmly gripped the small of my back, maintaining the towel's precarious hold on my body. Heat bloomed in my cheeks, and I breathed in his clean smell.

It should have been the last thing on my mind, but all I could think of was the night we met and his urgent lips on mine in the alley – the way he'd tasted and the way his skin had felt beneath my fingertips—

I let out a breath.

I needed to focus on remaining quiet. Kit and Yara had told me that some prisoners traded their bodies for favors, but I knew guards weren't supposed to fraternize with inmates – the Council thought it could create a bond and cause them to sympathize with us.

Vale would have difficulty explaining himself if whoever was in the locker room caught us.

Vale shifted his grip, fingers tracing comforting patterns along my spine, over the towel, and then over the damp skin of my upper back where the fabric ended.

'It's okay,' he breathed, the soft promise in his voice working to calm my rising panic. 'I've got you.'

My arms grew tighter around him, but instead of resisting, he leaned into my embrace.

Who are you? I wanted to ask again. It wasn't so much that he'd changed – more like he'd been hiding behind a mask ever since I was brought to Endlock. And, finally, he was showing me the man I'd first met at Vern's.

His hand trailed over the back of my shoulder, reaching the raised lines of my strike marks.

He stopped his perusal of my skin, his body going impossibly still as his fingers lingered on my scars. I couldn't even feel him breathing beneath me.

The footsteps grew distant, fainter and fainter, until we heard the creak of the locker room door once more, and they faded entirely down the corridor.

I sighed, the tension draining from my frame. I looked up, finding Vale's eyes mere inches from mine, our breaths entwined.

Vale seemed to shake himself from his thoughts. He flexed his fingers, moving his hand from my shoulder, and, at the same time, I remembered myself, jumping back to put space between us.

Vale was a *guard*. No matter what he said or how much he'd helped me, he wasn't someone to trust or to touch – he was someone I hoped to *use*, however I could, to get out of Endlock. I'd been starved of companionship while in solitary, but I couldn't let my craving for closeness distract me from my purpose.

'I'll go check everything out,' Vale said, voice hushed, even though there was no longer cause to whisper.

And then he slipped from the shower stall.

I discarded my towel and slid into the new jumpsuit Vale had left for me, its cold fabric sticking to my damp skin. I was yanking the zipper up when I heard his returning footsteps.

'All clear,' his rumbling voice came, cool and detached, with no trace of softness remaining.

I cleared my throat and stepped around the curtain, wiping my sweaty palms on my thighs as he guided me into the hall.

16

IN THE WEEKS that followed, much to Larch's chagrin, none of the hunters selected me for another hunt.

Groups of hunters rotated through our cellblock every few days, but most of them seemed uninterested in spending as many credits as Larch wanted for me.

The number eight shone from the digital display above my new Upper level cell, and I was still getting used to the comforts that came with my higher rank. A soft, twin-sized mattress with plush blankets and a fluffy pillow was pressed against one wall, and a dresser, courtesy of Yara, held my few belongings. A small privacy wall blocked a toilet and sink from the view of the other inmates.

The Upper shower room, too, was a welcome change from the Lower. Curtains lined each stall, and shelves at the edge of the room held fresh towels, shampoo, and bars of soap. A long mirror stood in the corner, giving me the first glimpse of myself in nearly a month. I'd lost weight on the meager rations given to the Grays, and purple circles weighed heavy beneath my eyes.

Perri tried cornering me in the showers, but she didn't have her group of minions by her side, and Kit and Yara stepped up to my defense before we could come to blows. Cyril pulled Perri away, not liking my improved odds.

The most surprising perk that came with being an Upper level inmate was the privilege of sending and receiving letters from loved ones outside of Endlock. I'd chosen Graylin as my primary contact. Of course, the guards reviewed all the communications, but when I finally worked up the nerve to send a letter, I'd use the code Gray and I had developed.

I watched as Jed struck up easy friendships with our group, seeming to grow particularly close to Kit and Momo. I'd catch him playing made-up games with Momo at dinner and listening intently as Kit talked about the part she'd played in Endlock's security.

My heart tightened at every interaction. Of course, Jed would build relationships in a place like this. He was sunshine incarnate.

I tried asking Kit and August about any progress they'd made toward escaping before I'd arrived at Endlock, but they answered evasively.

Which meant I hadn't gained their trust.

In an effort to remedy that, I told them about my plan to steal a pair of wire cutters from the workshop, and while they agreed it was worth a try, they told me that Vale took inventory of the tools at the end of every shift, before the inmates were allowed to leave.

If I was going to take the wire cutters, I'd have to time the theft perfectly.

And so far, I hadn't had a chance to take a pair – there were too many inmates around, and Vale paid far too much attention to us for my liking.

I hadn't made any headway with Vale since my release from solitary, and our interactions remained short and detached. It was partially a relief because if I kept him at a distance, I wouldn't need to worry about how my traitorous body reacted to his proximity – but it also meant my plan to get close to him would slip through my fingers if something didn't change.

At the back of my mind, a clock was ticking down faster than I was comfortable with. The number of days I had left until the North Settlement would refuse to take us in.

One afternoon during my shift in the workshop, Larch appeared in the doorway.

My head snapped up, and beside me at our shared workbench, August and Yara mirrored my reaction, their heads turning toward the door.

Vale glanced at Larch from behind his desk in the corner of the room, where he'd been supervising us.

My heart pounded in my chest as I waited for Larch to call out an inmate's number and have them hauled off to solitary, hoping beyond hope that it wouldn't be me.

I didn't know if I could take the darkness and isolation again.

But Larch turned his attention to Vale. 'Did you forget something?'

It was almost as if Vale didn't hear him. Instead of looking at the Warden, he shuffled the papers on his desk, and I watched Larch's face grow redder and redder until he loudly cleared his throat.

Vale turned to him, one brow raised. 'I'm not sure what you're referring to.'

Larch ground his teeth together and snapped, 'Come with me. Now.' Then he spun on his heel and disappeared into the corridor.

Vale's eyes narrowed, and he clenched his jaw. I thought he might defy Larch's order, but then he stood and left the workshop without another word. The door clicked shut behind him, but the barrier did little to muffle the voices on the other side.

'It was so *very* generous of you to spare time from your day to catch up with us. I certainly won't keep you long. You must have a very busy schedule if you couldn't be bothered to attend the board meeting.' A woman spoke the words with such vehemence that it took my breath away. Her voice was vaguely familiar, but I couldn't quite place where I'd heard it.

The board meeting?

Guards didn't attend board meetings. No one did except the executives of Endlock Enterprises and the Council.

'Yes, it's not as if we have busy schedules,' someone else answered, their words dripping with sarcasm. My eyes widened – it was impossible not to recognize the voice of Pharil Coates, the CEO of Endlock Enterprises. I'd heard his voiceover on Endlock commercials since I was a child.

'I wasn't aware there was a meeting today,' Vale drawled, addressing the speakers casually, his voice fading as the group's footsteps moved farther away.

I strained, wanting to hear more. *Needing* to hear more if I was going to learn the truth about Vale.

I stood, and nearly every inmate in the room looked at me.

'I need to use the bathroom,' I said, directing the words to August and Yara but ensuring the rest of the inmates heard.

August looked uneasy. 'Thorne—'

'It can't wait,' I told him and made quickly for the door, turning the knob and stepping over the threshold before I could change my mind.

I shut the door behind me.

'You can hardly claim not to have known about the meeting when I sent the communication over *three times*,' the woman's voice snapped from farther down the corridor. Her voice was as sharp as a dagger. 'And I know the Warden told you himself.'

I flattened myself against the wall, slipping through the shadows as I crept toward the voices, keeping an eye on the cameras to make sure no blinking red lights appeared.

'Do you know how many guards in your position would kill to be on the board, boy?' Pharil Coates chimed in. 'Endlock Enterprises is the *life* of this city. Dividium would be nothing without it.'

'Boy? Careful, Coates,' Vale murmured, dangerously low. 'You wouldn't want me to think you're being disrespectful, would you? Not when I know about your friend Blythe.'

Blythe? Blythe Levine?

As in, the reporter who had been sent to Endlock for stalking Coates several months ago? It'd been all over the live streams on my tablet and projected on screens across the Lower Sector.

There was a spluttering sound that I assumed came from Coates.

The truth of what had happened to Blythe was clearly different from what had been reported. And it must have been scandalous enough that just *knowing* the truth had given Vale a career boost at Endlock – though he must travel in the top circles of the Upper Sector to have gained access to that level of information. My best guess was that he had family on the Upper Sector's board of officials, the only leaders who came close to the Council's power.

Vale being part of the upper echelon of Dividium and having dirt on Coates *would* explain his strange authority over the other guards and the way he spoke to the Warden. Larch must have been under orders to keep Vale happy at all costs.

'Nevertheless, my apologies,' Vale mused, as if his exchange with Coates had never happened. 'I must have misunderstood the Warden. Was there something you needed from me?'

I took a few more steps.

Their voices were closer now, tucked into one of the rooms lining the corridor. From the sound of it, they hadn't bothered to close the door – they wouldn't have thought anyone would dare follow them.

'Show some respect,' Larch hissed as if reprimanding a child.

Vale murmured something under his breath, and I pressed my back against the wall, creeping closer until I was inches from the doorway. To my left, the stairwell that led to Endlock's main level came into view – if anyone came down those steps, I'd be caught.

The woman spoke again. 'The average length of each inmate's stay is becoming a problem,' she said, her tone grave. 'There are more arrests every day, but our citizens don't seem able to kill their targets as easily as they once did. Endlock is filling up at an alarming rate and will be over capacity soon.'

'As you can tell, Elder is worried about her reputation – I haven't heard the end of it,' Coates said.

My jaw nearly hit the floor. Elder. That's why the woman's voice sounded familiar. It was Councilor Caltriona Elder. She was the youngest of the Council, having inherited her position a few months prior when her predecessor and father, Gaius Elder, had passed away.

So not only was Vale invited to a meeting with Warden Larch and the CEO of Endlock Enterprises, but he was also having an intimate conversation with a councilor. Whatever he knew about Coates and Blythe Levine had to be damning.

'The *real* problem is that interest is down,' Coates continued. 'We used to have to turn hunters away from every hunt. Hell, last year we were looking into adding two more hunts in the evening just to meet demand, and now we can't even fill up the three we have every day. Profits are down nearly ten percent in the last two months alone.'

'Prices have gone up,' Larch said, slowly. 'What if we lowered them?'

Councilor Elder barked out a humorless laugh. 'The adults are talking, Roth. We don't pay you to help with business decisions. Especially when you can't even keep the inmates in check. Don't think I didn't hear about the hunter who was knocked unconscious a few weeks ago.'

Larch fell silent.

'We're not lowering the cost of hunting,' Coates hissed. 'I *just* told you that profits are down. This is about long-term growth. We need to add something that makes the experience worth the cost to the hunters – enough that they come back over and over, and bring new guests with them.'

Councilor Elder made a sound of agreement. 'Right now the inmates are making us look bad. One of them has been here for over *two years* now. It's unprecedented, and it's making a mockery of the Council and our laws. We must find a way to make the hunts more entertaining for the hunters when they visit Endlock. Give them better odds of making a kill.'

My hands balled into fists at my sides. I already knew these people didn't see us as human, but hearing them strategize about making our deaths *fun* was more than I could handle.

The door at the top of the stairwell slammed open, and I jumped, banging my elbow against the wall behind me. I froze as the conversation in the room ceased. I didn't dare to move – didn't even dare to run, in case my footsteps drew their attention.

Even as I heard the clear sound of a guard's boots slapping against the treads in the stairwell.

A throat was cleared in the room, and Vale's voice filtered out to me. 'And did anyone have any suggestions on how to make that happen?'

I was gone before I could hear a response.

By the time Vale returned to the workshop following his meeting with Larch, the alarm had gone off to call us to dinner.

He seemed distracted as he sat down and pulled out a new sheet of paper. He dismissed us without bothering to take inventory of the tools on the back wall. I stayed at the workbench under the guise of cleaning my station, gesturing Yara and August to go ahead. They shot me questioning looks, but I waved them off.

When the last inmate departed the room, Vale was still focused on the paperwork at his desk.

I swallowed, looking back and forth between him and the wall of tools as I sidestepped toward the back of the room.

He didn't look up once.

I slipped a small pair of wire cutters from the wall and into one of the deep pockets of my uniform.

With the weight of the tool in my pocket, there was a part of me that wanted to leave the room without drawing attention to myself, especially after I'd almost been caught eavesdropping in the corridor, but it wasn't as strong as the part of me that needed to ask Vale what the outcome of the conversation had been.

Vale had broken the rules for me several times over. While he'd yet to confide the full truth of what he was doing at End-lock, he seemed intent on helping me survive. I knew I couldn't trust him – could never trust a guard – but I also couldn't walk away without trying to learn more about his clandestine conversation.

In the end, Vale made the decision for me.

'What are you still doing here?' he asked, eyes snapping up from the document he'd been examining and noting the otherwise empty workshop.

'What was that about?' I forced the words past my lips before I could lose my nerve.

He turned to look over his shoulder at the camera I'd already confirmed wasn't recording and then met my gaze, his brow wrinkled. 'What do you mean?'

'Why would a guard be invited to a board meeting? Why are you important enough to that board meeting that the Warden, Councilor Elder, and the CEO of Endlock Enterprises came to speak with you when you didn't show up? Why do all the other guards defer to you, even though you're supposed to be on equal footing?' The questions spilled out of me, one after the other. Vale had practically avoided me in the time following my stint in solitary, and I'd been content to watch him in silence and attempt to piece together the truth.

But this was too much.

And while I *thought* I knew the answers to my questions, I needed to hear them from him.

Without another word, Vale was on his feet, sealing the workshop door, effectively cutting us off from the rest of the prison. His eyes bored into mine, a firestorm churning within them.

He stepped closer to where I stood. 'Lower your voice,' he hissed, molten eyes flashing to the door. 'If you could hear what was said out in the hall, don't you think anyone who happens to be wandering around would overhear the way you're speaking to me right now? Don't you think they would find it strange to know that you feel comfortable talking to me like this?'

'*I* find it strange that I'm comfortable talking to you like this. Don't you?'

He looked away, leaving yet another question unanswered. I let out a long sigh.

'I followed you,' I admitted, crossing my arms over my chest.

His head snapped up, but I didn't give him time to speak.

'If you won't tell me the truth about who you are, you can't expect me not to look for answers.'

'But I do, Raven,' he murmured, closing his eyes and pinching the bridge of his nose between his thumb and forefinger. 'I expect you to keep your head down.'

I let out a harsh laugh. 'Keeping my head down isn't going to keep my brother alive. If I don't know everything they plan to throw at us, we don't stand a chance.'

'But if you get caught listening to private conversations, Larch will kill you.'

'It's a good thing I didn't get caught, then,' I shot back. I couldn't bring myself to regret taking the risk. Not with everything at stake. 'I heard what Coates said about Endlock's profits being down, and needing to find a way to make the hunts entertaining to bring more visitors in.'

Vale gave a tight nod, confirming what I'd heard.

'Please,' I whispered, swallowing hard. 'I wasn't able to hear the rest, and I need to know if we're in more danger. I *need* to be able to protect Jed.'

There was a pause, an internal battle in Vale's gaze. He rubbed a hand over his jaw, and I could tell, even before he opened his mouth, that he'd accepted defeat.

'Most of the population from the Upper and Middle Sectors have already visited Endlock at least once over the years, and it seems like the novelty is wearing off. Endlock Enterprises is stagnant. Coates and the Council promised the shareholders a good year and they're worried about the implications of not delivering. Coates is a businessman, so it's all about profits for him. The Council has more at stake. Public perception can make all the difference in their control of Dividium.'

I nodded, though my stomach clenched. I knew there was more he hadn't shared yet.

'The board is working on a way to heighten Endlock's appeal for hunters.' Vale seemed to be carefully choosing each of his words.

'And how are they going to do that?'

He let out a harsh breath, shaking his head back and forth. 'I shouldn't be telling you any of this. It's dangerous. For both of us.'

No. I couldn't lose him now.

'There's a lot you shouldn't have done for me.' *But you did.* The unspoken words swirled through the air between us.

His eyes lingered on mine, assessing. 'You know the wristband every inmate wears?'

I nodded, looking down at the black band on my arm.

'Larch has suggested some upgrades – an option for hunters to purchase extra features for their target's wristband.'

'Extra features?' I repeated, tilting my head.

Vale grimaced. 'They're still working out some of the specifics, but so far they're on board with vital-signs monitoring, thermal imaging, proximity alerts, and . . . infliction of pain.'

Logically, I knew what his words meant, but I needed him to confirm. 'What does that mean for us?'

His eyes were steady on mine as he answered. 'The vitals monitoring won't have a big impact on you. The thermal imaging will allow hunters to see their targets through foliage and branches if they're close enough. In theory, with proximity alerts, your wristband would emit an alarm when a hunter is nearby. And the pain . . . they're talking to the engineers to figure out what's technically possible, but they want the wristbands to emit some kind of severe shock. Something that's painful enough to debilitate you, at least momentarily. They plan to offer the features as add-ons that the hunters can purchase to elevate their experience.'

'No.' My stomach dropped, nausea twisting my insides, and I slapped a hand over my mouth. If what Vale said was true, the prisoners would no longer stand a chance. Jed and I wouldn't stand a chance. There wouldn't be any hiding. The only survivors would be those who could outrun the hunters.

Vale gripped my shoulders, his thumbs rubbing in soothing circles. 'It will be a while before the engineers have the features up and running. We have time.'

We. Like we were a team.

Drawing a steadying breath, I tried to mask my emotions. 'Okay.'

I turned, deciding to seek out Kit in the mess hall and discuss our escape. I needed to get Jed out. Now.

'Wait.' Vale's voice was a low murmur, but it pulled me back. His fingers curled around my wrist, and I met his gaze, unable to ignore the feeling of his thumb moving back and forth on my skin – a caress over my hammering pulse.

'What is it?' I swallowed, the wire cutters heavy in my pocket. If he'd seen me take them . . . I didn't know what he'd do.

'There was something I wanted to ask you.' He hesitated, his mouth opening and closing twice before he finally spoke. 'Remember that day a few weeks ago, in the showers?'

As if I could forget.

I could still feel his fingers running up and down my back.

I nodded, ducking my head to hide the flush in my cheeks.

'I noticed . . .' He stopped, rubbing his free hand over the back of his neck before trying again. 'I noticed you have two strike marks on your shoulder.'

'Is there a question in there somewhere, or were you just trying to come up with an excuse to talk about being pressed against my body?' I drawled, giving myself time to decide how much of the truth I wanted to reveal to him.

'Stop stalling,' he said, leaning against the wall. His fingers were still clasped casually over my skin like my words didn't faze him. But I saw how he swallowed harshly, his eyes flitting over my frame. 'I don't need an excuse to talk about being pressed against you – I think about it every time I close my eyes.'

He did?

Here, he paused, seeming to savor my red cheeks and inability to form words.

'I want to know why you have two strike marks,' he continued when I didn't respond.

Subconsciously, my free hand moved to trace the edges of my scars, reliving that night with Jed seven years ago.

'Why do you care?'

Vale blew out a harsh laugh. 'I wish I knew the answer to that.'

Whatever that means.

I narrowed my eyes at him.

'A truth for a truth, then,' he said, giving me a small smile. 'Because I know you overheard what I said about Blythe Levine.'

I clenched my teeth together to keep my mouth from dropping open. But I only lasted a few moments before curiosity got the better of me. 'Deal.'

Vale gave me a crooked grin that did strange things to my stomach. 'You first.'

I stared at him for a long moment, then took a deep breath.

'Okay. My parents were arrested for hiding fugitives in our home,' I said, reciting the words as if I were merely spouting facts about Dividium's history and not reliving the worst night of my life. 'When they were caught, the guards wanted to give Jed and me a strike since we hadn't turned our parents in. The guards said we would have reported our parents if we were loyal citizens.'

Anger rose within me at the memory, my hand forming a shaking fist. As if any of them would have turned against their loved ones if put in the same situation.

Vale's eyes darkened, a shadow passing over his face, and I didn't miss the tic in the side of his clenched jaw. He pulled on my wrist gently until I stepped closer, our chests a mere inch from touching as his eyes roved over my face.

My breath caught in my throat, but I pushed on. 'I asked them to give me both strikes – to spare Jed. One of the guards took pity on me and agreed.'

'You were so brave,' Vale whispered, reaching up and tucking a strand of hair behind my ear. He let his fingers linger on my cheek, and it took all the strength I could muster to keep from shivering and pressing into the warmth of his touch. 'You took care of him, even then.'

I cleared my throat. It hadn't been bravery that had made me take that strike for Jed. If anything, it had been guilt. I'd deserved them – deserved the pain, and the reminder of my mistake.

'Now you,' I said, forcing a subject change. 'Tell me what you know.'

Vale frowned, but didn't refuse. 'I'm sure you saw what the news reported about Blythe, but it was a lie. She wasn't stalking Coates – she was gathering evidence. She'd learned something about Endlock that would've made Dividium revolt.'

'What did she find out?'

He paused, squeezing my wrist. 'You have to be careful once I tell you. You can't let Larch suspect that you know. It's one thing for me to find out – I'm from the Upper Sector. One of *them*.' His lip curled on the last word. 'But they'd kill you for knowing. Wouldn't even risk waiting for a hunter to do it.'

I swallowed. 'I'll be careful.'

Vale blew out a long breath. 'There's no real food shortage in the Lower Sector. It's a lie.'

A laugh slipped out of me before I could stop it.

'I'm serious, Raven.'

'Vale, I *lived* in the Lower Sector, remember? I can assure you that there's a food shortage. I don't think I've had three meals in one day in the last ten years.'

'Exactly,' he whispered.

I stared, waiting for him to go on.

'I don't know the details, or how they did it, but the crops never failed on their own. Endlock Enterprises and the Council worked together to create an artificial food shortage in the Lower Sector. Ten years ago.'

'No. No, they wouldn't—'

Wouldn't what? Starve their own citizens?

They let people pay to murder us for entertainment.

I swallowed painfully. 'Why?' I asked. Because there had to be a reason. I was sure they'd justified the move in order to live with themselves.

'Endlock hadn't picked up in popularity like they'd hoped – there weren't enough targets to hunt. Citizens were afraid of getting arrested, and the crime rate dropped to next to nothing across Dividium. But it seems like Coates realized that if people in the Lower Sector were hungry, *desperate*, they'd commit more crimes. And he was right.'

My mouth dropped open, my head spinning.

We'd been starving. My family, our neighbors. Nearly everyone I knew had struggled with food insecurity at one point or another over the last ten years, but it hadn't always been so bad. Until I was about thirteen, we had almost always had enough to get by. Until suddenly we hadn't.

I remembered something Loria had said, just before my arrest, about how there was more than enough food to go around if the Council allocated it correctly.

I hadn't believed her. Hadn't imagined, no matter how corrupt our society was, that they would *intentionally* starve us for profit. So they could arrest us and send us to our deaths for other citizens' amusement.

My stomach churned.

'Who knows about this?' I whispered.

'I'm not sure,' Vale admitted. 'Coates and Larch and the Council, for sure. A few of their most trusted guards. But the board doesn't know, and neither do the shareholders.'

So not everyone in the Upper and Middle Sectors knew.

'Okay,' I breathed. I couldn't process everything he'd said. There probably wasn't enough time in the world. And right now, I had to catch Kit before the end of dinner. 'I need to go.'

Vale went silent, his grip on my wrist loosening. His fingers brushed against my skin before his touch fell away entirely.

It wasn't until I reached the main floor that I realized Vale hadn't told me *how* he'd found out the truth about Blythe Levine.

I scanned the mess hall, then stalked over to where Kit and August were sitting.

'I got the wire cutters,' I said, once I was at their table, not bothering with a greeting.

August jerked his head up from his meal, and Kit glanced around, likely checking to see who might be within earshot.

'Good work, bounty hunter,' Kit said, grinning.

'Say I manage to smuggle them onto the hunting grounds and

cut the fence next time I'm chosen,' I whispered. 'Have you made any progress on the wristbands?'

'Why the rush all of a sudden?' August asked, looking around nervously. Our table was still relatively empty, but it would fill up soon. 'It's dangerous to talk about it here.'

'There's nowhere else to talk about it. And today . . .' I quickly filled the two of them in on what I'd overheard from Councilor Elder and Coates, and what Vale had admitted to me after – leaving out the part about the artificial food shortage.

Kit and August exchanged a long look.

'We need to know that we can trust you,' August finally said.

'Of course you can trust me.' I shook my head, exasperated. 'The only reason I'm in here is to help Jed. I would never do anything to jeopardize his safety.'

'It's not Jed we're worried about you betraying,' Kit whispered, looking almost apologetic. 'But we saw your face when we told you we were taking Yara and Momo with us. You don't want to take them along.'

'Of course I didn't. It makes things complicated with the North Settlement leaders, and even if it didn't, what we're doing is risky.'

'We can't leave them behind,' Kit answered fiercely. 'Gus and I agreed from the beginning that we each got to bring someone with us. Yara for me. Momo for him. And that was long before you got here.'

I raised my hands in surrender. 'I said *I didn't*. As in, when you first told me. I needed time to process. But I get it – you'd both do anything for them.' *Just like I'd do anything for Jed.*

'Don't pretend you don't care about them, too,' August insisted. 'I know you spend your days burying your feelings and acting like Jed's the only person that matters to you, but it's all a lie. That became obvious the moment you risked yourself for Momo.'

'I—' I didn't know what I planned to say in response, but August cut me off before I could decide.

'If we die trying, well, at least we'll know we went out doing everything we could to help them.'

I nodded. I knew it was a bad idea to bring more people along, but the more I thought about leaving Momo and Yara behind . . . *fuck*.

And Jed would be safer if he had a whole group protecting him.

'How are you going to disable the tracking?' I asked, trying to retain a modicum of authority over the situation.

'Say we can trust you, Thorne, and we'll find a way,' August promised.

I paused, looking them both in the eye so that they could see the truth in my gaze. 'We're in this together. I won't betray you.'

And I meant it. They were right that I hadn't wanted anyone else to leave with us. But my time at Endlock had changed things.

Kit grinned and leaned forward, putting her elbows on the table. 'So. At first we figured we'd just find a way to take our wristbands off, and save me the trouble of having to disable the tracking.'

I nodded. That did seem like the plan with the least amount of risk involved.

'But I've thought about it, and it'd be better to leave the wristbands on. That way I can disable the tracking and reverse engineer them so that any guards that come after us won't be able to shoot us. They'll be like the wristbands the guards and hunters wear.'

I whistled. I'd known she was an asset when she'd said she'd helped create some of the security systems, but being able to reverse engineer the wristbands from inside Endlock was an entirely different skillset. She was *dangerous*.

'What do you need?' I asked, rolling my lips.

'A tablet, for one,' Kit whispered.

'Oh, just that?' I stared at her, incredulous. She might as well have asked me to walk her out the front door.

Kit arched a brow. 'You stole a pair of wire cutters. What's a tablet?'

It remained to be seen if I'd actually gotten away with stealing the wire cutters or if Endlock would be on lockdown once Vale discovered they were missing. But I got her point.

'Where do they keep the tablets?' I asked.

Kit took a bite of stew and swallowed. 'All of the guards have one.'

'The—' I stopped, taking a deep breath and running a hand over my face. '*You want to steal a tablet from a guard?*'

She grimaced. 'I know. And once we manage to get our hands on one, we'll only have a few minutes before someone notices it's gone. Trust me – if it was easy, I'd have done it by now. But we're making headway on the second piece, at least.'

I raised a brow. 'And the second piece is?'

'I need a private space to work once we have the tablet,' Kit said under her breath. 'Somewhere the guards won't find me while I disable the tracking.'

I had to fight to keep my mouth from dropping open. I let my incredulous gaze flit back and forth between the two of them.

August's mouth twisted to one side. 'I've got it covered.'

My mind flashed to seeing August and Vale whispering on the hunting grounds. Was he using another favor to get Vale to help him?

'The tablet,' I started. 'Does it have to be from one of the guards?'

Kit pursed her lips. 'I mean, no. They have them in the security room, too. But aside from the front desk and Larch's office, those are the only tablets in the building.'

'What if we got one from outside of Endlock?' I asked.

Kit shook her head. 'Wouldn't work. I need one that's already connected to Endlock's network so that I can quickly go in and kill the tracking. Getting a tablet from the outside would require me to hack into the network first, which could take ages – not to mention set off alarm bells.'

My mind jumped to Vale, but I quickly shook off the thought. I didn't know enough about him, and I definitely didn't trust him enough to risk our entire plan. It was one thing for him to want to help keep me alive during hunts, but that was a long way from playing an active part in a prison break.

'There's a guard that's working with the Collective,' I said, thinking back to the woman who'd passed me a note from Gray while I was in solitary.

Kit and August exchanged a look I couldn't quite read before I continued.

'I don't know who she is, but she smuggled me a letter from a friend while I was in solitary. Do you know her?'

Kit shook her head. 'No. I've had someone slip me notes, too – tips for staying under the radar when certain hunters came to my cellblock for selection. But I never saw who left them. But if she is Collective – it would be too dangerous to use her tablet. If the Warden noticed any unusual activity on the prison's network, he'd be able to track it back to her.'

Great.

I'd have to swallow my pride and ask for help from the last person I wanted to speak with, then.

'Give me a few days,' I told them, thinking through how to use our code to write my first letter to Gray. Then, a thought occurred to me, and my lips twitched, unable to suppress a smile. 'Do you have experience working with weapons, Kit? I still have that rifle stashed out on the hunting grounds.'

Kit's grin matched mine. 'Maybe having a bounty hunter around isn't so bad after all.'

'What are you talking about?'

My head snapped around. Jed had filled his tray and was standing behind me.

I forced a smile onto my face. 'Just another potential escape route out on the hunting grounds.'

I didn't tell him about the wristbands or the tablet. I'd said I'd let him help, but that didn't mean he had to be involved in *every-thing*, right? If he focused on helping me with the escape route, and stayed out of Kit and August's part in the plan, I'd be able to keep an eye on him.

17

Dearest Gray,

It's so difficult to be away from you — if you were near, I could remind you that my second redeeming quality is the ability to give you a black eye without breaking a sweat. Then again, if you were near, I'd be subjected to your incessant lectures on how to be a perfect pain in the ass.

How dull.

Here's the deal. I need you to get me one of the guards' tablets. Prove to me you're more than just a pretty face, and help me, and I'll escort your precious asset to where she needs to be.

Kisses,
Raven

With Kit and August finally speaking to me about their plans, we might reach the North Settlement sooner than I'd anticipated.

The next evening, Hyde walked around delivering letters to the Upper level inmates and handed me one from Gray, written in code. When I deciphered it, my face reddened at Gray's words. It felt strange to be communicating with him in a way we hadn't in years. It felt like we were on the same side again when I'd never thought we could be.

Thorne,

My face isn't even the prettiest part of me.

Unfortunately, what you've asked can't be done. If any of our connections gave you their personal tablet, they'd be compromised. And if they were caught taking someone else's tablet to help you? They'd be compromised and tortured to the point of giving up everything they know about the Collective, and your plans.

You'll have to find another way.

Tick tock.
– G

Fuck.
It'd have to wait.

My next task was to figure out how to get the wire cutters out on the hunting grounds and cut an opening in the camouflaged part of the fence – that way, it would be ready when Kit disabled the tracking on all of our wristbands.

As it was, storing the cutters in my cell had kept me on edge.

I'd hidden them in the only spot I could think of – the tank of my toilet. I knew a guard could search my cell at any time and find them, but I couldn't get out on the hunting grounds right away.

Our cellblock was two days from being used to select targets in the rotation.

And while I was eager to use the time leading up to my next hunt to get more information out of Vale, I didn't catch sight of

him once, not even during my shifts in the workshop, where Mort
was supervising us in his stead.

I kept my head down, ignoring his lingering stares.

More visitors flowed through Endlock each day, but not just
hunters – Kit recognized engineers she'd worked with before
her arrest, and we guessed Larch had brought in specialists from
Dividium to work on adding his features to our wristbands.

We'd heard whispers that the Council was at Endlock as well.

There was also a change in the movements of the guards. Many
of them came and went throughout the prison, smeared with mud,
twigs tangled in their hair.

Yara paid one of them off with extra cigarettes, and he told her
that something had malfunctioned in the crematorium, and they'd
moved to burying the bodies of dead prisoners instead of inciner-
ating them.

I shivered at the thought of being forever entombed within the
hunting grounds.

But that wasn't all.

We found Perri crying in the showers one night, and Yara immediately ran off to ply the guards in exchange for information – but
cigarettes weren't enough. Only the promise of thousands of credits each, courtesy of Yara's mother, got them to tell her that Perri
had fallen out of favor with Larch.

He'd found out she was still running her operation at Endlock,
right under his nose, putting him in jeopardy of losing his job.
He'd sworn he was done protecting her from the hunters.

Some of the best news I'd heard since arriving, really.

On the morning of our cellblock's next hunt, a few days after
my conversation with Kit and August, I returned to my cell after
breakfast to find a tiny square of paper folded up on my bed, so
small that I hardly noticed it.

I shot a quick glance at the camera to confirm it wasn't recording, and then snatched the paper up and stepped behind the

privacy wall, where my toilet was, to read the note without fear of another inmate or guard catching me.

There were only ten words, written in neat lettering.

Hide the cutters in your uniform. You won't get caught.

The mystery guard again? Or had Kit or August written it?

My pulse kicked up in my chest, but I didn't hesitate. As quietly as I could, I lifted the lid from the tank on the back of the toilet and pulled the cutters free, shaking them lightly to remove some of the moisture.

I wrapped some toilet paper around my hand to get the rest of the water off, then slipped the cutters down the back of my uniform, my tight camisole and the cinched waistband of my jumpsuit keeping the tool pressed against my skin.

I flushed the toilet paper and scrubbed at my hands, then took the tie out of my long hair, shaking it out until it fanned across my back, hopefully obscuring any odd shapes from view if anyone looked too closely.

Moments later, Hyde entered our cellblock, his polished boots slapping against the cement floor, and announced it was time for another hunt.

A tall man in a business suit walked in behind him, flanked by five teenage girls who were whispering and laughing, their eyes wide as they scanned the cellblock. They wore matching black T-shirts with bedazzled lettering that read *Katarina's Killer Fifteenth*.

'*Dad*,' one of the girls addressed the man. She wore a sash that said *Birthday Girl*. 'When Melissa came here last month, she got to have her target's teeth shaved into a pearl bracelet.'

'Then you'll leave with a bracelet *and* a necklace, my dear Katarina,' the man promised, eyes swaying between the targets.

'And Endlock shirts for all my friends?' Katarina asked, brows raised.

'Of course.'

She threw her arms around him for a moment before walking farther down the cellblock with her friends.

Verona Shields walked in next, wearing her stacks of rings and necklaces and bracelets, but this time she also wore a thick black headband studded with teeth. I didn't let myself look too closely. Didn't want to believe what I knew in my heart – they were Torin's.

I didn't wait for her to show interest in another inmate.

Before she could make it past my cell, I baited her.

August seemed to have a similar plan, brazenly calling one of the hunters a coward when he walked past his cell.

We were selected immediately.

I watched as Katarina selected Perri, and one of her friends chose Cyril.

When August and I stepped into the prep room, my gaze went to Vale, who stood against the far wall, tapping at the screen of his tablet. He looked up at the sound of the opening door, and his face visibly drained of color when his eyes landed on us.

Hyde escorted us in, along with the other targets, and Vale motioned him over.

'Go inspect the stalls,' Vale said to the guard, who grunted in annoyance but obeyed, stalking toward the door to the hunting grounds.

Vale jerked his head, signaling us closer.

'You shouldn't be here,' he said, grabbing August's arm and looking at his wristband, pretending to inspect it.

'Why?' August whispered.

With a groan, Vale raked a hand through his dark hair. I couldn't help but notice the way the muscles in his arm flexed beneath his uniform with the movement, and I forced myself to look away.

Focus, Raven. On the task, not on forearms and golden-eyed guards.

'The Council is too impatient to wait for the engineers to develop the new features they requested.' Vale finally let go of August's wrist. 'They've made some adjustments to the hunting grounds in the meantime. Obstacles that are supposed to help the hunters succeed and have a more *enjoyable* time.'

'Obstacles?' My pulse quickened, my heart thundering in my chest, and I nearly forgot the tool hidden beneath my uniform.

Vale reached out, grabbing my arm and making a show of checking my wristband.

'The obstacles aren't meant to kill you,' he murmured, voice barely audible. His thumb stroked softly along my pulse point, sending it skittering even farther out of control. 'They're meant to incapacitate you long enough for the hunters to complete their kill.'

Bitterness coated my throat as I struggled to hold back the questions running through my mind. I couldn't risk drawing attention to our conversation.

'You can't tell anyone else,' Vale continued, his lips downturned at the edges. 'If Larch notices targets being extra cautious, he'll know one of us told you. He said he wants to see what happens if you all go in unprepared.'

Vale told us about the obstacles we could expect – leg snares and nets and spiked trenches. A hundred ways to die. I struggled to control my nerves, my free hand fisting at my side.

I narrowed my eyes. 'What about the hunters? The obstacles could hurt them.' Not that it would bother me, but I knew the Warden wanted to avoid more negative attention.

'Our team has updated their wristbands so they'll vibrate once the hunters start to approach an obstacle, like they do with the force field. And, since this is the first time and Larch doesn't want any mishaps, he's having a guard escort each hunter.'

Hyde's approach interrupted us.

'Start patting down the inmates,' Vale ordered.

Hyde narrowed his eyes, looking back and forth between us, but did as Vale told him.

Another show of the authority that Vale's dirt on Coates had granted him.

Pure panic shot through me when I saw the other inmates preparing for their mandatory pat-downs. My palms began to sweat, every nerve ending focused on the cool metal of the tool pressed against my skin.

But August caught my eye, holding my gaze for a moment and nodding as if he knew the exact thoughts flitting through my mind.

The note had been from him, then. But how could he ensure I wouldn't be caught?

I faced the wall, and though I knew what was coming, I felt a shock run through me the moment Vale made contact with my body. His hands glided over the fabric of my uniform, and I felt myself press, almost unconsciously, into his touch. He inhaled sharply, pausing in his movements for a moment before continuing. I took shallow breaths, the air growing thick and heavy against my flushed cheeks as the memory of his tight embrace in the shower flitted through my mind.

But then he touched the tool at my back, and I remembered myself. Stopped breathing as I waited for him to say something. To call another guard over.

The next moment passed like an eternity.

But then Vale's fingers brushed softly against mine before he stepped away.

I let out a breath. Had August called in another favor? Or was this Vale looking out for me, even though he had absolutely nothing to gain and everything to lose?

I didn't have time to linger on those thoughts as Hyde started shoving inmates into place.

I joined the others in a single line and proceeded out the prep room door, to where guards confined us within our stalls. The walls closed in on me, and my chest tightened.

I'd goaded Verona into selecting me as a target, knowing that it was what I had to do to take the next step toward escaping, by showing August the weakness in the fence and attempting to cut through the metal – but it wasn't lost on me that every hunt I participated in could be the one that killed me.

'Let me out!' the inmate in the stall next to mine screamed, his voice ringing in my ears. His nails screeched against the metal as if he were attempting to claw his way through. 'LET ME—'

The blare of the buzzer cut through his words. I lunged forward into the field, catching August's gaze, and the two of us came together, moving as a unit. Without speaking, we slowed our pace, placing ourselves at the back of the group, where we could observe any changes in the terrain.

The field was a vibrant green beneath the midday sun, and insects buzzed over the tall grass, celebrating a cloudless sky.

Within seconds, the first scream split the air. My eyes snapped to its source – a girl with her leg caught in a crude metal trap, its jagged teeth biting deep into her flesh. From the unnatural angle of the limb, I would've bet a month's rent that it was broken.

I shivered. The contraption was similar to those I'd seen in the history books at school. Game hunters used them to capture animals – bears, wild cats, and other beasts – sometimes for food, but other times for their pelts or sport.

If Vale hadn't risked telling us about the obstacles, it might've been August or me writhing on the ground, unable to run from the hunters.

The other inmates shifted, running in weaving spurts, avoiding the jaws of hidden traps. We all moved past the fallen inmate, knowing we could do nothing to save her.

From what Vale had managed to tell us, I knew Larch had riddled the woods with more of the same torture.

Another scream made my blood run cold. The prisoner ahead of us vanished as if the earth had swallowed him whole.

August and I exchanged glances.

Approaching cautiously, we found a trench dug into the ground. Its interior was hellish, lined with stakes, sharp as daggers, protruding from the earthen floor of the pit. The inmate had been skewered by several of the stakes.

Blood frothed from his lips, a coppery tang thick in the air as he took a final, heaving breath and then went limp.

My stomach churned at the sight, and I slapped a hand over my mouth to bite back a sob or a gasp or whatever strangled sound was attempting to claw its way past my lips.

Vale had said the traps weren't meant to kill us. It didn't make sense that Larch would craft obstacles that were lethal to the prisoners. Endlock would lose credits if the hunters didn't get to make kills themselves. I suspected he hadn't thought the pit of spikes would be as much of a death trap as it was.

Focus. If you don't focus, it will be you lying there next.

We cleared the field and entered the forest, rushing past dozens of mounds of freshly tilled dirt.

Graves, I realized, remembering what Yara had said about the malfunction in the crematorium. Most of the graves were dug in neat rows, but there was a break along one area in the makeshift cemetery, almost like a path running through the graves, though it was uneven and didn't seem like a logical route. It curved in multiple places, and there were a few spots where it looked like a guard had started to dig and then changed their mind, opting to leave the space untouched.

A sudden yank on my sleeve, courtesy of August's quick reflexes, stopped me a breath away from a net camouflaged by fallen leaves. It lay poised, ready to entangle any unsuspecting victim.

I let out a slow breath and stepped around the obstacle.

'I think Vale might've downplayed the gravity of the situation,' I ground out.

A bead of sweat trickled down August's forehead. 'That he did.'

We dodged half a dozen more death traps, but eventually the hidden section of the fence came into view.

'There,' I said, pointing. 'This is the spot. The foliage has covered it so long that the guards won't notice if we cut the fence and cover it back up, just like it was.'

August swallowed, betraying his nervousness, before he nodded.

A low hum pulsated through the air. It was not so much a sound as a sensation, scrambling my senses and making the hair on my arms stand on end. I wondered if it came from a concealed trap waiting to strike us before a hunter could.

I looked to August — he seemed wary of the sound as well, but he nodded, and we continued toward the fence with uneasy steps.

The hum grew in intensity, settling into my bones, practically vibrating my teeth as we moved the foliage away from the fence. I freed the cutters from my uniform.

'Were you going to leave the rest of us here to die, then?' a familiar, low voice asked from behind us.

I whipped around, muscles taut, ready to defend myself. I hid the cutters behind my back on the off chance they hadn't been spotted yet.

Cyril stood before me. His typically moon-pale skin now bore the angry blotches of sunburn, with his nose and cheeks taking the brunt of the sun's wrath. He impatiently brushed a loose strand of brown hair from his eyes as he stared us down, demanding an answer.

'Cyril?' August's brow wrinkled in confusion. 'What are you talking about?'

'You think we're stupid?' Perri stepped out of the shadow of the trees, glaring at us. 'We know you're trying to escape.'

'I don't think about you much at all, Perri, but if I did . . . I'd be inclined to think that you *are* stupid, considering you followed me out here where no one can protect you.' I smiled as I delivered the words, even as my mind raced. I stepped closer to her, away from the fence, hoping to guide her attention elsewhere.

'I saw the tool. No reason to keep hiding it.'

Fuck.

Perri would tell Larch what she'd seen – that she'd witnessed two prisoners trying to escape. She would ruin our plans before they were fully formed if it meant returning to his good graces.

'Don't insult our intelligence. You're so selfish that you weren't even going to let anyone join in on your little plan,' Cyril said, his sneer deepening.

'We're not trying to escape,' I lied, holding up my wrist and tilting my head toward the wristband. 'We can't. Even if we managed to get out, you know the wristbands would alert the guards.'

'It's true,' August chimed in. 'We were looking for a place to hide when we found those cutters on the ground. We were planning on turning them in.'

'Shut up, August,' Perri sneered. 'I didn't have any problems with you before, but now you're siding with a *bounty hunter*?'

Before I could react, Perri lunged at me, catching me off guard. The force of her shove threw me backward, my body connecting with the ground and pushing the breath from my lungs as I lost my grip on the cutters and watched them skitter across the ground. The coarse earth grated against my skin, and I felt a sharp sting on my forearm. My eyes darted to a fresh gash caused by one of the many jagged stones. The rock had torn the arm of my uniform, and my blood painted a crimson stain on the earth.

Anger, hot and heady, filled my veins, and I gritted my teeth.

But Perri wasn't done. She stalked closer, eyes wild with fury. Out of the corner of my eye, I saw August and Cyril engaged in their own battle, their fists flying and enraged insults shouted between them.

When Perri got close enough to touch, I lashed out, my foot

connecting with her shin and sending her flopping down to the ground beside me.

I sprang to my feet before she could catch her breath.

August cried out, and I looked over to see his nose gushing blood, his face smeared with red. Cyril's face was bloody, too; the two of them evenly matched. As they fought, they edged closer and closer to the fence.

And that's when I realized what the humming noise was.

'Wait! Stop!' My voice rang out with such urgency that, rather than lunging at me again, Perri followed my gaze.

The color leached from her face, and she cried out, scrambling to her feet and racing toward August and Cyril with her arms flailing above her head.

But it was too late.

August shoved Cyril with all his might. Cyril, caught off balance, reached for the fence to break his fall. But the moment his flesh made contact, it was as if the metal had a hold of him. His whole body shook, a violent dance, as electricity from the fence coursed through him. He convulsed, his muscles jerking uncontrollably.

'Cyril!' Perri's scream, raw and piercing, split the air as she crumpled beside him, her instincts strong enough to prevent her from placing her hands on his quaking body.

My eyes locked with August's, the horror in them reflecting the sickening scene playing out before us. The world seemed to slow, every agonizing second stretching into an eternity. We stood paralyzed, knowing that if we touched Cyril, we might die alongside him.

Cyril's grip on the fence weakened, though I couldn't say whether it was an intentional choice because as soon as he had nothing holding his body up, he collapsed to the ground in an unmoving heap.

Perri rushed to his side.

August reached for Cyril's wrist and seemed to search for a pulse.

'Cyril?' My voice wavered. 'Can you hear me?'

But smoke wafted up from his clothes, the charred scent filling my nose, and August shook his head, dropping Cyril's arm and watching it fall limply back to his side.

My heart plummeted.

That was two targets dead, neither at the hands of the hunters.

I hadn't known Cyril very well, and I was certain he would've killed me given a chance, but to die so close to what he'd thought was freedom . . . a weight settled in my chest at the thought.

And now my only plan for getting Jed out of Endlock was ruined.

'I heard they used to keep it electrified all the time,' August whispered, looking into the distance. 'But it was too expensive and pulled too much energy from the grid. Larch must have convinced the board to splurge on it.'

The fence, once harmless, was now coursing with fatal levels of electricity – another of Larch's obstacles.

Beside me, Perri choked on sobs, holding Cyril's hand like the smell of burnt flesh didn't point to a foregone conclusion, shaking him like he could possibly be alive after what he'd endured.

'Perri?' I whispered, placing my hand gently on her arm, shocking myself with my capacity to have compassion for the person who had beaten me to a pulp in the bathroom.

'Don't touch me!' Her scream echoed through the trees, and I cringed.

She would draw the hunters right to us.

'Perri, listen to me,' I said, removing my hand from her arm. 'We have to go. The force field will close in any minute.'

'I'm not going anywhere with *him*,' Perri screeched, staring daggers at August. 'He's a murderer.'

August's mouth dropped open. 'Cyril came at *me*. I was defending myself. I had no idea the fence was electrified.'

'Sure. Just like you two had no intention of escaping through the fence, right?' Perri looked back to the ground, and I pretended not to see the tears carving tracks through the dirt on her cheeks.

'I'm so sorry,' I said, trying again even as my eyes flitted about, searching for any sign of approaching danger. We had to go. 'I know Cyril was your friend. But he wouldn't want you to die out here.'

Perri wiped the wetness from her cheeks, locking her gaze with mine, her voice a deadly whisper. 'Let me say this slowly so you can get it through your thick skull. I don't want your help. I'm not going anywhere with you. Leave me the fuck alone.'

'Noted.' I pushed myself up, looking at August. He jerked his head toward the woods and then started walking. I left the wire cutters next to Cyril's still-smoking body, then jogged after August.

Once we were a few paces away from Perri, I asked, 'We're not seriously going to leave her, are we?'

August swallowed, not looking at me. 'We tried to help. She wouldn't listen. I'm not going to die for her – Momo needs me.'

He was right, of course. We had to look out for ourselves. For Jed. For our *friends*, because that's what they were to me now.

We couldn't feel guilt for doing what needed to be done to survive.

That was the first rule of bounty hunting, after all, and it seemed to be a good bit of advice out on the hunting grounds as well.

Never make eye contact.

I allowed myself to ignore the rule for a moment, glancing over my shoulder one last time at Perri's shaking form, meeting her unwavering gaze before we entered the forest, leaving her behind – though I wasn't able to leave behind the unease I felt at having caught her watching us, when I'd expected her to be focused on Cyril

The altercation at the fence had taken up too much time, and we were forced to abandon stealth in favor of speed to make it to the second segment. There, we climbed a monstrous pine, and waited in it until the force field moved in a final time. We managed to make it to the Blood Tree in second and third place, joining an inmate in a brown uniform who was taking gasping breaths and shuddering against the crimson bark.

She refused to acknowledge August when he tried to speak with her, and I had the impression she didn't even know we were there.

Two more inmates in gray uniforms burst from the forest with a pair of hunters on their heels – two of the teenage girls who were part of the birthday party.

'Faster,' the inmate in front got out through her heavy breaths. 'We're going to make it.'

The woman behind didn't answer, staring intently at the Blood Tree and pumping her arms.

'We're going to be okay, Suriah,' the inmate in front insisted, just as a shot rang out.

When Suriah didn't answer, the woman stopped and turned, finding her face-down on the ground.

'Suriah?'

Suriah's body remained motionless, but blood leaked from below her still form.

I bit my lip, blinking hard against the tears pricking the back of my eyes.

The first inmate rushed away from the Blood Tree and toward Suriah's body, but one of the hunters fired off three shots at her before she made it more than a few steps. She fell to the ground and didn't get back up.

I closed my eyes as a pair of guards dragged them away, with the teenage girls giggling behind them.

'What do you think they're going to do when they find Cyril's body?' I forced myself to ask August on the walk back to Endlock after the hunt, desperate to erase the image of the dead women from my mind.

'We left the wire cutters, so they'll assume Cyril was trying to escape. If Perri's smart, she won't mention being there. If she does, she'll risk Larch thinking she was trying to escape, too. As much as she hates us now, I don't think she'd implicate herself.'

I nodded, a bit of relief flooding my aching bones.

Perri had been the fifth and last inmate to make it to the Blood Tree.

The two women who'd almost made it, Cyril, the boy who'd fallen into the pit of spikes, and the girl who'd gotten caught in the leg trap. I ticked them off on my fingers.

A hunter must have finished off the prisoner with the broken leg, which meant that only three of the deaths had been at the hands of hunters. I didn't know whether Larch would be frustrated, or if the hunters had found the obstacles exciting enough for the Warden to consider the hunt a success.

When we reached Endlock, I noted Perri staring murderously at August. For once, I wasn't the focus of her hatred.

I was desperate to speak with Vale to see if any of the guards had found Cyril's body yet or mentioned the fence. But Larch emerged from the prison, a sheen of sweat on his forehead and a frown playing on his lips as he muttered a few indistinct words into the compact radio he held in his hand. He turned to address us.

'Inmates!' His voice cut through the murmured conversations. 'Line up against the wall. Now.'

No one hesitated.

'Two of Endlock's residents have been electrocuted to death,' Larch began, running a shaky hand over his dwindling strands of hair.

I snapped my head around. *Two people had died from the fence?*

Maybe the girl who'd gotten caught in the trap had escaped and crawled all the way to the fence.

'We believe an inmate was trying to escape,' Larch continued.

'And one of our guards tried to stop him, unaware that the perimeter fence carried a deadly current.'

'One of the guards died?' Hyde called from his post, eyes wide.

One of the guards.

No. *No.*

What if it was—

My heart dropped, and I gave up my calm facade, spinning wildly in search of Vale.

Larch gave a solemn nod. 'Mort. He died preventing one of these criminals from leaving Endlock – a hero's death.'

I closed my eyes. Vale was okay.

Mort's dead.

A current of relief washed over me. No part of me mourned the guard's death.

But Larch was wrong. Mort hadn't died trying to stop Cyril – he hadn't even been present during our altercation. He might have foolishly walked into the fence, but wouldn't Larch have warned all the guards about the obstacles?

My eyes finally found Vale standing by the building's entrance. The weight of his gaze felt tangible, like the warm caress of a hand running over my skin. Though his hands formed fists at his sides, I detected a slight tremor.

'Can anyone tell me more about this?' Larch asked, interrupting my thoughts. 'Did any of you witness these deaths?'

I met Larch's eyes, shaking my head and glancing around as if I expected another inmate to confess.

Silence.

I willed August not to look at me. Not to do anything that could give us away.

When my eyes flitted to Perri, she remained tight-lipped and unreadable. Save for her red-rimmed eyes, she looked much the same as always.

'It seemed like an isolated incident,' Larch said. 'But if we find out any of you are lying, you'll spend the rest of your miserable lives in solitary.'

Larch's gaze settled on Vale, who leaned casually against the wall. With a slight tilt of his head, Larch signaled him forward to escort us back inside.

Vale pushed himself off the wall and uttered a gruff, 'Follow me,' as he opened the door that led back into Endlock.

18

IN MY DREAMS, Jed raced ahead of me on the hunting grounds. He was years younger, around eleven – the same age as when our parents were arrested.

'Jed!' I screamed. But he didn't hear me.

He took another step and fell into the ground, out of sight.

The pit.

I screamed his name again, but there was no answer. And it seemed no matter how fast and hard I ran, I couldn't get any closer. Couldn't get to him. Couldn't *save him*.

A familiar clinking broke through my nightmares, jolting me awake.

I blinked, listening.

It was the sound of cells unlocking, though the blaring buzzer that typically accompanied the locks was strangely absent, and the lights didn't come on – the corridor remained enveloped in darkness.

I lay still on my bed, straining my ears for any other sign of life, but I heard nothing aside from the various snores of the sleeping inmates within the cellblock.

Maybe it was an accident. Maybe the night-shift guard fell asleep on top of the controls.

Silently, I rose, the chill of the cement floor harsh against my bare feet.

It had to be an oversight. Larch would never allow us to mill about freely in the middle of the night.

If he thought an injured hunter was terrible for his reputation, I couldn't imagine what the Council would think if they found out about his negligence in handling an entire cellblock of inmates.

My fingertips brushed the cold metal bars of my cell, expecting to meet resistance and find the door latched securely in place. But it drifted open effortlessly beneath my touch.

It made the lightest of scraping sounds, and my heart stopped.

When I glanced into the corridor, expecting to find the blinking red lights from the cameras that lined the tops of the cells, there was only blackness. None of them were recording. None of them would witness an attack.

I slid the cell door shut again and propped one of the novels Yara had lent me against the bars so that anyone trying to gain entrance would send it crashing to the floor. Then, I arranged my clothes on top of my mattress beneath my new, plush comforter, molding a crude silhouette of a sleeping figure as best I could in the dark.

Wrapping another blanket around myself, I sank to the floor between the foot of my bed and the farthest corner of my cell.

After what felt like an eternity, I heard the metallic groan of a rusty cell door rolling open. My pulse quickened.

Soft footsteps padded down the corridor. A predator stalking its prey. I clenched my hands into fists, my body tensing. What would I do if they opened the door to my cell?

If I could get past them and into the hall, I could shut them in my cell until help came.

My other option was to fight back. The attack in the bathroom hadn't been a fair fight, but I knew I'd have the upper hand if an inmate came at me one on one.

Soft footsteps sounded in the corridor, growing closer and closer.

I clenched my fists at my sides.

But the footsteps stopped before they reached my cell, and I heard another door slide open. I couldn't quite place the distance of the sound. I stood—

A sudden commotion in the cell next to mine sent my heart racing.

August's cell.

I heard a *thump*, a *crunch*, and then a cry so wretched it seemed to claw its way beneath my skin, burrowing into the marrow of my bones. I fought the urge to cover my ears, lunging for the door and bursting out of my cell as the lights in the corridor flickered on, illuminating the cellblock.

I glanced around wildly, catching Perri's cell door reverberating. Her hands clenched around the bars of her cell, and she peeked out into the corridor as if she were as shocked by the commotion as the rest of us.

Cell doors rolled open all around me, and inmates emerged, drawn to the anguished cries coming from August's cell.

My feet thudded against the cool cement floor, and I reached August's cell just as Yara did. She had a silky pink sleep mask shoved up onto her head, and her normally smooth hair was mussed and tangled. We shared a look before turning to face the scene before us.

Yara sucked in a breath and whispered, '*No.*'

I felt the blood drain from my face, and my legs grew weak as dizziness set in. I reached out and gripped Yara's shoulder to keep from dropping to my knees, blinking as if what I was seeing would disappear if I could only clear my vision.

Inside his cell, August lay crumpled, his ankle bent at an impossible angle. At his side was some kind of metal rod. His blankets and mattress lay in a heap on the floor as if he'd been yanked from his bed and had dragged the bedding right along with him.

'I think she broke my ankle,' August gasped, his breathing labored. 'It *hurts*. I can't move it at all. I'm not going to be able to walk.'

August's words continued to tumble out as he rocked back and forth.

I swallowed against the bile in my throat, stepping forward on shaky legs to examine the injury. I bit back a sob. August was right – maybe even conservative in his diagnosis. The way his ankle was bent, I imagined some of the bones had been shattered.

I looked over to find Yara shaking, mouth agape. Her hand was pressed to the wall, keeping her from collapsing. Seeing her shock mirroring mine had me swallowing the rising wave of panic and fury within me, and I let logic seep in instead.

Kit stepped into the cell, eyes wide with horror as she knelt beside me and grasped August's hand in hers. 'Momo,' she called, voice slicing through the small crowd of onlookers and their nervous chatter.

The young boy appeared, Jed at his back with an arm wrapped protectively around his shoulders. Upon seeing August, Momo let out a yowl and rushed toward us.

'Gus!' he cried, reaching out.

'It's all right, Momo,' August said through his teeth, clearly pushing through his pain and fear to set Momo's mind at ease. 'It's going to be okay.' August looked to Kit, a message in his eyes.

'Go see if Vale is on duty, Momo. Tell him we need Dr Row. Now,' Kit commanded.

Tears slipped down Momo's cheeks as he darted away, pushing

through the crowd of inmates who were clamoring to get a closer look at August.

I glanced up and across the corridor to where Perri was still gripping the bars of her cell, grinning. Rage simmered inside me.

I *knew* it had been her.

Kit was speaking in low, soothing tones to August, so I cast my attention around the cell, scanning the space for any clue that would prove beyond a doubt that Perri was behind this.

'Out,' I hissed at the other inmates, glaring. And my reputation might have helped me for once, as most of them backed up a few steps.

I checked the latch on the cell door, confirming it hadn't been forced open. It had been unlocked just like mine.

There were no other weapons in the room. Just the rod.

I leaned over, picking it up. It was copper and about an inch in diameter. I hadn't seen anything like it around Endlock, or really even in Dividium, and didn't know how Perri would've gotten access to it.

'It's an industrial water pipe.'

I turned and saw Jed looking at the pipe over my shoulder.

I blinked. 'How do you know?'

'We used them at the water treatment facility in Dividium,' he said, taking the pipe from me and rotating it in front of his eyes. 'They were just like this.'

I whirled around. 'Yara. What's Perri's work assignment?'

Yara had moved next to Kit, leaning against her for support and holding August's free hand, but her eyes snapped up to mine. 'She was in laundry. But when she fell out of favor with Larch he moved her into plumbing. She's assigned to Hyde.'

I shuddered at the thought of having to work with Hyde. But plumbing . . .

I turned back to Jed. 'You think she'd have access to these?'

Jed's mouth twisted to one side before he nodded. 'Yes. We had bins full of them at the facility. If one went missing, it would've been hard to notice.'

I ground my teeth together, my hands curling into fists as I made for the cell door. To confront Perri. To make her *pay*.

A hand wrapped around my wrist, yanking me back.

'No,' Jed said fiercely. 'Attacking her will only make it worse.'

'She did this to him!' I hissed. 'It's one thing to go after me for turning her in. But to do this? To *August*?' I'd known Perri was a force at Endlock, but this was a wild escalation from what I'd thought she was capable of. *She's as much as killed him.*

I couldn't say the last part out loud. Not with August writhing on the floor next to me.

'And what happens if you take out your anger on her?' Jed whispered. 'August's hurt. He's not going to be able to help with our *plans* for a while. And you think throwing a couple of punches is worth winding up in solitary, when we need you most?'

Jed finished, out of breath, and some of the fight left me. He was right. This wasn't about acting on my urges or getting revenge. This wasn't about *me* or what I wanted.

I knelt back down, close to August, checking for any changes in his ankle.

Vale burst into the cell, chest heaving, panicked eyes scanning the room. They caught on me, and his entire frame visibly relaxed as he exhaled. 'Are you hurt?' The words tumbled from his lips, urgent and unguarded.

His eyes raked over me, burning with intensity as if he were committing every inch of me to memory. His hand reached out, hovering in the space between us. Then, abruptly, he pulled back, shaking his head as if he'd forgotten himself – his role.

Kit's eyes flicked between us.

'I'm fine. It's August.'

Vale wrenched his gaze from mine with visible effort. His face went white at the sight of August's mottled ankle, and he made a choking sound.

He knelt on my other side, close enough that his arm brushed mine as he laid a gentle hand on August's shoulder. 'Dr Row is on the way, Gus,' he said softly. Then he faced me again. 'Tell me what happened.'

'The cells,' I began, an edge to my voice, even as my brain caught on how Vale had called August by his name, not his number. *Again.* 'They were all unlocked. I think it was intentional.'

I *knew* a buzzer sounded when they unlocked the cells during the day. The absence of that feature had to be deliberate.

Vale's eyes narrowed. 'I wasn't in charge of cell security tonight. Hyde was. I guess that was a mistake.' He leaned farther down to get a closer look at August's ankle, and his voice shook when he spoke again. 'Who did this?'

Hyde was in charge of cell security. After Perri had been assigned to him in plumbing. After she'd accused August of murdering Cyril.

'Perri,' I said firmly, leaving no room for argument. *Let's see how much she laughs once she's thrown into solitary confinement.* 'I heard a cell door open, and then August screamed. I rushed from my cell as the lights turned on, and I saw her door wobbling. She'd just slammed it shut. Like the coward she is.'

Vale's gaze darkened, his lips pressed into a hard line.

I pointed to the copper pipe Jed had returned to the floor. 'That's what she used to do it. Something she was able to get as a part of her new job in plumbing, where she's supervised by Hyde.'

The sound of the barrier door slamming open cut our conversation short. Larch strode in. He wore his usual starched shirt and dark pants, with his chains of teeth around his neck and a pearl-shaped tooth earring glinting from one ear. I wondered if he slept in the outfit in order to be prepared at all times. I imagined a row of black button-ups hanging in his closet, pressed and waiting.

'What happened?' he asked, his eyes flicking around frantically, as if Pharil Coates might appear from the shadows and fire him on the spot.

Vale straightened and got to his feet, meeting Larch's gaze. 'Hyde unlocked the cell doors. It's unclear if it was an accident, but none of the inmates were secured in their cells. Another inmate got their hands on this pipe and smashed 412's ankle.'

Larch was quiet, and I felt a smug smile creeping onto my face. He would finally have to punish Perri. It was one thing for him to favor her but quite another for her to openly defy Endlock's rules and walk away unscathed.

Though if Yara's intel was correct, Perri was no longer favored. Maybe he'd revel in the opportunity to punish her.

The silence stretched, taut as a bowstring, until Larch finally murmured, 'I see. And was anyone able to identify who did this? I assume it was dark, so it was likely impossible to see clearly.'

I gritted my teeth. 'When August called out, I rushed from my cell, and the lights came on. I saw Perri's door shaking. And this was the weapon,' I added, pointing to the pipe. 'Something only an inmate in plumbing would have access to.'

'So, you didn't witness her committing the act? And you didn't see her outside her cell?' Larch asked, a small smile playing on the edges of his lips.

I thought of telling the truth, if only for a moment. But Larch's smile, and the smug look on Perri's face, was too much for me. And what Perri had done to August was unforgivable. I opened my mouth—

'I saw her.'

My head snapped around, trying to locate the voice that had spoken.

An older man with graying hair nodded when I caught his eye.

Larch's smile faded, and when my eyes flitted over his shoulder to Perri, she was staring daggers at me.

Larch turned to the man. 'It was dark. How could you have been sure?'

I opened my mouth, gearing up to tear into Larch.

'I saw her too.'

This time, when I craned my neck to look farther down the cellblock, I saw it was a young girl who'd spoken. She'd said the words even as her hands shook at her sides.

And then there was a chorus of inmates chiming in, their voices blending together, and my heart swelled at the sound. All of them, willing to risk Larch's wrath to stand up for one of their own.

Larch's mouth opened and then closed again. 'I see.'

Dr Row's arrival interrupted his next words. She entered August's cell, arms laden with medical supplies, her silvery hair whirling around her in her haste.

She hissed as her fingers assessed the damage, and her face fell. 'If we were in Dividium, you'd have surgery for this, but the best I'll be able to do is set it and try to stabilize it. Put on a cast and give you some crutches. I'm sorry.'

She said the words low enough that Larch wouldn't have been able to hear them or reprimand her for her empathy.

August gritted his teeth. Getting around Endlock on crutches would be challenging enough, and his injury wouldn't keep him from being targeted by the hunters.

Dr Row instructed Vale to grab the spinal board leaning by the cell door, then softly spoke to August. 'I believe your ankle is the only part of you that's sustained an injury, but since you fell from your bed, we can't be too careful. We'll bring you to the infirmary for a full examination, okay?'

Vale loaded August onto the board, and then Dr Row gathered up her supplies and stood, addressing Larch. 'Could you call another guard to help Vale carry this inmate to the infirmary? My strength isn't what it used to be.'

'No need,' Larch said with a wicked smile, turning his withering

gaze on me. 'Since 224 has insisted on being so helpful this evening, I'm sure she wouldn't mind assisting you.'

I didn't let him see me hesitate as I stood and gripped the end
of the board opposite Vale. I'd lost muscle during my stay at Endlock, and even at my healthiest, carrying August would've been
difficult. But Vale caught my eye and nodded, and I schooled my
face into cool neutrality and lifted the board without so much as a
grunt, willing my arms not to give out.

We followed Dr Row out of the cellblock and through the corridor, and then down the stairs to the infirmary, my muscles shaking
for the entirety of the journey.

Once August was safely on the examination table, Dr Row
shooed us into the hallway.

'I need space. And quiet,' she told us unapologetically before
slamming the door in our faces.

Vale's gaze landed above the door, checking the camera, and
then he had me in his arms before I could say a word, squeezing
me against his chest so tightly that I could scarcely draw breath.

'I thought it was you,' he murmured, his lips pressed against the
top of my head. 'Momo was crying so hard he could barely speak.
He just said there was an attack and that Perri was involved. I
thought she'd killed you.'

'I'm fine,' I breathed against him, letting myself lean into his
warmth. 'I can take care of myself, you know.'

There was a clatter in the distance and then the sound of a door
slamming shut, like someone was headed for the basement, and
we jumped apart, Vale moving to block me from view.

'Do you have any idea how much scrutiny I'm under right
now?' a voice seethed, accompanied by two sets of footsteps.

It was Larch's voice.

'I'm sorry,' another voice answered. Perri. She was sobbing. 'I
was only trying to help.'

'Well, you didn't,' Larch hissed. 'There's a reason I told you I was done with you yesterday. You made me look worse. You made me look like I can't even handle a prison full of sleeping inmates. I'm *done* letting you get away with whatever you want. We'll see if solitary confinement teaches you a lesson.'

Perri's sobs grew louder as they got farther down the steps, and Vale grabbed my hand, pulling me down the hall and into the dark workshop. I blinked, my eyes adjusting to the space enough to see the camera in the corner wasn't recording.

He closed the door behind me and placed his hands on my shoulders, holding me at arm's length. His golden eyes bored into mine. 'Perri won't pass up an opportunity to hurt you. Especially after this. She knows no one saw her hurt August – that they lied, and she's getting thrown into solitary because of it. It doesn't matter that the other inmates spoke up; she won't place the blame on anyone but you.'

'You don't need to worry—'

He barked out a laugh, running a hand roughly through his hair to push the strands off his forehead. 'You think I can control this worry? You think I can just stop *thinking about you* every second of every damned day? All of this would be so much easier if I could get you out of my head, Little Bird. Don't think I haven't tried.'

His words washed over me, and all logical thought left my brain. I leaned closer to him, his hands falling from my shoulders to my waist as my eyes flitted up to his lips.

'Don't,' he groaned. 'Don't look at me like that.'

But he didn't look away. Like he was powerless to do so.

'Like what?' I whispered, emboldened, fully aware of each place where his body touched mine. His long fingers digging into my hips. My breasts pressing against his chest.

'Like you want me,' he breathed. 'Like you wouldn't kill me if I kissed you.'

I ran my tongue over my bottom lip, feeling a heady rush of

power as he tracked the movement with darkening eyes. 'I might kill you if you don't.'

And that was all it took for his restraint to slip.

One moment, we were looking into each other's eyes, each daring the other to break first, and the next, Vale had my back pressed up against the door, his lips finally on mine, his hands in my hair.

I needed him *closer*.

Our teeth clacked together in our haste, and I bit his lip, breathing in his groan.

His knuckles brushed up over my sides and back down to my hips, leaving little trails of fire anywhere he touched. I twined my arms around his neck, pushing up onto my toes and pulling him closer.

I ran my tongue along his, reveling in the fact that he tasted just like he smelled – clean and fresh – and it made me want to *consume* him.

His hands threaded into my hair once more, and he turned my head to get a better angle, deepening the kiss. I traced his lips with my tongue, then bit his bottom lip again, sucking it into my mouth.

'Careful, Little Bird,' he rasped.

That sense of power hit me again as I felt his lust, hard against his pants and pressing into my stomach. I moaned into his mouth, moving my hand between us to palm the front of his pants.

Vale growled, ripping his mouth from mine and moving to place scalding hot kisses along my throat, nipping and sucking as his hands moved down my body.

'Don't think you have all the power here,' he breathed into my neck, and I let out a whimper, letting my nails scrape along his back through his shirt.

I pulled at the fabric, desperate to remove the barrier keeping my hands from his deliciously warm skin, untucking it from his belt and dipping my fingers below the hem. Pushing my hands up over his stomach, I scratched the hard muscles there.

Then his mouth was back on mine, delving between my lips. I sucked in a sharp breath, nails pressing into him as he tasted me.

I was struck by how much I wanted him. The last person I should want, but somehow the only person capable of making me forget everything I'd gone through in the past weeks. His touch transported me, even as I stood in the most dangerous place in the world.

And maybe that was the most dangerous thing of all.

Because he'd managed to make me forget about August, and how catastrophically our escape plans had changed after what Perri had done.

I stepped back at the sobering thought, breaking our kiss.

Vale pressed his forehead against mine, breathing heavily as he looked into my eyes, lingering for a moment more. I breathed him in, but the ventilation system kicked in a moment later, the sound snapping me from my reverie.

I took a deep breath. 'I'd better get back.'

Vale walked me to Cellblock H and stayed on security duty for the rest of the night.

All the while, I lay awake in my cell, wondering what we were going to do now that August had suffered such a grave injury. How could he make the journey across the Wastes, now?

And I'd made the catastrophic decision to kiss a guard when I had far more important things to focus on, but I regretted only that I'd ended it so soon.

I was well and truly fucked.

19

AUGUST WAS RELEASED from the infirmary two days later, and Perri was let out of solitary confinement that same morning. I shouldn't have expected Larch to let her rot in there for a week as he'd done to me, but I'd been hopeful.

'Come *on*, August,' Jed said, exasperated, trying for the third time to grab August's tray so he could carry it to the table for him.

'I can't show weakness,' August murmured, refusing Jed's help. He balanced precariously on one foot. 'When you show weakness, you *become* weak. And at that point, you're as good as dead.'

Neither of us reminded him that his ankle was broken and that needing assistance carrying his tray since he didn't have three hands – one for each crutch and one for the tray – was perfectly reasonable. Instead, we stood one either side of him in case he got shaky and needed to lean on us.

August shifted, stuffing both crutches under one arm and holding his tray with the other, and began a precarious hop toward our table.

From the corner of my eye, I saw Perri's leg jut into our path.

I took a moment to measure the ferocity of my hunger. My stomach growled, but that was normal. I'd gone longer with far less food. My need for revenge was more potent than my desire to bite into the spiced porridge in my bowl.

I stumbled deliberately over Perri's outstretched foot, sending my tray and its contents flying into her face.

The hot, gooey porridge dripped from her hair and chin, and she shrieked through gritted teeth. The other inmates at her table stared, open-mouthed and silent.

'I'm sorry, Perri,' I cooed, words coated in syrupy sweetness. 'Here, let me help you with that.'

I took a napkin and smeared some of the porridge, pressing it deeper into her dark tresses.

'Enough!' she snarled, shoving me away. 'You did that on purpose.'

'I didn't see your foot there,' I said. 'I'll try to be more careful next time.'

She let out a screech and stood, shoving past me to get to the room's exit.

I grinned all the way to our table, and August's muted chuckle reached my ears as we settled down onto a bench.

Kit smiled at me from her space across the table, and she divided her helping of porridge between the two of us without a word. 'Not bad, Thorne.'

'Not bad?' Yara laughed, scooping a few spoonfuls from her bowl into mine. 'That was amazing. Plus, you've given me a great idea. Oats are *so* good for your hair. I'm bringing this back to my cell to make a hair mask. You're a genius.'

Kit laughed, her eyes soft as they fell on Yara, and I noted how their knees knocked together beneath the table. It filled me with warmth, the idea of them finding something beautiful in a place defined by its cruelty.

When we exited the mess hall, I didn't miss the smile Vale tried to hide by staring at his shoes. I flushed, my mind flashing back to our moment in the workshop – his mouth on mine, his hands sliding over my hips, the hard length of him pressed up against me.

I let out a breathy sigh, and Vale's head snapped up, gaze meeting mine and eyes darkening before I stepped out the door and out of sight.

The guards herded us into our cells, and unease burrowed a hole in my stomach when Larch entered our cellblock. It wasn't supposed to be our day in the rotation, and he'd said he didn't usually preside over the hunt selections.

I wondered if the talk of new obstacles had drawn more hunters in, and they'd had to host more hunts, leading to them getting through the rotation more quickly than usual.

I hadn't even had time to discuss an alternative escape plan with Kit and August now that the fence was out of the question.

'Some of the Council have graced us with their presence for today's first hunt,' Larch declared, voice shaky. A bead of sweat trickled down his temple.

You have no idea how much scrutiny I'm under.

Larch's words, whispered to Perri the night of her attack on August, came back to me.

I struggled to believe the Council's passion for hunting was enough to take them away from their busy schedules so soon after Larch had made a mistake. It had to be some kind of test – Endlock was struggling, and, after everything I'd witnessed since arriving, Larch had to be at risk of replacement.

Larch cleared his throat. 'Councilor Baskan and Councilor Elder are here today, along with Councilor Baskan's son.'

Roald Baskan.

'No,' I said before I could stop myself.

My mouth went dry, and I gripped the bars of my cell, looking across the corridor and meeting Jed's eyes.

He swallowed, taking measured breaths. *It's okay*, he mouthed.

But it wasn't.

'*Quiet*,' Larch snapped, glaring at me before he continued. 'The Councilors have tasked me with selecting their targets for this hunt. They desire a challenge – prisoners who have eluded death many times before or possess a fighting spirit. Or arrogance.' His eyes flicked to mine once more.

'We want to be sure our selection meets our guests' standards. Their entertainment is of utmost importance,' Larch mused, pacing back and forth along the cellblock. He wiped his palms on the front of his pants, leaving wet marks behind. 'First up is 412. Your record speaks for itself. No inmate poses a bigger challenge than you.'

Murmurs filled the air, spreading through the cellblock like wildfire. But I'd known Larch's choice as soon as he'd announced he would be the one selecting targets. As much as he'd been angry at Perri for injuring August, Larch was obviously hoping to use it to his advantage. The hunter who killed August would receive a serious reputation boost.

And if it was a Councilor who took August down, they might be pleased enough to convince Coates to overlook Larch's recent mistakes.

'224,' Larch sneered, breaking me from my thoughts. 'I think your attitude is precisely the kind the Councilors would enjoy snuffing out.'

Not exactly subtle, but that had never been his strong suit.

Larch selected four more targets, then turned back to me, leveling a grin at me that told me he was about to wield a killing blow. 'And for the last target, inmate number 203. Roald Baskan's personal request.'

I'd known it was coming from the moment Larch had mentioned Roald's name, and I just barely managed to keep my expression neutral, even as my stomach twisted and writhed.

Because choosing Jed was the worst thing Larch could do to me.

I was terrified to have him out there with Roald Baskan on the loose. There was nothing like a vendetta to help accomplish one's goals, and I knew Roald's overinflated ego wouldn't rest until Jed was dead.

'May the Council watch over you,' Larch crooned, motioning for the guards to haul us from our cells as he waited for us to give the required response.

But his words were met with silence.

I shouldn't have been surprised, not after the way the inmates in our cellblock had stepped up to hold Perri accountable after August's injury.

But there was another kind of strength in directly defying Larch with their silence.

Larch frowned, placing a hand on the gun holstered at his side, and I gritted my teeth. But the other inmates remained silent, maybe betting, as I was, that Larch wouldn't dare to kill us all. Not while the Council was at Endlock, waiting to see if he'd make another mistake.

A few of the guards looked at each other, uneasy, and seemed to come to a decision. 'May they guide us to eternal peace,' they chanted in unison, snapping Larch out of the worst of his rage.

He stomped ahead of us, and our group let out a collective breath, sneaking glances at one another and sharing small, hesitant smiles.

This time, Larch sent several guards, including Vale, out ahead of the targets to monitor the forest. Undoubtedly, he wanted to avoid any surprises while the Councilors were on the property. A small smile tugged at my lips, imagining the shock on his face if I managed to hit one of the Councilors over the head with a sturdy tree branch.

When the buzzer went off, releasing us from our stalls, I braced myself for the sight of Jed quaking with fear. After what he'd witnessed during our first hunt, I worried he'd dissolve into panic.

But Jed's hands were steady as he wrapped one of August's arms around his shoulders – despite August's protests. I took August's free arm and the other half of his weight, and with the two of us as crutches, he moved with surprising speed, hobbling off the field a minute shy of the others.

Jed caught my eye, and I found that instead of dread, there was a spark of defiance in his gaze, the blue of his eyes matching the cloudless sky.

As soon as the thick canopy of trees enveloped us, hiding us from the eyes of the watchtower guards, Vale appeared from the shadows.

I jumped at the sight of him, and Jed's eyes widened, wary.

'What are you doing here?' I asked, looking around to see if the other targets had spotted him.

But we were alone.

Vale didn't answer, and his gaze shifted to August. 'You're sure? Are we doing this? Bringing them in?'

I reared back, eyes flitting between them and finally settling on August. 'What's happening here?'

August grimaced, his mouth opening and then closing without answering me. I snapped my gaze to Vale. 'Start talking.'

Here it was. My confirmation that the relationship between them was more than just Vale granting August favors. While I'd suspected that was the case since I'd first seen them whispering on the hunting grounds, it was another thing to be presented with proof.

'Gus?' Vale whispered, prompting him instead of answering me.

August hesitated, then gave a firm nod.

'Are either of you going to clue us in?' Jed asked, pulling August's arm more firmly over his shoulder.

Jed hadn't had nearly as many interactions with Vale as I had, and while I'd told him about Vale saving me on our first hunt, he was much warier of the guard than I'd grown to be. I couldn't imagine what was going through his head.

Vale finally met my gaze. 'We'll tell you everything. But not here. We have to get to safety first. Just trust me, Little Bird.'

Jed's eyes narrowed at the nickname, and my face flamed.

A battle raged inside me as I looked deeper into Vale's eyes, searching for any hint of deception. Any hint that I should be afraid. But he'd had so many chances to throw me to the wolves. And if August trusted him . . .

'It's okay,' I told Jed, sighing. 'He'll help us. You can trust him.' *For now.*

'To the tunnels, then,' Vale murmured.

The tunnels?

But there was no time for questions.

With each step, August's weight seemed to press harder on me. Fatigue crept in, and sweat dripped down the curve of my spine.

I felt a soft hand on my arm, and then Vale gave me a slight push and took up my position under August's arm. I didn't bother arguing – my back nearly cried out in relief.

The whine of the buzzer quickened our pace, all of us thinking of those who wanted to take August's life.

The guards had dug more graves for the inmates since the last time I'd been on the grounds, and we tried to avoid them as best we could. My eyes caught on that strange, curving path again, wondering where it might lead.

Eventually, we reached a cluster of bushes laden with blood-red berries. Vale nodded for us to push through, and we waded into the prickly stalks. Thorns stabbed through the fabric of my uniform, and I maintained careful steps to avoid disrupting the foliage or leaving a trail.

Midway through the thorns, Vale stopped. He confirmed August was steady on his feet, and then he knelt, fingers tracing over a patch of greenery. I exchanged a look with Jed, but a moment later, Vale lifted a neat square of moss, revealing a make-shift lid of interwoven sticks beneath. Once he removed it, I took a step back.

I swallowed. 'What's down there?'

Beneath the lid was a hole in the ground, so dark that it was impossible to discern what it held.

'A really good hiding place,' August whispered, urgency pushing his words out in a rush. 'We use it for emergencies.'

'We?' My voice was barely above a whisper.

Vale looked around, likely calculating how long we had before a hunter jumped out of the trees and ambushed us. 'Look, can we discuss this down there? Please.'

I looked at Jed.

He stared back at me, his eyes narrowed, but finally gave a reluctant nod. 'Okay. But they're explaining themselves once we're safe.'

After stepping closer, I noticed the handmade ladder poised against the pit's edge. It seemed steady enough. Jed carefully maneuvered August down its rungs, and then I followed, my heartbeat quickening as I entered the musty darkness, several degrees cooler than the air above. Vale came last, resealing the cover above us and plunging the pit into total darkness.

The click of a switch pierced the silence, and then a beam from Vale's flashlight illuminated the dark.

My eyes adjusted, and I sucked in a sharp breath. The space was about the size of my cramped apartment bedroom back in Dividium.

Unlike my bedroom, the pit was filled to the brim with dust-covered artifacts from a forgotten time. Wristbands – relics compared to the technologically advanced devices used now – lined a table in one corner, and shelving units held an array of blankets, first-aid kits, and jugs of water.

'They wanted to be prepared for every situation,' August explained, getting the words out before I could ask.

'Who's *they*? What the hell is going on?' I demanded, sidling closer to Jed, who crossed his arms over his chest.

Vale and August exchanged glances.

Jed scoffed. 'Tell us what's going on.'

I let out an exasperated sigh. 'Look, for a while now, I've suspected that you and August have a connection beyond an inmate bribing a guard for protection. And you've helped me too many times to count. I know you try to do the right thing when you can. But this? Some sort of secret hideout that I'd have to assume Larch knows nothing about?'

It was one thing for there to be . . . whatever there was between Vale and me, for him to want to make life at the prison easier for me, to help me *survive*. But it was another thing entirely for him to have some sort of underground bunker where he hid inmates beneath Larch's nose. It was a move a rebel would make, but he'd made his disdain for the Collective clear.

'What do you mean you've suspected it for a while now?' Jed asked, hurt flashing in his eyes.

'Later, Jed.' I spun in a slow circle, taking in more detail. The flashlights and oil lanterns stacked on a high shelf. A box of candles. The scent of damp earth.

'I think we've already established that I don't enjoy watching people die,' Vale replied, avoiding giving me any actual answers. 'I can't help everyone, but I do what I can.'

'And what about Mort? Did you enjoy watching him die?' I said it before I could stop myself. The accusation wasn't based on anything but the feeling in my gut and the look in Vale's eyes when Larch had announced Mort's death – but I had to know.

August and Jed looked back and forth between us, but neither of them intervened.

The corners of Vale's lips turned down, and he moved closer

until we were barely a step apart. 'Maybe I did. Maybe killing that fucking rapist was the best thing I've done since becoming a guard. Everyone acts like the inmates here are monsters, but Mort? He was the real monster. And he kept getting away with it. Day after day, and he was never going to stop.'

I stared at him. He'd killed a guard and had just openly scorned everything Endlock stood for. The revelation thrummed through me.

'I didn't plan it.' Vale shoved a hand through his hair, his voice gruff. 'But then I walked up to see him pulling the teeth from Cyril's body. He was *laughing*. Just like he was laughing when he cornered you in the hallway. I couldn't stop thinking about how if I hadn't—' He swallowed, his whole body shaking. 'I'd seen him put his hands on so many others. There were probably a half dozen times *I couldn't stop him*. And I snapped. I won't lie to you and say I didn't know what I was doing – I knew that piece of shit would burn to a crisp before he knew what hit him.'

August, Jed, and I stared at Vale, open-mouthed, for a few moments before I collected myself enough to speak.

'How did you feel after?' I whispered.

'I didn't regret it.' His eyes were only for me.

And I didn't feel disgusted.

I felt some strange combination of gratitude and . . . something I couldn't quite place. But I no longer had to worry that Mort would find me, or Kit, or Yara in an isolated corridor and take what he wanted from us.

'Okay. So you want to help us, but how?' Jed asked, standing tall despite the slight tremor I detected in his voice. I reached out, laying a hand on his arm before he continued. 'Sure, we can hide out in this hole in the ground. But we have to get to the Blood Tree eventually. I doubt being underground will stop the force field from touching us.'

'It won't,' August confirmed.

I hung my head. What was Vale's goal, anyway? He could help us get through whatever hunts we were assigned to, but to what end? He couldn't keep us alive forever. Not inside Endlock.

Something about the darkness of the space made it easier for me to be truthful with myself. I'd tried to stave off my doubts as best as I could, but the reality was that I was nowhere near to coming up with a solution for getting out of Endlock. And hiding in a hole in the ground wouldn't bring us any closer to freedom.

Vale and August exchanged another glance that set my teeth on edge.

'Larch knows about this place,' Vale admitted.

'He knows you dug a pit in the ground to help hide inmates from the hunters?' Jed asked.

I narrowed my eyes.

Vale barked out a laugh. 'No. Of course not. He knows there was an emergency tunnel system here decades ago, dating back to the original prison. It ran beneath the entirety of the grounds so that the guards had an escape route in case of uprisings or riots. Some of the entrances and sections have caved in, so the Warden thinks the tunnels were destroyed. Collapsed from disuse.'

'The tunnels run beneath the whole expanse of the grounds?' I asked, my voice tinged with disbelief. The possibility of something like that existing had been beyond my wildest dreams. If it was true, it meant the fence might no longer be a factor in our escape.

I stared at August. He'd known about this and hadn't bothered to help me while I'd been floundering in my search for a way out?

'Mostly,' Vale answered. 'Some parts of the tunnels *did* collapse. This entrance is closest to Endlock, so we rarely use it. Too many hunters pass by, so we have to stay quiet or risk them catching us.'

'This entrance point connects to a tunnel that brings us to the edge of the Blood Tree's clearing,' August said, motioning to the other side of what I'd thought was a pit. When I looked to where he pointed, partially obscured by a stack of boxes, there was an opening in the dirt wall.

That's how he'd survived for so long, then. He'd used the tunnel to get to the Blood Tree.

'Actually, we need to get moving,' Vale announced. 'The force field will be closing in soon, and we need to make it into the next segment.' He walked over to one of the shelving units, grabbing several flashlights and tossing one to each of us.

We clicked on the lights, and followed him into the cobweb-coated tunnel.

'But *why* are you helping us?' I asked Vale, not daring to believe the conclusion that my mind was leaping to.

I turned, meeting August's gaze, trying to ask him without words if what my heart wanted to believe could ever feasibly be the truth.

Is this what I think it is? I tried to convey the words through my eyes, and maybe it worked because August's lips pulled to the side in a smirk just as Vale answered me.

'Because I don't want you to die here. I'm going to help you get out.'

20

'YOU'RE *WHAT*?' MY voice came out a strangled whisper, and I stumbled before catching myself on the tunnel wall.

I couldn't have heard Vale right – wouldn't get my hopes up until he confirmed I hadn't hallucinated.

'I'm going to help you with your plan to get out of here,' Vale repeated, easing back to walk beside me. 'And go with you to the North Settlement.'

'You do remember the part where you're a guard, right?' I asked, incredulity woven through my words. 'In case you've forgotten. You *want* to escape with a bunch of inmates?'

I didn't give him time to answer, instead turning my accusatory glare over my shoulder and onto August. 'And you. We're supposed to be working together. But you conveniently failed to mention that you planned on bringing a guard along. Didn't you think that was an important detail? Do the others know about this?'

'They all know about Vale,' August answered, leaning heavily against Jed and limping along after us. 'You need to understand

that I would never do anything to jeopardize Yara or Kit or Momo.
When you first arrived, I didn't trust you. You're a *bounty hunter*,
Raven. And more than that, your desperation to save Jed made
you a liability. How did I know you wouldn't turn us in for your
own gain if it would help Jed?'

My mouth fell open, but no words came out. August was right.
It would have been foolish of him to tell me anything. Before
I'd gotten to know them, I probably would've turned them in
if it had meant gaining some sort of leverage that I could use to
escape.

Silently, I turned to Vale, seeking an explanation on his part.

'I asked August not to tell you,' Vale admitted. 'I didn't know if
I could bring myself to help you when I thought you were a rebel.
And by the time I knew you weren't . . . I didn't think you'd be
able to trust a guard. It wasn't until I got to know you that I was
willing to risk the truth.'

His instincts had been right. I would've spat in his face if he'd
tried to convince me he wanted to help me when I'd first run into
him at Endlock.

I shook my head. 'So what *is* the truth, then? You told me you're
not with the Collective, and you just want to help people. That
extends to helping inmates escape?' I paused. 'Or does this have
something to do with you being indebted to Eris? The night we
met, you said you owed him. Is this you paying your debt?'

'You met him before Endlock?' Jed hissed behind me.

I cringed. 'At Vern's. I'll explain later.'

'I didn't say I owed him,' Vale answered. 'I said I needed to
repay him.'

I stared, eyes narrowed. 'We don't have time to argue over
semantics, Vale.'

'He killed my father.'

My heart clenched in my chest at the raw grief in his eyes.

'I'm so sorry,' I whispered, unable to stop myself from reaching for him. But he stepped ahead of me again, and I clenched my jaw to keep the hurt from showing on my face.

I knew what it was like to lose a parent, though. Knew how hard it was to share your grief. Even still, his words swirled through my mind, the puzzle pieces working to click into place. If Eris had killed *my* parents, I'd hold no love for the Collective, either.

'Were you at Vern's to kill Eris?'

I whipped around, surprised at Jed for asking the question I'd been too afraid to voice.

Vale paused for a moment and then nodded. 'I was, but he never showed. I had to come back to Endlock the next day.'

'Do you still plan on going after him?' I whispered.

Vale didn't hesitate. 'I won't pass up an opportunity to kill him. A life for a life.' None of us had an answer for that, and a long silence ensued before Vale spoke again. 'As for helping you . . . I never wanted to be a guard. I was raised on the idea that everything the Council did was for the greater good – at least, that's what I heard from my mom. But we had a rough relationship, and hardly anything in common, and as a teenager all I wanted to do was rebel against her.'

He let out a harsh laugh. 'My mom got fed up and asked my dad to talk some sense into me. Only instead, he told me he was part of the Collective. He'd been hiding it from my mom for years, and asked me to keep it a secret from her, too.'

I gasped, turning to look at Jed. Vale was the child of a rebel, just like us.

'My dad—' Vale broke off for a moment and cleared his throat, the glow from his flashlight bouncing off the tunnel walls. 'We were close. I wanted to be just like him, really. But he didn't want me anywhere near the Collective. Said it was too dangerous to join the cell in the Upper Sector, and he wanted me to keep my head down instead. Look for small ways I could help Dividium citizens without being part of the Collective.

'About a year and a half ago I was given the chance to become a guard,' Vale continued, eyes far away, living in the past. 'I didn't want to do it, but I knew it was what was right – it was the kind of opportunity my dad had told me to look out for. I knew I could use my status as someone from the Upper Sector to work my way up through the ranks and have access to conversations that other guards wouldn't.'

I shook my head. I could hardly keep myself from insulting Larch for the few minutes I had to be in his presence, let alone imagine going undercover and having to pretend I *agreed* with what went on at Endlock.

'How did you go from wanting access to high-level conversations to helping a group of inmates escape?' I asked.

'We knew each other,' August supplied, out of breath behind me. 'Before Endlock.'

I inhaled sharply, jerking to a stop in the middle of the tunnel. Jed slammed into my back, nearly knocking me to the ground, but Vale grabbed my wrist, pulling me into him and holding me upright.

His golden eyes scanned my face, but I could only shake my head, my mouth slightly parted.

They'd known each other.

I'd been so careful in my conversations with Vale, trying not to give too much away, and they'd *known* each other.

Jed barked out a harsh laugh behind me, and I turned to find him shoving his hair back from his face, his forehead wrinkling in the way it did when he had a lot to say, but didn't know how to put it into words.

I knew how he felt.

But I also knew that this was another thing Vale and August had kept to themselves until they were sure they could trust me.

'I told you I was a doctor at a Middle Sector health center.'

August cleared his throat. 'Vale volunteered there for a while before I was arrested. We became friends.'

I scrubbed at my eyes, frustrated that I hadn't managed to piece any of this together. Of course, they'd known each other before Endlock. Vale called August by his nickname. They whispered together like old friends. Because they *were*. And I remembered how Vale's face had lost all color when he'd first laid eyes on August's injury.

'I stopped volunteering after August was arrested,' Vale said, and he gripped his flashlight tighter, his knuckles whitening. 'I couldn't walk into the medical center, let alone stomach a career in medicine, while I knew he could die any day at Endlock.'

I softened. If I hadn't followed Jed straight to Endlock, there's no way I'd have been able to go about normal life without him back home, either. I put a hand on Vale's shoulder, and this time he leaned into my touch.

There were so many questions I wanted to ask, but I knew we had to be running out of time, and my focus had to be on our escape.

'How did you find the tunnels?' I asked, waving my flashlight toward the earthen walls surrounding us.

'We knew they existed,' Vale said, some memory turning his lips up at one side and making my stomach flutter. 'But I wasn't able to find any maps to tell us how to access them. August and I started taking turns searching the grounds during hunts when he was a target or when I was on duty. It felt like a ridiculous task at the time, given how vast the grounds are. Miles to cover. But one day, I fell through the opening to the pit we just came from.'

A small smile tugged at my lips at the image.

'I followed the length of this section of the tunnel, and it led me to another entrance near the Blood Tree.'

'Vale showed me,' August chimed in. 'And we started using the tunnels during hunts, when we could. We don't use them all the time – we're too worried about drawing attention to them. But we've used them to help Momo, Kit, and Yara survive a lot of their hunts. When we use them, we split up at the beginning of the hunt and then meet up at a rendezvous point and access the tunnels together from there. That day you saved Momo . . . a hunter must have caught up to him before he got to the meeting point.'

August shook his head, his eyes haunted.

'We believe there's another segment of tunnels that leads completely off the grounds,' Vale whispered.

'Then I don't get it,' I said. 'Why even entertain my idea of escaping through the fence if you knew this place existed?' I paused, and then another thought dawned on me, and I looked at Vale. 'You risked letting me bring the wire cutters onto the hunting grounds to try and cut through the fence.'

Vale grimaced. 'That was before I knew the Warden had gotten permission to electrify the fence.'

'We wanted to see if the fence was a viable option because we haven't been able to access the other tunnels,' August said. 'Or even find them. If there was another escape route, we would have taken it.'

So that was what we had to do, then. Find a way to access the tunnels. It sounded simple enough, but Vale and August had already spent months trying.

I blew out a long breath. 'So you know everything, then?' I asked Vale.

Vale shared a glance with August, then nodded.

I pinched the bridge of my nose between my thumb and forefinger. So much time wasted, all because my efforts to gain their trust hadn't been enough.

But it was pointless dwelling on what I couldn't change, especially when we had a path forward.

'Okay,' I said slowly. 'Let's assume this all works out, and we find a way to access the other section of tunnels. How are seven of us going to slip out of Endlock without anyone noticing?'

Jed watched us all in brooding silence, and I could tell from the look in his eyes that I'd be in for it later.

August grimaced. 'Once Kit disables the wristband tracking and we access the other tunnels, the only thing I can think of is to make sure we're all selected for a hunt while Vale's on duty. It sounds ridiculous, I know, but I just don't know what other option we have. We're open to suggestions.'

'If we can even manage to get Kit what she needs to disable the tracking. I thought I'd be able to get a tablet for her, but my lead fell through,' I grumbled. Then, my eyes shot to Vale. 'Wait – she can use your tablet.'

'She can't,' Vale responded, and I frowned. 'I would've handed mine over ages ago if it wouldn't have put us all at risk. If someone looked into the activity log before we had a chance to escape, and saw that my tablet had been used to disable the tracking, we'd be fucked. There's no lie in the world to explain why I would disable the tracking on six active wristbands.'

I groaned.

'But she can use Mort's tablet.'

My gaze snapped to Vale's face, only to find him *grinning*.

'I . . . What?' I couldn't have heard him right.

'I took it. Before anyone found his body.'

Jed laughed. 'I guess we *can* trust you.'

We stepped into a new cavern that looked similar to the first pit we'd entered. It had an old ladder leading to an exit in the earthen ceiling. Vale pulled out his tablet, tilting the screen in my direction so that I could see the tiny red dots that were moving across a map of the grounds. The hunters.

'No hunters nearby.' Vale pointed to our location, then climbed the ladder first, poking his head out of the ground and scanning every direction to double-check before signaling for us to follow.

Jed scampered up the ladder, and then I pushed August up before me to where Vale was waiting to help pull him out of the hole.

After so long in the dark with only the artificial glow of Vale's flashlight, the sunlight forced me to squint.

I scrambled up the rudimentary ladder, edging closer to the lip of the hole. But as my fingers closed around the final wooden rung, it gave way, splintering, and I fell backward onto the hard-packed ground below.

'Raven!' Jed cried out.

I groaned, lying in the dirt and allowing the breath to return to my lungs.

'I'm fine,' I croaked reflexively, not wanting to worry Jed.

There was a thud, and I glanced over to see that Vale, now dimly illuminated by the light above, had jumped back into the hideout without the ladder's assistance. 'Are you all right?' He knelt in front of me, scanning my body.

I assessed myself for injuries, feeling a rush of sticky warmth seeping from the fleshiest part of my palm. I lifted my hand toward the light filtering in from above, wincing at the gouge left by the splintered rung.

Ouch.

Vale sucked in a breath, taking my wounded hand gently in his. His hand was warm against my skin, the rough calluses he'd earned over the years rivaling my own.

'You'll need stitches for that,' he said, shaking his head. 'I could do it right now, but then they'd know I helped you today.'

I nodded. 'I can wait until we get back. I'm sure it's nothing.'

But the wound was steadily oozing blood, and I felt a hint of dizziness creeping over me.

'Take your shirt off,' Vale said abruptly.

My breath caught, and my gaze flew to his face. 'What?'

The smile that lit his lips was devastating, and his warm eyes glittered in amusement. 'To stop the bleeding, Little Bird. I'd

enjoy watching you take your shirt off under much different circumstances, too, but I think you knew that already.'

A small thrill coursed through me as I painstakingly unzipped
my jumpsuit and removed the shirt beneath with my uninjured hand, noticing that Vale was struggling not to stare at my
bare skin.

I wrapped the garment tightly around my bleeding hand, then
zipped my jumpsuit.

'Okay, I think that will do for now,' I whispered, looking up.

Vale was staring at me. Or, more accurately, staring at my
mouth. He was close enough that his breath mingled with my
own. And just like that, all sense of reason disappeared, like it had
in the basement a couple of nights before. I thought about how
easy it would be to lean in.

But he was already leaning in.

I licked my lips, anticipating how his skin would taste.

His mouth was just a breath away from mine—

Someone coughed above, and I jumped back from Vale as if
struck by an electric current.

'You two coming up?' August asked. 'The tunnel will have
given us a lead on the hunters, but they can't be too far from the
Blood Tree now that the force field has moved to the center of the
grounds.'

Vale closed his eyes, letting out a long, slow breath. 'Yeah.' He
cleared his throat. 'Yes. Of course.'

What am I doing?

We were in the middle of a hunt. Jed and August were barely
ten feet away from us.

Vale touched my shoulder, gently urging me toward the broken
ladder.

August reached for me, and Vale spotted me from behind. His
fingers pressed into my waist until I emerged into the early afternoon sunshine, in the middle of another berry-laden bush.

Vale stuck his head out of the tunnel exit, checking his tablet one more time before nodding. 'Get to the Blood Tree. I'll be waiting at Endlock, and I'll get you to the infirmary once you're back.'

He gave me a lingering look before he ducked back into the tunnel, replacing the pit's cover. I leaned down, covering the lid with sticks and dead leaves, ensuring it blended seamlessly with its surroundings.

As the three of us staggered from the cloak of the forest and across the clearing to the Blood Tree, I knew if any hunter were within shooting distance, we wouldn't have stood a chance — August limping and leaning heavily on Jed and me, my hand clutched to my chest, my now-ruined shirt already soaked through with blood.

This time, only one other target joined us at the Blood Tree. Three of the seven of us selected had fallen to the hunters or Larch's obstacles.

When we returned to the prison, I caught a brief glimpse of the Councilors in their impeccably tailored, specially designed hunting attire as they stormed back toward Endlock.

Councilor Elder was tall and wraith-like, striding toward the prison with graceful movements, the light breeze blowing her black curls from her face. She bared her teeth at Larch, the whiteness contrasting with her ruby-red lipstick and brown skin. She was young for a Councilor. Her father's death had been unexpected, and Caltriona had taken his spot on the Council at fifty-three years old.

Councilor Baskan, on the other hand, was approaching seventy. His silver hair was neatly knotted atop his head, his mouth stretched to the side in a sneer, and his lips were like a thin slash of blood on his milky white face.

I loosed a breath when I didn't see Roald with them.

Following a terse exchange, the Councilors retreated into the building, leaving the door to slam shut behind them, inches from Larch's nose.

They must have been embarrassed that they hadn't been able to kill August, even with his injured leg.

It brought me no small satisfaction that three citizens from the Lower Sector had outsmarted some of the most powerful people in Dividium.

Instead of berating us, Larch entered the prison without a word, presumably to follow the Councilors and plead with them to forgive him for their experience.

We lined up against the side of the building, waiting to be escorted inside. The sun-warmed stone soaked through my jump-suit, and rivulets of blood ran down my forearm, mirroring the veins beneath my skin.

'What happened to you, 224?' Vale asked, his voice devoid of emotion.

'I was climbing a tree, and the branch I grabbed snapped in half. It sliced my hand,' I stated.

'Clumsy.' He blew out a harsh breath, rolling his eyes. 'Come with me.'

I shot a glance at Jed and August before following on Vale's heels. I didn't like leaving them alone. Now I'd all but confirmed that Perri was actively trying to kill August, it didn't seem wise to let him go anywhere without a few of us by his side. But given I'd gone from slight wooziness to feeling like I was moments from passing out, my first priority had to be getting my hand stitched up.

Vale led me into the prep room and through two locked doors before we reached the staircase leading to the basement.

The halls of the sublevel were lit up with the warm glow from the sconces, but no trace of natural light reached its depths. The darkness left an uneasiness in my stomach each time I ventured to the basement, reminding me of what might've happened with

Mort if Vale hadn't shown up. Or, worse, the darkness of the apartment in Dividium the night my parents got arrested. Jed and I had sat in the living room for hours after they were taken, silent, the only sound coming from the blood dripping off my back from the two fresh strike marks on my shoulder.

We stopped outside the infirmary, and Vale pounded on the door. 'Amelia? I have an inmate here to see you. Hand injury. Stitches are needed.'

As Vale raised his fist to knock again, the door swung open. Dr Row came bustling out with an armful of medical supplies.

'Oh!' She jumped, nearly dropping her supplies. 'Vale, dear, you scared me half to death! What is it?'

Vale gestured to me and my hastily wrapped injury. '224 was wounded during the hunt just now. She needs stitches.'

'Goodness – with all that blood, it certainly looks like it,' Dr Row said, distracted. She bent her head, using her shoulder to push her glasses higher on her nose. 'A guard called me to the mess hall. There's been a fight, and one of the inmates is in bad shape. Can you stitch Raven up? You know where all my things are.'

Without waiting for an answer, she hurried past us toward the stairs leading to the main level. I didn't know why her use of my real name and not my inmate number threatened to bring tears to my eyes.

Vale waved me toward the infirmary, and I stepped inside.

I raised an eyebrow at him once the door shut behind us, and we were alone in the small room. 'Did you learn to stitch wounds when you were volunteering at the medical center?'

He nodded. 'I was attending the medical academy in the Upper Sector. I was in my second year, which is when they have the volunteer requirement for their students. After everything that happened, I never got my degree.'

He motioned for me to sit. I did, choosing one of the wheeled chairs that occupied the space, and he settled across from me.

'Let's take a look at that hand,' he said in a low voice, hooking his hand around the back of my calf and pulling gently to bring my chair closer to his.

My breath hitched at the unexpected touch. The warmth from his fingers leaked through the fabric of my jumpsuit and pressed into my skin, and the memory of his lips on mine filled my head.

I flushed, and my eyes flicked up to his and then higher, over his head to the corner of the room where a camera was pointed directly at us. A red light was blinking at steady intervals.

Watching us.

I stopped breathing, trying to remember everything we'd said since entering the room. Had we implicated ourselves? Betrayed an intimacy we shouldn't have?

Vale's brow wrinkled at the look in my eyes, and then he looked over his shoulder and spotted the camera. He tensed, releasing my leg like it had burned him.

He took hold of my wrist, unwinding the soiled shirt from my injured hand.

I sucked in a sharp breath as the fabric pulled at my tender flesh.

Vale paused, eyes flitting to my face before he began again with far gentler movements.

He moved away to the attached washroom, returning with a stack of gauze pads. He used the gauze and some saline solution to clean the wound. When he finished, he picked up the needle and sutures.

'Wait. Aren't you going to numb the area?'

'We don't stock numbing agents for inmates, 224,' Vale answered, but his eyes said *I'm sorry*. 'It would be a waste of Endlock's resources.'

Of course it would.

I swallowed, bracing myself, and he began the painstaking process of stitching. As the needle pierced my skin, I bit my lip to keep from crying out.

Just breathe.

Breathe.

Keep breathing.

Vale's eyes moved between my face and my hand, and he worried his bottom lip between his teeth as he worked. I could feel the tension in his muscles even as his hands remained steady each time the needle pierced my skin.

Every few moments, he met my eyes, urging me to see the apology in them. His jaw was clenched so tightly I half expected to hear his teeth crack.

He tied off a suture, his hands steady as they deliberately brushed against my fingers, soothing me.

I watched his face, not his movements, letting my eyes trace over his strong jaw and dark hair. I remembered taking his hair down and knotting my fingers in his locks. I remembered things I shouldn't be remembering, but I allowed it just the same. I needed something to draw my attention from the throbbing in my hand.

He caught me staring and stopped, pausing for almost a full minute as if he could sense my thoughts. He licked his lips, took a deep, shuddering breath, then looked down at my hand again, forcing himself to focus.

I watched as his lips twisted into a teasing smile, and warmth pooled in my stomach.

Without speaking, I knew he was remembering our kiss, too.

Wondering what would have happened if we'd been allowed one more uninterrupted minute.

Vale's shoulders blocked most of my body from the camera's view, so I allowed my free hand to loosen and slip from where it rested on my thigh. It dangled between us for a few moments before I brushed my fingers, feather-light, across his knee.

It might have been an accident, except that I wasn't sure I'd ever done something so purposeful in my life.

Vale leaned forward into my touch under the guise of scrutinizing my wound. His breath mingled with mine as he worked.

I rolled my lips together, fighting a smile.

He tied off a final suture, then dropped his hand from my skin, letting out a shaky breath as he turned his back on me to clean up the healing supplies.

21

I CLOSED MY eyes, relishing the warmth of the scalding water raining down from the shower. Sloughing the dirt from the tunnels off my body with a cloud of jasmine-scented soap swirling in the steamy air almost made me forget where I was.

I could practically taste freedom. With Vale on our side, I knew it wouldn't be long before we were out of Endlock.

A sharp tug on my hair yanked me back to reality, tearing me from the privacy of the shower stall I occupied. The cool air of the bathroom replaced the hot stream of water, sending shivers through my body. My scalp screamed in protest.

Perri stood there, holding me at arm's length, strands of my wet hair clamped in her meaty fist.

'You think you and August can get away with what you did to Cyril? You killed him!' Her voice erupted into a raw, furious scream. I'd been concerned about leaving August alone, worried that Perri or Larch might target him again, but I hadn't given my safety a second thought.

She didn't bother to lower her voice, hinting that she'd taken care of the guards who usually monitored the bathroom – bribed them or distracted them in some other way.

Perri reared back to punch me in the face, but I pulled against the hand she had knotted in my hair, and moved enough that her fist grazed my skin instead of landing a direct hit. Still, a stinging sensation spread across my cheek, followed by a warm trickle of blood sliding down my chin. She had a shard of glass in her hand, and when I looked across the room, I found the tall mirror in the corner shattered.

Her hands shook, and her eyes were wild. 'You've ruined *everything*. You're the reason I'm here. The reason Cyril's dead. The reason the Warden dropped me.'

She screamed the words in my face, spit flying from her mouth, and her cheeks going red.

I should've been afraid, but Perri had made a mistake this time. Before, she'd had other inmates backing her up. Now, it was just the two of us.

A grin unfurled across my face.

Perri's blow had loosened her grip on my hair, and as she pulled back for another strike, I turned my head to the side and out of her grasp, letting her arm fly past me. My hands shot up, locking around her wrist, and I pulled, redirecting her momentum and sending her crashing into the wet shower wall.

She managed to stay on her feet and lunged forward, swinging the shard of glass wildly. I ducked, backing away, and she tried to match my steps.

She was strong, but I was faster than her.

I pretended to stumble, and she took the bait, shoving the glass forward to slice my neck – but I caught her wrist again, twisting until she dropped the shard, and it shattered into pieces against the damp floor.

Without hesitation, I slammed my knee into her groin.

Hard.

It was a dirty move, but if anyone deserved it, it was Perri.

She doubled over, gasping in pain. My scalp still throbbed from the force of her grip, and my teeth clenched together, anger thrumming through me.

Before she could recover, I lifted my knee again, this time driving it straight into her nose. I couldn't help the tiny thrill of satisfaction that ran through me when I heard the crunch of breaking bones.

She fell to the wet tiles, yowling in pain.

I snatched my clothes from the floor, hopping into loose pants and then pulling a camisole from Yara over my head. I didn't bother towel-drying my hair, and water droplets dripped down my back and over my chest as I headed for the exit.

Two guards stood watch outside the bathroom, barring other prisoners from entering. Their mouths dropped open when they saw me relatively unharmed, but they didn't say a word or move to stop me from leaving.

I offered them a tight smile and a bow of my head. 'I think someone in there might need your help,' I whispered conspiratorially.

'What did you do?' one of the guards asked, gripping her baton – a woman with shiny black hair I'd seen hanging around Hyde; terrible taste in company.

'The guard that usually waits inside and monitors the showers was gone,' I said, crinkling my brow. 'An inmate attacked me, and I defended myself. There's a lot of blood. I don't think one towel will cut it.'

The guards stepped into the bathroom, and I rushed away before they changed their minds and decided to question me further. When I rounded the corner, I nearly collided with Vale, who was hurrying toward the bathrooms.

'What's the rush?' I said, using his arm to steady myself.

'Kit said she tried to go into the bathroom, but guards stopped her. I had a feeling Perri was up to something and—' He stopped mid-sentence, staring at my cheek. 'What the fuck happened? Who did that to you?' he demanded through gritted teeth, moving his hand up to my face and tracing the skin beneath the cut with the pad of his thumb.

I glanced around, noting the cameras in the corridor were down – Perri's doing, most likely. It seemed that even if Larch had dropped her, she still held some sway over the guards. She might even be desperate enough to still be calling the shots on her business beneath Larch's nose.

I leaned further into Vale's touch, even as I told myself I should be shaking him off. 'It's nothing. A scratch,' I murmured.

His eyes darkened further, but the sound of heavy-booted footsteps around the corner had him clamping his hand around my arm and dragging me into the nearest supply closet.

It was nearly black inside, and there was barely enough room for one person, let alone the two of us.

The door pressed into my back, and there wasn't an inch of space between Vale's chest and mine. I was all too aware of my heavy breathing. And his.

My eyes slowly adjusted to the sliver of light seeping in under the door, and I saw Vale staring intently at me.

I cleared my throat once I heard the footsteps pass by our hiding place and move farther down the corridor.

'I really am okay,' I whispered. 'The blood makes it look worse than it is.'

Vale's jaw was still hard, his eyes flicking over every inch of my face, fingers prodding gently along my skin as if worried I'd hidden more injuries from him. Finally, he nodded, letting out a breath. 'Those guards are still losing their jobs – and they should feel lucky to keep their lives.'

I went still for a moment, an unexpected thrill coursing through me at the idea of Vale unleashing his wrath on my behalf. I shook my head to clear the sensation.

'I can take care of myself, Vale,' I murmured.

He chuckled. 'I've known that since the day I met you,' he said. 'It doesn't mean you don't deserve protection.' His eyes stayed on mine. 'From what I can tell, you've always been the one protecting those around you – you've never been taken care of.'

'My parents took care of me once,' I whispered, without quite meaning to.

'I'm so sorry, Raven.' The words were so soft I felt them like a caress over my skin.

'Everyone in the Lower Sector has a sad story.'

'That doesn't mean that yours doesn't mean anything.' He tucked a strand of hair behind my ear.

'And what about your story?' I forced the words past the tightness in my throat before the memories of my parents could choke me. 'What was your father like?'

Vale shook his head, pausing for almost a full minute, seeming to weigh up whether he wanted to answer. He took a deep breath, his jaw clenching. Eventually, he let out a sigh.

'I loved my father very much.' Vale's voice came out fragile. 'When I was a child, he was like the sun. Bright and happy and bursting with light. In the safety of our home, he would tell me of the kindness of all people – how the only thing that separated us from those in the Lower Sector was the number of credits in our account. That we could easily be in their situation instead of ours and that we needed to help each other.'

Vale's face thawed beneath his vulnerability, his brow smoothing out and his full lips softening.

'But as I grew older,' Vale continued, 'I noticed he only said those things when my mother wasn't around. They had completely different beliefs. It all made sense to me when he confessed to being a rebel, but I still have a hard time reconciling myself to the fact that my mother supports this system.'

'Do you think your mother would have turned your father in

to the guards, if she'd known?' I couldn't imagine having to hide such a big part of myself from a life partner.

'I think she would have,' Vale whispered. 'She never had the chance to do it, but somehow, I can't forgive her anyway. And yet, I'm doing the same as my father did – I'm too cowardly to challenge her beliefs to her face.'

'It's not always easy doing what you know is right,' I whispered. 'I always knew being a bounty hunter wasn't right – but letting Jed starve wouldn't have been right, either.'

'You didn't have another choice.' Vale rubbed a hand up and down my arm.

'Still. There are things I would've done differently. Fears I would've faced.'

'You would have,' Vale agreed, nodding. 'Endlock has changed you.'

He was right.

I'd spent the years before my arrest pushing everyone away just to face my biggest fear and have it bring more community into my life than I'd imagined I could have again.

They made me want to *live*, instead of just surviving.

And together, we'd become the first to leave Endlock.

'There's no way I'll give Larch the satisfaction of letting this place kill me.' I smirked. 'I can't wait until we get out of here. My only regret is that I won't see the look on his face when he realizes we've bested him.'

Vale chuckled, but the sound was cut off abruptly, and I watched how his eyes flicked to the top of my camisole, and then away so quickly I almost missed the movement. He sucked in a sharp breath, and when I looked down, I noted how the water from my wet hair had soaked the already-thin fabric, leaving little to the imagination.

His eyes darkened, and I knew we were both thinking about what had happened in the workshop a few nights ago.

My mind flashed back to his mouth on mine, and my cheeks grew hot.

'Vale . . .' I bit my lip, and his pupils dilated.

'Say you want me to kiss you again,' he whispered, and my breath hitched.

I licked my lips and noted the way his eyes tracked the movement. 'It doesn't matter what I want. What matters is getting out of Endlock. Thinking about anything else right now is too dangerous.'

And it *was* dangerous. I couldn't get him out of my head, and it was consuming me. Consuming my every waking thought and my ability to focus on escape.

Vale brushed a strand of hair away from my eyes and trailed his thumb slowly down my cheek, carefully avoiding my fresh cut. The hair on the back of my neck stood on end, and goosebumps rose on my arms. I tried not to stare at his lips. And failed.

'Too dangerous?' he asked, looking into my eyes. I felt like I'd been put under a spell, making it impossible to look away from him.

He leaned closer, never moving his gaze from my eyes, giving me enough time to pull away if I decided to.

But I didn't want to pull away.

Vale brushed his mouth against mine, slow and sensuous, coaxing my lips apart with a languid caress of his tongue until I opened for him.

He pulled away from me slightly, looking into my eyes as he trailed his hand down my arm to interlace our fingers.

He kissed me again, harder this time, and caught my bottom lip between his teeth, nibbling lightly. A shiver snaked its way up my spine.

My hands found their way into his hair, and then I was pulling it as his hands ran down my body to the backs of my thighs. He picked me up and helped me wrap my legs around him, pressing my back harder into the door.

I ran my tongue lightly over his bottom lip, and he pulled me more fully against him, his hands tightening over my hips. My fingers trailed down his back, playing with the hem of his shirt before I worked up the nerve to slip my hands under the fabric and place them against his bare skin.

Already, the hard length of him pressed against my core through our clothes, and an ache pulsed through me. I nipped his lower lip, eliciting a growl from him. And then his hands were under my shirt, cool against skin that had caught fire.

I grabbed his hand and urged it higher, and he bit my neck.

'Fuck, Raven,' he murmured against my lips, his voice roughened with desire, breaths fast and shallow and warm against my skin.

His words sent a bolt of heat straight through me, and I rolled against him, moaning at the friction of him against my core.

I nudged him, trying to move his lips back to mine, but he moved his hands to my shoulders and held me there, slightly away from him. I raised an eyebrow, my eyes meeting his.

A question swam in those depthless pools of liquid gold.

'I don't want to stop,' Vale said earnestly. 'Trust me, that is the last thing I want. But even now that you know I'm on your side, I'm still a guard. And you're an inmate. And I don't want you to think you have to do anything you don't want to do. I still want to help you no matter what.'

Perhaps the softest words I'd heard him speak in the short time I'd known him.

And it had been so long since I'd felt I had control over what was happening around me. I couldn't protect Jed. I couldn't guarantee a future for our friends. I couldn't even take a shower without another inmate waging an assault on me.

But this.

This I could control.

And I wanted him.

'I want you to touch me,' I breathed.

Once the words left my lips, there was chaos.

Vale's eyes darkened impossibly, teeth biting into his plush bottom lip as he pulled me to him. He kissed his way down my neck. When he reached my chest, he flicked his tongue over the peak of one of my hardened nipples through the material of my camisole, and I let out a muffled cry, arching my back and pushing against his mouth.

He chuckled, low and rumbling against me.

My breath caught as he pressed me harder against the door, the surface cooling my skin but doing nothing to douse the fire burning within me. The tension between us all these weeks had finally boiled over, threatening to incinerate me.

He moved to untie the string of my pants, claiming my lips with his once more. I knew my mouth would bruise from the urgency of his kiss.

I curled my fingers into his hair, yanking until he let out a low groan.

'I know you've dreamed of hurting me for ages now,' Vale mused, scraping his teeth over my earlobe. 'But is now really the time for that?'

A shiver wracked my body, rendering me incapable of speech.

His fingers slipped beneath my waistband, and my breath quickened, my grip on him tightening, keeping him close, as I rolled against him, seeking out his touch. I felt like I might die without it.

Vale made a sound low in his throat and dipped his face down, his tongue darting out and licking a line up the column of my neck.

'Please,' I breathed, not caring how desperate I must have sounded to him.

Footsteps.

Right outside the closet door.

Vale's hand covered my mouth, and his free arm wound around my waist to hold me tight against him.

There were muffled voices from what sounded like two guards, and they stopped walking just outside the closet, continuing a conversation I couldn't quite make out.

My heart kicked up an erratic beat in my chest as I caught Vale's eye, not daring to move a muscle.

But instead of nerves, something dangerous was reflected in Vale's gaze. He gave me a wicked smile and then, keeping one hand over my mouth, his other hand ventured down, inching toward my throbbing core.

My breath hitched in my throat. What was he *doing*?

A guard laughed on the other side of the door just as Vale caressed the most sensitive part of me through the fabric of my underwear.

My eyes went wide with shock, even as I released a desperate breath behind his hand. Instead of dousing my arousal, the fear of being caught seemed to heighten it.

Vale's hand clamped tighter over my mouth as he whispered, 'You have to stay quiet for me. You wouldn't want someone to catch us, would you?'

I shook my head back and forth, grinding into his excruciatingly light touch, needing more. So much more.

His forehead pressed against mine as he slowly tortured me with the barely-there touches of his fingers against my sensitive flesh, watching my face as I squirmed and panted into his palm. 'Do you want me to keep going?'

I squeezed my eyes shut.

I shouldn't want him to keep going.

But my traitorous body arched toward him, and I nodded against his hand.

His golden eyes darkened, shining with triumph even as he

rewarded me, rubbing harder against me and wringing another muffled moan from my body. I ground down onto him, relief mixing with increasingly desperate need as the guards' voices finally faded down the corridor.

But then Vale's radio crackled to life.

'There's been an incident in the Upper showers.' A tinny voice came through the device. 'Vale, are you available?'

Fuck. Perri must have been in worse shape than I'd thought.

Vale growled, pausing in his movements, and removing his hand from my mouth.

'Vale?' the voice called again. 'If you're not available we'll need to call the Warden.'

That brought me back to reality. 'Go,' I urged Vale, though I had to bite back a whimper as he moved his hand away from me. The last thing I needed was Larch knowing I'd been involved in another incident.

Vale picked up his radio, pressing the button on the side, even as he watched me with heavy-lidded eyes. His voice was rough when he finally spoke, like gravel scraping along my skin.

'Don't call the Warden. I'll be right there.'

22

VALE CHECKED TO be sure the coast was clear before ushering me back into the corridor. Under the fluorescent lights, he remembered the cut on my face.

Anger darkened his honeyed eyes. 'You're still bleeding.'

I met his gaze. 'Not as much as Perri's bleeding on the bathroom floor.'

He groaned, throwing his head back. 'You beating the shit out of people shouldn't turn me on as much as it does.'

I grinned. 'Definitely not. You should work on that.'

'It'd be useless to try.' He brought his thumb up to caress my full bottom lip. 'I think we can stop pretending I have any control when it comes to you,' he said, before releasing my face and walking past me, presumably to give the guards a piece of his mind.

I stood rooted to the spot, dazed and tingling from his touch. It took a full minute for my legs to remember how to move, and, even then, a grin lingered on my face all the way back to my cell.

When I returned, Jed was moving into the Upper level cell

across the corridor from mine. The digital display above showed that his rank had increased to an eight.

'Promoted,' he said when he turned and saw my grin, though he didn't return my smile.

I followed him down the corridor to his Middle level cell and watched as he gathered a few books into his arms – more gifts from Yara.

'Jed . . .'

'We talked about this after our first hunt together,' he snapped. 'You were supposed to stop treating me like a child.'

'And I have,' I insisted. 'I've told you about all of the leads I've had on an escape so far.'

'No.' Jed let out a harsh laugh and slammed the books down. 'You've been trying to have it both ways. Maybe you told me about the details *you* were working on, but you left out the fact that you've grown close to a guard. That Kit is working on our wrist-bands. You're still deciding what's safe enough to tell me.'

'Giving you these kinds of details puts you at risk,' I whispered, touching his arm.

He stepped away from my touch. 'I get to decide whether I want to be involved in that risk. Not you.'

'You know I'm only trying to protect you.'

'Your version of protection is what got me arrested in the first place,' he hissed. His voice was low and yet the words hit me like a punch to the stomach.

My mouth opened and then shut. I had no defense.

'I didn't mean that,' Jed whispered, eyes on his feet. 'I really didn't. You just have to let me be in charge of my own life, Raven. Trying to do everything on your own is far riskier than letting people help you. I can contribute.'

I swallowed past the lump in my throat. 'You're right. And I'm sorry.'

He stared at me for a long moment. 'I can forgive you if you promise this time. Promise to stop treating me like a child and let me make decisions for myself. Let me *in*.'

I closed my eyes, taking a deep breath.

Jed was right. My version of protection – of keeping him blind to difficult decisions and situations – hadn't done us any favors so far. And he'd weathered Endlock as well as, perhaps even better than, I had. He hadn't backed down when I'd expected him to and had gotten me through moments of paralyzing fear.

It was time to start thinking of him as the asset he was.

Pride warmed my chest, and tears pricked at the back of my eyes. I blinked furiously to keep them at bay before nodding at Jed. 'I promise.'

That night, I dreamed I was being carried through the hunting grounds by Hyde and another guard I didn't recognize. I was tossed over his shoulder like a rag doll, my eyes open and taking in my surroundings, but I couldn't move.

My fingers refused to clench into fists, and my mouth wouldn't form the shapes of the words I wanted to scream.

'Crematorium's not back up and running yet,' Hyde grumbled, directing his words at the other guard. 'I'm sick of breaking my back burying these bodies.'

The other guard grumbled in assent, dragging her shovel across the ground and trampling directly over fresh graves. 'Let's get this over with. Try and find a spot without too many roots and rocks.'

My body bounced against Hyde's back as my eyes scanned the countless graves. They followed the same strange pattern I'd seen during my hunts – for the most part, the bodies were buried in uninterrupted rows, save for a break, about five feet wide, that wound through the graves and farther into the forest.

If it was a path, then why didn't the guards bother to walk along it?

'We need to find another clearing,' Hyde said.

The other guard stopped behind him, within eyesight, and pointed at the winding break in the graves. 'What about here?'

'Can't.' Hyde turned and stomped his foot hard in the middle of the opening. The ground rumbled and shook like it would cave in beneath us. 'See?'

The guard nodded, and they began walking farther into the forest.

An alarm blared through the cellblock, ripping me from my dream. My eyes flew open, my breath coming in heavy gasps as I sat bolt upright on my cot, the sound of cell doors grinding open filling my ears. I sat there, heart pounding, feeling the remnants of fear from my nightmare.

But then, a fragment of my dream returned to me, a piece of the puzzle.

'Of course,' I whispered, wondering how it hadn't occurred to me before.

I raced ahead of the other inmates on their way to their workshop shifts, hoping for a private moment with Vale to share my revelation. The basement corridor seemed more shadowed than usual, the lights muted to a soft, almost non-existent glow.

A hushed conversation from within the workshop stopped me before I could get too close.

Slowing my steps, I inched closer to the wall, allowing the surrounding darkness to cloak me as I strained to hear more.

'When are you going to let me be honest?' Vale's voice was barely above a whisper, but it held a harsh edge that caught me off guard.

Honest? My brows knitted together.

'When the time is right,' August responded, a hint of annoyance in his tone. 'When it's safe. A little time won't change anything.'

'Maybe not for you,' Vale said, the rest of his words trailing off.

The sound of footsteps on the basement stairs urged me forward, and I tucked the conversation away for later examination.

I knew I only had minutes away from prying ears to explain my plan to Vale. I gave up on eavesdropping, treading heavily the rest of the way to the workshop to announce my arrival.

I shoved open the workshop door. August stood leaning against the wall, his injured leg lifted, while Vale stared intently at a notebook behind his desk. I could practically smell their feigned innocence, but I didn't have time to question them.

My eyes flitted to the camera in the corner. Off.

'Have you buried any bodies since the crematorium malfunctioned?' I directed the question at Vale, setting aside formalities and any lingering thought of what we'd done together in the closet the night before.

'Hi.' Vale glanced up, gaze flitting over my face and a sly smile pulling his lips up on one side. 'No, I haven't.'

'Hi back,' I said, allowing him a small smile.

'I'm right here,' August said flatly, with a weak wave.

I shook my head, dispelling the distraction. 'Right. When we were out on the hunting grounds, there seemed to be a grid-like pattern that the graves were dug in. Except there's a break in that pattern.'

Vale bit his cheek. 'The path?'

I shook my head. 'But I don't think it's a path. They don't care if we tromp all over those graves.'

August tilted his head. 'If it's not a path, then what is it?'

'I remember seeing some marks on the ground. Like someone had tried to dig a grave in the break and then changed their mind. What if they tried digging, and the ground collapsed beneath their shovel? Or Larch told them to avoid a certain area.'

August whistled. 'Council above.'

'They're avoiding the tunnel,' Vale whispered, understanding lighting his eyes.

A short burst of laughter pushed its way past my lips, uncontainable. 'We're going to get out of here.'

Vale grinned at me, eyes glinting.

'We just need to find a good spot to access the tunnel system,' I declared, hope surging. 'And make sure that there are no collapses between wherever we enter and where the tunnel ends on the other side of the fence.'

Vale was silent for a minute, running his hand over his face and resting it beneath his chin. His brow wrinkled. 'That could work.'

August kicked off from the wall, limping over to us. 'It makes sense,' he agreed. 'Provided we can figure out a way to get out on the grounds and dig down into the tunnel without arousing Larch's suspicion.'

I thought for a moment. 'Vale, you said Larch didn't intend for the obstacles on the hunting grounds to kill us, right?'

Vale shook his head. 'No. They were meant to trap the inmates. Make them easier targets.'

As if being weaponless didn't render us defenseless enough.

'And how did he react when two inmates were killed by the obstacles?' I asked.

'At first, he was worried,' Vale said. 'But a lot of the hunters enjoyed the spectacle. They all watched that one girl die – the one who got her leg caught in the trap in the field. Some visitors never make a kill or witness a death, so it was a big deal. The Council wants Larch to keep the obstacles in place until the new wristband features are ready.'

My stomach churned at the thought of that inmate having to die surrounded by hunters who were *cheering* for her death. She must have been terrified.

I cleared my throat. 'How long before the wristbands are ready?'

Vale frowned. 'Any day now. They plan to select inmates for trials soon to test the new features.'

August and I locked eyes across the room.

'You need to make sure we're selected for the trials,' I told him.

Vale's mouth fell open as he stood and stalked toward me, his eyes flitting between August and me.

'No,' Vale said, eyes now intent on mine. 'No, I won't do that to you.'

'It's the only way,' August insisted. 'What other excuse will we have to be out on the grounds outside of a hunt? It's our only chance to get into the tunnels.'

Vale gripped my wrist, pulling me toward him and shaking his head. 'You don't understand. These new features are inhumane. Extremely painful. I'm not putting you through that.'

He spoke to both of us, but his eyes remained on me, and a fire surged within them, embers flitting through molten gold.

'A little pain isn't a bad trade for freedom,' I argued.

'If we see what the features are like in a trial, we'll be more prepared to face them in a hunt,' August added. 'Otherwise, the shock could kill us.'

'I don't want to hurt you,' Vale whispered, his hand coming up to cup my face. His thumb stroked along my jaw.

'If you don't, we'll die.' I crossed my arms. 'And if you don't help us get selected . . .' I hesitated. 'If you don't help us, I'll piss Larch off enough that he'll choose me himself.'

23

IT DIDN'T TAKE Vale long to convince the Warden.

Before lights out, Vale led August and me out onto the hunting grounds while the rest of the inmates were herded back to their cellblocks.

The sun had long since sunk beyond the horizon, leaving the grounds blanketed in darkness and starlight. I looked over my shoulder at every sound, even though I knew no one had followed us – it had been weeks since I'd been outside without the immediate threat of being killed.

I realized, for the first time, that the forest was beautiful.

Concrete, glass, and metal had been my day-to-day view for as long as I could remember in Dividium. Now, I found myself inhaling lungfuls of crisp air and marveling at how the moonlight played over the needles of the towering pines.

We reached the break between the graves quickly, and followed the makeshift path deeper into the trees.

'We want to get as far from Endlock as possible before we dig down,' Vale whispered. 'Less risk of someone stumbling across the entrance that way.'

The crematorium had only been broken for a week, and nearly a hundred inmates had been buried on the grounds in that time.

My stomach churned at the number. So much life, *gone*.

The deeper we got into the forest, the more scattered the graves seemed, and the more difficult it became to keep track of where we thought the tunnel was.

Eventually, we stopped near the base of an ancient oak, August gasping for air, worn down from the long hike and his injury.

'Gus, it's fine. Just stand watch,' Vale said, hands raised in a placating gesture. The moon cast a dim glow over where we stood, and a cool breeze rustled the leaves. Autumn was creeping up on us with each passing day.

August arched a brow. 'You think I'm useless.'

'No, that's not it,' Vale replied. 'But if we don't give that ankle a rest, you're not going to be able to make it very far once we get out of here. You know Raven and I can dig faster right now. We need someone watching our backs.'

August glared at him before finally giving a consenting nod. He limped over to a nearby pine and leaned against it, rustling the boughs as he slid down the trunk to sit on the ground.

'But what about the features? Won't the engineers know if we don't test them?' I asked.

'After,' Vale said. 'If we test them first, you won't have the strength to help dig.'

I swallowed at his words, my feet rooted to the spot.

'Come on, then,' Vale called over to me. 'We have a tunnel to explore.'

A small smile curved my lips at his words.

We were going to escape, and the pain from the wristband would only be temporary.

I lifted my spade as Vale clicked on a flashlight, and my eyes caught on a spot of red.

'Wait,' I hissed, dropping my shovel.

Vale was at my side in an instant, hand on my arm, while August's gaze snapped to my face.

'What is it?' Vale asked.

I shook my head, staring at the blood-red berries that had caught my attention. Clusters of them hung from a thorny bush – a variety I'd only seen in two other places on the hunting grounds.

August followed my gaze. 'It's like those thickets that are outside the entrances to the Blood Tree tunnel,' he whispered. 'You don't think . . .?'

'No,' I whispered. 'It couldn't be that easy.'

But could it? The guards from the prison before would've wanted some kind of landmark near the tunnels' entrances, something to easily identify them in an emergency.

Vale stepped into the thicket and crouched down, running his hand along the ground and brushing away dead leaves and old, dried berries. He felt around for several moments to no avail, and my face fell.

I tried for a small smile. 'It's all right. It was worth a—'

The flashlight slipped from Vale's hand, hitting the ground, but instead of the thump I'd expected from an object hitting hard-packed dirt, there was the clang of metal on metal.

I rushed into the thicket, leaning down next to Vale.

August hobbled over to us. 'Is that what I think it is?' He voiced the question I hadn't dared ask.

Vale didn't answer. Instead, he felt around the flashlight before gripping the edges of some flat, square object we hadn't seen before – he pulled on it, straining until, finally, there was a popping sound, and the square came free, sending Vale stumbling backward.

A cloud of dust rose from the ground, dancing in the glow of the flashlight, and when it cleared, I clapped a hand over my mouth.

August and Vale exchanged glances and laughed.

The entrance to the tunnels.

'It can't have been opened for decades,' I mused, staring into the hole. It was pitch black.

Vale stepped forward with his flashlight and shone it into the space. 'There's an old ladder,' he confirmed, passing me the flashlight. He grabbed the ladder, leaning his weight onto it and shaking. 'I think it'll hold.'

I grinned. 'What are you waiting for, then?'

August cleared his throat, nodding to his ankle. 'I think I'll wait up here. It was a long walk.'

'No hero shit, okay?' Vale told him. 'If you hear someone coming, put the lid back on and hide.'

'No hero shit,' August repeated, lifting his palms.

We turned back to the entrance and lowered ourselves in. Vale led the way, flashlight in hand. As I followed, my foot caught, and I stumbled. Vale's hand found my hip to steady me, his fingers pressing into my skin. My breath hitched.

'Are you all right?' he asked, close and concerned. The moonlight from the pit's opening illuminated his eyes enough that I could see my shaky expression in their reflection.

I swallowed, my voice caught in my throat. I needed to get a grip.

'Fine,' I managed to reply, gulping. My foot hit the ground, and I turned, taking in the space in the glow of Vale's flashlight.

The cavern was a near-replica of the space below the first tunnel entrance I'd seen, complete with emergency supplies, but I noted a thicker coat of dust and cobwebs.

The air was heavy with the scent of damp soil.

Vale rotated to face north, the direction of the fence. And the settlement. On that side of the cavern, the wall gave way to an even deeper darkness.

The tunnel.

'Are you ready?' he asked, sliding his hand down my arm to intertwine our fingers. He squeezed my hand.

I nodded, not trusting myself to answer.

We stepped into the tunnel, Vale tugging me after him, his flashlight hardly penetrating the darkness more than a few feet in front of us.

The tunnel was practically identical to the other one I'd been in – earthen walls and packed dirt floors. Once in a while, we'd pass an abandoned rifle or a crumpled wrapper from a ration bar, relics from a time long since past.

A clump of dirt fell from above, and I jumped, picturing the tunnel collapsing on top of us.

'Can I ask you something?' I began, eager to shift the focus away from darker thoughts.

'Anything.'

I watched the side of his face as we continued walking. 'I've heard that the North Settlement isn't a fan of outsiders. They're only expecting Jed, Kit, and me. How do you know they'll let the rest of our group in?'

Vale gave me a sad smile. 'First, you have to know that we've been fed lies about the North Settlement our entire lives. The Council puts Dividium on a pedestal. They want us to think that they've learned from past mistakes and formulated the best possible way to live. But they don't want us to know that the people in the settlements live peacefully. They don't want us to know that a successful society could exist without something like Endlock.'

'How do you know that's true?' I asked, narrowing my eyes. Surely, Aggie would've told me if the North Settlement was some utopian society.

'Some of my . . . sources have been in communication with the North Settlement,' Vale said.

My mouth dropped open. 'Why? What do they talk about?'

'The Council wants the North Settlement to grant them access to visit. I don't know the specifics of why, but I'd imagine they only have an interest in something if they think it will make them credits,' Vale said.

I believed him. If the North Settlement agreed to a visit from the Council, I had a feeling they'd come to regret it.

'And I can't guarantee the North Settlement will let us in,' Vale continued. 'But there are no other options. If they hesitate to accept us, we'll offer to help wherever possible. We can help with manual labor or with specialty services. August's a doctor. Kit's an engineer. Yara was an agriculturist. You're already part of the deal, but even if you weren't, your combat skills are an asset. We have a lot to offer if they don't want to take us in out of the kindness of their hearts.'

He was right. It wasn't like we could go back to the city. And attempting to live on our own, out on the Wastes, would be a death sentence. The North Settlement was the only option.

From what Aggie had told me before I left Dividium, the North Settlement *did* lack access to certain resources, and having people around with August's and Kit's experience might be enough for them to take in the rest of us.

Vale stopped suddenly, passing me his flashlight and disentangling our hands to reach into his pocket and pull out his tablet. He touched the screen, and it lit up. He scanned it.

'You'll need to stay here,' Vale whispered, finally looking at me again.

'What?' I shuddered, thinking of being alone in the oppressive dark.

Vale reached up, brushing a strand of hair behind my ear. 'We're only a few steps from being directly beneath the fence. If your wristband passes over the perimeter, an alarm will sound inside the prison. You'll be caught. My wristband doesn't have that feature, and I need to make sure the tunnel really will get us to the other side of the fence. Make sure there's an exit on the other end.'

He was right. There was no other choice.

I swallowed, rolling my shoulders back, forcing a tight smile to my lips. 'Of course.'

He held his hand out, and I stared at it for a moment before I realized he wanted the flashlight I was still holding. The only light source in the tunnel aside from the slight glow emitting from his tablet.

I held back a groan. *Fuck me.*

I placed the flashlight in his hand.

'I'll be right back,' he promised, walking backward a few steps, eyes intent on mine before he turned.

For several moments, I stood, back against the wall, as he got farther down the tunnel, and the space around me grew darker.

Until he turned a corner, and I was left with no light at all.

I slid down the wall until I was sitting, squinting my eyes, trying to see anything.

I'd never been afraid of the dark, but the dark had never been so complete.

And the silence.

Was this what it would be like to be buried alive? I drew in a sharp breath at the thought, curling into myself and wrapping my arms around my bent knees. My chest grew tight, and it felt like there was something stuck in my throat, stopping me from pulling in full breaths.

I heard my mother's voice in my head. *Breathe, Raven.*

In*, two, three, four.*

Out*, two, three, four.*

I didn't think I'd drawn a full breath since my parents were taken. Something had lodged itself in my chest that night, and my lungs had been forced to adapt ever since.

In, *two, three, four.*

Out, *two, three, four.*

It had gotten worse when Jed was arrested.

In, *two, three, four.*

Out, *two, three, four.*

And worse, when I'd been forced onto the hunting grounds for the first time.

In, *two, three, four.*

Out, *two, three, four.*

I pictured our friends sitting around our assigned table in the mess hall, laughing despite where they were, and something stuttered in my chest.

In, *two, three, four.*

I pictured Vale, pulling Jed and me into the tunnel.

Out, *two, three, four.*

And I realized, somewhere along the way, these people had made it easier for me to breathe.

Made me feel almost whole again.

I pictured all of us, making our way across the Wastes.

I took a deep breath, the rhythm evening out.

By the time we returned to the tunnel entrance and back up to the land of the living, half an hour had passed.

'Tunnel's clear.' Vale filled August in. 'Exit on the other side of the fence is wedged shut, I'd guess because it hasn't been used for so long. But we can't risk breaking it open until we leave – another guard might notice a gaping hole in the ground on the other side of the fence.'

A wide grin unfurled across August's face. 'We're really doing this.'

We started to walk back toward the prison, but I froze, remembering something. I turned to Vale. 'While we're out here, I should show you where I stashed that rifle I stole from the hunter. That way, you can get it to Kit. She said she could modify it for us to use.'

Vale grinned. 'Lead the way, Little Bird.'

I frowned. 'The thing is, directionally, I don't know how to get there.' All the trees looked the same, and while I was getting used to the hunting grounds, I hadn't returned to that specific spot since my first hunt.

'Do you remember anything about it?' August asked.

'It was in a sort of clearing,' I mused, thinking back. 'Actually, I watched you two meet up right where it happened. You were whispering to each other, and then you heard a scream and took off.'

Vale chuckled. 'Putting the pieces together, even then.'

'I think I know where that is,' August interjected.

We followed him for several minutes until we reached a clearing. I wasn't sure it was *the* clearing until I spotted a blood-stained rock.

August caught me eyeing it and raised a brow. 'Damn. Momo said you cracked that hunter's head pretty good. I guess I should've believed him.'

August and Vale followed as I retraced my steps from that day, finally approaching the hollow tree where I'd stashed the gun. I reached inside, wary of being bitten by some creature that had made the tree its home, but my fingers met cool metal. 'Still here,' I whispered.

'I'll come back for it later,' Vale promised, punching the coordinates into his tablet.

I couldn't keep the smile off my face as Vale directed us nearly all the way back to Endlock, stopping at the edge of the field. Lights winked at us from the watchtowers around the perimeter, but for the most part, the prison was wholly dark, everyone tucked in for the evening.

'Why do you want to test the new features this close to the prison?' August asked, leaning against the nearest tree. Sweat trickled down his temple, and he rested his weight solely on his uninjured leg.

'Because I don't know what state you'll be in after the experiment is done,' Vale confessed, fiddling with a handheld rectangular device with a glowing screen. 'I might be able to drag you across the field if you're unconscious, but I wouldn't be able to carry you across the entirety of the grounds.'

I swallowed against my dry throat.

'How does it work?' I asked, though I didn't really want to know the answer.

Vale cleared his throat, finally meeting my eyes. 'I'll scan your wristband and add the features. The hunters who pay for the features will likely only add one or two at a time, but Larch insisted that we test them all today.'

'He's efficient, I'll give him that,' August grumbled.

I huffed out a laugh, clenching my hands into fists at my sides to stop their shaking.

'One of us at a time or . . .?' I trailed off.

'Together,' August answered before Vale could, stepping up beside me with a wince. I reached an arm out, offering to take some of the weight off his leg, but he waved me off. 'Best to get it over with.'

Vale nodded, his jaw clenched tight. He scanned August's wristband and then tapped a few times on the screen of his device before reaching for my arm. His fingers closed around my wrist, and his golden eyes looked into mine, warming something low in my belly.

He scanned my wristband and then, rather reluctantly, released my arm.

'I'm sorry,' he said, tapping the device screen again.

The words slipped from him so softly that I could've convinced myself it was my imagination.

Vale pulled a pair of dark-lensed glasses from the pocket of his pants and, after seeing my scrunched brows, said, 'It's for the thermal imaging. When the feature is activated on your wristbands, these glasses will allow me to see where you are – whether in the dark or through the foliage of the trees.'

A death sentence for any inmate it was used on.

But not us. Not Jed. Not now that we'd found a way to leave.

'Are you ready?' Vale asked, sliding the sunglasses onto his face.

I nodded and, out of the corner of my eye, saw August doing the same.

'It will be over soon,' Vale promised. 'I'm going to head about a hundred yards in that direction' – he pointed away from us – 'to make sure the features work from a distance. I'll head back toward you slowly, tracking your vitals and the accuracy of the thermal imaging. Once I'm close enough, we'll be able to see if the proximity alerts work. We'll save the pain infliction for last.'

Vale grimaced as if the last of the words tasted sour. But he said nothing else before turning his back and walking away from us.

I was glad.

I could no longer hide the fear coursing through me as I watched Vale's retreating figure.

August and I were silent as we waited.

'Vitals and thermal imaging are good,' Vale called, waving his device in the air. 'Proximity alerts should be—'

But a high-pitched alarm was emitted simultaneously from my wristband and August's, cutting him off. I slapped my hands over my ears as the sound of the alarm rattled through my skull, piercing to the point of pain.

I saw August leaning against a tree, covering his ears.

The alarm cut out, and Vale jogged the rest of the distance between us.

'Too loud,' August grunted through his teeth. 'It will hurt the hunters, too.'

'Let it hurt them,' I seethed, shaking my head from side to side to clear the ringing in my ears.

'August's right,' Vale said, touching my cheek. 'We'll have to work on the decibel level. Larch will know I'm sabotaging him if we set that loose on the hunters.'

August coughed. 'Let's get the last part over with before you two start making out ten feet from me.'

I bit back a laugh.

Vale dropped his hand, composing himself. 'For the pain infliction, I'll press a small button on my tablet, and it will make your wristbands shock you. I don't know how painful it will be, but it's supposed to be strong enough to debilitate you.'

'So it's going to fucking suck,' August said. 'Noted.'

I gritted my teeth. I'd had plenty of injuries, and this was only going to be temporary. And it was all worth it now that we'd found our way out.

'Just do it,' I told Vale, meeting his eyes. 'We're ready.'

He bit his lip, watching me intently for a moment before nodding. He lifted his hand and tapped his screen, just once.

I felt something like a pinprick against my wrist.

'Okay,' I breathed, staring at it. Waiting. My brow wrinkled. 'It hurts, of course, but it's n—'

I screamed.

And screamed.

My arm was being torn off. The prick had spread like a disease, burning through flesh and sinew and severing bone.

'Make it stop!' I yelled, refusing to look at my arm. Tears streamed from my eyes, leaking into my mouth. Choking me.

The pain burned up into my shoulder. It was consuming me. I wouldn't survive it.

There were hands on my back, on my head, brushing against me, but those hurt too. I tried to step away, to escape the hands and the hurt, but I couldn't move – the attempt had me falling flat on my face, and I wanted to *die*.

'Kill me,' I whispered. 'Please.'

I repeated the words until the world around me faded to black, and I escaped into blissful nothingness.

24

'I'M SO SORRY.'

I felt the words as much as I heard them, as the lips that spoke them were pressed against my ear, and then my temple, and then my forehead.

'Little Bird. Can you hear me?'

I was comfortable where I was, curled against something solid and deliciously warm.

'Mmm,' I hummed, nestling into the warmth.

'Council above,' the voice murmured. Arms clenched tighter around me, cradling me into a solid chest. 'Are you in pain?'

Pain?

What an odd question. Why would I be in pain here? Everything was warm and—

Pain.

It all flooded back, and I wrenched my eyes open, needing to see if my arm had been permanently damaged.

But it was fine.

The limb was curled over my abdomen, slightly red, but otherwise completely normal.

And if it had hurt me that much, then—

'August?' I called, shifting in Vale's arms and scanning the shadowy trees.

'Here, Thorne,' August called back, and I whipped my head in the other direction, a breath leaving me when I saw him. His hairline glistened with sweat, and he sucked in breaths like he'd been running for miles, but otherwise he appeared unharmed.

'You didn't pass out?' I asked.

'I did,' he confirmed. 'I woke up two minutes ago. I guess pain tolerance is one thing I kick your ass at, bounty hunter.'

He finished his words with a wink, but he was right. We were supposed to find a way to leave through the tunnels during a hunt, but the idea of trying to escape while under the haze of so much pain . . . I shuddered.

I turned back to Vale, who pressed another feverish kiss to my brow, his eyes flitting over my face.

'I'm okay,' I told him.

'I can't believe I did that to you,' he whispered, brow furrowed and lips turned down at the corners. He didn't meet my eyes, and his own were heavy with regret.

I reached up, resting a hand on his cheek. 'You didn't have a choice.'

'You asked me to *kill you*.'

I didn't know what to say to that. I had. I'd never felt such pain in my life.

I bit my lip. 'So make sure I never have to feel that pain again. Make sure we're out of here before the features go live.'

I watched Vale intently as I spoke, and he finally met my eyes, staring into them for a long moment before giving a firm nod. He placed me gently on my feet, a hand pressed solidly against my back until I proved I was capable of walking.

We headed back for Endlock, walking in silence for a few minutes before August spoke up.

'How are we going to make sure all six of us get selected for a hunt at the same time when we're ready to escape? Kit needs to know the exact day, almost down to the hour, that we're going to leave so that when she hacks into the security system, she can set a time for the tracking on our wristbands to expire.'

It'd been something I'd been thinking about too – how uncomfortable it was that a huge piece of our escape plan was going to be left up to chance. We could taunt the hunters all we wanted, but it didn't guarantee they'd select us as targets.

'I think we have to leave at night,' Vale said, stopping August and me in our tracks.

'At night?' I hissed, and, at the same time, August asked, 'How would we get out on the grounds without anyone noticing?'

Vale held his hands up in a placating gesture. 'I know it's hard to picture, but leaving at night is the only way to make sure no one gets left behind. We'll have to make sure everyone's passed out.'

'*How?*' I asked, sharing an exasperated look with August. Of course, leaving at night would be preferable. If we left during a hunt, Larch would notice much sooner, and we wouldn't have much of a head start before he sent search parties after us.

'I don't know,' Vale admitted, rubbing the back of his neck. 'I was thinking of drugging the food in the mess hall, but I can't figure out a way to make sure everyone eats it. There's more than one dinner shift, and a lot of the time the guards and Larch don't even eat the food from the mess hall. And then, I'd have to figure out which drug to use.'

'Concentrated ironroot.'

The words slipped off my tongue before I knew I was going to say them. As he'd spoken, I'd pictured Aggie – she'd smoked ironroot for years, had built up something like an immunity so that it took longer for the herb to lull her to sleep, but for most people the effects were nearly instantaneous.

August nodded. 'That would work.'

'But there's still the question of how to get it into anyone's system,' I mused. Vale was right – attempting to put it into the food was too risky.

We tossed ideas back and forth all the way back to the prison, eventually deciding to loop our friends in and see if they could come up with a solution.

By the time we tucked ourselves within Endlock's walls, I was aching for a shower. After passing Larch, who seemed immensely pleased by our disheveled appearances, I was granted a blissfully private shower in the bathrooms. The guards had already confined the other inmates to their cells for the night, and I allowed myself to linger under the hot stream of water.

No matter how vigorously I scrubbed, and regardless of my memory of the pain infliction feature, I couldn't wipe the smile from my face.

Because soon, we would be tasting freedom.

'The ventilation shafts.'

My spoon stopped mid-air, halfway to my mouth with a bit of porridge, and I stared wide-eyed at Jed. 'What?'

'Assuming we could figure out a way to vaporize concentrated ironroot,' Jed said, biting at his thumbnail, 'we should be able to push it through the ventilation system and into every area of the prison.'

August and Yara and I exchanged looks, all of us wearing matching slack-jawed expressions. A bubble of laughter left me.

August let out a low whistle. 'Council above.'

'That could work,' Kit said, scraping the last spoonful of

porridge from her bowl. 'We'd need an ultra-concentrated ironroot tincture. And then I'd need to install a diffuser in the ventilation system – the system should do the rest, and push the vapors into the rooms across the prison.'

'Jed,' I whispered, shaking my head in awe. Just days ago I'd thought the best course of action had been to leave him out of these important conversations, and now . . . I didn't know if we'd have a solution without him.

His cheeks reddened, and he ducked his head.

'Uh, two problems,' Yara said, pointing her spoon at Kit. 'Where are we going to get concentrated ironroot tincture? And how are we going to keep from breathing it in along with every-one else?'

'Well,' Kit started, shooting me a sheepish look. 'Our resident bounty hunter might have to step up again for this one. The Col-lective has access to respirators.'

I blinked. It wasn't like the Collective was dropping bombs or walking through irradiated areas where they'd need to wear something like that.

'Why do they have—' I started, but Kit cut me off.

'We need seven,' she continued. 'And I'd guess your connection should also be able to get us the ironroot tincture, too?'

I grimaced. Gray probably could get us what we needed, but it was a risk.

'Vale can't help?' I asked.

August shook his head. 'He risks enough as it is. If he got caught, we'd be done for.'

I frowned. If Vale were caught, he'd be locked in a cell like the rest of us.

'I'll write to my connection,' I whispered. 'We need to get out. Soon.'

'Get me what I need, Thorne, and then we can choose a day,' Kit promised.

Gorgeous Gray,

You failed to meet my last request, so I'm giving you a final opportunity to redeem yourself.

I need seven respirators.

And ironroot tincture. Of the highly concentrated variety that would send an entire prison into an uninterruptible slumber.

Can you do that for me, Gray?

If you can, I can send you a departure date that's well within the settlement's deadline.

Xoxo,
Raven

Thorne,

You wound me.

I can get you all of the respirators and ironroot tincture in the world, though if I were my mother, I would be questioning why you need seven respirators when you should only need three.

Give me a few days. Stay alive.

– G

'224, come with me.'

I looked up from my workbench, and the project I was working on with Yara, to see the blonde guard, Anya, standing in the doorway, beckoning me.

'Inmate 224 is on duty,' Vale said, brows raised, before I could open my mouth.

'She's being put on kitchen duty today,' Anya responded, stiffly. 'One of the inmates on prep died in this morning's hunt and she's to replace them temporarily. Warden's orders.'

Warden's orders.

The words sent a shiver down my spine. Why would Larch

have specifically asked for me to be put on kitchen duty? He'd seemed frazzled since my last hunt, when the Councilors had walked away unsatisfied, so choosing me for a shitty job could've been a way for him to take out his anger on me.

Still, there was no universe in which I wanted Larch scrutinizing me. The best thing to do was follow his orders without complaint.

My eyes met Vale's and I watched as he clenched his jaw. I could tell he was about to protest, so I shook my head at him, barely discernible. The camera in the workshop was on today, but beyond that, he needed to be more careful around me if we hoped not to arouse suspicion.

Vale must have seen the movement because he closed his eyes and let out a soft breath.

'You heard her, 224,' he said, voice gruff. 'Get moving.'

I trailed behind Anya, through the corridor and up the steps and toward the mess hall. All the while, she didn't say a single word.

Anya shoved through the kitchen doors, pushing me ahead of her.

In one corner, sitting on a stool and not paying attention in the slightest, a guard with a white scraggly beard was engrossed in a novel. We walked past him, and a few inmates scrubbing dishes, to the back of the kitchen.

I looked at each of them, trying to take in as much detail as possible in case it would help me through whatever came next.

Anya threw open another door that led to a chilled room, much like the root cellar attached to the Collective's meeting space at Vern's. There were sacks of grain and baskets of root vegetables. Aside from dry goods, there were a few cooler boxes that held specialty foods and perishables that I imagined were for Larch or some of the higher-ranked guards.

There was, however, an absence of one thing – cameras.

I stiffened.

There was no good reason Larch would have me brought to a room with zero chance of being recorded.

'What's going on?' I asked Anya, waiting for her to give me some direction.

'Wait here,' she responded, not bothering to answer my question. She turned and left, closing the door behind her.

An hour later, when I was sure all the other inmates on kitchen duty had finished their work, the door at my back opened again, and I huffed out an annoyed, 'It's about time.'

'That excited to see me? I didn't expect that from you, Thorne.'

I placed my hands on the counter for support. No, it couldn't be. I turned and saw—

Gray.

I ran to him, wrapping my arms around him and squeezing hard. I was shocked by how emotional I was to see a familiar face.

Gray stood still, unmoving for a moment, then finally returned my embrace.

'I didn't think you were capable of expressing anything but annoyance toward me,' he whispered, amusement lacing his words.

I hadn't, either. And while there was still so much left unsaid between us . . . I was ready to talk about it once I got out of End-lock. We could never go back to what we used to be, but maybe we could move past hating each other.

I heard a voice through the door that led to the kitchen and froze, stepping back. 'Gray, you have to go,' I whispered. 'A guard brought me here to do a task for the Warden. She'll be back any second.'

He tilted his head. 'Anya brought you here to meet me.'

'She what?'

'She's Collective.'

'No,' I said, laughing. 'Anya is not Collective. A few weeks ago, I saw her bash in another inmate's head with her baton.'

Gray didn't try to hide his grimace. 'That's what it takes to be undercover here. You think she could pretend to be on their side without engaging in some kind of violence?'

I frowned.

'And who do you think delivered that note while you were in solitary?' Gray asked.

I shook my head. 'I thought it was too dangerous to reveal Collective assets. Why tell me?'

'Someone had to get you in here to speak with me,' Gray said, a smile pulling his lips to one side. 'And besides, my mom's pulling Anya back into the city. She's done her time at Endlock. She'll be gone in a few days.'

I nodded. If Gray said it was true, then I believed him. We'd had a lot of issues over the years, but trust had never been one of them.

He pulled back farther, holding me at arm's length, and his eyes darkened as they traced my face and the fading bruises there. He raised his hand as if to touch them, then let it fall back to his side.

'What happened to you?' he said, jaw clenched, as if he'd expected me to get through our mission unscathed.

'Which time?' I joked, and then rushed on when he narrowed his eyes. 'It's Endlock, Gray. I'm as good a bounty hunter as it gets, but these guards and inmates are ruthless. I've managed to hold my own.'

He looked away for a moment, a muscle ticking in his jaw. 'I'm sorry this happened to you. That you're in this situation in the first place, and in danger of dying every single day.'

'It's not your fault, Gray. I chose this when Jed was arrested – being a bounty hunter is what got us here, and you warned me against that years ago.'

'None of that matters right now,' he whispered, turning back to me and placing his hands on my shoulders. His eyes were filled with an emotion I couldn't name. 'You need to be careful. You're so close.'

'I will,' I promised, my mind racing. 'But how are you here? You need to leave before the guards see you.'

'Relax.' He shook his head. 'I came to bring you these.'

Gray released me, dug a hand into his pocket, and showed me a few tinted glass bottles.

'Ironroot tincture,' he explained when I raised a brow. 'Concentrated enough to knock out an entire prison. As requested.'

I clapped a hand over my mouth to hold back the giddy smile forming there.

'And respirators.' He pulled a small drawstring bag out of his other pocket. 'Care to explain why you need seven of them, Thorne?'

I looked down at the floor. 'They're my friends, Gray. I can't leave them behind.'

If we all look out for each other, we might have a fighting chance of survival.

Gray's words, from all those years ago, hit me like a punch to the gut. He'd been right from the beginning.

He was silent for so long I thought he wouldn't speak, but when I looked up and met his gaze, he gave me a soft smile. 'This place has changed you.'

'Maybe it has,' I whispered, and, inexplicably, I felt tears pricking at the back of my eyes. I cleared my throat. 'Care to explain to me why you're here in person? Seems like a risk.'

'I had to make sure they got to you.'

My smile flipped into a frown. 'I don't understand. If you could get in here so easily, how haven't you been able to get anyone out?'

'I wouldn't say I had an easy time getting here,' he said. 'The Collective had to make sure the usual guy didn't come into work. Then came the part where we had to forge a convincing employee badge. And then I had to deliver medications to the prison infirmary, and the guards looked through everything I brought in.

Luckily, you're dealing with a pro, and I replaced the labels on the ironroot tincture to make them look like antibiotics.'

'How'd you get the respirators through?'

'Endlock's doctor actually requested a case of them to be brought in from Dividium. Mentioned something about a group of inmates coming down with something highly contagious and wanting protection for her staff.'

I bit my lip. 'We're going to get out.'

'You're going to get out,' he responded, smiling. 'And I'm going to meet you on the other side of the fence – get you to the settlement.'

'What's going on here?'

We both jumped, and I reached my hand out to the nearby counter, searching for a weapon as we looked toward the door. My shoulders slumped in relief when I saw it was Vale.

'Vale,' I breathed out. 'This is a friend of mine from the Lower Sector. He's with the Collective. He delivered the things we need to leave.'

Gray inched toward me as if Vale were a threat.

'It's okay,' I told Gray as I went to Vale. 'He's an ally – he's friends with Kit. He's helping us escape.'

Vale placed a hand on my waist, pulling me in closer, and then flicked his gaze up to meet Gray's. They were caught in some kind of standoff for long enough that I almost spoke, but eventually Gray stuck his hand out, and Vale clasped it in his own and shook.

'Thank you.' Vale nodded at him, clenching Gray's hand tightly, far harder than was necessary for a handshake.

I rolled my eyes.

'No need,' Gray answered, and I saw the tendons in his arm stand out as he squeezed Vale's hand back. He smirked. 'I better go.'

He clasped my shoulder, squeezing for a moment, and then he was gone.

Vale wedged a chair beneath the door handle, sealing the two of us into the back room.

'I had to check on you,' he said softly, running his hand over my cheek and brushing my hair behind my ear. 'When Anya said Larch had requested you to be here, something didn't feel right. I came as soon as the shift ended in the workshop.'

'You got me in the closet one time, and now you think it's your duty to protect me?' I smirked, my sarcasm battling with the fluttering in my stomach.

But Vale didn't laugh.

Instead, he stepped toward me, walking me backward until my back hit the counter, and I had nowhere to go. He ran his tongue over the top of his teeth, and when he spoke, his voice was thick and raspy. 'Duty implies honor, but there's nothing honorable about my intentions.'

I swallowed. 'Which are?'

'To watch you come undone.'

I sucked in a breath, my pulse quickening. 'That seems pretty honorable, compared to last time.'

Vale reached up, toying with the zipper of my jumpsuit. 'Then let me make amends.' He gave me a wicked smile that had my toes curling.

'For?' I tilted my head to the side, ever so slightly.

'Leaving you unsatisfied,' he breathed, pulling my zipper down, keeping his eyes on mine to see if I would object. 'Can I make it up to you?'

It was becoming embarrassingly easy to shove aside my survival instincts where Vale was concerned.

Was I at risk of being thrown into solitary confinement, or worse, if we were caught?

Mm-hmm.

Was I going to stop him?

Definitely not.

'I don't know – *can* you?' I said, biting my lip and letting my eyes flick over him until my meaning sank in.

He growled, finishing with my zipper and pushing my uniform down to my waist, and then his lips were at my ear, brushing against my skin as he spoke in a throaty whisper. 'You're about to find out just how capable I am.'

Once his mouth met mine, I forgot myself entirely, giving in to the feel of his lips, and teeth, and tongue on mine. There was nothing slow or gentle about the way he touched me, and it was exactly what I needed to escape into him.

Vale pulled back, and I gasped at the raw, molten heat in his eyes.

He kissed his way down my neck, lowering the straps of my camisole and pulling the fabric down until my breasts were fully exposed to the air and his attentive fingers. My nipples hardened into sensitive peaks beneath his touch, and I arched into him.

I moved one hand down his chest toward the hardness that strained against the front of his pants and pressed into my stomach through our clothes. The full size of him became apparent as I rubbed against his length through his pants, and I swallowed.

Vale stopped me before I could get any closer, making a sound low in his throat.

'Not this time. This time, it's all about you.' He didn't wait for my response. Instead, his hands trailed down, and he lifted me onto the counter so I was sitting, and he was between my legs.

I gasped as he dipped his fingers into the waistband of my underwear. 'Still think you can't trust me to make amends?' he whispered against my mouth.

'That remains to be seen,' I said stubbornly, through panting breaths.

Vale made a sound low in his throat, giving me no warning before he brushed his fingers over my core.

I moaned, my thighs widening of their own volition, arching into his touch.

This time, he didn't make me ask, and I had to grip the edge of the counter for support as he plunged a finger into my wetness. I cried out, grinding into his finger, forcing him deeper, though I ached for him to stretch me with the length that was still straining against the fabric of his pants.

'Is this what you wanted?' he purred, thrusting his finger in and out of me as I battled to keep my moans in check, pleasure building low in my belly.

'More,' I ground out, still moving against him.

He growled and ripped his finger from me, and I cried out at the loss of him. The sound was cut short when he pulled me off the counter and spun me around so my back was to him.

'What are you—'

'Bend over,' he commanded, interrupting me before I could string together a simple question.

I narrowed my eyes but quickly flattened myself on the counter, my body desperate to regain the pleasure I'd lost. Leaning my bare arms against the cool stone, I bent over until my cheek pressed to the surface.

I was opening my mouth to ask what he was doing when I felt him pushing down my uniform and undergarments until they were wound around my ankles.

'Do you still want me to touch you?' Vale's voice sounded strained, as if he were barely in control.

'Yes,' I breathed, though I felt more vulnerable than ever with my naked ass exposed to the frigid draft coursing through the room while he remained completely clothed.

My nipples were still painfully hard, waiting in agony where they pressed against the cold surface of the counter.

He didn't hesitate this time as he sank his finger back inside me, moving in and out as I tightened around him. His other hand came around to caress my breasts, giving attention to one and then moving to the other.

I arched my spine, pushing back into him as far as my body would allow, my hand slipping down my front until it fell between my legs to caress the bundle of nerves there.

'That's it.' Vale added another finger, stretching me, and I pressed my face into my arm to muffle my cries.

I moved my ass back and forth, making him thrust deeper and faster into me, all the while circling my clit with my fingers and coiling my pleasure tighter.

'Just like that,' Vale murmured, rolling my nipple between his forefinger and thumb as I strained for his fingers to go deeper. 'Fuck my fingers.'

I moaned and bit my arm as his fingers curled lightly, hitting that aching spot deep within me. I had to remove my hand from my sensitive flesh to grip the side of the counter and keep myself balanced and upright. My pleasure built inside me, higher and higher, until it bordered on pain.

He continued working inside me even as he leaned close to whisper in my ear. 'How about now, Little Bird? Have I passed your test?' His free hand reached between my legs to deliver a gentle flick to my clit, and then he rested his fingers there, moving them in a lazy circle. 'Or do you want me to stop?'

My back arched farther, and I shook my head violently.

Vale leaned over me, pressing hot, open-mouthed kisses along the column of my neck as he increased the pressure on my clit, even as his fingers continued to dip in and out of me in a torturous rhythm.

The ache between my legs intensified, throbbing, and Vale curled his fingers—

I cried out as I reached my peak. I fisted my knuckles between my teeth so no one would hear, pushing back into Vale's fingers and touch even as my whole body shook with the waves of my release. When the pleasure eventually abated, I collapsed, my weight supported by the counter and the arm Vale had banded around my waist.

I looked over my shoulder to see Vale removing his fingers from me and inserting them into his mouth, licking them clean, and then running his tongue over his lips as he released a low growl. 'Even better than I dreamed.'

I felt my cheeks flush despite myself. Though I had plenty of experience with men, most of it had come from quick trysts. And there had never been nearly as much talking – nothing like the filthy words Vale had spoken to me.

My breath hitched. 'So, you've dreamed of me, then?'

'Since the first night I saw you,' he confessed, his eyes never leaving mine.

25

THE MORNING BUZZER was still blaring when Yara flopped onto my bed, nearly crushing me beneath my blankets.

'Good morning,' she sang out, snatching my pillow away from my eyes, exposing me to the harsh fluorescent lights and a cloud of expensive, floral perfume.

'You are insufferably cheerful in the mornings,' I groaned, draping an arm over my eyes to block out the light.

'Not just the mornings. I'm *always* insufferably cheerful.'

I sat up, squinting against the glare, suddenly suspicious. 'No. You're always in a good mood. But this is something else entirely. You're practically vibrating.'

'Well, you know I love a good bit of gossip, and . . .' She leaned in until her face was inches from mine. 'Word on the street is you slept with a *guard*.'

My mouth flapped open, and I forced it shut, my teeth clicking together audibly. 'What are you talking about?'

She sat back on her elbows, looking up at the ceiling. 'Let's see – a guard grabbed you from your shift in the workshop yesterday.'

She began ticking off on her fingers. 'Vale looked anxious for the rest of the shift and sprinted out of there as soon as the alarm rang, presumably to check on you. And ever since, the two of you have been glowing so brightly that I miss my designer sunglasses.'

My cheeks blazed, and Yara smiled impossibly wider. I pushed myself up, leaning against the wall with my arms folded across my chest. 'I didn't expect it to happen.'

Yara grinned at my admission. 'Maybe, but the rest of us did.'

'The rest of you?'

'We've been taking bets on when it would happen,' she admitted, then laughed. 'Well, except for Jed. He covers his ears every time we bring it up.'

'For strike's sake,' I groaned, covering my reddening face. The last thing I needed was for Jed to be involved in gossip about my sex life. I looked at Yara again. 'Why are you acting like this is so normal? For me to be doing . . . whatever I'm doing with Vale.'

She shrugged. 'Nothing here's normal. I have to pay off the guards just to get enough privacy to have sex with my girlfriend. My father was horrible, but at least he was rich. Otherwise, Kit and I would never get a moment alone.'

I laughed. 'It *is* hard to find privacy around here.'

'Tell me about it,' she whined, then sobered, watching me intently. 'You like him, then? Vale?'

'I don't know,' I answered honestly. Or as honest as I was willing to be with myself. 'I like being around him. But I don't like getting close to people, especially those I'm not sure I can trust.'

Yara nodded. 'You do have a "fuck off, I'm not here to make friends" kind of energy.'

I rolled my eyes. 'And with Vale,' I continued, my words muffled by the sounds of slamming cell doors and boots slapping against cement as the other inmates made their way to breakfast, 'I know he's keeping things from me.'

Something flashed in Yara's eyes but vanished before I could examine it further. She looked down at her hands, picking at her cuticles and avoiding my gaze. 'He's a good guy. If he is hiding something, he'll tell you when he's ready.'

'Yeah. I'm sure you're right.'

'If he doesn't, I can always poison him,' Yara whispered, trying to hold a straight face.

'I'll keep that in mind.' My lips twitched, and then I grew serious again as I thought over her words. 'That's how you killed your father, isn't it? Poison.'

When Yara didn't immediately answer, I tried to take the words back. 'I'm sorry I asked. It's none of my business, and you don't have to t—'

'Yeah. It was poison,' she blurted, without looking at me.

I blew out a breath. Yara had told me her father had deserved to die, and I believed her. But killing him herself? It had to have taken a toll.

'Why?' I asked, needing confirmation. 'Because he worked at Endlock?'

She shook her head. 'He had put his hands on my mother and me all my life. But one day, he hit my little sister. After that . . . well. I killed him three days later.'

I processed the rest of her words. 'I'm sorry you had to do that,' I eventually managed. I couldn't fathom it. Having to live in fear of the people who raised you. The people who were supposed to love you unconditionally and keep you safe. Maybe that was part of why Endlock didn't seem to faze Yara as much as some of the other inmates – she'd grown up terrified of being in her own home, continually fearing she'd be hurt. At least the hunters were upfront about their intentions.

'Don't be.' She shrugged. 'I wish I could relive it. The fucker deserved worse and I should've killed him long before that. His work at Endlock should've been enough to make me do it.'

'He was your dad,' I whispered. 'I'm sure you hoped he'd change.'

'He was never going to change – the man was a fucking *monster*,' Yara hissed. 'When Pharil Coates promoted him to Chief Financial Officer, Endlock had only been around for five years, and citizens were *terrified* of getting arrested – Dividium had the lowest crime rate in the city's history.'

I nodded, thinking back on my conversation with Vale. 'I remember what it was like then. My parents thought Endlock would get shut down because it seemed to be failing.' There weren't enough inmates to hunt, which meant Endlock wasn't generating enough income. It'd been a time of hope in the Lower Sector.

Yara swallowed, looking down at her hands twisting in her lap. 'It would have if it wasn't for my dad. He came up with a strategy to introduce an artificial food shortage to the Lower Sector and presented the plan to Coates and the Council. Once they saw the financial forecasting numbers and how much his strategy would increase arrests and Endlock's revenue, they had news streams going out to the Lower Sector within the week, spreading lies about crop failures.'

I froze. *Yara's father* had been the one to come up with the strategy.

'I didn't know until I killed him. My mother told me everything once he was dead – everything she'd been too afraid to voice before. I don't know why I'm telling you about this now, but it's been eating at me. I guess I just needed you to know.'

She picked at a cuticle, and as casual as she tried to come across, there was tension in the line of her shoulders and a wrinkle between her brows. When I didn't answer right away, she looked up at me, and she must have read the thoughts I couldn't keep off my face because her mouth dropped open.

'You knew.'

I shook my head. 'I only found out recently, but I didn't know it was your dad who came up with the idea.'

'Vale told you?'

'He did. I guess a reporter dug up the story last year, and Coates got her arrested to cover it up. But—' I frowned. 'Vale didn't seem to know it was your dad who was behind the food shortage.'

'It's not something I talk about,' Yara whispered. 'But you're from the Lower Sector. You were directly impacted by his choices, and it makes me sick. The Lower Sector *needs* to know, Raven.'

How would the Lower Sector respond? Would the truth finally be enough for everyone to work together to fight back?

For the first time, I thought about what it would be like to help take the Council down.

A strange thrill coursed through me.

I reached out, placing my hand over hers. 'Thank you for telling me. When we make it to the North Settlement, we'll talk to the Collective. Find a way to make sure *everyone* knows the truth of what Endlock's done.'

A small, hopeful smile touched Yara's lips.

Even as my mind was full of everything she'd just told me, a bubble of warmth formed in my stomach because I wasn't processing the information alone.

Yara had trusted me enough to tell me what she knew.

Before Endlock, I hadn't known what it was like to have friends, and despite what Aggie had told me, I didn't consider them a weakness. They were the reason I stood a fighting chance of escaping in the first place.

Yara grabbed my hand, yanking me to standing and motioning me to follow her out of the cell.

'Start thinking about what you're going to bring with you when we leave,' she whispered, completely changing the subject and angling her head close so none of the inmates on their way to the mess hall would hear. 'Vale's working on getting Kit swapped into my spot in the workshop so he can send the two of you off to install the diffuser in the ventilation system.'

Smart. It shouldn't raise too many eyebrows for him to send us off under the guise of a maintenance project.

'And what about hacking into the security system?' I asked. 'August said he was trying to find Kit a private space to work.'

Yara cringed. 'We already have a private space; we just couldn't tell you about it until you knew Vale was helping us. She's using Vale's private quarters.'

I stopped short, and an inmate ran into my back. I sheepishly apologized, and he cursed at me as he walked around.

I'd forgotten Vale had mentioned having his own room.

I raced to catch up with Yara. 'That's perfect.'

She smirked. 'Eye on the prize, bounty hunter. Just not the one you're thinking of.'

My cheeks reddened, and I knocked her shoulder with mine. 'I wasn't thinking about that.'

She stared at me until I grinned. 'Fine, I was. But now I'm not. Now I'm one hundred percent focused on the plan like the mature adult I am.'

'I believe you,' Yara said in a sing-song voice. 'But like I said, things are moving quickly now that you found the other section of the tunnel – Vale's going to start gathering supplies and food. I left some more stuff from my mom in your dresser, so pick some sturdy clothing that will fit in a small pack, and he'll smuggle everything into the tunnels before we leave. Choose wisely, though. The Wastes can be scorching during the day and drop below freezing at night.'

I nodded, shivering as we stepped into the mess hall. No matter my situation, even at Endlock, I'd always had a roof over my head. And we were about to spend weeks sleeping outside.

After breakfast, the guards herded us back to our cellblock, and I couldn't help but remember how I'd been willing to leave without these people a few short weeks ago. The Council had wronged them as much as they had my family. They all had people they loved and were willing to risk themselves for, and not just blood relatives. They were willing to risk it all for *each other*, their chosen family, and I wanted to be a part of that. I wanted Jed to have that.

My thoughts scattered when Larch slammed through the barrier door, snarling at us to move faster, to get back into our cells and prepare for the hunt selection. He seemed more irritable than usual, shoving inmates impatiently and snapping at others.

After our last hunt, my rank had increased to a nine. The number glowed proudly from the digital display above my cell. Not as intimidating as August's solid ten, but higher than many of the inmates in the cellblock — and hopefully, that meant that hunters would choose me over Jed.

Kit and Yara were ranked at eight and nine, respectively.

Momo's rank had sat at an eight since I'd been at Endlock. Only the cruelest hunters selected children as their targets.

The guards ushered a group of hunters into the cellblock, and my heart plummeted when I recognized a familiar face — Councilor Elder. She wore a scarlet pantsuit with the sleeves rolled up to reveal a tattoo on her forearm — three interlocking circles inked in black to represent the three sectors. All of the Councilors and their families bore the marking. She walked on a set of heels so thin and sharp that they were practically weapons. The shoes added to her generous height, and she towered over Larch. The outfit was finished off with a crimson ribbon, decorating her neck like blood flowing from a slit throat, and a gold chain weighed down by a single, polished molar.

Arrogance rolled off her in waves, her head swiveling back and forth as she peered through the bars of our cells, her lips twisting in disappointment.

I understood Larch's mood now. He didn't want to look bad in front of the Councilor. Couldn't disappoint her.

Not again.

'That's the one I told you about, Caltriona,' Larch said, shocking me by casually addressing the Councilor by her first name and directing her attention toward my cell. 'The bounty hunter.'

She strode to my cell.

'Nice necklace,' I said dryly.

'Shut your mouth,' Larch growled, his hand going to his baton.

'It's fine, Roth,' Councilor Elder said, placing a hand on his chest. 'We're just having a conversation.'

She turned back to me. 'It was my husband's.' She stroked the tooth lovingly, and I blanched. Normally, citizens only took teeth from those they'd killed in a hunt – wearing the tooth of her husband who'd recently died in a fire . . . it was an interesting choice. 'Raven Thorne, is it?'

'The one and only.'

She nodded. 'Only a formidable opponent could've evaded us like you did during the last hunt. Unsurprising for the daughter of Melody and Keaton Thorne, I suppose.'

Don't talk about them.

I swallowed the words, my teeth clenching from the effort of keeping them inside.

'They raised me well,' I said instead.

Councilor Elder nodded, studying me. 'It was brave of you to take a strike for your brother the night Melody and Keaton were arrested. Not many citizens your age would've done so.'

My eyes widened, but I didn't let my surprise show anywhere else on my face. She knew my parents' names and something I'd done for Jed *seven years ago*. I knew some hunters got off on researching their targets ahead of time, finding out as much as they could about them to make for a more satisfying hunt, but I hadn't expected that from a Councilor.

'You almost turned it around,' Elder continued, shaking her head. 'Becoming a bounty hunter – one of the top bounty hunters in the city, at that. It's an admirable job, especially for someone with a strike record. But it's not surprising that you wound up here in the end. It's why we maintain such a heavy guard presence in the Lower Sector. Criminals raise criminals.'

Or is it because you intentionally starve them?

I clenched my fists at my sides, taking a deep breath. With what I now knew about the artificial food shortages, the biggest criminals of all were those involved in the inner workings of Endlock. But I couldn't reveal what I knew – if she knew *I knew*, she'd have me killed on the spot.

Information gave me more power than anything else could.

And for the second time in just one day, I was able to think of something except making sure Jed survived.

I wanted to play a part in destroying Endlock.

And at that moment, it was like my parents were standing by my side, each of them holding one of my hands, urging me.

Don't let her see your rage.

I wouldn't. Not yet.

'My parents would be proud,' I said instead, feeling the truth of the words deep in my gut.

Elder studied me for a moment, surprise flashing in her eyes and one corner of her lips twitching up to the side. She nodded. 'I suspect you're right. Just as I am proud, as a Councilor, to have a son who has dedicated his life to Endlock's mission. Children tend to follow in their parents' footsteps.'

I took in a sharp breath. 'You have a son who works here?' The question was out before I could stop it. All of the Councilors had children, but I'd imagined them all in the vein of Roald – spoiled and sheltered and content to never leave the Upper Sector except for a hunt.

Elder smiled, seeming pleased that I'd asked. 'I do. He's very dedicated. Even when his father died, he only came home for a few days. Couldn't stand to be away from work.'

She continued speaking, but her voice grew muffled and far away as I zeroed in on five words.

Even when his father died.

My head spun, and suddenly I was back at the Lower Sector jail, delivering Torin to Captain Flint and overhearing the news stream from his tablet.

'*. . . the Council has reported findings that Eris Cybin, known terrorist and leader of the rebel organization called the Collective, is the culprit behind a fire that destroyed a large portion of the city's coming harvest and resulted in the death of several field workers, as well as the death of Silas V. Elder, the husband of Councilor Caltriona Elder.*'

My heart beat like a drum against my chest, and I sifted through memories, faster and faster, until I landed out on the hunting grounds. Seeing the tunnels for the first time. Hearing Vale confess he was going to help us. Hearing Vale explain what he'd been doing in the Lower Sector the night we met.

He killed my father. Eris Cybin.

It couldn't be. I tried to ignore the puzzle pieces fitting themselves together.

Silas V. Elder.

Silas *Valorian* Elder.

Vale was Councilor Elder's son.

Valorian Elder.

And I couldn't breathe, because of course he was. It explained everything. How he'd managed to get dirt on Coates. His authority over the other guards. The way he addressed the Warden. His invitations to Endlock board meetings.

And I was a fool.

Councilor Elder was still talking. 'Nevertheless, I'm here to perform my duty as a citizen and Councilor to the great city of Dividium. We cannot let crime run amuck, lest we repeat the mistakes of our ancestors. Criminals must be extinguished.'

She stared at me for a few moments, pointedly, before I gathered myself enough to respond. 'You're selecting me as your target, then?' I asked, weakly.

'I am.'

'Then I'll see you out there.' I was so numb that the prospect of being hunted couldn't even summon fear.

Councilor Elder frowned, walking away without another word.

I watched, as if from far away, as August was selected, along with a few other prisoners I vaguely recognized, trying to force the unwanted truth of Vale out of my mind so I could focus on surviving.

And suddenly, I knew what Aggie meant when she'd said having friends would make me weak.

26

I MOVED ROBOTICALLY through the prep room, submitting to a pat-down for contraband while trying not to breathe in the scent of Hyde's unwashed body, then listening to the recitation of the rules for what felt like the thousandth time.

August was off to the side, where Dr Row was checking his cast. I cringed. *Don't think of him. Not right now.*

'Hey.'

And there he was.

'Hi,' I said, voice low, eyes flicking to the camera in the corner that was recording. Now wasn't the place to talk, or even reveal what I knew. I had to get through the hunt. Then I could process. Then I could decide how I felt.

Dark circles marred the skin beneath Vale's bloodshot eyes, and his uniform was rumpled as if he'd slept in it. Dirt stained the fabric of his clothes. I realized, for the first time, how much he *looked* like Caltriona, and the thought was like a dagger through my heart. Warm, golden-brown skin. Honeyed eyes. Glossy, black hair and that wide, pearly-white smile.

'Larch tasked a crew of us to go out on the grounds last night,' he explained, misreading my expression as he turned slightly away from me, staring at his tablet and pretending to go through his checklist.

'For what?' I asked stiffly as I knelt and pretended to knot my already-tied boots. Busying my hands to keep myself from slapping him or grabbing him by the collar and forcing him to look me in the eye while he confessed he'd been lying to me this whole time.

'He found out Councilor Elder was coming for a hunt today, and asked us to dig more trenches. He's been fucking up left and right lately and wanted to give her a better shot at a kill. You need to watch out. Some of the trenches closer to the Blood Tree have camouflage covering the openings – I almost fell into one last night. A fall like that could break bones. And with Councilor Elder out there . . .'

'I'm sure she likes to think she's dangerous,' I interrupted, impulsively, watching him closely to gauge his reaction. 'But take away her gun and she'd realize she's just like the rest of us.'

I'd expected him to grimace or look away but he gave me a soft smile. 'That's not quite true, Little Bird. They're nothing like you. You're truly dangerous.'

I looked away, throat tight. 'I'm not.'

'Tell that to my heart.'

He was gone before I could respond, before I could even begin to process his words and everything else that was swirling through my head and my heart.

'Line up!' Vale commanded.

I filed out of the prep room and into my designated stall alongside the other inmates. The claustrophobic metal walls no longer caused panic to simmer within me. They were a sanctuary compared to the hunters that awaited us on the grounds.

This time, when the buzzer sounded, and the walls slid away

to let us out into the dazzling brightness of the mid-morning sun, August allowed me to help him across the field but shrugged me off as soon as we entered the tree line.

'I need to be able to get around on my own,' he explained when I wrinkled my brow in confusion. 'When we get out of here, I have to be strong enough to make the trek to the settlement.'

A new thought struck me like a punch to the gut. Did August know? He'd kept information from me since I'd arrived, slowly feeding me piece by piece as he began to trust me. But he couldn't know that we were working with a Councilor's son, could he?

But he'd known Vale before Endlock.

Had worked with him, when Vale volunteered at his medical center.

I shook my head. Now wasn't the time.

Focus, Raven.

'August, that's ridiculous,' I insisted. 'You're still recovering. And we'll be with you the whole way to the settlement. We can help.'

I tried not to let him see how supporting him the small distance across the field had winded me. I'd lost muscle since entering Endlock – the smaller rations and strenuous workloads, not to mention the stress of being hunted, had taken their toll on my strength.

August bent down and picked up a stick, studying it. He tossed it aside, deeming it unfit for his purposes.

'I don't want to rely on anyone,' he said, selecting another stick. This one was nearly as tall as him, and he wrapped his fingers around it with a nod of approval. 'We don't know what we'll face out there.'

'August—' I started to protest, but he interrupted me, using the stick as an improvised crutch to support his weight.

'Let me do this, Thorne, okay?' he pleaded. The wind kicked

up, sending ripples through his curls and filling the air with the scent of crisp pine needles. 'I'll tell you if I need help.'

Hearing the desperation in his tone, I didn't argue further. The walking stick might have actually offered more support than my shoulder because August kept pace with me easily. And I couldn't fault him. I would've wanted the same independence if I were in his position, though I wasn't sure I could have made it look as effortless as he did.

The next buzzer sounded, signaling the release of the hunters.

'Should we head to the tunnels?' I asked, scanning our surroundings for any sign of the approaching hunters.

'No.' August shook his head, his brow slick with sweat. 'We don't want to draw attention to them. It's too risky when we're this close to leaving.'

'Okay,' I conceded, nodding. He was right, but I also didn't want him to push himself to the point of worsening his injury.

He gritted his teeth. 'I think my best bet is to put as much distance between myself and Endlock as possible and keep aware of my surroundings. Get to the Blood Tree as quickly as I can. You don't have to stay with me, though – you're faster.'

'As if I'd leave you behind,' I said, rolling my eyes. Last month, I might have done it. But even with what I'd just learned . . . I felt betrayed by Vale. Betrayed by August. And yet I still believed that we were on the same side, somehow.

We picked up the pace, August in the lead. I trailed behind, keeping my eyes and ears peeled for any hint of danger.

Just get through today.

I repeated the words to myself. If we could survive this hunt, we'd be on our way to the North Settlement in a few days.

But I couldn't stop thinking about what I knew. That the person I'd been falling for was the son of my *enemy*. Didn't that make him my enemy, too? Wouldn't he have told me the truth if he wasn't?

Ahead of us, the landscape opened into a meadow surrounded by trees. Rays of sunshine filtered through the leaves, casting a golden glow over the multitude of wildflowers and tall grass. The clearing was interrupted by a small bed of moss at its center.

Strangely out of place among the grass.

'Wait,' I cried out, my heart in my throat.

Too late.

August's foot plunged through the moss, and he tumbled into the trench below. The sickening snap of bones and his muffled cry of pain reached me from where I stood rooted to the spot.

I hadn't told him.

Vale's warning about the trenches had entirely slipped my mind – my head had been swirling with other thoughts – and it had taken me a heartbeat too long to recognize the mossy covering. A groan broke me from my wild thoughts, and I rushed to the edge of the pit, heart pounding.

'August?' I whispered, true terror gripping me, the likes of which I hadn't felt since I'd learned of Jed's arrest.

Another groan was my answer. I scrambled to pull the rest of the mossy covering away and peered into the trench, gripping its side and waiting for my eyes to adjust.

It was bad. Really, *really* bad.

August's injured leg was twisted grotesquely, a shard of bone piercing through the skin below his knee.

'It's okay,' I said, swallowing my nausea. 'It's going to be all right. I'll get you out.'

'Raven, I can't stand,' he said, matter-of-fact. A sheen of sweat coated his forehead.

'It's all right, it's okay,' I said again, as if repeating the words would make them true.

My mind raced, rushing to find a solution before a hunter stumbled upon us. Dirt broke off and tumbled into the trench from where I was gripping the edge, and I scrambled back to avoid falling in.

'Listen to me,' August rasped, his breath coming in ragged bursts. 'You need to leave me here.'

'What are you talking about?' I protested, baffled by his words. 'I'm not going to leave you. I'll get you out.'

'Raven, don't be stupid. Listen to me. You need to get Momo out of here. *Promise me.*'

'Stop,' I whispered. 'Everything's going to be fine.'

This time, I didn't even believe my own words.

They sounded shallow and breakable like the lie they were.

But this was August we were talking about.

'Even if you manage to get me out, the force field will be closing in soon and there's no way a hunter wouldn't catch up to me in this state. And if I survive this hunt, I can't make the trip to the settlement like this,' August murmured, defeated but leaving no room for argument.

'You deserve to get out of here alive,' I whispered. He was the person who held us all together. He was the reason we'd made it this far. 'I can't let you die.'

'This isn't about you,' he hissed. 'You don't get to decide what happens here. I'm *never* leaving Endlock, but that doesn't mean I just have to sit here and wait for a hunter to kill me. But I need you to *listen.*'

My mouth snapped shut. Of course he was right. Of course he couldn't make the trip across the Wastes, and me refusing to acknowledge that wasn't helping anything.

'I'm listening,' I whispered, furiously blinking away my tears.

'First, swear to me you'll get Momo out of here,' August insisted, staring into my eyes intently. 'He has to get out. He has to *live*. Protect him like you'd protect Jed.'

'I swear,' I vowed. 'I won't let anything happen to him.'

August closed his eyes, nodding, a small, impossible smile touching his lips. 'Okay. Then I need your help.'

'Anything.'

'Councilor Elder's out on these hunting grounds. Right now. I'm never getting out of this alive, never going to get to see Momo grow up. But I can do something for him. I can *kill* Elder.'

My mouth dropped open. 'August . . .'

'Gus,' he whispered.

I felt my forehead wrinkle. 'What?'

'I think it's about time you call me Gus. All my friends do.'

My throat tightened, and I had to look away for a moment. 'Okay. Gus,' I whispered, nearly choking on the words.

'Good. Now go. You need to hide,' Gus insisted. 'She's good at this, so she'll be nearby. Tracking us. I'm going to call out for her. If she hears me, she'll come.'

'She'll shoot you from above,' I whispered, shaking my head.

'Not if you shove her into the trench, Thorne.'

I paused, picturing it. Gus calling out to her, and Elder rushing to the edge of the pit while I snuck up behind her.

He could do it. He was strong enough to kill her with his bare hands, and it would send a message. It would ripple through Endlock and Dividium and the Lower Sector and they would *know* the Council wasn't as invincible as they'd like us to believe.

'I'm doing this with or without you,' Gus told me. 'Though I'd prefer it to be with you.'

'Okay,' I said, nodding, even as more tears pricked the back of my eyes. I swallowed hard against the lump in my throat. 'Of course I'll help.'

He turned his head, meeting my gaze. Something flickered in his eyes, and he let out a sigh. 'You're a good friend.'

My heart clenched.

'Not as good as you,' I whispered, getting to my feet. 'Once she's dead I'm going to find a way to pull you out of there.' The words felt hollow, even as I tried my best to believe them.

'Okay, Thorne,' Gus whispered, giving me a sad smile.

I bit my lip, turning before he could see the tears collecting in my eyes. I sprinted into the nearby woods, throwing myself against the side of an ancient pine. I shut my eyes as my chest tightened and struggled to keep my breathing even.

In, *two, three, four.*

Out, *two, three, four.*

'Come and get me, Elder!' Gus's shout split the air.

I choked on a sob.

In, *two, three, four.*

Out, *two, three, four.*

'I'm right here!' Gus's voice came again. Louder.

He kept yelling, taunting, a siren call to anyone who might be around. I prayed it was Councilor Elder.

In, *two, three, four.*

Out, *two, three, four.*

Movement, to my left.

I turned, tracking the hunter as they stepped through the trees.

Not just any hunter – Councilor Elder, with her black curls bouncing as she strode through the clearing, rifle raised, sunlight glinting off her pearly teeth. She'd changed out of her glamorous red pantsuit and heels in favor of a black uniform and matching leather boots.

I stepped out of my hiding space and took off at a run back into the clearing.

I would reach him in time. I had to. I panted as I ran – great, gasping breaths. Sticks snapped beneath my pounding feet, but the Councilor was so focused on her quarry that she didn't seem to register my presence.

I was strides away. A few paces and I would knock her down like I had with the last hunter who'd tried to hurt one of my friends.

Her finger tightened on the trigger. I leaped into the air.

A gunshot split the silence as my body collided with hers. The rifle slipped from her grip, and she flew forward, head first, into the trench, landing with a satisfying *thump*.

I tried to stop from falling forward, my arms pinwheeling at my sides to keep me balanced, but it was no use. I careened into the pit, landing hard enough to knock the breath from my lungs. I found myself lying on my back, on something sturdy but pliable, gazing upward at a sliver of blue sky framed by over-hanging leaves.

I groaned, hesitantly moving my arms and then my hands. I concentrated on my body, waiting to feel the sharp pain of a broken bone. Aside from an ache in my ribs, there was nothing.

I turned my head to the side to find a mess of black curls spilled across the dirt beneath my arm. Curls that led to a head that belonged to Councilor Elder.

Her body had broken my fall. And she was either dead or close to it.

I burst into hysterical laughter.

'That was way too close.'

Silence.

'Gus?'

Still no answer.

Terror gripped me, and I rolled onto my stomach, the ache in my ribs blossoming into a widespread throbbing pain in my abdomen. I wrapped an arm around myself, holding my body together, and moved to standing.

My eyes closed instinctively. Perhaps to shield me from what was to come. I took a shaky breath.

'Gus?' My voice was barely a whisper as I peered deeper into the chasm.

Gus stared back at me with unseeing eyes, a pool of blood oozing from the gaping wound in his chest.

So much blood.

I jerked my head away as if refusing to look would make the scene disappear. But my eyes landed back on Councilor Elder. She lay still, her arm twisted at an impossible angle. I was shaking too much to tell whether her chest was heaving with breaths or if she'd joined Gus in the land of the dead.

August.

Dead.

I doubled over, emptying the contents of my stomach onto the ground, retching over and over until my body convulsed with dry heaves.

It's not real. I'll open my eyes, and I'll be on my bed in my cell. It's a nightmare. It's not real.

The world spun behind my eyelids as I counted down from three and then forced my eyes open.

Gus's lifeless, accusing eyes still met mine, his blood seeping into the soil beneath him.

My chest cracked open, spilling my heart onto the ground at my feet. Somewhere, far away, someone was screaming. One long note. A never-ending wail.

There was a thud.

Hands grabbed my shoulders, shaking me, but I didn't care. If it was a hunter, let them kill me. There was no defeating them. No fighting the Warden or the Council. They would always win. They would kill us all eventually.

Arms clamped tightly around me, squeezing to bring me back up from underwater, and as I surfaced, I realized the screams were mine. I shut my mouth, and the world became quiet again.

Too quiet.

Vale held me close. 'Raven, shhh. You're all right. I've got you.' His voice was a desperate whisper, his fingers digging into my back, and when I turned my head, I met eyes that were wide and frantic.

Some strange feeling crept over me at the sight of him, but I couldn't *think*.

'Vale, Gus, he – he's . . .' My voice cracked, my shaking knees threatening to send me sprawling onto the ground. My stomach churned, though there was nothing left to expel. 'He's dead,' I whispered.

'I know.' Vale's voice cracked, too, and utter devastation flashed in his eyes.

'It's my fault.' I couldn't stop shaking. My legs finally gave out, and I sank to the ground. Vale dropped down beside me, pulling me into his lap and rocking us back and forth.

'It's not your fault,' he insisted. He looked around the trench, and hatred filled his eyes. I wouldn't blame him if he hated me. *I* hated me. But instead, he pulled me closer, nestling me against him. He breathed into my hair and rubbed soothing circles along my back. 'You're okay. Everything is okay.'

'No, it's not,' I said into his neck. 'Just leave me here, Vale. We can't do this without him. And even if we could, I wouldn't want to. Not after what I've done.'

Vale leaned back, cradling my face in his hands and forcing me to meet his gaze. 'This didn't happen because of anything you've done.'

I opened my mouth to argue, but a twig snapped in the distance and Vale slid me off his lap. 'You need to get down. Someone must have heard the shots.'

I sat frozen, staring at him until he crouched down, tilting my chin up with his fingers and leaning in until his face was inches from mine. 'I can't lose you, too,' he whispered. 'And neither can Jed. You have to survive for him. *For me.* I'm begging you. Get down on the ground and play dead, and I promise it will be okay.'

It *wouldn't* be okay, but the mention of Jed's name snapped something within me. I had made a promise to Gus. To protect Momo like I'd protect Jed. I wouldn't fail him again. The pain and horror were still there, but I shoved them to the back of my mind. I needed to make it through the hunt before I could fall apart. The hunters' shouts were drawing nearer, closing in on us.

I lay down next to Gus, a mixture of warm blood and gritty earth meeting my skin as I pressed my cheek into the ground, staring into Gus's vacant eyes. A single tear slid down my face, soaking into the soil.

Static filled my ears, and then Vale was speaking into his radio. 'Councilor Elder needs help. Send a unit of guards, and bring a spinal board.'

'What happened?' a voice called down to us in the trench.

I squeezed my eyes shut.

Vale ignored the affirmative reply from his radio, instead calling out to the voice above. 'Looks like 224 fell into the trench, and 412 came to help her. The Councilor must have gotten into an altercation with him – she shot him, but he pulled her into the trench with him as he went down. The inmates are dead. The Councilor's alive but badly injured.'

I bit my lip to keep from sobbing. *She was alive.* Why hadn't I killed her before Vale showed up?

'Shit,' the voice replied. 'Let's get her out of there.'

More guards arrived and jumped into the trench, and there were grunts and groans and the sound of Councilor Elder's body sliding onto the spinal board, and then being lifted out of the pit.

Vale heaved Gus's body up and handed him to a waiting guard.

'Give that one to me,' one of the guards said above. 'The crematorium's back up and running. I'll take her there, and you can help the Councilor.'

'No,' Vale said, too quickly. 'No, I've got her. You help the others with Councilor Elder. Get her back to the infirmary. I've called ahead to Endlock, and Dr Row is ready to receive her.'

There was a pause. 'But don't you want to—'

'I said *go*,' Vale snapped, and I heard the guards gathering

Councilor Elder, several of them clamoring to grab the handles of the spinal board, as if she would reward them handsomely for carrying her to safety.

A few stragglers grunted, and I pictured them hefting Gus's limp body.

Vale scooped me up in his arms once the others started to retreat. I kept my eyes shut. My breathing was shallow as he set me on the lip of the trench and then hauled himself out before gathering me into his arms again.

I wondered which guards were carrying Gus and what would become of him. Would they burn him to ash and scatter his remains to the wind? Or simply bury him on the hunting grounds, where his soul couldn't possibly find rest?

Vale carried me gently, not so much as jostling me in his arms.

'It's not your fault,' he said softly, his lips brushing the shell of my ear.

He repeated the words endlessly, grief coating his voice until it was rough enough to scratch. I wasn't sure if the reassurance was meant for me or himself.

27

BY THE TIME I reached the infirmary, I had remembered myself—remembered who Vale was.

His mother had killed Gus.

'You're the Councilor's son,' I whispered, once Vale had laid me on a bed in the infirmary.

His eyes widened, and he looked away for a moment. I wondered if he'd deny it, hoped he'd inexplicably prove me wrong. But, of course, that's not what happened.

'I am,' he breathed, running a hand through his hair. 'But it doesn't change anything, Little Bird.'

'It changes *everything*,' I cried, my hands fisting in the sheets on the bed. 'You lied to me.'

I felt like I was drowning, the air too thick to breathe. It filled my lungs, choking me with grief and betrayal.

Or perhaps I was dreaming.

Anything but living in reality.

Vale's mother stood for everything wrong with Dividium — everything my parents had fought against.

And Councilor Elder had murdered Gus.

I swallowed. 'Who else knows about this?'

His silence was all the confirmation I needed.

All of them, then. Yara. Kit. Even Momo.

My heart felt like it was being ripped apart by the betrayal.

'Your mother killed Gus,' I ground out, the words tearing at my throat. 'How am I supposed to trust you? Is *anything* you've told me true? What's the real reason you're here?'

I held my breath, willing myself to listen to his explanation, hoping his words could offer some sort of redemption. Maybe all wasn't as it seemed.

'Everything I've told you is true,' Vale insisted, reaching for me. I turned away, wincing as the sudden movement sent a spike of pain through my head. 'I took this position as a way to help people without joining the Collective, just like my father wanted. But . . . it didn't hurt that my mother wanted me here, too.'

I turned back to him, unspeaking.

'She's grown paranoid. She thinks Coates might be trying to shut her and the Council out of Endlock's profits. I'm supposed to listen and report back to her.'

Councilor Elder's communications. The ones the Collective had wanted me to intercept before Jed was arrested. Now I knew they were letters she'd written to Vale.

'So you've betrayed me and your father's beliefs?'

He cringed. 'No, Raven, no. Of course not. I only give her the barest pieces of information to keep her from becoming suspicious of *me*. Only enough that she continues to believe that I'm supportive of the Council.'

I refused to look at him. I didn't want to believe him. Hated that I did.

'I'm not like her,' he whispered, his voice catching. 'My mother's a Councilor, but my father was a rebel. Why are you more inclined to believe that I'm like her rather than him?'

'Then why did you lie?' I hissed, fighting back tears.

'I wish I hadn't. But I was scared, Raven. I thought you'd hate me. That you'd never trust me, never work with me to get our friends out of here. It seemed too risky to tell you before we escaped. I swear I was going to.'

And now I didn't know if I'd ever be able to trust him again.

'I need time,' I told him, shutting my eyes. I didn't open them again until I heard his booted steps shuffle across the room and out the door.

Minutes later, Dr Row entered the infirmary and was surprised to discover I wasn't dead but had miraculously survived my treacherous fall into the trench.

Lucky me.

Dr Row diagnosed me with a concussion based on my feigned unconsciousness on arrival and my lack of responsiveness to her examination.

Truthfully, I was too numb to answer her questions or follow the path of her finger with my eyes. Hyde knocked on the door, interrupting us as he escorted an inmate who was shivering and coughing and scratching at their arms into the room.

Dr Row sent me on my way, mentioning something about a bacterial infection going around the prison that she didn't want me to catch.

The guards deposited me in my cell after I begged them to let me skip dinner. The thought of eating and facing the others, of seeing a red X next to the number 412 on the live screen, made me feel nauseous all over again.

I sat on my cot, looking at my hands resting on my thighs, my fingernails encrusted with dirt from gripping the edge of the trench, some of them cracked from the force I'd used.

The alarm must have signaled for the others to return to the cellblock because I looked up to see Yara, Kit, Momo, and Jed waiting at the entrance to my cell.

Yara entered first, sitting on my bed. Jed came to sit on my other side, and Kit and Momo remained by the entrance, staring at me warily.

It was a long while before I could muster the strength to speak.

I looked down at my hands, inhaling deeply. The scent of iron and rust filled my nose, and I bit back a sob. Was that Gus's blood staining my cheek? I had the sudden urge to peel the skin from my bones.

'Is it true?'

Kit was the one to break the silence.

I nodded, squeezing my eyes shut against the tears that were welling up.

'How?' Yara whispered.

My hands formed fists, my fingernails digging sharply into my palms until the sting of it prompted me to speak.

'Larch took some heat after Au— *Gus* and me embarrassed Councilor Elder and Councilor Baskan when they visited,' I began, my voice so low that Kit and Momo moved closer to hear. 'He had the guards dig more trenches last night and camouflage them, hoping it'd make hunting us easier.'

Yara nodded, encouraging me to continue.

'Vale warned me this morning before the hunt to watch for the trenches, but Gus wasn't there to hear him because he was getting his ankle wrapped.'

The others remained silent, staring at me intently.

'I forgot to tell him,' I said, voice catching. Jed placed a hand on my shoulder, and I cleared my throat, fighting against the tears that pricked the back of my eyes. 'I'd just found out that V—' I stopped, turning and looking at Jed. He stared back, unflinching, waiting to take on *my* pain if I'd only let him.

I *had* to let him.

'I'd just found out that Vale is Councilor Elder's son. I wasn't in my right mind, and I completely forgot about Vale's warning. The hunters had just been released onto the grounds. Gus was walking ahead of me and fell into one of the trenches.'

Jed's eyes widened at the revelation, but he didn't say anything.

Yara leaned closer to me, slipping her hand into mine.

I continued, my voice a whisper. 'When he fell, it broke his leg again. Badly. I said I wanted to help get him out, but he wouldn't—'

My voice cracked, and I broke off, clearing my throat. Momo's eyes filled with tears, and I had to look away.

'He knew he was going to die. He wanted to try and kill Councilor Elder. He asked me to help him and then made me promise to get Momo out of here alive.'

Momo ran from my cell, and Kit stood frozen for a moment before calling out and rushing after him.

But the words were coming fast now; I couldn't make them stop.

'Gus made a plan to call out to Councilor Elder. I was supposed to hide until she got there and then sneak up and tackle her into the pit so he could kill her. But I was too late. I tackled her as she fired her weapon. But she . . . she . . .'

The words wouldn't come out. I couldn't say it.

If I said it, it would be *real*.

'Say it,' Yara whispered, voice rough as sandpaper. 'Please.'

I closed my eyes. 'She shot him. And then he was gone.'

The words should have tasted bitter. They should have grated along my tongue, clawing at my mouth until they were free and I was a bleeding mess, the sound of them wreaking as much havoc on my ears as the truth was wreaking on my soul.

Instead, they spilled free like any other words, settling into the air with finality.

Stop it. You don't deserve to cry. You did this. You forgot to tell him.

'I can't believe he's dead.' Yara got to her feet and paced the cell. 'He survived this place for years. No one's as good as him.'

'I know.' My vision blurred with tears, and my eyes fixed on my hands once more, now twisting in my lap.

'I have to—' Yara let out a choked sob and spun, racing for the cell door. 'I have to go.'

Jed lingered until lights out, holding my hand in silence until the guards forced him back to his cell. Soon after, I watched as they ushered a newly promoted inmate into Gus's cell.

Like he'd never been there at all.

I lay awake long after the cells were sealed and the lights in the cellblock had been switched off, listening to Momo's muffled sobs a few cells down.

Listening to the silence in the cell next to mine, where Gus should have been snoring.

It's your fault.

It's your fault.

It's your fault.

The words flitted through my head over and over. I couldn't escape them as they mingled with the haunting image of Gus's unseeing eyes, searing every detail into my memory.

The following morning in the mess hall, I had no appetite. I sat as far from Yara, Kit, and Momo as I could at our assigned table, angled away from them. They all bore the signs of grief – bloodshot eyes lined with deep circles. Shaky hands that could barely grip a utensil long enough to scoop up a mouthful of porridge.

I couldn't watch, knowing what I'd done. Knowing that this was what it felt like to get close to someone and lose them. That I could lose *all of them*.

Jed sat beside me and took my hand under the table, giving it a light squeeze. He didn't speak. He knew me well enough to know I didn't want to talk and that his presence was enough.

I glanced across the room and saw Vale leaning against the wall, purple shadows lining his red-rimmed eyes, like the rest of us.

The other guards probably thought he'd been up late gambling and drinking, but I knew better.

28

VALE TRIED TO catch my eye, but I avoided him during my shifts in the workshop and averted my gaze when I passed him in the corridor.

I couldn't even face the swirling mass of grief that had taken up residence in my bones, let alone try to work out how I felt about Vale's lie.

Any discussion of escape plans stopped.

As it was, it was hard enough to get out of bed and go through the motions each day.

After Councilor Elder's near-death experience, Pharil Coates called an emergency meeting of the board to figure out a way to spin the accident that wouldn't incite public backlash.

Councilor Elder didn't remember the fall or the moments leading up to it but didn't want the incident to keep Endlock from raking in credits. That much became apparent once Coates publicized a story explaining that Gus had gotten into a fight with the Councilor and yanked her into the trench with him just as she pulled the trigger on her gun.

There was no mention of me.

Larch looked like he was on the verge of a breakdown, stalking around Endlock and hollering at anyone who so much as looked at him. His uniform was rumpled, his minimal hair flat with grease, and stains marred the fabric of his shirt beneath his armpits.

I overheard Yara saying the board was looking to remove Larch from Endlock, and they were only keeping him on until they could find a suitable replacement – something that would have made me smile before but barely broke through my consciousness now.

But Councilor Elder's brush with death drew even more people to Endlock to partake in the hunts. The live screen in the mess hall showed that the daily hunts were full, and after Elder accepted a live interview, streaming the story to every tablet and screen in Dividium, I overheard Larch saying he had to turn dozens of guests away each day.

The hunters flocked to Endlock like vultures, eager to pick at the meat and bones of the disaster.

In the end, the event made Councilor Elder look *good*. She was the one who had finally taken Gus out. The story rallied Endlock's most loyal supporters. The company's financial forecast had improved, which meant that Elder's own stake in the company had to be up, too. She was profiting from Gus's death.

Two days after his death, the rotation had moved back to our cellblock, and I'd lifted my head only long enough to confirm that the hunters hadn't chosen Jed or Momo or any of my friends as targets.

When a new group of hunters came through our cellblock a couple of days later, I hardly noticed.

I sat on my cot, slumped forward with my elbows resting on my knees and my face buried in my hands.

'I'll take number 203.'

I stood, rushing over to look into the corridor and wrapping my hands tightly around the bars of my cell, my heart in my throat.

Hyde was unlocking Jed from his cell and corralling him down the hall with the rest of the targets.

'Hey!' I slammed my palm against the bars, the reverberation coursing up my arm. 'My rank's higher than his. Don't you want more of a challenge?'

Hyde chuckled, peering down from where he towered above me. 'Shut up before I make you. Selection's over.'

Jed looked back over his shoulder, catching my eye. *It's okay*, he mouthed.

But it wasn't okay. I'd been so wrapped up in my grief and guilt that I'd failed to hear what was unfolding during the selection process until it was too late.

I stared down the corridor long after Jed had been ushered out of the cellblock, hoping he'd return to me if I just kept watching.

But life at Endlock didn't stop on account of my worry.

During my shift in the workshop, images of Jed out on the hunting grounds flashed through my mind – Jed running and hiding. Jed screaming, and dying.

I swung my hammer, intending to hit a nail, but instead I brought the tool down directly on my thumb.

I yelped.

This was what our lives would be if we didn't escape. An endless cycle of being chosen for hunts until one of us failed to return. Until *all* of us did.

I'd foolishly made friends and allowed myself to open up. Allowed myself to care for others. And I couldn't wait around and watch the rest of them die.

I wouldn't. I'd sworn to Gus that I'd get Momo out of Endlock, and I intended to keep that promise.

Yara cast a worried look in my direction before returning to her work.

We hadn't spoken since the day Gus died.

I hadn't seen her talk to Vale, either. Instead, she formed a close-knit trio with Kit and Momo, as Jed remained glued to my side.

The radio on Vale's desk crackled to life, nearly making me jump out of my skin. At first, there was static, and then Hyde's tinny voice came through.

'You should be jealous you're not out here with me on the grounds. I might have witnessed the most entertaining kill of the year.'

There was a prolonged pause before Vale finally picked up the radio and pressed the button on the side. 'What do you want, Hyde?' A frown turned his lips down at the corners.

More static. 'What's gotten into you?' Hyde retorted. 'Don't answer that. It doesn't matter – this will give you a laugh. I watched some kid fall out of a tree and snap his spine. He saw the hunter coming for him, but he couldn't move to get away. Not so much as a finger. All he could do was cry.'

I shot to my feet, the stool screeching against the floor as I pushed away from my workbench.

Vale pinched the bridge of his nose, closing his eyes for a long moment.

More static. 'Vale? You there?'

Vale blew out a breath. 'That's horrifying.'

'Oh, it was.' Hyde sighed dreamily, and bile climbed up my throat. He sounded as if he were salivating at the memory.

'Who was it?' I called across the room, my voice unsteady. 'Which inmate?'

The other inmates stared in disbelief, their tools held in various positions of use, stunned that I dared to speak to a guard without being addressed first.

Vale's head snapped up. For a split second, I saw something like relief in his eyes. But then, seeming to remember himself and noting all of the witnesses around us, his eyes narrowed.

He held my gaze, biting his lip for a moment. But then he shook his head, standing. 'Shut your mouth and sit down, 224. Speak to me like that again and you'll regret it. Do you understand?'

I gripped my uniform to keep my hands from shaking as I nodded and sat back down.

The buzzer rang out, signaling the end of the hunt.

I leaned heavily against the workbench, my breath coming in ragged gasps.

I couldn't lose anyone else. Not Jed. I wouldn't survive it.

A hand touched my shoulder, and I turned.

'It's okay,' Yara said, wrapping her arm around me. 'It's not him.'

'How do you know?' My voice broke, tears threatening to spill over as I leaned into her, letting her support my weight.

Her gaze was unwavering. 'Because you would feel it. He's your brother, and you would know.'

'Hey.'

I whipped my head around to the entrance of my cell. I'd been engrossed in counting the cracks in the wall to keep from driving myself mad thinking about Jed – waiting for him to return.

I hadn't heard Yara's approach.

'How are you doing?' she asked, stepping tentatively into my cell.

'Every minute he's not back in his cell, I lose a little more hope.'

'He's fine, Raven,' she said, resting on the mattress beside me. 'There was only one kill. I heard the guards talking.'

'It could still be him.'

'It's not.' Yara bit her lip. She looked at me and then away.

I took a deep breath. 'I'm sorry.'

'What?'

'For shutting you out,' I clarified. 'I just felt so betrayed, knowing that you all knew about Vale and didn't tell me. And Gus's death was too much. I thought if I pushed you all away—' My voice cracked, and I dropped my gaze.

'Let me guess,' Yara cut in. 'You thought if you pushed us away now, you wouldn't have to feel this pain again if something happened to us later on.'

I turned back to her, wide-eyed.

'I guessed as much, and then Jed confirmed it,' she explained.

'I didn't even say anything to him.'

'Please. You two practically read each other's minds. You think he couldn't tell what was going on with you?'

My lips twisted to one side. I'd always felt like I could read Jed's mind – every expression and move and inflection of tone. Of course he could read mine, too.

'There's nothing to forgive,' Yara whispered. 'We were never upset at you – we felt guilty for lying. And we've all been in too much pain to address it.'

'What if we can't trust him?' I whispered. Tears welled in my eyes, overflowing as I looked at her.

Yara placed her hands on my shoulders, meeting my eyes as tears continued to stream down my cheeks. 'Of course we can trust him. Do you think Gus would've risked Momo's life on blind hope alone?'

I looked away.

No. Gus would never have put Momo's life in danger, and now I wouldn't either. I was done being selfish and wallowing in feelings of betrayal.

'We can't let his death be for nothing,' Yara whispered when I didn't answer. 'Once we know Jed's safe, we *have* to get out of here.'

I shook my head, feeling the heavy weight of helplessness. 'I know, and we will. I won't break my promise to him. It's just that Gus being a doctor was a huge advantage for us and our chances of the North Settlement leaders letting us all in. What if they won't take us all without him?'

'We'll have to find another way in,' Yara declared, as if it were the simplest thing in the world. 'Make them an offer they can't refuse.'

I was trailing Yara to dinner when Vale rounded a corner and locked eyes with me. '224. Come with me. I need an extra set of hands in the workshop.'

I froze.

'Should I come too?' Yara asked.

'No. I only need one of you.'

Only me.

There could only be one reason Vale would risk pulling me aside. I swallowed against a lump in my throat, my pulse racing.

I caught Perri eyeing the two of us as I stepped numbly away from Yara and followed Vale down the hall.

He was silent, his eyes remaining straight ahead as we reached the steps that led to the basement.

My breath started to come in short spurts, and I gripped the railing to keep myself from falling. If I stayed where I was, I could pretend that Jed was okay — that Vale wasn't bringing me to see his lifeless body. But if I walked any farther, if I took another step closer to the infirmary, I'd have to come to terms with the truth.

I didn't think I could face it.

'Raven?' Vale turned to look at me, his face tight with worry. He looked around before placing a hand low on my back to steady me. 'What's wrong?'

'He's dead, isn't he?' I choked out, trembling.

Vale's brow wrinkled, but then his eyes widened in understanding. 'No. Council above, no, he's alive,' he whispered, moving his hands to my shoulders.

'He's alive,' I breathed, letting out a hysterical trill of laughter. 'He's alive.'

I closed my eyes, taking deep breaths to steady myself. But then I blinked. 'If he's alive, where are we going?'

'To the infirmary. He sprained his wrist. Dr Row stepped out for a meeting with Larch about a sickness that's circulating, and I double-checked that the camera in the infirmary is off, so you can visit Jed.'

I nodded, regaining my composure. I could deal with a sprain. A sprain wouldn't keep Jed from making the journey to the North Settlement – the journey that we *would* figure out how to make.

Vale reached out as if to take my hand, but I pushed past him, running down the stairs and through the basement corridor.

'Jed!' I cried out as soon as I opened the door to the infirmary. I rushed for him, throwing my arms around his neck. 'I was so worried.'

'I knew you would be. But I'm okay. I made it.' He hugged me back fiercely, careful of his wrapped wrist.

'What happened?' I asked, reluctantly letting him go and scanning him for any other injury.

'Had a hunter on my tail,' Jed explained, grimacing. 'I used the first set of tunnels Vale and Gus showed us, but I fell off the ladder on my way down. Runs in the family, I guess.'

I rolled my eyes, finally able to breathe again now that Jed was in front of me, well enough to make a joke.

Jed sobered. 'If I'd known being in danger would be the thing to wake you up, I'd have pissed Larch off days ago.'

'That's not funny,' I said, looking away.

'Neither is dying before we can get out of here,' Jed whispered.

I nodded, looking at my feet. 'You're right. Gus isn't here to help us get into the settlement.' My throat tightened painfully, and I swallowed against the lump that had appeared there. 'But he would want us to keep trying. We have to get ourselves in. I promised him I would protect Momo, and I need you to help me.'

Jed placed his good hand on my shoulder. 'I will. What do we have to do next to get ready to leave?'

'Kit is being reassigned to the workshop tomorrow. I told them I needed a replacement for Gus.' Vale's voice cracked at the end, and he looked away, clearing his throat. 'If you're up for it, Raven, I'll sneak you and Kit into my room during your shift in the workshop so Kit can disable the wristband tracking – she said something about reverse engineering them, too, so if any of the guards aren't affected by the ironroot, they won't be able to shoot at any of you.'

Yara's words flowed through my mind. If Gus had trusted Vale to help us, then I could, too. I could work with him if it meant getting out of Endlock.

'Okay,' I said. 'I'll be there.'

A label on one of the medication bottles on the counter caught my eye, and I crossed the room, picking it up and turning it over in my hand.

Antibiotics.

Aggie had told me that one of the things that separated the North Settlement from Dividium was its lack of technology and medical advancements.

People died of conditions they never would've succumbed to if they'd resided within the city and could have afforded medical care – conditions many Lower Sector citizens also didn't survive due to the treatments being too expensive.

'I don't need those,' Jed called out to me. 'Nothing broke my skin. Dr Row said I'd be fine.'

'They're not for you,' I murmured, turning on my heel, intentionally looking Vale in the eye for the first time in days.

He met my stare, arching a brow, but then understanding filled his molten eyes. 'You want to bring them to the North Settlement.'

Jed nodded, catching on. 'Because Gus's not with us anymore. We have to find another way to convince them to let us all in.'

I hummed. 'Will it be enough?'

Vale rubbed the back of his neck. 'If we bring a pretty good stockpile. Medication, supplies, and medical textbooks.'

'I'm guessing Endlock has some kind of backstock?' Jed asked, the paper on the examination table crinkling as he shifted.

Vale nodded thoughtfully. 'Dr Row does keep a significant inventory. She likes to stay prepared.'

I frowned. 'Will anyone notice if you take them, Vale?'

Vale grimaced. 'Dr Row would be suspicious of me coming and going. I could reassign you to the medical stockroom if you're up for it, Jed.'

I had to bite my tongue to keep from arguing as Jed nodded. He was more than capable of the job. And it was his decision.

'How long do we have until the new features are live on the wristbands during the hunts?' I asked. Jed was right. Seeing him alive *had* woken me back up. And we had no more time to waste.

Vale frowned. 'A little more than a week, I'd guess. If we're lucky.'

'Let's give ourselves five days, then, to be safe,' I said, my gaze hovering between Jed and Vale.

'Five days,' Vale confirmed.

'We'll trust you,' Jed murmured, looking at Vale. 'But if you lie to my sister again, you'll find out there's more than one Thorne sibling that should scare you.'

My eyes widened, and I bit my lip to keep from smiling. Vale, on the other hand, was deadly serious as he met Jed's eyes and inclined his head. 'You have my word.'

The doorknob rattled, and we fell silent as Dr Row entered the room, her eyes flitting between us.

'You two wait in the hall while I finish up with my patient,' she told Vale and me. 'Then Vale can escort Jed back to his cell.'

Jed nodded at me, and I followed Vale into the corridor.

'And you still want me to go with you?' he asked quietly once the door had shut behind us, his warm eyes pinned on mine, full of an emotion I couldn't read.

'I need time, Vale,' I whispered. 'To figure out how I feel. But I don't need time to know that if Gus trusted you to help us, not to betray us, then I can trust you too.'

Vale gave me a sad smile and leaned against the wall. 'Take all the time you need, Little Bird.'

29

Gray,

We've done it. We've found a way to leave, at last. Add that to my tally of redeemable qualities, will you? Though I'm loath to admit it, I've already added resourcefulness to yours.

We'll escape in five days, on the night of the full moon. We'll head north and plan to meet you at sunrise at the top of the last mountain before the Wastes.

Don't be late.

Xoxo,
Raven

'Yara would be mortified,' Kit mused, spinning in a circle as she took in Vale's room.

I nodded in agreement. 'She'd take the lack of decor as a personal attack.'

Vale's bed was meticulously made, with a navy blue duvet and a single pillow. A side table held a lamp and a dog-eared book, and a small dresser occupied the room's far corner, next to the door that led to an attached bathroom. The only other pieces of furniture were a wooden desk and a chair. Mort's tablet sat on the desk next to a notebook and pencil.

'I have decor,' Vale huffed out.

I arched a brow, and he pointed to the book on his nightstand.

Kit shut her eyes, blowing out a long breath. 'There is *no world* where that is considered a decoration, Vale.'

I hid my laughter behind my hand, plopping down on Vale's bed, effectively wrinkling his perfectly smoothed duvet.

'All right, you two, this isn't a fair fight,' Vale complained. 'I need to get back to the workshop – one of the inmates was coughing and acting off, and I need to get them to Dr Row in case they have that bacterial infection that's going around. I'll be back in an hour.'

Kit pulled out the chair and sat at the desk. 'I'll only need thirty minutes.'

Vale rolled his eyes. 'I'm sure you can find a way to entertain yourselves for the rest of the time. Just stay quiet.'

He slipped out the door, shutting it carefully behind him. I stretched my arm out, turning the lock on the doorknob.

'Need anything?' I asked Kit. I was there as the muscle in case someone who wasn't Vale tried to come into the room.

Kit was already tapping away at the tablet. 'Nope. I'm in. Disabling the tracking will be the easy part.'

'Right. The easy part.'

'Reverse engineering the wristbands will take longer. But for both pieces, I'm essentially setting a timer that ends the night we leave. The tracking will stop working then, and the guards won't be able to shoot at us.'

'Have I told you how brilliant you are?'

'No.'

I laughed. 'Right. I'll have to say it more often.'

She went back to tapping.

'And there's nothing I can help with?'

She stopped but didn't turn to face me. 'Raven?'

'Yes?' I leaned forward.

'You can stop talking.'

I bit my lip to keep from laughing. 'Noted.' I flopped back on the bed.

We were really doing this.

I tried to imagine Larch's face if he even lasted long enough as Warden to be blamed for our escape. I hoped he would. I hoped it was the thing that would push him over the edge.

I hoped we were the thing that would give the other inmates hope. And everyone in the Lower Sector. They had to know that Endlock was survivable. That the Council and Pharil Coates weren't infallible.

I stared at the ceiling, letting the minutes tick by with each tap of Kit's fingers on the tablet.

'Gus told me about Vale as soon as we agreed to work together to escape.'

I sat bolt upright, blood rushing to my head from the sudden movement. I'd been so lost in thought I hadn't even noticed when Kit had stopped tapping the tablet, but now it was sitting at the back of the desk, screen black, and Kit had turned the chair around to face me. She watched me, waiting for my reaction.

I frowned. 'Why are you telling me this?'

'Because when Gus told me . . . I completely backed out of our escape plans.'

'When was this?'

Kit nodded. 'It was months ago. Before Yara got here. Gus was insistent on getting Momo out, and I wanted to help, but I quit on them when I found out about Vale. My mother is dead because of the Council – she found out the food shortages in the Lower Sector were a lie and tried to organize a protest. They sent her to Endlock before she could. She was the only family I had left. When I found out who Vale was, I couldn't fathom working with him.'

'I'm sorry,' I whispered, somehow still able to feel shocked at how every one of us had experienced a tragedy at the hands of the Council.

'If I'd been able to think about it rationally, we probably would've escaped by now. Long before Yara or you ever got here.'

And I'd be nowhere without them. Jed and I would've died at Endlock.

'What changed your mind about Vale?' I whispered.

'Seeing Gus and Momo trust him, for one. He saved them over and over during hunts – saved me, too, when he could. Then Yara got here, and our relationship grew so quickly. Everything's intensified in here. But loving her . . . I couldn't let her die in here. And despite my distrust, Vale has never done anything other than help us.'

'It would take anyone time to adjust after learning that. You didn't do anything wrong.'

'I know I didn't,' Kit said, looking intently into my eyes. 'But you have to see why Gus asked Vale not to tell you. Every moment in here is a moment closer to death, and after what happened with me . . . how could he let Vale tell you who he was and risk another setback?'

'I . . .' I didn't have an answer.

'Think about all the times you kept things from Jed, even in here, because you thought it was what was best to keep him safe.'

I cringed.

Of course, she was right. Of course, I understood why they didn't tell me, but that didn't change the fact that it hurt. It hurt that I'd been falling for someone without ever really knowing them.

Although, maybe I *did* know Vale. I knew his history. I knew his father was a rebel. And I knew that he believed in what was right.

I knew that from the moment I'd met him I hadn't been able to get him out of my head. Even now. Even with everything that had happened, I still wanted him.

'Isn't it possible for me to understand why Vale didn't tell me while still feeling hurt by it?'

'Of course it is. But is him not telling you really so unforgivable? Or is it more of a self-inflicted punishment because you blame yourself for what happened to Gus and don't think you deserve to have anything good?'

My mouth dropped open. I hadn't been consciously aware of what I'd been doing, but Kit was right. The idea of doing anything that would bring me happiness had kernels of guilt blooming deep in my stomach.

'How did you know that?' I asked her.

She touched her chin. 'What was it you called me again?'

'I—' I frowned, thinking. 'You mean when I said you were brilliant?'

'Your words, not mine, bounty hunter.'

I rolled my eyes.

There was a sound at the door, and we both froze.

Tap.

Tap. Tap. Tap.

Tap.

'Just Vale,' I breathed, my muscles relaxing. He'd used the series of knocks we'd agreed on.

I stood, unlocking the door and stepping back to allow him in.

'Is it done?' he asked, eyes flitting between Kit and me, though I noticed he lingered on me.

'Of course it's done,' Kit said. 'I told you I could do it. The timer will set off the changes in the wristbands the night we leave.'

Vale grinned. 'Never doubted you.' He grabbed the tablet from the desk and slipped it beneath his mattress. 'Workshop shift's over. I can make sure you get into the main corridor, and then I'll send you off to dinner on your own.'

Kit stepped toward the door, and I made to follow her, then stopped. 'Vale.'

He stared at me, head tilted slightly to one side.

'Can I talk to you?' I whispered. 'Alone.'

Kit didn't even try to hide her smile as Vale's eyes widened.

He nodded. 'Stay here. Let me get Kit back into the main hall, and I'll be right back, okay? Lock the door.'

I did as he said, locking the door and sitting at the desk as I waited, tapping my fingers against the wooden surface.

Tap.

Tap. Tap. Tap.

Tap.

I blew out a long breath and let Vale back in, his body sliding just barely against mine as he brushed past me and sat on his bed.

I sat back in the chair, turning it to face him.

'I've been thinking,' I blurted before I could lose my nerve. 'About Gus and how he only surrounded himself with the best people. He only lied or kept things from me to keep the people he loved safe until he knew he could trust me. If I'd had a bad reaction to something, it could've compromised everything you've been working toward.'

I'd tried my best to place myself in Gus's shoes, and it was so easy to see my love for Jed reflected in how he'd felt about Momo. I knew beyond a shadow of a doubt I would've lied to Gus if our roles had been reversed.

'Still,' Vale whispered, watching me intently. 'From the moment things . . . changed between us, I should have told you the truth.'

'You should've,' I agreed. 'It also wasn't fair for me to assume that you're like your mother just because you're family. For the better part of the last ten years, I've been *nothing* like my own parents, and you've done nothing but show me that you're more like your father than anyone else. But it hurts that you lied to me, Vale. We need to be able to trust each other if we're going to make it through this. Not just to escape, but through the trip across the Wastes.'

'You can trust me,' he said, reaching forward and grabbing my hands, his eyes staring into mine.

'Promise me,' I implored, squeezing his hands back. 'Promise me that there are no more lies. That you won't keep anything from me again.'

He swallowed, hesitating for only a moment. 'I promise.'

'Then I forgive you.'

A river of relief seemed to course through him, his rigid shoulders lowering and the creases smoothing from his forehead. 'I thought you'd hate me forever.'

I reared back. 'Why would I hate you?'

'Because it's my fault Gus died.'

'It's not your fault.' I enunciated each word. He must have been trying to take the blame off me. To make me feel better. 'It's mine. I should have warned him about the trenches.'

'I could've told him myself. The blame is just as much mine. More.'

I shook my head but didn't press him further. It was an unwinnable argument.

His gaze locked onto mine. As always, his golden eyes held me captive. He opened his mouth, seemingly ready to argue, but the words that slipped out next weren't what I expected. 'I missed you, Little Bird.'

Hearing his use of the nickname eased some of the tension in my stomach, and I let out a small breath. Losing Gus had been the most painful thing I'd experienced since my parents died, and I'd been afraid that his death meant that I'd lost Vale as well.

'Do you still want me?' I whispered, baring my heart.

Vale closed the distance between us, slipping his hand beneath my chin, tilting my head until my eyes met his.

'I'll never stop wanting you, Raven. I don't even know if I was alive before I met you – I was just going through the motions. The first time I saw you, it was like you lit me on fire. And maybe, after you were arrested, I mistook the flames for hatred. I know better now.'

And then he kissed me. Soft and sweet and slow, his hand gentle on my skin.

But I didn't want slow or gentle.

I wanted everything while I still could have it – before we risked our lives to leave Endlock.

I claimed his bottom lip, sucking it gently into my mouth, and he growled, his hand on my face tensing. 'Careful.'

I stood, forcing him to widen his legs as I stepped between them, where he still sat at the edge of his bed. 'Or what?' I whispered.

'Or I'll forget how dangerous it is to have you alone in my room.' The words came out low and raspy, tickling my skin like his calloused fingers that were running up and down my arms.

I let my fingers sink into his lush hair, pushing his head back until it was tilted up, his eyes meeting mine. 'Show me what you're like when you're not careful, Vale.'

He paused for the barest fraction of a second before reaching up and grabbing the zipper of my jumpsuit. He pulled it down, inch by slow inch, until it reached my waist. I shrugged the fabric off my shoulders, shoved the uniform down past my hips, and stepped out of it entirely.

I stood before him in my underwear and a thin camisole.

His mouth parted, his eyes darkening as they scanned every part of me, and I shivered, reaching for the collar of his shirt and undoing the first button. I was done with stolen kisses and having to be careful all the time.

I reached the last button and pushed his shirt off his shoulders,

drinking in the sight of his bare chest and the hard plane of muscles below. My tongue darted out, wetting my bottom lip, and he
tracked the movement, his throat bobbing as he swallowed.

Vale gripped my hips, then splayed his fingers and pushed them
up and under my camisole, driving the fabric up until my abdomen was exposed. He pulled me closer and leaned down to place a
kiss on my navel, then moved higher, nipping at my stomach and
leaving a trail of kisses up and up until we were at eye level again.

I knotted my fingers tighter in his hair, pulling his mouth to
mine. But I wasn't close enough. Needed to be closer.

I kissed him harder as I climbed onto his lap, my core brushing
against the erection straining against his pants as I straddled him.
I let out a harsh breath at the contact, and he inhaled, tasting me,
his tongue delving into my mouth.

I moved my hands to his chest, scraping my nails down along
his skin until I reached his belt. He let go of me for a moment,
leaning back on his elbows to undo the buckle and then staying
there as I unbuttoned his pants.

He helped me pull them down slightly, and then I reached up,
pulling his arousal free. My throat went dry as I stared at the hard,
thick length of him. An almost pained sound left him, his head
falling back as I wrapped my hand around him.

I swallowed, gripping him tighter and running my hand up
and down his shaft, reveling in his groans as he rocked against
my hand.

'Fuck, Raven,' he rasped, sitting up and claiming my mouth
again, even as I continued to pump my hand.

He nipped my lip and then moved his mouth to my neck, licking
and biting along the column of my throat. He reached between us,
his fingers dipping between my thighs and rubbing me through my
underwear, where I'd soaked right through the fabric. I moaned,
letting my eyes flutter closed and my head fall back.

'So fucking wet for me,' he breathed into my neck. He moved

the fabric of my underwear aside, running his fingers over my bare flesh, hovering just short of my entrance. I pushed harder against him, nearly begging, as I increased the pressure of my strokes on his length.

He used his other hand to shove my camisole up farther, freeing my breasts and exposing my hardened nipples. He took one of them into his mouth, flicking his tongue over the tip just as he pushed a finger inside of me.

'Vale,' I gasped, my eyes rolling back as he pumped his finger inside of me and scraped his teeth over my nipple, rolling the other between his fingers. My free hand went to his hair, pushing him tighter against me.

He added another finger, and I cried out, rocking against him.

'You like that?' he breathed, tilting his head back and watching the look of rapture on my face.

'Mhmm,' I moaned, wetting my lips as he pumped his fingers in and out of me. At my answer, he curled his fingers, hitting that spot deep inside of me, and my mouth opened on a silent scream.

'More,' I whispered, still rocking against him and squeezing his length.

He growled, pulling his fingers free of me to reach between us and position his cock at my entrance.

'Is this what you want?'

'Yes,' I whimpered, rubbing myself against him. 'But—'

'I take my monthly tablet,' Vale said, reading my mind. 'It's safe.'

I didn't know if I'd ever been so relieved in my life.

I wrapped my hands around his neck, kissing him as I pressed myself against his naked chest. He kissed me back, tongue tracing my lips before delving between them. His length slid against my core, getting closer to my entrance and then moving away.

I groaned in frustration, and he chuckled, the low sound raising goosebumps on my arms.

I smirked and gripped his shoulders, lifting myself and positioning him right at my center before slowly sinking down onto his cock. The smirk left my face as his thick length entered me, stretching me – and I'd only gotten past the first few inches.

I closed my eyes, sucking in a deep breath as I worked to get used to the size of him.

Vale's hands gripped my hips, and I could feel him straining to keep from driving into me. 'That's it, Little Bird. You can take it.'

His words undid me, and I sank all the way down, crying out as the full length of him entered me, filling me. I bit my lip.

And then I started to move, using Vale's shoulders as leverage to lift myself up before he drove his hips back up into me, impaling me.

'Fuck,' I moaned, bouncing up and down as Vale watched, drinking me in. He gripped my hips, pushing deeper, hitting that elusive spot again. My legs began to shake from the pleasure, a pressure rising deep in my belly.

I scraped my nails over his back, leaving marks behind, and Vale growled, pumping harder. He moved one hand until it was between our bodies and pressed the pad of his thumb against my clit, rubbing circles against the sensitive flesh.

I arched into him, the pressure driving me higher. 'Please, Vale,' I breathed.

He swirled his thumb faster, driving into me with punishing strokes until the pleasure was too much.

'That's it,' he growled. 'Come for me like a good girl.'

He lifted me up, pulling out of me, and then drove me back down, all the way to the hilt, and the pleasure reached a crescendo, exploding. Vale kept pumping as I moaned, riding the waves of my pleasure until he reached the top, too, tangling his fingers into my hair and coming alongside me.

When we came down, both still breathing heavily, he pulled

me down onto the bed with him until we were lying side by side, facing each other with his arm curled comfortably over my hips.

His eyes flitted over my face, studying me until I smiled. 'What?' I asked, suddenly self-conscious.

'You're beautiful.' The words came out deadly serious, his golden eyes searching mine.

I couldn't help the small smile that lit my lips, and I reached out a hand, lightly pushing his chest. 'Don't get all soft on me.'

'Too late for that – you've ruined me.' He leaned closer, running his nose up the column of my neck and inhaling, and my breath caught in my throat. 'You smell so good. I can't get it out of my head and it drives me wild. I'll be going about my day and get a whiff of jasmine and who the fuck knows what else, something so distinctly *you*, and suddenly you're all I can think about.'

I bit my lip.

'I tried to keep my distance from you, you know. Tried to banish you from my mind, for both of our sakes. But fighting what I felt for you was more of a distraction than giving in. It was over for me from the moment I saw you punch that guy in the face at Vern's.'

I winked, my insides warming at his words. 'You're lucky it wasn't you I punched.'

He laughed, sitting up before I could respond and shifting his pillow. The movement caused my gaze to land on his forearms. His tattoos.

In the heat of the moment, I hadn't been particularly focused on the ink, but now I took in the three interlocking circles of Dividium on his right arm, and the family crest on his left – the outline of a fox, ready to pounce on unsuspecting prey. Both tattoos were done in simple black ink.

Vale followed my gaze and grimaced. 'I got them when I was eighteen. It's mandatory in my family.'

I reached out a tentative finger to trace the tattoo of his family crest, and he shivered. Then he blew out a breath, turning away, and I put a hand on his cheek, forcing him to look back at me.

'This isn't who you are,' I breathed, looking into his eyes. 'I know who you are.'

He stared at me for a long moment, leaning into my touch and nodding.

'It's getting easier to believe that,' he murmured, lowering himself next to me once more. And then: 'Look who's being soft now.'

I lightly flicked his nose, earning a grin before I said, 'Says the man who hasn't stopped thinking about me since the moment he laid eyes on me.'

His lips were on mine before I'd finished speaking.

30

'THE WARDEN WANTS to see you in his office.'

My head snapped up from the bench Yara and I were building, a replacement for one that had broken in the mess hall.

Vale stood before me, his posture rigid. He'd freed his hair from its leather tie, and it framed his strong jaw in waves. I resisted the urge to reach out and brush a dark lock back from his forehead, imagining how I'd gripped it in his bed the day before.

A swell of pleasure washed through my body at the memory.

At his words, tools ceased clinking, and conversations paused. The other inmates watched me with pity, but Kit and Yara only looked curious.

'What?' I asked, though I'd heard Vale's words. It was a desperate attempt to stall – to brace myself for whatever new form of cruelty Larch intended to inflict on me. I had no idea what I'd done to deserve his scrutiny. Had he somehow realized that Councilor Elder's injury was my fault?

'The Warden asked to see you in his office,' Vale repeated. His voice was harsh for the benefit of the onlookers. 'Now.'

'Of course.' I cleared my throat, swiping my sweaty palms down the front of my jumpsuit and squaring my shoulders.

Vale trailed me to the door. 'No one is to leave this room,' he announced, eyes sweeping over the inmates. 'I'll return shortly. I need to escort 224.'

There was a chorus of 'Yes, sir's around the room, followed by the sound of the heavy door swinging shut behind us. We walked through the dimly lit corridor, my pounding heart louder than the thud of my booted footsteps on the cement floor.

When I was sure we were out of earshot of the other inmates, I dared to whisper, 'Is he throwing me back into solitary? If he is, you need to take Jed and Momo and the others and leave this place without me. You might not get another shot.'

The idea of being separated from my brother, from Vale and the others, sent a sharp ache through my heart. But that small shard of pain was far better than the alternative of watching them die. I couldn't survive that.

'What? Raven, no. Hold on,' Vale said. We stopped at the entrance to the infirmary, and before I could question him, he shoved the door open. He caught my elbow, pulling me into the room after him, and then shut the door to seal us in. The lock clicked into place.

The room was pitch black. I couldn't see an inch in front of me, and if Vale hadn't been holding onto me, I likely would've walked into one of the rolling chairs or medicine cabinets.

'What's going on?' I asked. 'You realize being late will make Larch even angrier at me than he already is, right?' He was vindictive enough to add days or weeks onto my punishment if I kept him waiting.

Vale pulled me against him, so close I felt the heat radiating off his body, flames licking sensuously against my chilled skin. His scent filled the air around us, a cloud of soap and fresh pine. I wanted to burrow into him – curl up and pretend we were far from Endlock.

'I'm sorry,' he said quietly. 'I thought you understood. There is no meeting with Larch. I needed a believable excuse to get you out of the workshop without making the others suspicious.'

His words rendered me speechless, and my thoughts raced to catch up. Then, a laugh bubbled from me. 'You pulled me out of the workshop to spend time with me in a dark room? Vale, I want to spend time with you too, but don't you think it's too risky when we're so close to leaving? We can't draw extra attention to ourselves.'

Given what we'd done yesterday, it was utter hypocrisy for me to say so, but it was one thing to be intimate in his private room and another for him to pull me out of the workshop in front of witnesses.

Vale chuckled, dark and rumbling. 'As much as I want to spend more of *that* kind of time with you' – he traced a hand down my waist and over my hip to emphasize his words, and my breath caught – 'that's not what's going on here.'

He flicked a switch on the wall, flooding the room with harsh fluorescent light. I blinked, disoriented. I turned from Vale to hide the flush that had crept into my cheeks at his words and my gaze shifted around the room. The first thing I noticed was the camera in the corner that was, thankfully, off. The second was the stainless-steel countertop on the other side of the room.

Atop the surface sat a device that made my blood run cold.

I twisted from Vale's grip and turned for the door. I needed to get away from that thing.

The branding iron on the counter brought me back to my first day at Endlock, when Vale had pressed the searing metal against my skin, leaving a permanent scar. Even now, I could hear my scream echoing and feel the molten heat consuming me.

Before I could reach the door, Vale stepped in front of me, blocking the exit.

'Hey, stop. It's okay.' Vale's voice was soft and tinged with regret. He placed his hands on my cheeks, forcing me to look at him. 'You're okay. I'm not going to let anything happen to you.'

His words registered slowly, and the tension coiling in my stomach began to unspool. 'What's it doing in here?'

'I need you to use it on me.'

My mouth dropped open, but Vale's eyes met mine, and he spoke again before I could. 'Last night, I couldn't sleep. I was going over our plan, thinking about how to convince the settlement leaders to let us in. I realized something. They'll never let a guard from Endlock enter their territory.'

I bit my lip, thinking. 'We can lie to them and create a different backstory for you. You don't have to mutilate yourself.'

Vale's eyes drifted to my wrist, where the brand still marked my skin. A ripple of guilt washed over his features. Taking my hand, he looked me in the eyes, his own brimming with sincerity. 'I never said I was sorry for doing that to you, Raven. And I am sorry. I wish I'd never hurt you, and I'd take it back if I could. I'd take on every bit of pain that's been inflicted on you if it were possible.'

'You had to,' I said, softening. 'Someone would have noticed if I was missing a brand.' It wasn't as if he'd wielded the branding iron for pleasure. I knew now that he hated inflicting pain on us.

'Probably. But I still should have tried to get around it.' He cleared his throat, entwining our fingers. 'I need you to brand a number onto me. If we're going to lie to the leaders at the settlement, we need to have our stories straight. Not having a brand like the rest of you could be what gives me away.'

His eyes were steady, solid in his resolve. As much as the idea of branding him, of pressing that torture device to his beautiful skin, made me cringe, I knew he had a point. We couldn't give them a reason to doubt our story – it could be the thing that ended our lives.

'Okay,' I conceded, my voice quivering despite my efforts to remain calm.

He dropped my hand and crossed the room, taking up the device. He waved me over, then flipped the switch on the side of the branding iron. 'It'll need a minute to heat up. After that, press it to my forearm for about five seconds.'

Nodding, I watched as he settled onto one of the wheeled chairs, the seat creaking beneath his weight.

'You don't think you'll need restraints?' I asked, arching a brow. I might've killed him if he hadn't restrained me when he'd branded me.

'If we had a chair like that in here, believe me, I would use it,' he said. 'But getting you into that examination room without anyone noticing would have been too risky. And Dr Row's there now, examining new arrivals.'

It made sense. An inmate getting escorted across the prison, nearly to the building's entrance, would raise far too many questions. I hadn't been back in that area since my first day at Endlock.

As my hands found Vale's wrist, I rolled up his sleeve until his forearm was exposed, then released him, taking the branding iron from his outstretched hand. The device shook in my grasp. 'Are you ready?'

I wondered whether I was more nervous than he was, with the way my breath came in short bursts, and my heart pounded desperately against my chest in a futile attempt to escape the cage of my ribs.

I looked down to see the number 242 glowing up at me, an angry orange.

'I am.' Vale steeled himself as he stretched his right forearm across his thigh. His left hand reached out, seeking comfort in gripping the curve of my waist.

'I'm sorry,' I murmured, bringing the scorching branding iron down onto his arm.

A deep groan emanated from his throat, giving sound to his pain, piercing my heart. But he didn't scream.

'Almost there,' I whispered, knowing I could provide no real comfort. I avoided looking directly at where the branding iron touched his arm, but the acrid smell of burning flesh made it impossible to forget what I was doing.

His fingers dug painfully into my waist, but I knew it was nothing compared to what he was feeling.

Finally, my mental countdown ended, and I lifted the branding iron from his skin, hurling it onto the countertop. My hands seized the nearby bucket of water that Vale had prepared, and he plunged his forearm into it.

His head slumped forward against my abdomen, and he released a sigh heavy with both pain and relief. I wove my fingers through his thick hair, soothing him as his free arm encircled my waist.

'It's okay,' I said. 'It's over.'

We stayed like that for several long minutes, not speaking but wrapped up in each other. The idea that soon we'd be on our way to a new life, able to touch freely instead of in darkened alcoves or behind closed doors – I'd never thought I would find myself longing for those things.

Maybe it was okay to want someone who would look out for me. Someone I could turn to when things got hard instead of bearing the impossible weight on my own.

After a while, I tenderly bandaged Vale's branded arm, taking care not to apply any unnecessary pressure.

'Thank you,' he whispered.

'For melting your skin off?' I asked incredulously.

'For helping me,' he replied. He stood up, cradling my face gently in one hand, and his lips met mine in a soft kiss.

My breath hitched in my throat. Vale was gentle, his tongue

grazing my lower lip before coaxing my mouth open. His fingers ran up my neck and tightened in my hair.

It terrified me, this intimacy.

I opened up as if he were peeling away the layers of my soul. It made me feel more vulnerable and exposed than when I was stripped naked in his room with him.

'You don't have to be afraid of me, Little Bird,' Vale murmured, as if he'd read my mind.

But I didn't know how to stop.

31

'wrench.'

'Ugh. Which one? There are, like, a million of them in here.' Yara dug through the portable toolbox Vale had procured for us.

'I need the three-eighth,' Kit called, her voice muffled. She stood on a ladder, her head not visible from where it was inside the ventilation shaft.

Yara's brow furrowed. 'I'm going to need you to repeat that as if I have no idea what you're talking about. Which I don't, in case you were wondering.'

A snort from Kit. 'Your talents lie elsewhere, darling. Raven?'

I grinned. 'Let me have a look.'

Yara shrugged and slid the toolbox across the mechanical room's checkered tiled floor, and I dug through the pile of tools until I found the three-eighth wrench. I stood, crossing the room and pressing the tool into Kit's outstretched hand.

The sound of metal clanging against metal flowed from the ventilation shaft, and I shifted my weight, eyeing the locked door and waiting to see if someone would attempt to force their way through.

It was the day of our escape.

Kit had insisted it was too dangerous to install the diffuser any earlier in case another guard happened across it before we could leave.

That morning, Vale had made a show in front of the other inmates from the workshop, asking us to follow him for a maintenance project and then leaving us alone in the mechanical room.

It was a large space, but it was stuffed to the brim with equipment, making it feel cramped. Numerous pipes and electrical wires lined the ceiling and crisscrossed the room while industrial-sized boilers and backup generators sat against the walls.

'Since when do bounty hunters know anything about tools?' Yara asked, slipping a bottle of baby-blue nail polish from the pocket of her uniform and unscrewing the cap.

The chemical smell of the polish swirled through the room, and I wrinkled my nose.

'My father was a handyman for the landlord that owned the apartment buildings in our neighborhood,' I explained. 'He serviced hundreds of apartments. I'd go with him on jobs when I wasn't in school. Picked up some stuff, I guess.'

I'd loved working with him. I'd done the same as I was doing for Kit now by carrying around his toolbox and selecting the tools he needed. Sometimes, if our mother was working late at the factory, Jed would come with us, too, and I'd be in charge of keeping an eye on him. I'd loved that our parents trusted me to look after him.

'What about you?' I asked, shaking myself from the memory. 'You must have learned some useful skills as an agriculturist.'

'I was mostly in the lab,' Yara said, finishing her first hand and examining the perfectly painted nails before moving on to the next. 'Working with soil samples and testing compounds to make it more fertile. But then, when my father died . . . well. I told you about the artificial food shortages. I don't know if everything I did in the lab was completely useless – if they were giving us contaminated soil samples the whole time so we'd believe their lies.'

I blanched. It'd been beyond horrifying to learn that the Council and Endlock Enterprises were willing to starve Lower Sector citizens to drive up crime rates, but I hadn't thought about what keeping up the appearance of that lie meant. They'd had to sell an illusion.

'Even if they lied, it doesn't mean that the things you were doing weren't useful,' I told Yara. 'Think about the Wastes – they're almost completely barren. But maybe one day they won't be, thanks to people like you working to restore the soil.'

She shrugged as if it weren't a big deal, but I saw the corners of her lips tilt up, ever so slightly, before she ducked her head.

'Diffuser,' Kit called.

Yara held up her hands, waving her wet nails at me. 'Do you mind?'

We sat at our usual table at dinner, our trays laden with biscuits and stew.

I looked over to my right, where Momo was sitting, leaving a gap between us.

Gus's spot.

Momo stared at the empty space on the bench, blinking rapidly. I reached over, grasping his hand in mine and giving it a quick squeeze.

I swallowed the lump that had taken up residence in my throat. 'You know, one of the last things Gus said to me was how important it was for you to get out of here,' I whispered. 'He loved you. So much. He was so excited for you to live the rest of your life away from Endlock and Dividium.'

Momo looked up at me with his big, brown eyes. 'He made

me promise him every day that if something happened to him, I wouldn't give up. And I won't. I'll make it to the North Settlement but—'

A few tears leaked from his eyes and he turned, pulling his hand free of mine and swiping roughly at the tears.

'But what?' I asked gently. I didn't reach over to touch him – holding his hand had been risky enough with all the guards around, and I couldn't draw attention to our table.

'But I won't forget what Elder did to him,' Momo said, his words surprisingly steady with the wetness still glistening on his cheeks.

'Neither will I,' Jed added, from where he sat on Momo's other side. I watched as he scooted closer to the boy, and my heart clenched in my chest.

Yara and I both nodded in agreement.

'We won't forget or forgive,' Kit promised. 'And if I have anything to say about it, the Collective will be helping us take her down.'

I gasped. 'A direct hit on a Councilor?' The Collective engaged in a number of illicit activities and missions, but as far as I knew they'd never waged a direct attack on the Council. Yet . . . Because of course it meant something that they were trying to learn as much as possible about Endlock's security.

Kit shrugged. 'They need me, don't they? They've risked plenty to get me out of here, which leads me to believe they'd do plenty more to make sure I'm on their side. I never said my help wasn't conditional.'

Yara sighed, resting her chin on her hand and staring dreamily at Kit. 'You might be the most badass woman I've ever had the pleasure of laying eyes on.'

'I'd have to agree,' Jed said, and out of the corner of my eye I watched as he slipped his uneaten biscuit onto Momo's tray. 'But you all better start eating. This is our last good meal.'

'Oh my dear, sweet Jed.' Yara clucked, shaking her head as she swirled her spoon through the cloudy stew. 'If this is your idea of a good meal, I'd hate to hear what you think is bad.'

My gaze flew to Jed's and we both blurted, 'Rat.'

'Come on, that's not so bad,' Momo joined in, smiling. 'My mom used to bake it into a meat pie that even Yara would've liked.'

Yara watched us, grimacing. 'I'd never disrespect your mother, but if you ever bring a rat pie close to me, I will not hold back in defending myself.'

Kit cleared her throat, rolling her lips together to hide a grin. 'Darling, you have to realize that Pharil Coates isn't wasting his precious credits feeding us beef. What do you think we've been eating in here all this time?'

Yara's mouth formed a perfect O and I had to slap a hand over my own mouth to keep from laughing out loud.

'No,' Yara whispered, horrified. 'Why didn't you tell me before, Kit? You've betrayed me.' She shoved her tray in Jed's direction, and he gladly slipped her bowl of stew onto his tray, pouring half the food into Momo's bowl before he dug in.

'Let's see. Because I love you, and I knew that given the choice between eating rat and starving, you'd choose death.'

Yara huffed, crossing her arms over her chest. 'You know me too well.'

After what felt like an eternity, we finished our meals and returned to our cells, settling in early to get some rest before the timer went off and the diffuser began pumping ironroot through the vents.

I found myself tossing and turning. Given the circumstances, I should've known that sleep would elude me. A few cells down, I heard Yara stirring on her cot. I stared at the ceiling, going over the plan in my mind until the guards turned out the lights.

It was time.

I rose from my cot, careful not to disturb anyone, and reached under my bed for the satchel that Vale had told me would be hidden there. I unzipped it and pulled my respirator free, placing it over my nose and mouth, where it seemed to suction against my skin, leaving no space for unfiltered air to sneak through.

I began to pack my remaining possessions into the bag as quietly as possible.

First was a set of thermal leggings and a long-sleeved shirt that Yara had handed me at the last minute. There would be frigid nights on our journey, with body heat and the threadbare blankets stowed in the tunnels as our only armor against the cold.

A hat, gloves, and a half-decent jacket followed, then socks and undergarments. Most of it had been gifted by Yara or stolen from the guards' quarters by Vale.

Everything else we needed or could scrape together was already stashed in the tunnels. All we had to do was get ourselves there.

I zipped up the pack, slung it over my shoulders, and sat back down on my cot, waiting.

It was several hours before I heard the barrier door open amid the snores of the other inmates. Vale hadn't been able to cut the power entirely – that would have triggered alarms at the security office in Dividium. But he'd worked with Kit to place Endlock into the low-energy mode that was typically used on days when blackouts wreaked havoc on the energy grid in Dividium and the city had to pull from Endlock's reserves.

The lights were all dimmed to the barest glow, none of the cameras were recording, and Vale could override the electric locks and unlock our cells with a manual key. Without the usual systems running at full capacity, it would be difficult for the guards to get organized and come after us if someone woke up early.

I heard the metallic sound of a key turning as Vale unlocked the cells before mine – Jed's, Kit's, and Momo's. Their footsteps padded softly across the concrete floor. Then, there was a quiet click, and my cell door rolled open.

I stepped out, barely making out Vale's shadowed figure. He

reached for my hand, squeezing it tightly for a second before releasing it to let Yara out of her cell.

The six of us made our way to the slightly ajar barrier door, slipping through. Behind us, no one stirred; the only sound in the cellblock was a chorus of snoring inmates.

We wound our way through the prison, stopping periodically to survey our surroundings, but all was quiet. Guards were slumped on the ground in various positions, some snoring loudly with their mouths hanging open, some crying out in their sleep as if they, too, were plagued by nightmares.

Our plan was working.

Almost too well.

We continued until we reached the prep room, the last obstacle before the hunting grounds.

Vale clicked his flashlight on, casting a hazy glow over the bare space. He pulled several sheathed daggers out of his pouch and handed one to each of us.

'Kit,' Vale said, his voice low and urgent, 'when are the wristband settings supposed to change?'

Kit lifted her arm, staring it her wristband. 'It should be right about . . .' The green light on the band clicked off for a moment, then switched back on. Only it was red. When I looked at my wristband, the color had changed as well. 'Now.'

'That's my girl,' Yara said, grinning and slinging a casual arm around Kit's shoulders.

'Incredible,' Jed chimed in, looking at Kit. She didn't meet his eye, but I caught a glimpse of the small smile she flashed before ducking her head.

Vale reached down and lifted up the rifle I'd stashed on the grounds, all those weeks ago. 'You haven't even seen the gun yet.'

'Oh,' Kit spoke up, a grin spreading across her face. 'I made the modifications we talked about. Now we can aim it at anyone — whether they're wearing a wristband or not.'

I shook my head at her. 'We'd be dead without you.'

Kit smiled. 'It's not much against a horde of guards, but it's better than nothing.'

'All right,' Vale said as we gathered in a circle. His fingers brushed lightly against mine, and my breath caught. 'From here, it's a straight shot to the tunnels, and then we're out. No talking once we're out on the hunting grounds unless it's essential.'

We nodded back at him, and the gravity of our actions settled into my bones, making me almost giddy with adrenaline. What we were about to do could set the tone for the future – it could be the start of dismantling Endlock, brick by brick.

Vale opened the door, and cool night air greeted us like an icy kiss pressed to my flushed cheeks. I tilted my face up and drew in a deep, steadying breath. Above me, the sky stretched out in an endless expanse of ink-black dotted with millions of glittering stars that seemed to twinkle in silent encouragement.

We pressed ourselves against the prison's rough exterior, scanning the watchtowers for signs of movement. There were none – no hint of life. The guards inside must have surrendered to the ironroot and slumped over their stations in deep slumber.

Once we deemed it safe enough, we bolted across the open field. My heart raced in my chest as I ran, my breath coming in ragged gasps, the frigid air like shards of glass scraping against my throat. Every nerve in my body screamed at me, reminding me how exposed and vulnerable we were. The light of the full moon lit up the field like a spotlight. A single alert guard who was immune to the ironroot, a chance glance from a window, and it would all be over.

But no alarms blared, and no shouts chased us. Instead, the dark, enveloping arms of the forest reached out to receive us.

I let out a long, shaky breath as the trees closed around us. We were hidden from view, cloaked by the gloom of the woods. The tunnel entrance was a fair distance away, but anyone trying to follow us would be hard-pressed to do so in the dark. Even still, we moved in silence, mindful of Vale's warning.

Time seemed to crawl as we made our way through the forest. I felt a small hand slip into mine and instinctively closed my fingers around it. Momo – seeking comfort. In the moonlight, the branches of the trees appeared to reach for us like ghostly arms, and shadows danced eerily over the forest floor.

I squeezed his hand reassuringly as we pressed on, and as we reached the tunnel entrance, a small smile curved my lips.

One by one, we descended the ladder. We waited until the cover was securely in place above us before allowing the weak beam of Vale's flashlight to pierce the darkness.

Several packs lined the wall of the cavern, stuffed to the brim with medicine, books, and food.

The rest of the tunnel curved into the distance, the end shrouded in darkness.

Our final task was to break through the exit at the end of the tunnel, something we'd held off on for fear of raising suspicion if a guard managed to spot a hole in the ground on the other side of the perimeter fence.

Vale and I grabbed the pair of spades that he'd stashed inside the tunnel, in case we couldn't get the lid free and needed to dig a new exit.

'All right,' Vale said, blowing out a breath as he met each of our gazes in turn. 'Raven and I will work on the exit. I need the rest of you to stay in this main chamber and get your personal belongings distributed among our packs.'

The four of them nodded, and I handed my extra clothes to Jed.

He raised a skeptical brow. 'This is a lot of supplies. Are you sure we can manage them all?'

It *was* a lot of weight to divide between the six of us.

'We can't afford to leave anything behind,' I cut in before Vale could respond. 'There's no way of knowing what the leaders at the North Settlement will find the most valuable, so we need to bring it all.'

'We'll find a way to fit the rest of it,' Kit assured me.

Yara nodded in agreement, sinking to the floor and grabbing a satchel. 'I may look like just a pretty face, but I pack some muscle, too. This won't be a problem.'

Another smile tugged at my lips despite my nerves. The others dropped to their knees, grabbing their packs.

Vale and I made for the other end of the tunnel, walking for several long minutes through the passageway that twisted and turned like the worms residing in its earthen walls.

By the time we reached the end, we could no longer see our friends' flashlights.

We shoved against the exit. First with our hands, before slamming into it with our shovels, but it didn't budge, and we decided we had to dig our way out.

We got to work, the minutes ticking by with each movement of our shovels. Sweat poured down my back, soaking into my jumpsuit. Eventually, the last bites of dirt gave way to reveal the night sky.

I stuck my spade in the dirt and swiped the back of my hand across my upper lip to relieve some of the moisture there. I looked over at Vale, and then we stood, grinning stupidly at each other.

We were almost there.

He reached out a hand and tenderly brushed a stray strand of hair behind my ear, and then he took my hand and guided me back into the tunnel. We were almost back to the main cavern when we realized that the noises from the chamber had ceased. We'd left to the quiet sounds of Kit, Momo, Jed, and Yara stuffing the last of the supplies into our packs, and now there was only an unsettling silence.

32

VALE MADE TO step toward the main chamber, but I placed a hand on his arm, halting him. I said nothing, only signaled for him to remain in place, pressing a finger to my lips.

If there was an intruder in the tunnels, I didn't want him to give himself away. I needed him as backup in case things went wrong.

Vale clicked off his flashlight as I rounded the bend in the tunnel.

I stepped farther into the blackness, my fingers trailing against the cool earth of the tunnel wall for guidance, bits of dirt crumbling away.

I couldn't see an inch in front of my face.

When the glow from the others' flashlights came into view, I stopped, listening intently. I heard Vale's light footsteps behind me but nothing else.

I took a few more steps and saw the beginnings of the cavern. Yara, Jed, Kit, and Momo sat quietly, staring at the ground.

Why weren't they packing?

I stepped into the cavern, and Jed's head snapped up, his eyes widening. 'Raven, wait—'

But then there was a dagger at my neck, and an arm around my torso, and Larch's voice whispering into my ear, 'Did you think I wouldn't find out?'

His words sent a chill down my spine.

'Imagine my surprise,' Larch continued, amusement lacing his tone as he pulled me tighter against his chest, and pressed his blade into my throat, 'when I started feeling drowsy in my office. It was the exact feeling I get every night when I smoke ironroot to help me fall asleep. I've been smoking it for years – the stress from working here won't let me fall asleep without it – so I've built up quite the tolerance.'

I stared, wide-eyed, at the others.

'I went to check on the patrolling guards and found them all slumped on the ground,' Larch continued. 'Now, I know most of them can't stay away from liquor, but this many? I knew it had to be more than a drunken stupor.'

My hand shook as I calculated whether I could reach for the dagger sheathed at my side before Larch sliced my throat.

'I searched the prison further,' he went on, 'and could not find a single soul awake, save for Dr Row, who was wearing a respirator to keep from catching a bacterial infection from the patient she was treating. It stopped her from breathing in the ironroot that you managed to pump through the ventilation system.'

My throat was dry as bone, and swallowing felt like sandpaper running along my insides.

'I still haven't figured out how you did it,' Larch continued. 'Dr Row and I were discussing the possibilities when the power went out.'

Larch's low chuckle raised the hair on my arms.

Vale had yet to show himself.

'A group of inmates couldn't possibly orchestrate something like this alone,' Larch mused. 'It got me thinking about how one guard in particular has become close with this little group. How he brought you to the infirmary to visit your brother. How Hyde and Perri came to me, insisting Vale played a part in Mort's death.'

Fuck. We should've been more careful. Should've known Hyde was onto us after he unlocked the cells and allowed Perri to attack Gus that night.

Think, Raven. Think. Is there a way to get out of this?

'So. I had my colleagues in Dividium review the tracking logs tonight,' Larch said, 'and discovered that two inmates and a *guard* spent a large amount of time in this area before testing the proposed wristband upgrades.'

I hadn't contemplated the possibility that Larch or anyone else would bother examining the records until we were long gone.

It seemed Vale hadn't, either.

Our mistakes were stacking up. Mocking us.

'Where does this leave us?' I finally spoke, breaking my silence, feeling the blade press closer with each word. 'If any other guards were awake, you would have brought them with you. But you're here alone.'

'For now. Dr Row is working on waking them up.'

There was a pause. 'They can't be woken up,' I said, though my words shook, lacking their usual confidence. 'They have to sleep the drug off.'

'Do you really think there isn't a way to counteract a simple herb?' Larch chuckled. 'Though, to be fair, Dr Row resisted helping me at first. I had to threaten her child's life to get her to agree. Not that I'll let them live when this is all over. If she were a loyal citizen of Dividium, I wouldn't have had to threaten her at all.'

Fucking monster. I had to bite my lip to keep the words from slipping free.

'As you can see, even without the guards, I have the upper hand.'

'Let her go, and we won't have to hurt you,' Vale said, his voice steady as he stepped out of the shadows.

'Let her go?' Larch repeated, ridiculing Vale. He laughed as if it were the most hysterical thing he'd ever heard. 'You must be joking. The moment I release her, you'll be on me. No. I don't think so.'

'If you let her go,' Vale persisted, 'you have my word that we'll let you walk away from this unharmed.'

'I don't think so,' Larch repeated icily. 'Here's what's going to happen. You're going to do exactly as I ask, or I will slit this girl's throat right here.'

'Larch, listen—' Vale started.

'Not another step! Your mother will hear of this! I'm warning you!'

Larch pressed his dagger harder into my throat, breaking my skin, and I felt a warm trickle slide down my neck.

Vale froze, eyes widening in panic. 'Okay. Okay, please. I'll do anything you want – just don't hurt her.'

Larch smiled. 'That's more like it.'

'What do you want?'

'I want to keep my job.'

Vale paused, brow furrowing. 'Larch, I have no control over that.'

'Bullshit.' Larch's laugh was mirthless. Sinister. 'For someone intelligent enough to devise a plan to escape this place, I can't believe you're so foolish as to think I'd buy that.'

Vale's mouth snapped shut, and he shook his head back and forth. 'It's the board's decision. They said you've made too many mistakes in recent weeks.'

'Recent weeks,' Larch spat. 'As in, when this bounty hunter arrived and began *ruining* my life?' He pushed the blade against me again, drawing a soft cry from my lips.

Vale took a step forward.

'Ah, ah, ah,' Larch sang. 'Not another inch. It took until tonight for me to be sure that you were working with them. Working against me. Destroying my reputation. And if you can destroy it, you can fix it.'

'How?' Vale asked, talking to Larch even as his eyes bored into mine.

'Simple, really,' Larch hissed, his breath hot against my ear, making my skin crawl. 'Come with me. Convince your mother. And I'll let the rest of them leave.'

I opened my mouth to argue.

And then the alarms went off.

33

THE ALARMS BLARED through the dimly lit tunnels, a piercing siren that seemed to run its sharpened nails along the inside of my skull.

Dr Row had woken the guards, then.

Time was running out.

Larch jumped at the sound, loosening his grip on the dagger at my throat.

Momo lunged forward. In one fluid movement, he drove his dagger into Larch's thigh.

Larch cried out, lowering his weapon long enough that I slipped from his arms and put some distance between us. His arm flailed, knocking Momo out of the way and sending his blade skittering across the pit, and then Yara was there, tackling Larch to the ground and holding vigil over him with her own dagger.

Larch chuckled as the alarm continued to sound. 'Tick tock.'

'We need to go,' Yara said to me and Vale through her teeth. 'Or we'll all die here.'

Fear coursed through me, and a raging headache was blooming

behind my eyes, but I nodded. 'Were you able to finish transferring everything to the packs?'

Yara bit her lip, shaking her head. 'Not before he got here, no.'

Voices called from outside the pit, dangerously close to our position. Guards.

'I'm here!' Larch yelled out, trying to capture their attention, a grim mirror of the way Gus had called out to Councilor Elder in his last moments in the world of the living.

Without flinching, I stalked over to him, shoving Yara aside and pressing the edge of my dagger to his throat.

Larch laughed. *Laughed*. Right in my face.

'You've never killed before, girl,' he got out. 'You bounty hunters all think you're so strong, but you've never had the strength of a true patriot. You've never paid to hunt the criminals that ruin our great city.'

'You have no idea what I'm capable of,' I ground out, red filling my vision. *I* didn't know what I was capable of – not when we were this close to escaping and he'd gotten in the way.

'I do,' Larch answered, lips curling into a smile. 'It's why I know you're going to end up back in your cell and eventually killed like an animal. Like your whore of a mother.'

My hand clamped tighter around the handle of my dagger, heart pounding so furiously that it blocked out all other sounds.

And then – choking.

I looked down to find Larch's body thrashing uncontrollably. He gasped, the sound wet and labored, and his hands flew to his neck. Crimson seeped between the fingers that he held over a gaping slash in his throat.

A slash that I'd made.

I dropped the dagger.

Larch took a final, heaving breath, and his eyes shuttered. He was quiet.

Dead.

'I killed him,' I whispered.

Hands squeezed my shoulders, pulling me away from Larch's body.

I turned to the rest of the group. 'I killed him,' I repeated.

'It's okay,' a soothing voice breathed in my ear. 'He had to die. He knew too much.'

Vale.

I turned, placing shaking hands on his chest, leaning into him even as I smeared Larch's blood on his clothing.

'I'll go buy us some time.' Jed's voice came from the corner, quiet but firm.

Vale looked over his shoulder at Jed. 'I'll go with you.'

'What are you talking about?' I protested, my voice rising as he snapped me from my numb state. I moved to block his path. 'You two can't go out there. You could be killed.'

'We'll be fine,' Vale said in a low, soothing voice. 'No one else knows I'm involved in helping you escape.'

'He's right,' Jed mused, nodding. 'Vale can pretend that he caught me escaping, and we can lead the guards in the opposite direction.' He rolled back his shoulders and moved toward the ladder that led out of the tunnels.

'Jed, wait!' I called out, grabbing him by the shoulders, leaving wet red prints on his jumpsuit. 'Let me go instead.'

'No, Raven,' Jed said. 'They need you here. If something happens to me, you'll all be fine. You're a fighter. You can protect them. This is *my* contribution. This is bigger than us. If we get out of here, we could save everyone in that prison.'

This is bigger than us.

He was right.

The situation had evolved beyond breaking Jed out of Endlock, and my time within the prison had solidified my understanding of how vital it was to stop the Council. That would never happen if we didn't escape.

Years of my life flashed before me. Jed as a child without a care in the world. Jed, after our parents died, with perpetual purple circles adorning the spaces below his eyes. Jed growing several feet, nearly overnight, and announcing his job at the textile factory. Jed staying up until dawn to work, striving for a better life, and still finding the time to stand up for those around him.

'Okay,' I finally said, and I saw Jed's jaw drop. 'Take the rifle and be as quick as you can.'

Jed stepped toward me, wrapping his arms around me in a fierce hug that stole my breath. 'Thank you,' he breathed, letting go of me before I was ready. Then he grabbed the rifle from where it leaned against one of the dirt walls and scrambled up the ladder, his long legs taking the rungs two at a time.

'I'll keep him safe,' Vale whispered, voice fervent, eyes intense enough that I nearly looked away. He brushed a soft kiss across my lips. 'If we're not back in thirty minutes, leave without us.'

I didn't even hide my eye-roll.

We switched off our flashlights, and the two of them lifted the mossy cover enough to scan the area before they slipped away into the night.

I held my breath, listening to their retreating footsteps, but heard no sign of commotion.

After securing the lid, we flipped the flashlights back on, bathing the chamber in artificial light.

Larch's body lay sprawled in one corner, his blood pooling on the hard-packed dirt.

I sat frozen with worry. Pretending my hands weren't shaking – pretending I wasn't a murderer.

Momo placed a hand on my arm, but I was afraid I would cry if I met his eyes.

'We need to finish packing,' Kit said, voice soft and kind. Her gaze was filled with pity, and I knew that tears would slip from my eyes if I stared at her for too long.

I cleared my throat, struggling against the tightness that had embedded itself there.

I turned to see Yara sitting on her knees, watching me timidly as if I were a rabid animal that might lash out and bite her if she was foolish enough to turn her back to me.

I knelt beside her and Momo, and started transferring the clothing from my satchel into one of the larger packs with the medical supplies, trying to distract myself by thinking of the journey ahead – it would be grueling, and we'd have to move quickly to put distance between us and the pursuing guards who would follow without the hindrance of weight on their backs.

But without supplies of their own, the guards would be forced to turn back to Endlock before long. We might have a chance if we could put enough miles between us.

The four of us worked quickly, until all that remained was to hoist our packs and walk to the end of the tunnel so we could climb to the surface on the other side of the fence.

But first we sat on the cold floor, breath held, waiting for Jed and Vale to return.

With each passing minute, my mind conjured increasingly grim scenarios, imagining all the ways they could be dying alone on the hunting grounds.

'We need to leave,' Yara said, her voice taut, after what must have been nearly thirty minutes.

I gave her an incredulous look. 'Not without them,' I replied, firm, allowing no space for argument.

'They're our friends,' Momo whispered fiercely.

'Of course they are,' Yara whispered. 'But you heard Vale. Every second we stay here, the guards draw closer to finding us. Do you want them to capture us? To kill us? Vale and Jed wouldn't want that for us. We can wait for them on the other side.'

'They're risking their lives for us, and you want to leave them behind?'

A flash of guilt crossed Yara's face, but she had no time to answer. The entrance creaked open, and Jed's face appeared, pale but unharmed, though a frown marred his features.

I had to close my eyes against the potency of my relief, and the tears that welled up.

Kit and I flicked off our flashlights to prevent light escaping our hideaway.

'Vale needs help,' Jed said, descending into the tunnel in a heartbeat. I heard a groan and then the thump of something heavy falling to the floor.

We switched our lights back on and—

'Vale!' I cried out, rushing across the space and kneeling next to where he was sprawled on the ground. His teeth were bared, and he had a hand pressed to his shoulder with blood seeping from a wound beneath his fingers.

'What happened?' I asked, panic filling me as I took in the wound.

'We pointed a group of guards in the opposite direction, and we thought they'd all left, but . . . Hyde was with them. He must have known we were lying,' Jed said. 'He snuck up on us. His gun wasn't firing because of our wristbands, but he managed to grab the rifle right out of my hands. He got a clean shot through Vale's shoulder, before we took care of him.'

I swallowed, grabbing Vale's wrist and pulling gently at it. 'Let me see.'

He gritted his teeth as he slid his hand away from the wound. As soon as the pressure was gone, blood flowed freely from it.

'Fuck,' I hissed, ripping a shirt from a nearby pack and pressing it against the wound, applying pressure.

There's too much blood. The words crept through my head uninvited.

'Someone get me a first-aid kit,' I snapped. 'I know it's in one of these packs.'

'Raven,' Vale whispered, placing his bloodied hand on top of mine where it was pushing the shirt into his wound.

I forced a smile that I was sure looked like a grimace. 'Don't worry. I just need to get the bullet out and then get you sewn up and you'll be good to go.'

'Raven . . .' he said again, but I ignored him, turning back to the others.

'I need that first-aid kit now,' I told them. They were already digging through the bags, searching.

'*Raven*,' Vale hissed, and I finally looked him in the eyes.

'What?' I whispered.

'You need to leave without me.'

I narrowed my eyes, incredulous. 'Don't be stupid. We're not leaving without you.'

'You have to,' he insisted, squeezing my hand as if to soften the blow of his words.

'I can stitch a wound, Vale – I've done it dozens of times.'

'I've lost too much blood, Little Bird. I won't be able to make the trek. Not like this. I need a doctor.'

I moved my free hand, pressing my palm into his cheek. He'd grown pale, and his skin was cool and moist to the touch.

'He's right, Raven.' Kit had sidled up beside me and was bent over, her eyes flitting over Vale. 'He'll die if he doesn't get to a doctor.'

'I— *No*,' I whispered, my throat tightening as I pressed my forehead to Vale's.

He held my gaze, and I soaked in those golden eyes. 'It's okay, Little Bird. You have each other. You'll make it.'

'I can't leave you,' I breathed, my voice cracking. My heart wrenched in my chest. Like I'd already left. Like we were already apart.

He lowered his voice until I was the only one who could hear. 'You have to. For Jed. For Gus and *Momo*, like you promised. For all of them. I'm going to be okay – Hyde is dead. Larch is dead. I'll make up a story – say I tried to stop you all, then point anyone who decides to go after you in the wrong direction.'

He was panting by the end of his speech, and I felt his quickening pulse where I touched his skin. I looked away, wanting to argue, but my eyes fell on Momo, wide-eyed and terrified, and I shut them again, taking a settling breath. I had made a promise.

I opened my eyes, and he must have thought I was going to argue again, because he spoke before I could.

'Damn it, listen to me, Raven. I can't watch you die here. I lov—'

'Don't.' I stopped him, breathing heavy, my heart nearly beating out of my chest. 'Don't say it. Not now. If you mean it, you'll wait. If you mean it, you'll leave here when you're better. You'll come after me. And *then* you can say it.'

'Nothing could keep me from you.' He met my gaze, his eyes molten and burning in their intensity, and he brought a hand up to cup my face. 'I swear it. As soon as I'm better, I'll follow you.'

'Raven, we have to go.' Jed laid a hand on my shoulder, his tone apologetic.

Vale traced my face with his hand, slipping his fingers into my hair and brushing his lips softly against mine.

I didn't care that we weren't alone – I lost myself in his touch, kissing him back with all of the pain scorching through me. My hands were in his hair, and then roving over his back. I brushed my tongue against his, breathing him in as tears dripped down my cheeks.

The moment was over far too soon, and we pulled apart, breathing heavily.

Jed and I helped Vale to his feet, and then through a shaky climb up the ladder.

Just before he slipped outside, Vale reached back, fingers brushing my hand and eyes boring into mine. 'I'll find you,' he breathed.

And then he was gone.

34

AT FIRST WE ran.

Stumbling over roots and rocks, panting terrified breaths as Endlock's alarms echoed around us, pressing at our backs and urging us onward.

Every snapping twig, every rustle of leaves in the wind, each time a tree dropped a pine cone to the forest floor – we jumped.

But after several hours of trekking in the silvery light of the full moon, the alarms faded from piercing, to a dull drone, to nothing. And then there were miles between us and the prison.

We exchanged tentative glances and small smiles, though now we missed two of our friends. Gus's absence weighed heavily on us. I could almost hear his encouraging words, hear him laughing at something Momo said and affectionately palming the boy's head.

Vale's absence was too fresh for me to pry at the wound.

Our escape didn't feel quite real, and we'd fallen into a silence, broken only by the soft rustling of our footsteps treading over pine needles.

After a long, uphill journey, we arrived at a clearing, and I couldn't help but gasp at the sight that greeted me. Bathed in a brilliant midday sun, the world spread out before me – below the conifer-adorned mountain where we stood was a barren flatland, dried and cracked as far as the eye could see, akin to the deserts I'd read about from the world before. The Wastes.

In the distance, I could just make out the bare outline of a magnificent mountain.

The world beyond.

And somewhere, the North Settlement.

It was there that I finally let the tears stream down my face. Tears for those I'd lost. Tears for what I'd done.

Standing there, looking out over the world that had been kept from me for so long, I felt a rush of emotions. Fear. Exhilaration. Hope. Hurt.

Determination.

'Crying tears of joy just at the sight of me, Thorne? I never thought I'd live to see the day.'

I turned, and a wide grin spread over my face as Gray and Opal stepped out of the forest, the latter surveying our ragtag group.

'Crying because I'm going to have to spend an entire month listening to your righteous bullshit,' I told him, but I threw my arms around his neck just the same, breathing in the familiar scent of leather and soap.

'That's more like it,' Gray murmured against my ear. 'I was getting worried. Thought you'd gone soft on me.'

'Why – because I called you pretty?' I leaned back and winked.

Jed came up beside us and Gray released me to sling an arm around his shoulders and rub his knuckles over his already mussed hair. Jed laughed and I looked over at Opal, who gave me a hesitant smile.

'You did it.' She laughed. 'You actually did it.'

'It was a team effort. I don't know why you all thought you

needed me – Kit did most of the heavy lifting,' I admitted, turning and introducing the two of them to the rest of our group.

A bounty hunter, an engineer, an agricultural scientist turned poisoner, a factory worker with a will of steel, and a dagger-wielding twelve-year-old. It sounded like the start of a joke.

We sat in a circle, not daring to kindle a fire as we passed around a couple of ration bars, munching on them and leaning over the map of the Wastes that Opal spread before us, weighed down by a handful of stones.

'We need to get moving,' she insisted. 'There's not enough space between us and Endlock. We need to make it at least a few miles into the Wastes before we sleep.'

'Agreed.' I nodded. 'The farther we get from this place, the better.'

We gathered our belongings, hoisting our packs. I paused, turning back to Endlock just for a moment, picturing the distance between where I stood and where we'd left Vale.

Nothing could keep me from you.

I closed my eyes, letting Vale's words wrap me in a warm embrace.

And then I stepped into the unknown.

Acknowledgments

To Cage a Wild Bird began as a short story – an assignment for a creative writing class I took in my freshman year of college. It sat in my head for seven years after that, watching and waiting. It never would have made it this far without the help of some amazing people.

Thank you to my husband, Solomon, for your unwavering love and support. I love you always.

Thank you to my brilliant agent, Rebeka Finch, for believing in me and this story, and helping shape it into what it is today. I couldn't do any of this without you!

A massive thank you to the entire Darley Anderson team, especially Francesca, Georgia, Sarah, and Ilaria, for championing this story and just generally being the absolute best.

Thank you to my editors, Laura Schrieber and Lara Stevenson, and their wonderful teams at Avon and Transworld, respectively.

A special thank you to my Fronch writing crew. Without you, I don't think this story would be here today.

Thank you so much to my friends and family for your support – from your words of encouragement to checking in for updates and helping spread the excitement, it all means the absolute world to me.

And thank you, dear reader, for taking a chance on me and this book. I hope you can feel how much of my heart I put into this story.

About the Author

BROOKE FAST is a lover of dystopian, fantasy, and all things romance. When she's not writing new worlds, you can find her curled up on the couch with her husband and their pups in their self-built tiny house in the mountains of Maine. She'll either be consuming copious amounts of coffee and thumbing through the latest romantasy release or sharing book reviews and writing snippets under her alter-ego, @librarybrookes.